A Mistletoe Kiss

Katie Flynn

A Mistletoe Kiss

arrow books

Published by Arrow Books in 2010

2 4 6 8 10 9 7 5 3 1

Copyright © Katie Flynn 2010

Katie Flynn has asserted her right under the Copyright, Designs and Patents Act, 1988, to be identified as the author of this work.

First published in Great Britain in 2010 by Arrow Books
The Random House Group Limited
20 Vauxhall Bridge Road, London, SW1V 2SA

www.rbooks.co.uk

Addresses for companies within The Random House Group Limited can be found at: www.randomhouse.co.uk/offices.htm

The Random House Group Limited Reg. No. 954009

A CIP catalogue record for this book
is available from the British Library

ISBN 9780099550471

The Random House Group Limited supports The Forest Stewardship Council (FSC), the leading international forest certification organisation. All our titles that are printed on Greenpeace approved FSC certified paper carry the FSC logo. Our paper procurement policy can be found at www.rbooks.co.uk/environment

Mixed Sources
Product group from well-managed forests and other controlled sources
www.fsc.org Cert no. TT-COC-2139
© 1996 Forest Stewardship Council

FSC

Typeset in Palatino by Palimpsest Book Production Limited, Falkirk, Stirlingshire

Printed and bound in Great Britain by
CPI Mackays, Chatham, ME5 8TD

For Eileen and Jim Greenwood,
with many thanks; how nice to
do one's research over a delicious
meal at a canalside pub!

Acknowledgements

First and foremost, my sincere thanks go to Jim and Eileen Greenwood, who put in a great deal of time and thought into my various problems whilst I was writing this book. Without their help I should still be tearing my hair out over the layout of the Everton Library (as it was when I knew it) and the finer points of narrow boats on the Birmingham to London run. Despite their endeavours, however, I may have made mistakes and if I have done so, the mistakes are mine; the details I got right are thanks to Eileen and Jim. Thank you both so much!

I should also like to thank the late Eily Gayford, who wrote *The Amateur Boatwomen*, and Margaret Cornish, who wrote *Troubled Waters*, marvellous books in the Working Waterways series, and essential reading for anyone interested in the role canals played during WWII. And the staff of the Ellesmere Boat Museum were, as always, both knowledgeable and helpful.

Chapter One

July 1934

Hetty Gilbert wandered slowly along St Domingo Road, trying to look completely casual, completely indifferent, but when she reached the library she could not help turning towards it and staring at the imposing doors with their big glass panels with the gold writing upon them. She had looked at these doors often; enviously for the most part. She had seen men and women going in and coming out, positively laden with books, and she had thought, rebelliously, that it was extremely unfair. Why should adults be able to borrow books, when they had no real need of them, whereas she herself, who *needed* to read . . .

But if her teacher's words were correct then the librarian had no right to turn her out, which was what had happened on the only two previous occasions she had braved the big glass doors and slid inside. Then, she had stared with awe at the shelves and their burden of what must be many thousands of wonderful books, but had barely taken half a dozen steps towards the nearest display when a voice had sounded far too close to her ear, and a hand had descended on to her shoulder. 'Out!' the voice had announced, and she was

1

given a painful shove in the direction of the exit. 'This is no place for children!'

'Oh, but I were only looking . . .' Hetty had begun.

However, the owner of the voice – the shover in fact – had taken no notice, merely repeating the word 'Out!' as Hetty had been propelled through the glass doors and on to the pavement.

Now, Hetty walked past the library, then turned casually and retraced her steps. Today, she reminded herself, today would be different, thanks to her teacher. Miss Marks took her class, and had decided to give them as a holiday task an essay written on the subject of 'Children in Foreign Lands'. Upon her announcing this, however, a number of blank faces had been turned towards the teacher, who had said impatiently: 'Whatever is the matter, children? Surely you know that there are French children, Dutch children, Indian, African . . . good gracious, I'm giving you just about the widest choice of subject . . .'

'But Miss,' Hetty had said plaintively. 'We don't know nothin' about kids in – in other lands. Oh, I know Millie's Chinese and there are black kids an' all, but . . .'

Miss Marks was a large woman, whose short dark hair, round pink cheeks and black, snapping eyes always reminded Hetty of a Dutch doll she had once seen in Bunney's window. At her pupil's words, however, she had gone red and screwed up her mouth into a tight little bunch, answering scornfully: 'Have you never heard of books, you foolish child?' She had seized a copy of *Treasure Island*, which had been lying on her desk, and had waved it so vigorously under Hetty's nose that Hetty had jumped back, blinking. 'As for Millie and young Bert, they've neither of them got nearer to China nor Africa than I have myself. It's books you come to school to study, and it is to books you should turn for information.'

'But my – my aunt doesn't have any books, and school will be closed for the summer when we're doing our holiday task,' Hetty had pointed out. 'And when I join my grandma and grandpa on the canal there's even less chance of finding a book, particularly one about foreign kids. There's no room on a barge for anything but . . .'

Miss Marks had given an impatient sigh and raised her eyes to heaven, or rather to the ceiling of the class-room. Hetty, who rather liked the teacher, had had to hide a smile because the older woman looked so very odd. 'Hester Gilbert, I used to think you had *some* intelligence, but it seems I was mistaken,' Miss Marks had said, infusing her voice with disbelief. 'Have you never heard of libraries? I suppose you'll tell me you've never visited one, and thought the term applied to purveyors of pork chops or – or smart shoes! Really, child, your ignorance horrifies me. Is there anyone else in the class who believes that libraries sell pork chops?'

There had been a sycophantic snigger from the pupils sitting in the front row of desks, but Hetty had decided it was time to cast her own eyes ceilingwards. 'Of course I know about libraries, Miss,' she had said quickly, before anyone else could put in their two penn'orth. 'There's a big one on St Domingo Road. But I'm not allowed in there; the librarian told me so.'

'Then the librarian was not speaking the truth,' Miss Marks had said in a slightly milder tone. 'Children are certainly allowed to visit the library, and to become members if they so wish. So if you want to borrow books, you'd best tell the librarian that you need them for your schoolwork, and I'm sure she'll see reason.

'But what if she don't, Miss?' Lucy Arnold, who shared a desk with Hetty, had said boldly. Lucy was tall for her age and pretty, and always smiled sweetly at Miss Marks, whilst digging Hetty in the ribs as soon as the teacher's attention moved to someone at the back of the room. 'What if she just tells us to gerrout, which is what she said to Hetty an' meself when we tried to go in one day.'

Miss Marks had seemed to swell with indignation and Hetty had thought, gleefully, what if she bursts? Only she's not a bad old stick . . .

Her thoughts had been interrupted by the ringing of the school bell and Miss Marks had promptly begun marshalling her class into line and herding them out through the door in the direction of the cloakrooms. As she turned to leave them, however, she answered Lucy's question. 'If the librarian tries to say you can't enter the library, then recommend her to explain to me why my pupils can't be trusted amongst books. But I think you'll find she's not unreasonable.'

So now here was Hetty, walking back and forth outside the library and wishing that she had had the forethought to ask Lucy to accompany her, because she knew she would have been a lot bolder with her friend beside her. But Lucy had gone shopping with her mother, so Hetty would have to brave the fierce and terrible librarian alone.

And then, whilst she was still trying to pluck up courage, something occurred which made her bolt like a rabbit into its burrow at the approach of a dog. Coming up the street, clouting one another and shouting, came her cousins Bill and Tom with their neighbour, Gareth Evans. Gareth was a freckled, red-headed lad, three years older than Hetty. He was at the stage when he disliked all girls, and teased Hetty unmercifully, making fun of her mousy hair, her skinny legs and the fact that she was a dreamer who seemed to have her head in the clouds most of the time. Hetty knew from past experience that if Gareth spotted her he would begin to jeer and make rude remarks, and naturally Bill and Tom would join in, though they were friendly enough as a rule. Her cousins looked up to Gareth, who had stayed on an extra year at school and hoped to become an engineer one day. And since Hetty was not in the mood for teasing, she looked wildly round her, then dived for the nearest refuge, which was, of course, the library. Neither Bill, Tom nor Gareth would dream of entering its portals, so she would be safe from them once she was through the big glass doors. And even facing the cross librarian would be better than having either her cousins or her next-door neighbour scoffing, tugging at her untidy hair, trying to trip her up . . .

Once inside the doors, Hetty looked round for

somewhere to hide, then chided herself for cowardice. The teacher said she had the right to visit the library and she was doing just that. It was a piece of luck that the librarian had a short queue of elderly ladies who had chosen their books and were waiting to check them out at the long wooden counter. Hetty noticed that the woman at the front had opened her books at the first page, and even as she watched the librarian picked up a rubber stamp, clicked it down on both books and smiled at her customer. 'You've got three weeks to read them in, Mrs Burrell,' she said. 'But I know you; you'll be back here in a week looking for two more.'

Hetty, listening avidly, thought how lovely it would be to have two books for three whole weeks. And the choice was enormous! Books of every shape, colour and size jostled each other on the shelves, and seeing that the librarian had not even noticed her as yet and would probably be busy stamping books for some time, she set off to explore her surroundings. To her left, in one corner of the large room, was a notice reading *Children's Books*, but though there were a number of adults browsing at the shelves there was only one child beside herself in the place and she must, Hetty assumed, be simply accompanying her mother since she was paying no attention at all to the books.

Hetty sidled past the counter and made for the children's section. She began to examine the books, then reminded herself that this was not wholly a pleasure trip. She was supposed to be finding books about children in other lands; best get that over with first, then later she would pick something she really wanted to read. Goodness knows, there was enough choice. Presently, she found what she was looking for. She selected a book about Eskimos, then one about Red Indians.

Tucking them under her arm, she suddenly saw a title with which she was familiar: *Treasure Island*, by Robert Louis Stevenson. She knew the book well, for Miss Marks was reading it to the class, or rather sharing the reading with the class. The teacher would read a few pages, then hand the book to one of her pupils. It wasn't too bad when Hetty or Lucy or one of the other brighter children had to read a few pages aloud, but it was misery when it went to someone who found reading a chore, and prolonged the agony by mis-pronouncing all the longer words and making a nonsense of half the sentences. Hetty had got over the suspense of not knowing what came next by closing her ears to the dreadful, painful renderings of the slower readers and racing ahead, so that by the time the class were about a third of the way through the book Hetty had already finished it. She suspected that Miss Marks knew what she had done, but the teacher must have understood the temptation, for she had neither commented on Hetty's knowledge of the story, nor upbraided her pupil for reading ahead.

Right next to *Treasure Island*, however, was another book by the same author, entitled *The Black Arrow*. Hetty slid it off the shelf, retreated to the very back of the children's section, sat down cross-legged on the hard wooden floor and began to read. She was well into the second chapter when a shadow fell across the page and looking up she saw the librarian glaring down at her. 'Just what do you think you are doing, child?' the woman said, her voice cold as ice. 'I recognise you! I've turned you out of my library twice already; have you no respect for your elders? This library is a place for those who wish to borrow books. Children have other places of amusement.'

'If children aren't allowed in here, why do you have so many books especially for us?' Hetty asked boldly, but she scrambled to her feet as she spoke. 'And anyway, my teacher told me to come here so that I could get information for my holiday task.' Highly daring, she added: 'She's called Miss Marks and she said that you had to let me into your library and let me borrow books as well.'

The librarian glared, put out a hand as though to seize Hetty's shoulder, then seemed to change her mind. 'Yes, we do let children borrow books occasionally,' she admitted grudgingly. 'But not scruffy little girls with grubby paws, and toes sticking out of ragged plimsolls. I am responsible for keeping all the books in good order, and I don't want the covers ruined by dirty fingerprints.'

Hetty drew an outraged breath, pushed *The Black Arrow* back on to the shelf, and held out her hands, palms uppermost. 'I scrubbed my hands before I came out this morning, Miss,' she said indignantly. 'If they're dirty, which they aren't, it'll be dirt off your books. And if they're dusty, which they are, it's because the books don't get handled enough. As for my plimsolls, I've never heard of anybody reading books with their feet.'

For the first time, the librarian looked flustered. 'Very well, as your hands are clean you may choose two books,' she said, after a short pause. 'But first, of course, you must fill in a membership form. I take it you can write, and know your name and address?'

Hetty could think of a number of cutting replies to this nasty question, but knew it would not be wise to utter any of them. Instead she said, quite meekly: 'I live with my aunt, except for when I stay with my grandparents. Will my aunt's address do?'

The librarian sighed and cast her eyes up to the ceiling, reminding Hetty momentarily of Miss Marks, though no two women could have been less alike. Miss Marks was stout and rosy, the librarian thin and pale, with black hair pulled back into a tight little knob at the nape of her neck, soulful black eyes and a slight but definite black moustache. 'Your aunt's address? You don't live with your parents then?' she said, leading the way across to a large mahogany desk behind the counter.

Hetty, following her, the books on Eskimos and Red Indians tucked once more under her arm, said briefly: 'My mum and dad died when I was two. I live with my Aunt Phoebe and Uncle Alf.'

'I see,' the librarian said. She sat down in a chair, pulled open a drawer and selected a form from within. She thrust it across the desk at Hetty, added a pencil and said impatiently: 'Fill in the form – read it carefully first, mind – and then bring it to me. I've some ladies wanting their books stamped, so I must get on.'

She arose from the chair and went across to the

counter. For the first time, Hetty noticed that she had a very bad limp. Her skirt was so long that it brushed her ankles, but even so Hetty could see that she wore a great ugly boot on her right foot, though she had a perfectly normal low-heeled shoe on her left. Odd, Hetty thought, but then dismissed the matter and began to read the form carefully, sucking the end of her pencil as she did so.

The form seemed straightforward until one reached the very end, and then it said that if the would-be library member were under twenty-one years of age, he or she would have to provide the name of a guarantor willing to take responsibility for the library books they had borrowed. Here, Hetty's pencil remained poised. What on earth should she do? She was fond of Aunt Phoebe, but she could not imagine that hard-pressed person agreeing to pay for a lost or ruined library book. Why, some of them must be worth several shillings, possibly even several pounds! She could ask Gramps or Gran of course, but they wouldn't be calling for her in the *Water Sprite* for at least two weeks and she wanted to borrow the books now so that she might get her holiday task completed before she set off for a whole glorious month on her grandparents' canal barge.

Chewing the end of her pencil and praying for inspiration, Hetty looked around her. She had seen a flight of stairs leading up to a sort of gallery overhead, and a sign saying *Reference*, but since she did not understand the meaning of the phrase she did not glance up again but looked hopefully across the room to where the librarian was just finishing with her customers and coming back towards the big mahogany desk. 'All done?' she said briskly, holding out her hand for the form. 'I'll just check your answers and then you'd best run home and get your mother – I mean your aunt – to sign at the bottom here.'

Hetty sighed. 'My aunt isn't too flush right now,' she said apologetically. 'I don't know that she'll sign. My grandpa would, but he won't be in Liverpool for another two weeks and I need the books to get my holiday task written so's I can help out when I go aboard the *Water Sprite*. That's the name of Grandpa's canal barge,' she finished.

She handed the almost completed form to the librarian and was horrified when she saw that lady begin to scrumple it into a ball. Hetty had been sitting on a hard wooden chair, facing the librarian, but now she stood up and shot out a hand to grab back the form. 'Oh, Miss, suppose I read the books in the library?' she said desperately. 'I'd be ever so careful, and you could see no harm came to them. I wouldn't try and take them out, honest to God I wouldn't.'

The librarian sighed and began to shake her head, but she must have read the despair in Hetty's eyes and suddenly seemed to change her mind. She smoothed out the form and bent a piercing gaze upon Hetty. 'Do you see that door over there? It leads to what we call the Reading Room. There are a great many people who come here to read newspapers and periodicals – that's another name for magazines – and some who merely want to look up some reference or other in one of our books without wishing to become members of the library. I don't believe I've ever seen a child go into the Reading Room, probably because there are strict rules governing it, the main one of which is silence. Whilst you are in there you may not talk or laugh, or hum a tune beneath your breath, because that would disturb others. But if you promise me you'll abide by the rules, I see no reason why you shouldn't use it.'

Hetty was so excited that she gave a little hop and clasped her hands before her. 'Oh, Miss, what are the other rules? Do I have to take the books into the Reading Room one at a time, or can I take a pile? Can I take notes? Can I write my whole essay in there, come to that? It would be a lot easier than trying to do it at home, because the boys are awful noisy . . .'

'You may take two books at a time into the Reading Room, and you may make pencilled notes,' the librarian told her. 'The other rules are written up on a placard by the door and I'm sure you'll find them both sensible and easy to follow. You may not take any of the newspapers and periodicals out with you, for instance, nor turn down the corner of a page to mark your place . . .'

'Oh, I wouldn't do that – turn down the corner of a page, I mean – because that would spoil the book for someone else,' Hetty said righteously. 'But suppose someone speaks to *me*, Miss? It would be rude not to answer.'

'Rude or not, it's one of the rules. You'll find the word *Silence* on several boards suspended from the ceiling, and all you have to do is point to one of them and make your way out of the Reading Room. Once the door has closed behind you, you can speak, but please keep your conversation as brief as you can, and if possible any such talk should be conducted in whispers. And, of course, you must obey any command given to you by a member of staff.'

'Who are they? You don't wear uniform, so how am I to tell a member of staff from anyone else?' Hetty asked timidly. So far, she had only seen the librarian herself.

'At present, there are only two of us: Mr Gower, who runs the reference section in the gallery, and myself. But we shall have an assistant librarian quite soon, and on a Saturday we have a young lady from college; you will be able to recognise her because she'll be on this side of the counter.'

'Right. And as for the silence rule, I shall be quiet as a mouse, because I like quiet when I'm reading,' Hetty promised eagerly. 'Oh, Miss, you are good! I do think my grandfather would sign the form – he loves books so he does – but I'd much rather go to your Reading Room and take notes and study in the quiet there.'

'Very well then, for the time being at least that is what you may do. And my name is Miss Preece; I very much dislike being called "Miss" all the time.'

'I'll remember, Miss Preece,' Hetty said fervently. 'It's very kind of you to let me use the Reading Room; thank you.'

'Well, abide by the rules and I'll be satisfied,' Miss Preece said. 'I must ask Mr Gower whether he agrees, but I'm sure he will, if I vouch for you.' She glanced at her watch. 'We close the library at four on a Saturday, though it's open until later on weekdays. It's only three o'clock now, however, so if you'd like to spend an hour in the Reading Room, you may choose yourself a couple of books.' Hetty displayed the books she had selected, and Miss Preece approved her choice with a nod before leading her towards the door of the Reading Room. 'You may pick a desk – there's bound to be one vacant this late in the afternoon – and start reading. Will you be returning on Monday?'

'Oh yes, Miss Preece, as soon as I can after school,' Hetty said eagerly. Then they entered the Reading Room, and Hetty was unable to repress a gasp. It was huge, and contained a number of polished wooden tables, and stands with newspapers and periodicals spread out upon them, but what caused Hetty to gasp was the room itself, with its vast domed glass ceiling. Wordlessly, for she remembered the silence rule, she gestured around her and raised her eyebrows, and Miss Preece, mindful of her own previous remarks no doubt, led her outside again before she spoke.

She smiled at Hetty, and for the first time Hetty thought that Miss Preece was regarding her with kindness. 'What do you think of our Reading Room?'

'It's wonderful,' Hetty breathed. 'May I really come here on Monday afternoon?'

'If you are free after school on Monday, and if Mr Gower agrees of course, you can come in then,' Miss Preece said, and this time Hetty thought she could read approval in the eyes that met her own. 'I know this will sound foolish to you, but we have to keep a watch on some of the people who use the Reading Room in case they have brought in scissors or penknives hidden upon their persons, to enable them to cut out a particular paragraph or item of news and save them the trouble and expense of buying a newspaper. So if you see anyone with such items, you would be doing us a great service if you came quietly out and told whoever was manning the desk.' She smiled suddenly and delightfully, and Hetty wished she would smile more often for she thought it improved her no end; made her seem, for a moment, almost pretty. 'If you can watch out for suspicious behaviour, you would be repaying the trust I'm placing in you.'

'Oh yes, I'll certainly warn you if I see someone misbehaving,' Hetty said eagerly. 'And I'll come back on Monday, after school, with my exercise book, and write my essay when I've read the books. It'll be a deal quieter than at home, 'cos me Aunt Phoebe's two big sons, Tom and Bill, what I told you about, are never what you might call quiet.'

'Very well; and I don't need details of your home life,' Miss Preece said loftily, making Hetty give an inward gurgle of amusement. If only the librarian knew! Aunt Phoebe worked as a home laundress, and in that capacity was meticulous and highly regarded by her employers. But apart from her work she was easy-going, almost slapdash, whilst Uncle Alf was the exact opposite. He expected his wife to keep her sons in order, a task Aunt Phoebe thought unnecessary, so that quite frequently chaos reigned at No. 7 Salisbury Street, with Uncle Alf bawling that he wanted his meals regular and was that too much to ask, Aunt Phoebe saying plaintively that she would see what she could do, and the boys grabbing any food that was going or taking money from the housekeeping purse on the mantelpiece to buy themselves two penn'orth of chips or a shop-made meat and potato pie.

Now the librarian limped back to her counter and Hetty returned to the Reading Room and settled down with her books. She was alone in the huge room, and soon became so absorbed that Miss Preece actually had to come into the room and give her shoulder a shake to get her attention. 'You've had your hour,' she said, but to Hetty's surprise she did not speak unkindly. 'Time you were off; Mr Gower and I are about to clear away and close up. Give me your books, and I'll return them to their places on the shelves.'

'It's all right, I'll do it,' Hetty said at once, not wanting to be a burden to the librarian, for now that the day was drawing to a close she could see lines of pain etching themselves on Miss Preece's face whenever she had to take a step.

The woman, however, shook her head. 'I'll put them back myself all the same,' she said. 'Fiction is in alphabetical order according to author, but non-fiction is catalogued differently: under subject matter.' She raised her eyebrows as Hetty stood up. 'How's the essay coming along?'

This seemed like an attempt at friendship, so Hetty gave the librarian her sweetest smile and explained that she had just been taking notes in her head, since she had not brought her exercise book with her.

Miss Preece began to answer, then stopped short with an exclamation of dismay. 'My dear child, whatever have you been doing? Oh, don't say you've been *eating* . . . but no, I'm sure you've read the signs forbidding anyone to eat or drink on the premises. Only – only your tongue is bright purple, and so is your lower lip; you look quite dreadful.'

Hetty glanced round, then giggled. 'You must have give me an indelible pencil to fill in that form,' she said. 'I reckon I always suck my pencil when I'm thinking, but don't worry, I haven't licked none of the books.'

The librarian, who had been bending over her, straightened, a hand going to the small of her back even as she took the books Hetty was offering. She sighed, then gave what might have almost been a smile, though all she said was: 'Bring your own pencil on Monday,' before turning away and taking hold of a large trolley piled with books.

Hetty realised that these were some of the volumes the library borrowers had returned, and hurried over to where the librarian stood. 'You tell me where they's to go and I'll put 'em up, then you'll be through a whole lot quicker,' she observed. 'I'd like to do it, honest to God I would.'

She expected to be turned down and was genuinely delighted when Miss Preece handed her a book and told her that it had come off the top shelf and should be placed amongst other works by the same author.

Very soon they were working in harmony, and when Mr Gower came down the stairs he said 'Good night' to Miss Preece in a very formal manner, but raised his eyebrows at the sight of Hetty replacing the books on the shelves.

Miss Preece answered his unasked question. 'We had a great many readers bringing their books back today, Mr Gower; if it hadn't been for my little helper, I'd not have been able to close at four,' she explained.

Mr Gower nodded. 'Very well, Miss Preece. Is this the young person who wanted to become a member but . . .'

'Yes, that's right, but we've sorted the matter out,' Miss Preece said rather hurriedly. She handed Hetty a large and imposing tome. 'Bottom shelf, next to the red book with gold lettering,' she said briskly.

It was a good walk from the library to Salisbury Street, but Hetty was used to walking. Grandpa's barge was still pulled by Guinness, the big piebald cob, so when she was living on the canal she walked long distances leading him, and of course lacking a penny for trams she walked a good deal in Liverpool as well.

She had emerged from the library with considerable caution, just in case the boys might still be hanging about, but there was no one she knew on the crowded pavement and presently she forgot all about her cousins and the telling-off she would probably get for not offering to do her aunt's messages before she had set out for the library.

All Hetty could think about as she trudged along

were the wonderful books she had read and handled. She was sure her essay would win her a star, possibly even a gold one, and really and truly if her work was commended, it would be thanks to Miss Preece. Hetty thought about the older woman's strange boot and heavy limp, and now that she seriously considered it she realised that this might be the cause of Miss Preece's bad temper. She herself had been caned several times at school for inattention and knew how difficult it was to concentrate when your palm was red raw and stinging whenever you moved your fingers.

Hetty glanced at her school as she walked along William Henry Street, but of course on a Saturday the only people in the building would be the cleaners and the caretaker. She headed for the jigger that ran between the houses on Salisbury Street and those on Stitt Street. She reached the back gate of No. 7, hurried across the tiny paved yard, ducked under her aunt's washing hanging on the line and went through the back door and into the kitchen. Her aunt was ironing and the room smelt pleasantly of starched linen. Hetty smiled at her aunt. 'Sorry I slipped out early this morning, Aunt Phoebe, but me teacher told me to go to the library so's I could get my holiday task written up before I join Grandma and Gramps on the *Water Sprite*. I thought Bill and Tom would probably get your messages for once, if I weren't about to do it.'

Her aunt looked up and gave Hetty an absent-minded smile. Her face was very red and her light brown hair hung over her damp forehead, for it was a hot day and though Aunt Phoebe was always saying how much she would like one of the new-fangled electric irons she was still using the old-fashioned flats. You needed to be 'on the electric' as they put it before you could use an electric iron, so Aunt Phoebe would have to wait until the happy day arrived when electricity came to their part of the city.

In the meantime, she had to do her work the hard way. Two or three times a week she did the rounds of small cafés and restaurants collecting tablecloths, napkins and tea towels, which she then bundled up and took along to the washhouse on Netherfield Road. There she would wash all the linen she had collected, using starch when necessary, and hang it to dry on the indoor lines which criss-crossed the large space. Later she would bring everything back to her own home when it was still just damp enough to iron. She was always careful to see that all the linen, right down to the tea towels, was marked with the owner's initials so that her customers knew she could be trusted to return exactly what she had taken.

But how much quicker and easier the task of ironing such large quantities of linen would have been had she owned an electric iron, Hetty thought now, eyeing her aunt's red and sweaty face with real sympathy. Once, when her aunt had been ill, Hetty had undertaken the ironing herself sooner than risk losing customers, so she knew from personal experience what very hard work ironing starched tablecloths could be. However, at present the wonderful electric iron was out of the question, so her aunt laboured on and all

Hetty could do was help by delivering her work and collecting the money due.

Now, Aunt Phoebe changed irons, but did not put the cooling one back in front of the fire, so Hetty deduced that her aunt had almost finished her day's work and would presently pack the laundry up into two or three bundles and suggest that her niece should deliver them before the restaurants and cafés closed. Hetty, anxious to please, went over to the sink and filled the kettle, then put it over the fire. 'You look as though you could do with a cuppa, Auntie,' she said cheerfully. 'When you've finished I'll deliver the stuff for you, and if there's any messages I'll do them then. Or did Bill and Tom do everything this morning?'

Aunt Phoebe stood back from the ironing board for a moment, then wiped the back of her hand across her forehead. 'Oh aye, the boys did their share,' she said tiredly. 'There's no more messages, but I don't deny I'd be glad of that cuppa, and it 'ud be a help if you'd deliver me work.'

Aunt Phoebe was a plump and pretty woman, usually cheerful and chatty, but right now her niece could see that she was too tired to do anything more than fold the last tablecloth, stand the second iron back in the hearth and slump into a chair. Hetty bustled about, making the tea and handing her aunt a cup. Sadly, this was not simply from a wish to ease the older woman's burden, but because Hetty wanted to tell her all about the librarian, and the fact that she was to be allowed to use the Reading Room to study

21

the books she needed, and realised that her aunt was more likely to show interest with a nice cup of tea inside her. She still had the form Miss Preece had given her and meant to show it to her aunt, but had no expectation that the older woman would sign it for her. And if she were honest, she much preferred using the Reading Room.

Hetty sorted the linen and bagged it up, carefully checking the initials to ensure that the linen went to the correct owners, then poured herself a cup of tea, sat down opposite her aunt and began to tell her where she had been all day, explaining that she had to have a responsible adult's signature before she could borrow books from the Everton library.

'Oh aye?' Aunt Phoebe said. 'I seem to remember something o' the sort were the rule in my young day. Of course, I never joined the library meself, but Sukey, your mam, was a great one for books. She and her pals were forever in and out, borrowin' books on all sorts. She had to get special permission, mind, 'cos she couldn't always get what she borrowed back in time because of being aboard the *Water Sprite*.

Aunt Phoebe rarely talked about Hetty's mother, who had died ten years earlier. Now, Hetty pricked up her ears and smiled hopefully across at her aunt. 'Oh, so my mam was like me, and enjoyed reading? Did she go to the Everton library then, or was there another one nearer the canal?'

Aunt Phoebe, who was beginning to recover from her exhaustion, tutted. 'Remember, queen, our pa were your grandpa, and thought education important. Like yourself, we lived ashore wi' an old aunt from the time we were ten until we were old enough to earn. Well, that were me; your mam was clever – she and her pal Agatha were the brightest in the class, though they were almost two years younger than the rest of us – and they both went on to what they called further education. Your mam were all set to be a teacher, only then along came James Gilbert . . . and that were the end of her wantin' to teach and the beginning of her talkin' of nothin' but marriage.' She chuckled. 'It comes to us all, queen; you'll be just the same, see if you ain't.'

Hetty compressed her lips; she had no intention of getting involved, even in friendship, with any boy, but knew she could scarcely admit to it. Bill and Tom were her cousins, and when they weren't teasing her she liked them well enough, but she could not imagine wanting either of them to take Lucy's place as her bezzie. However, it would never do to say so; instead she smiled sweetly and began to probe for more information. 'I knew Mam and Dad died of the flu when I was only two, but you don't often talk about them, Aunt Phoebe, and nor do Gran and Grandpa. I used to try to get them remembering, but it made Gran cry, so I had to stop. All I know about my father is his name, and the fact that he was a seaman.'

Aunt Phoebe heaved a sigh. 'It were a long time ago,' she said vaguely. 'Your dad stopped wanting to be a seaman when he married your mam and started on the canal himself, working for the Company. We didn't see much of either of them after that, because they weren't on the Leeds and Liverpool, but on the Grand Union, plying between Birmingham and London. I remember they came back to Liverpool when you were a couple of months old, just so we could all see you. But after that, except at Christmas when we all met up somewhere, we'd begun to live our own lives, if you understand me.' She smiled at her niece, shaking her head sadly. 'No, of course you won't understand because you're too young, and nothing like it has happened to you yet. But give it a few more years, queen, and Bill and Tom will have left home and may be miles away, livin' with their wives and kids. If you were to pass 'em in the street, you'd scarce reckernise them.'

Hetty opened her mouth to say what a pleasant prospect this was, and closed it quickly. Bill and Tom weren't so bad. When they weren't tripping her up or scoffing at her urge for books they weren't any worse than other lads; in fact the three of them got on pretty well.

She was about to say so to her aunt when the older woman reached out a hand and took the form Hetty had been holding. She scanned it for a moment, then clicked her tongue and pointed to the sideboard. 'Fetch me spectacles, there's a good girl,' she said. 'I can't read the small print without some help.'

Hardly able to believe her luck, Hetty fetched the spectacles and watched hopefully as her aunt perched them on her nose and began to read. She realised that just the mention of her mother had softened her aunt's attitude to reading; perhaps she really would sign the form so that she, Hetty, might bring books home to study at her leisure.

However, her aunt sighed and handed the form back to her niece. 'I wish I could sign it, but I dare not,' she said rather plaintively. 'I spend me life makin' sixpence do the work of a shillin', and books . . . well, they're a luxury, especially if you go losin' one or puttin' finger marks on 'em. No, you'll have to get someone else to sign this, someone wi' a bit more cash to spare. I'm sorry, queen, because I know you love to read, but your uncle would be that mad if we had to pay for a book you'd lost . . .'

'It's all right, Auntie,' Hetty said ruefully; it was only what she had expected, after all. She tucked the form into her pocket, and her aunt heaved herself to her feet and went across to the pantry, beginning to take potatoes from the sack so that when she spoke again her voice was rather muffled. 'I'll start on the perishin' spuds while you're taking the laundry round. There's a bill for each of the four cafés I've done today, so mind you makes 'em pay up.' She looked rather doubtfully round at her niece. 'By rights, one of your cousins should go with you, seein' as how you're handlin' cash, but they're off some-where, goodness knows where.' She glanced out at the bright sunshine and smiled. 'Not that anyone's likely to try to take my laundry money, but stick to the main roads, chuck; don't go takin' no short cuts.

Only remember your supper'll be on the table at six, an' seein' as how it's Saturday it's egg and chips followed by stewed apple an' conny-onny, and you don't want to miss that.'

Chapter Two

Miss Preece came out of the library, locked the double doors and took a deep breath of the warm, early evening air. She loved her job and thought her workplace delightful, but she had been on her feet almost without a break since eight thirty that morning and she moved away from the library with a distinct feeling of relief. She was free now until Monday morning, and though she meant to attend morning service the next day she would be able to lie in a little longer than usual, which would be nice. Always assuming that her mother would allow it, of course. Old Mrs Preece was a tartar, as her daughter knew well.

Now, Miss Preece slung her bag across her shoulder as though it were a school satchel and picked up her stick, then joined the people hurrying along the pavement. She did not mean to catch a tram despite her tiredness, for at this time of the day the trams would be crowded, and though someone would see her stick and offer her a seat she decided that on such a lovely evening she would far rather walk.

As she limped along St Domingo Road she thought back over her day. It had been different from most of her days in the library because of that odd little girl, who had refused to be turned out of the library, had answered back, had dared to argue. Of course children did come into the library from time to time, but mostly they belonged to better-off parents, people who borrowed books as a matter of course so that their offspring respected the volumes they borrowed. Some of her readers in the children's section were neat, uniformed little girls from the private schools which abounded in the area. Others were older, needing information which Miss Preece was sometimes able to supply. But this child . . . well, she wore ancient plimsolls with holes in the toes and a faded and none-too-clean gingham dress. She had explained that she needed books for her holiday task and had quoted Miss Marks, a teacher at her school, who had told her that she had every right to enter the library to borrow books. I was cross at first, of course I was, Miss Preece reminded herself, trudging along. I had to let her come in and look at the books, but I doubt very much if she'll ever get anyone to sign that form, so she won't be taking them out. The thought should have cheered her, but, strangely, it did not. She realised she was sorry for the child, and told herself that this was because she would have to keep coming into the library to consult books on the spot, but knew she was fooling herself if she believed that. She had actually *invited* the child to return to the library after school on Monday, so that she might use the books in the children's section to write up her holiday task. Turning into Priory Mount, Miss Preece wondered what people would think if she had to admit she had actually encouraged the girl. Why

28

did I do it, she wondered. I could easily have told her she might only return when she had found someone to sign the form. If I'd done that, I don't suppose she would have come back. It was what I meant to say . . . only there was something about her . . . she made me remember being young and poor and wanting books desperately . . .

Someone barged into her, knocking the stick out of her hand. It was a youth, red-haired, snub-nosed, with a great many freckles and a rueful grin. 'Sorry, missus,' he said, bending to pick up her stick and handing it back to her. 'But it were you bumped into me, you know. You did oughter be more careful; look where youse goin' and stop dreamin'.'

The words were accompanied by a disarming twinkle, and despite herself Miss Preece could not prevent an answering smile from touching her lips. She knew he was right, that she had not been watching where she was going, so she took the stick with a word of thanks and told herself to concentrate because her leg was aching dreadfully and it would never do to bump into someone else – or into a lamp post for that matter – and do herself an injury.

She turned left into St George's Hill, and as she did so happened to glance down a small alleyway. She stopped short. A young girl carrying a large canvas bag, which looked heavy, was trying to push past a group of youths in the mouth of the alley, and Miss Preece realised with considerable surprise that it was her would-be borrower of earlier in the day. And it looked as though the girl was in some sort of trouble, for the youths were crowding close and she was clutching her bag and expostulating, though the librarian could not hear what was being said. She took a couple of undecided steps away from the alley, then turned back. Even as she did so, one of the three youths swung his fist and struck the girl on the side of the head, causing her to momentarily lose her hold on the canvas bag, and as it slipped from her grasp another of the youths grabbed it and made for the alley entrance, by which Miss Preece stood.

Before she had thought twice Miss Preece had wielded her stick, not high, to hurt, but low, to trip. The end went straight between the boy's feet, causing him to crash spectacularly to the ground. The girl did not wait for the other two to attack her but leapt on the canvas bag, picked it up and grabbed Miss Preece by the arm. 'Thanks, Miss,' she said. 'You'd best come along o' me, though; the feller on the ground ain't none too pleased wi' what you just done.'

Miss Preece smiled grimly and swung her stick in a half-circle, which whistled dangerously close to the youths' noses and caused them to cringe hastily back. 'It's all right. When I was your age some people thought I was an easy target too, so I had to learn to defend myself,' she said rather breathlessly.

She poked the recumbent youth hard in the chest with her stick; he had been trying to get to his feet, but now he slumped back on the cobbles, grumbling that it weren't fair. 'I were just goin' to help the gal wi' that big canvas bag . . .'

Even his mates sniggered at this blatant lie, but no smile crossed the librarian's face. 'Oh really?' she said, and there was a world of sarcasm in her tone. 'Well, my young friend doesn't need any help so just you clear off and take your pals with you, or I'll give a yell which will fetch every scuffer for miles around.'

Hetty gazed at the older woman with awe; for a moment she had sounded really fierce, and the youths were obviously cowed by her tone, for they made off, muttering, and did not attempt to justify themselves further.

'Thanks ever so much,' Hetty said awkwardly as she fell into step with her rescuer. 'In a way it were my own fault, though. I've been delivering Aunt Phoebe's laundry work and collecting the stuff to be washed so of course the lads guessed I'd have money on me. As a rule, when I'm collecting and delivering, I stick to the main roads but' – she jerked her head at the alley she had recently quitted – 'this is a short cut, and since it's getting near supper time I thought I'd take a chance for once.'

'Well, don't do so again; I might not be around another time,' the librarian said lightly. 'Don't you have a brother, or a friend, who could go with you?'

'I've got cousins who would have helped, only they were off somewhere,' Hetty admitted. 'So it were a lucky thing for me that you were passing.' She looked up at her companion and gave her a rueful grin. 'If we were in a book, it would be me who rescued you from losing your money and getting a beating, not the other way round. Then you'd be so grateful that you'd adopt me as your own child, or turn out to be rich as . . . as whatsisname . . . Midas, wasn't it? And set my family up in business . . . or you might empty your purse into my hands with a warning not to spend it all at once. But I'm afraid all you'll get from me is thanks.'

Miss Preece smiled, though a trifle warily. 'I imagine you mean Croesus; he was reputed to be rich beyond the dreams of man. As for thanking me, you've done that already. How far do you have to walk to get back to your aunt's house? Can I take it that you'll stick to main streets?'

Hetty's reply was cut short as a red-headed boy whom Miss Preece recognised as the lad who had spoken to her earlier came up to them, grinning cheerfully at Hetty. 'Awright, Het?' he said breezily. 'Your aunt were gettin' in a fair old state, 'cos it ain't like you to be late for your grub. I said I'd tek a look round on me way to the flicks and if I saw you I'd send you off home wi' a flea in your ear.'

Hetty grinned back at the boy and turned to the librarian. 'This is my next-door neighbour, Gareth Evans; he don't like me much, except to tease me, but he'll see me safe home . . . not that I mean to go down any more jiggers today, not even if it 'ud save me half a mile o' walking.'

'Good evening, young man,' the librarian said, smiling slightly. She addressed Hetty. 'Then if you're quite happy, I'll leave you.' She spoke primly, relieved that she would not have to warn the girl that their recent encounter did not mean she would accept Hetty as a member of the library. Yet despite this resolve, as she turned away to continue her walk home, she added: 'And I'll see you on Monday, after school. Unless you have other plans.' Behind her she heard the girl promising to be at the library as soon as she could after school finished, but Miss Preece neither replied nor looked back. What was happening to her? She did not *like* children, did not want them coming in and out, untidying her nice tidy library. But to be fair the girl had made it pretty plain that she was not going to presume on their acquaintance. Perhaps it would be all right; perhaps the girl would grow tired of the library before her presence became irritating. She knew that many senior librarians felt as she did about children in the beautiful building which was Everton library.

Miss Preece limped on; a little more slowly perhaps, but with just as determined a gait. Soon she reached Everton Terrace and went up the short path leading to her front door, which she unlocked to let herself into the dark little hall. Immediately, she heard her mother's voice. 'Is that you, Agatha? Agatha, is that you?'

'Yes, Mother, it's me,' Agatha Preece called, taking off her jacket and hanging it on the hallstand. Trying to hide the annoyance she always felt, for her mother asked the same question each evening, she added with an attempt at humour: 'Who else has a key to the front door? Even Mrs Simpson has to come round the back.'

She entered the kitchen as she spoke. Her mother, a small woman with beautiful white hair and a determined expression, was sitting at the table and cast her a malevolent glance. 'You're late,' she said accusingly. 'Here am I, trying to do my best to give you a bit of a helping hand' – she gestured towards a bowl of peeled potatoes – 'even though I know I shan't get a word of thanks. And in you come, a good hour or two after your usual time . . .'

'Sorry, Mother; I was kept late at the library,' Agatha Preece said, crossing her fingers behind her back. She did not like to admit that sometimes she stayed at work after closing time for the sheer pleasure of the peace and quiet to be found in the company of books.

Mrs Preece snorted and eyed her daughter up and down as though she were about to find fault with her appearance. Instead she said accusingly: 'You didn't hurry yourself, did you? Here am I, alone all day, dying for a cup of tea . . .'

'Mother!' her daughter exclaimed. 'You know very well Mrs Simpson comes in at least twice a day. She makes you a nice lunch at around noon, then gets you a cup of tea and a piece of cake at four o'clock. And she's always telling you to knock on the wall if you need her.'

The old lady sniffed. 'Oh, she pops in, I grant you that,' she said disagreeably. 'But what's five minutes, twice a day? I know you'll say I've got the wireless, but I don't understand these new-fangled things. What I want is a bit of human company. Any other daughter would hurry home to tell me about her day, what she's done and who she's seen, but not you. Oh no, you'd rather hang around that great conceited Gower fellow, hoping for a word of commendation for working late. You don't give a thought to your poor old mother, alone in the house for hours at a time and counting the minutes to your return. Why, my poor old bones have been so bad that I've not moved out of this chair all day, just you imagine that!'

Miss Preece tightened her lips but knew better than to try to argue. She crossed to the sink, filled the kettle, put it on the stove and lit the gas. She knew very well that it was Mrs Simpson who had prepared the vegetables, knew also that their fat and friendly neighbour would have spent a good deal longer than five or ten minutes with the old lady, but once again previous experience told her that it would be fatal to say so. She paid Mrs Simpson to spend an hour, morning and afternoon, with old Mrs Preece and knew that, if anything, Mrs Simpson would stay longer, and would never dream of hurrying away before her time was up. However, her mother's irascible temper could never stand contradiction or argument; if Miss Preece wanted a quiet life she would simply agree with every word the older woman uttered and get on with preparing the meal.

She put the saucepan of vegetables on the stove and then checked the meat safe in the larder. She found two small pork chops beneath the wire gauze cover, slid them into the roasting dish which their neighbour had left standing ready and returned to the kitchen to put the dish into the oven, reminding herself that it was her mother's state of health which made her so difficult. For many years now, Mrs Preece had been a martyr to osteoarthritis and if it had not been for their family doctor, a young and energetic man who was a great believer in encouraging his patients to help themselves in every way possible, Mrs Preece would probably have become bedridden years before. As it was, though she grumbled and constantly complained that the younger woman was both cruel and selfish, her daughter helped her up and down the stairs morning and evening and refused to let her remain in bed unless some ailment other than the arthritis attacked her.

'If she once takes to her bed for a lengthy period, her limbs will speedily become immobile and she'll be stuck in that bedroom for the rest of her life,' Dr Browning had warned Miss Preece. He had run a hand through his untidy, hay-coloured hair and grinned at her. 'You don't want to spend the rest of your life traipsing up and downstairs, because your mother won't get easier as her pain increases. I know movement is painful, but at the moment she can potter about, make herself a cup of tea, push the Ewbank across the carpets, and even prepare vegetables for your evening meal. She may not realise it, but it's little tasks like that which give meaning to her life, so we will both discourage any suggestion of Mrs Preece's taking to her bed.'

Miss Preece had thanked him from the heart, for what she dreaded more than anything else was having to give up her job. She had worked very hard to acquire the necessary qualifications and had gone to university to obtain her degree in the teeth of her mother's objections, which had been frequently voiced even in the days when Mrs Preece had been pretty well, with only an occasional twinge.

Thinking back to that delightful time, for she had been very happy at university, Miss Preece smiled to herself. She had made several good friends during her years there, though she had never been able to share her friends' social life, being far too conscious of her club foot. Many fellow students had urged her to go with them to dances and parties even if she could not participate, but she had resolutely refused to do so. She was an only child and not at ease with young men, considering them rough and unreliable. At school, boys and girls were strictly segregated and naturally she had gone to an all girls' college to gain her degree. She had watched with horror as friends climbed out of the dormitory window in order to go out with young men, and even when she was fully qualified and working at Everton library she seldom managed to act naturally towards Mr Gower, the reference librarian, though she admired his scholarship and if any man entered her dreams it was he.

In some peculiar way, her mother seemed to have realised that her liking and respect for Mr Gower went a good deal deeper than the surface and to Miss Preece's horror the older woman frequently brought his name into the conversation. She had actually told Mrs Simpson that her daughter had a crush on some fellow at the library, causing Miss Preece agonies of embarrassment. Naturally, as soon as she got Mrs Simpson alone, she had explained that this was 'some of the old lady's imaginings', but Mrs Simpson had merely chuckled and patted her hand. 'Your mam can be that spiteful she'd turn milk sour,' she had observed. 'And why shouldn't you admire your boss, for heaven's sake? It ain't as if you're a young gal what's on the catch for a husband . . . tell me, queen, is your boss married?'

'I haven't the faintest idea,' Miss Preece had replied coolly, if untruthfully.

She knew very well that Mr Gower was unmarried and likely to remain so. He had once confided, as they ate their sandwiches in his small office, that he was supporting his mother. 'She has a pension, but it's a tiny one, so my salary is stretched to its limit. That is why I've agreed to do the greengrocer's books,' he had said rather stiffly, and Miss Preece had realised he had only told her because he had seen her eyeing the ledgers spread out upon his desk. Nevertheless, she told herself that he would not have mentioned the matter had he not trusted her, and the thought gave her a good deal of quiet pleasure.

Now, Miss Preece made the tea, poured two cups and handed one to her mother, who received it without a word of thanks. 'Did you put two sugars in?' she asked suspiciously, staring at the brown liquid in the cup.

Miss Preece sighed. 'Of course I did,' she said wearily, and then her annoyance got the better of her. 'I've been making you cups of tea for most of my life, so I'm not likely to forget that you like two sugar lumps,' she said almost crossly. Then, seeing her mother's mouth drop open, she hastily continued. 'Would you like a ginger nut? I bought some yesterday. And I got some squashed fly ones as well since I know they're your favourites.'

'No thank you,' old Mrs Preece said frostily. 'The tea will do nicely.'

'Well, I wouldn't mind a biscuit, since supper won't be ready for another half-hour,' Miss Preece remarked. She went over to the larder, fetched the biscuit tin and opened the lid. 'Are you sure . . .' she began, then stopped short, staring wide-eyed at her mother. The tin, which she had filled with ginger nuts and Garibaldi biscuits only the previous day, was empty.

For a moment, sheer puzzlement kept Miss Preece open-mouthed but silent, then a smile curved her lips. She simply couldn't help it. Her mother, claiming to be unable to move from her chair, had managed to cross the kitchen, open the pantry door, go inside, and eat not just one or two biscuits, but the whole lot. Unable to prevent herself, she gazed accusingly at the older woman. 'Mother, did you . . .' she began, then stopped short.

Mrs Preece, without so much as a groan or grumble, had risen to her feet and was making for the door. Over her shoulder she said: 'I got peckish. Mrs Simpson was late with my lunch . . . and come to think, I gave her some biscuits for her grandchildren. They're spending the day with her tomorrow so I thought it would be a kindness . . .'

'Mother! If you . . .' Miss Preece stopped speaking because she was doing so to a firmly closed door.

Chapter Three

Although the incident with the laundry money had left her somewhat shaken, Hetty would not have dreamed of admitting it to either Miss Preece or Gareth. Gareth would jeer and tell her cousins that she was a little ninny, and the librarian might withdraw her offer to let Hetty use the Reading Room. After all, the librarian had intervened before the three lads had had a chance to do more than thump her on the side of the head. With a couple of boy cousins such blows were by no means unusual, and Hetty had learned to give as good as she got. But her attackers had been unknown to her, and a good deal brawnier than either Bill or Tom – brawnier than Gareth too, come to that – and she had no desire to find herself the object of a vendetta. Large lads who had been vanquished by a middle-aged librarian, and furthermore one with a limp, would not relish the news of their defeat getting around, so might take steps to ensure that their victim did not tale-clat.

However, Hetty had no illusions about her personal appearance. She was small, plain and unremarkable, so having thought the matter over she decided that she was safe enough. She realised that if she met any of her attackers again she would not know them from

Adam, and was pretty sure they would not know her either. Accordingly, she trotted along beside Gareth, telling him of her day, though with certain omissions, for she supposed, rightly, that he would not understand her urge to join the library or her pleasure when Miss Preece had agreed to let her study the books on the premises and would immediately call her a stupid little swot, or teacher's pet.

What he did understand, however, and wanted to talk about, was her grandfather's barge, the *Water Sprite*. 'There ain't no job I'd enjoy more,' he said, his greenish-grey eyes wistful instead of mocking. 'Imagine it! Carryin' excitin' cargoes all the way from the Liverpool docks to the other side of them hills . . . what's they called?'

'The Pennines,' Hetty told him. 'Not that the cargoes are excitin', not really. My grandpa takes all sorts, but mostly it's grain, or wool, though sometimes it's what they call a mixed cargo. That means calling at all the villages along the way; I like that best. It means a lot of stoppin' and startin', and carryin' stuff up from the canal and into the villages themselves, but you get to know the locals, same as me grandparents does.'

Gareth sighed enviously. Hetty wondered why he was sharing his interest in the canal with her, a despised girl, but then she put two and two together and knew the answer to her unasked question. Gareth would be looking for work when he left school. He had hoped to go to the technical college to pursue his dream of becoming an engineer, but had had to give up that idea since his father had been injured at a football match and could no longer work full time. She thought that most boys must think life aboard a canal barge fascinating, but she knew better than to advise him to try the Company, or indeed any of the other barges owned by their Number Ones. Folk worked the canals for generations, son succeeding father, and newcomers were rarely employed. Indeed, had she been a boy she would have taken it for granted that, upon leaving school, she would have a permanent place aboard the *Water Sprite*, but since she was a mere girl she doubted that she would ever be considered for a berth.

'Hetty? Did you hear what I said? Would you purrin a good word wi' your grandpa for me? I'm real strong and I've been hangin' about down by the wharf, helpin' to load and unload the barges when they tie up. Honest to God, I'd work for me keep alone until they thought I were worth a wage.'

Hetty grinned at her companion. 'How polite you are when you want something,' she said. 'As for working on one of the Leeds and Liverpool barges, you have to be jokin'. Why, Gramps could take his pick of fellers who've spent their perishin' lives aboard. If I were you I'd forget it.' She felt mean, but it would not have been fair to encourage him when she believed his cause was hopeless.

'You're just sayin' that because you don't like me,' Gareth said, suddenly moody. 'You're just a stupid little kid what don't know the first thing about work. Forget I ever mentioned it, why doncher?'

Hetty tightened her lips but spoke with all the patience she could muster. 'I wish I could help you,

Gareth, honest to God I do, but it wouldn't be no manner of use me tellin' Grandpa you were after a berth aboard the *Sprite*. He'll be wantin' another hand as he an' Gran get older, but that won't be for a while yet. Of course, if they had the old *Sprite* converted from horse-drawn to engine they'd be lookin' for someone who understands engines as well as someone who knows the Leeds and Liverpool canal backwards, but Grandpa says that will be over his dead body.'

Gareth cast her an unfriendly glance from beneath his eyelids and heaved a disappointed sigh. 'Me older brother, the one what moved out five years back, has a motorbike; I'm going to get him to show me how engines work,' he said, and Hetty realised that he was still hoping to find a way of joining a canal barge as a member of her crew.

However, it would not do to say so; instead she glanced into the nearest shop window, pretending an interest in the display therein. 'That's a real smart dress,' she said. 'Why not learn all you can from your big brother? If you truly get to know how engines work, there's all sorts of jobs you could try for, apart from canal barges. Why, only the other day Bill was talking about joining one of the armed forces. He says they teach fellers to drive and service the vehicles and so on. You might have a go at that, Gareth.'

Gareth was beginning to reply when they reached the jigger and turned into it. Bill was coming towards them and Hetty guessed that he had been sent to find her. The two boys grinned at one another. 'Found her dreamin' along as usual, the way you said she'd be,'

Gareth called as soon as they were close enough to exchange a few words. 'She were with some old woman, so of course your mam's laundry money were safe. I did like your mam said an' dragged her home by her straggly hair, for all she kicked and screamed.'

Bill, reaching Hetty's side, looked at her keenly. 'What old woman?' he asked. 'Was it her gave you a thump?' He laughed. 'You'll have a black eye by tomorrer, mark my words.'

Hetty's hand flew to her bruised cheek; it was tender to the touch. 'Fancy you noticing, Bill!' she said ruefully. 'And no, it weren't the lady I were with – who is not an old woman, you cheeky beggar – what hit me. It were three lads who must have guessed I were collectin' laundry money. In fact it was the lady Gareth saw me with who scared them off.'

'Well blow me down, and her with only one good leg,' Gareth said, his tone a mixture of admiration and amazement. He turned to Bill. 'It were that old gal from the library – Limpy Liz they calls her.'

'Not in front of me they don't, unless they want a bloody nose,' Hetty said at once. 'I tell you, she saw three fellers hemming me in and tripped one up and whacked t'others. She were really brave.'

She expected her cousin to make some comment, for it was his mother's money which the librarian's prompt action had saved, but by now they had reached the back yard of No. 7 and Bill merely hurried her across it, shouting a farewell to Gareth as he hustled her in at the back door. 'Here she is, Ma, and she's still got your cash, as well as the linen for washing,' he bawled cheerfully. 'Gareth found her.'

Aunt Phoebe, dishing egg and chips out on to the waiting plates, smiled at her niece, then put down her spatula and came across the kitchen, frowning. 'You've got dirt on your cheek,' she said accusingly. 'Is it dirt? Or . . .'

'She got thumped . . .' Bill was beginning when Hetty hastily cut across him.

'It's all right, Auntie,' she said quickly. 'I nipped down a jigger, 'cos it's a short cut – I know you told me not to – and some fellers must have guessed I were collectin' laundry money and tried to take it off me. But that Miss Preece from the library saw, and came to my rescue.' She put the canvas bag full of dirty tablecloths and napkins down on the kitchen floor and smiled ingratiatingly at her aunt. 'So no harm done, you see . . . oh, is that plateful for me? I'm that hungry I could eat a perishin' horse.'

'It is,' Aunt Phoebe said. 'Well, if you've gorra black eye by Monday mebbe it'll teach you to do as your elders and betters advise. Wash your hands, then you can dig in.'

Her uncle, seated at the kitchen table, nodded approvingly. 'Good gal, our Hetty,' he said through a mouthful of egg. 'You stick up for your pal. And Billy, don't call names.'

Happy to have escaped without a lecture – for she knew very well that she had nearly lost not only her aunt's money but also the dirty laundry – Hetty sat down at the table and began to eat, reflecting as she did so that it had been a good day. Tomorrow was Sunday, which meant church in the morning and Sunday school in the afternoon, but on the Monday she would tell Miss Marks that she had indeed visited the library and had been given permission to return there after school, even though she could not become a member without an adult's signature. Finishing off her plateful with a large slice of bread and margarine, she could not help thinking how nice it would be if Miss Marks offered to sign the form for her, but she knew that such an action was very unlikely. If the teacher did it for her she would feel obliged to do it for others, and, as Hetty knew all too well, there were girls in her class who would have sold their library books to anyone willing to buy, thus putting the teacher in a very difficult position.

So on second thoughts I won't say anything about Miss Preece or the library to my teacher, Hetty told herself. If she asks me I'll explain, but it really isn't important. What is important is writing the best possible essay, and since it's a holiday task Miss Marks won't even see it until we go back to school in September. By then, of course, she will have forgotten having told me to join the library. And I shall have had my summer holiday on the canal . . . oh, how can I wait?

On Sunday morning, Miss Preece got up later than usual and took a cup of tea to her mother in her pleasant airy bedroom, with its wide bay window overlooking Everton Terrace. She did this every

Sunday, and every Sunday old Mrs Preece grumbled that she was worn out and saw no reason why she should not have a day in bed. Miss Preece reminded her that she would not want to miss the eleven o'clock service, and as soon as the old lady had drunk her tea began the difficult task of getting her out of bed and dressing her in her best. The Preeces were fortunate in that they had an upstairs bathroom, but the old lady always grumbled that it was cold, despite her daughter's carrying up a couple of jugs of hot water since, on a warm July day, it was scarcely worth lighting the fire in the range.

Presently, with both of them washed and dressed in their church-going clothes, Miss Preece helped her mother down the stairs and settled her at the kitchen table. Then she cooked bacon, eggs and toast, made a pot of coffee, saw that her mother had salt and pepper to hand, and began to eat. Only when the last piece of toast and the last cup of coffee had disappeared did Miss Preece take her mother's coat from its place on the hallstand and embark on the arduous task of getting her ready for the outside world. She then donned her own coat and hat, gave her mother the big black handbag without which the old woman would not have dreamed of leaving the house, and handed her her black ebony stick.

Throughout the short journey to the church, Mrs Preece kept up a continual grumble: the paving stones were uneven, the sun was in her eyes, her daughter had not tucked her silk scarf sufficiently tightly around her neck, her hat was too far forward . . .

However, her whole attitude changed as soon as they were within sight of the church, and when the service was over and the curate waited in the porch to greet his flock she became gracious, hailing old friends and acquaintances with equal warmth, and telling the curate that no one could have a better daughter than hers. The curate, a skinny young man with a stutter and a pair of tiny pince-nez glasses, agreed eagerly that Miss Preece was indeed a pearl past price. He gave Miss Preece the benefit of a rather watery smile and invited her to come to the vicarage on Tuesday evening to listen to a lecture from a parishioner recently returned from Palestine. Miss Preece smiled with false gratitude, said that she could not leave her mother who never went out in the evenings, and congratulated the young man on his sermon.

The curate smiled sadly, murmured that Miss Preece was an example to them all and moved away, and the Preeces, having exchanged a few remarks on the warmth of the weather and the excellence of the sermon with other churchgoers, began to make their way back to Everton Terrace. Miss Preece intended to prepare a cold luncheon, for she did not see the need for a hot midday meal at this time of year.

As soon as they were far enough away from the church, the grumbles began again, as though a tap had been turned on. Usually, this depressed Miss Preece, but today she scarcely heard her mother's whining, discontented voice. She was thinking back. Once she had looked forward to Sundays, had gone with friends to Prince's Park or into the country where they had picnicked, gossiped and laughed a good deal. Why had such pleasant pastimes ceased? Surely all her friends had not married or moved away? When had she begun to let her mother rule her so completely? And why was she now querying that rule, when she had not done so for the past four or five – no, ten or twelve – years?

'Agatha? Whatever is the matter with you, girl? Don't say the curate's pretty words have turned your head. He's not interested in you; he simply wants a good audience for this friend of his who means to bore anyone who will listen with tales of his doings in Palestine.'

Miss Preece opened her mouth to reply and was astonished when her voice, apparently of its own accord, began to sing: 'Onward, Christian so-oldiers, marching as to war.' As she sang she dragged her mother up and down the kerbs and along the uneven paving stones. Her mother raised her voice and Miss Preece sang louder. Gloriously, the spirit of rebellion rose in her. The worm has turned, she told herself exultantly, and oh goodness, what a worm I have been; but no longer! She still felt sorry for her mother, would still continue to do everything she could for the older woman, but she would not let herself be bullied.

They reached the house and Miss Preece unlocked the front door and threw it wide. She almost expected to hear a voice cry querulously: 'Is that you, Agatha? Agatha, is that you?' But of course only silence greeted her. Instead she heard her own voice saying cheerfully: 'Here we are, Mother, home again! I thought we'd have a nice ham salad for luncheon today, followed by stewed apple. Would you like that?' As she spoke, she took off her mother's hat and began to unbutton her coat. She did not do this roughly, but speedily, taking both garments across to the hallstand and shedding her own coat and hat before returning to help her mother on to a kitchen chair. She saw that the old woman was staring at her, round-eyed and drop-jawed, and felt the first faint stirrings of compunction. Most of the time she and her mother got on well, but now and then the old woman vented her frustrations on her daughter and could be thoroughly difficult. If only they could have a good relationship all the time, how happy she would be! But she knew her mother of old; give her an inch and she would take a mile. 'Mother, did you hear what I said?' she asked, keeping her tone as neutral as possible. 'Do you fancy ham salad for your luncheon?'

Mrs Preece gave her a sour look, but her daughter recognised uncertainty in her dark and beady eyes. 'If that's all there is, I suppose it'll have to do,' she said ungraciously. Miss Preece, going into the larder to collect the makings of their meal, smiled to herself and presently, putting the two plates of ham salad down on the kitchen table and beginning to slice and butter bread, she told herself that she should not expect too much. It would take time, patience and a good deal of courage to stop her mother taking out her bad temper on her daughter, but stop it she must. On the thought, Miss Preece handed her mother a round of buttered bread. Then she closed her eyes, bowed her head and clasped her hands together. 'For what we are about to receive, may the Lord make us truly thankful,' she said. 'Eat up, Mother, because when we finish luncheon I'm going to take you through to the parlour where you can have a little nap. I'm going out, but I'll be back in time to make a nice pot of tea and to cut the cake Mrs Simpson has left.'

Mrs Preece stopped eating, a forkful of tomato and lettuce halfway to her mouth. 'And just where might you be going, my lady?' she enquired, her eyes glittering. 'I don't recall my saying you could go gadding off and leave me stuck in that stuffy parlour . . .'

Miss Preece smiled. 'I'm going out,' she said succinctly. 'Would you like a glass of lemonade, Mother?' Mrs Preece glared at her but did not answer and her daughter knew that the old woman was searching for a crushing reply. Quickly, she got to her feet, went to the larder and came back with a bottle of Corona. She fetched two glasses from the sideboard, popped open the stopper, then raised her eyebrows. 'Well? Will you join me in a glass of lemonade?'

For a moment the old woman stared at her, her eyes hard and calculating, and Miss Preece could see that she was still searching for a devastating reply. With an inward sigh, she poured lemonade into two glasses, pushed one across to her mother, and began to eat once more. Rome wasn't built in a day, she reminded herself; take one step at a time, Agatha Preece, and maybe you'll win in the end.

* * *

Hetty was awoken on Monday morning when sunlight, coming through a gap in the curtains, fell on her face. She sat up and twitched the curtain back. She had no clock in her room but experience told her that light came early at this time of year and it was probably between six o'clock and half past. Her Uncle Alf was a shipyard worker at Cammell Laird's and had to leave the house soon after six if he was to catch the early ferry, so she listened hard and was rewarded when she heard the back door bang, closely followed by her aunt's voice shouting that he had forgotten his butties.

Hetty snuggled down again and closed her eyes until she was woken once more by her aunt, calling that breakfast was ready. Then she scrambled out of bed, washed, dressed and set off down the stairs, banging on the boys' door as she passed. She was aware that today was different from most Mondays because it was today that, as soon as school finished, she would take her exercise book and go along to Everton library. There she would start her holiday task, with the aid of the books in the children's section, and perhaps she might chat to Miss Preece, thus cementing good relations.

She entered the kitchen where Aunt Phoebe, having cleared away her husband's and her own breakfast dishes, was setting out bowls for the boys and Hetty. Hetty took her place at the table and began to eat her porridge. 'Am I to do your messages before school?' she asked and was relieved when her aunt shook her head.

'No, not today, chuck,' Aunt Phoebe said. She grinned at her niece. 'Off with you now!'

Hetty, already putting on her coat and about to head for the back door, turned towards her aunt. 'I'm awfully sorry, Auntie, but I won't be home till late; I'm going to Everton library to work on my holiday task. It closes at six, so I'll probably be back around half past . . .'

'You're a good girl, Hetty,' her aunt said. 'You're doin' so well at school that the last time I met your teacher she was talkin' about a scholarship again. It 'ud mean you could stay on at school like your mam did. Still, that's two years away, so no point in discussin' it yet.'

Hetty's eyebrows shot up. She would have liked to question her aunt further, for no one had mentioned the possibility of a scholarship to her, but even as she opened her mouth the kitchen door burst open and her cousins erupted into the room. Her aunt immediately seized the porridge saucepan and began to fill their bowls. She turned to Hetty, starting to ask her to pour mugs of tea, but Hetty, coated and hatted, was already halfway out of the door and managed to escape.

As she entered the playground, she wondered what Miss Preece was doing at that moment and thought how lovely it must be to have no one to please but oneself. When I'm grown up I shan't have a husband, or kids, I'll just have a nice little house and an interesting job, Hetty told herself. I must ask Miss Preece how one sets about becoming a librarian. Imagine spending all day surrounded by books; why, it would be even better than being a teacher!

* * *

54

'Tomorrow, did you say? Goodness, how the time has flown! And how long did you say you would spend on the canal?'

'A whole month,' Hetty said, smiling at the librarian. 'Well, I suppose it will be a whole month; it usually is. It's a good thing we get six weeks off school, because Grandpa would never dream of letting me stay on the *Sprite* if school was open. As it is, he'll probably have to bring me back on the very last day of the holidays. But of course I shan't know for certain until I get aboard.'

Miss Preece nodded her comprehension. She knew that her companion's holiday should have started two weeks ago, and that Hetty had been desperately disappointed when a note had arrived from her grandfather telling her that the *Sprite* was out of commission for a fortnight, during which time he and his wife would move into cheap lodgings in Leeds. However, he had said that they would be in Liverpool in plenty of time to pick Hetty up at the wharf, and promised her 'a nice surprise' when he saw her again. Miss Preece had been delighted that her small companion was not to be wrested from her as soon as she had expected, but had known better than to say so, merely commiserating with Hetty and using the extra time to introduce the girl to a great many of her own favourite books.

Now the two of them were in the tiny office at the back of the library with Hetty's holiday task, satisfactorily completed, spread out on the desk. Miss Preece had read it and been impressed. The girl before her had used all the information the library could provide on her subject, yet had managed to do it so cleverly that the completed essay read more like a story than a stiff and formal piece of research.

'A whole month, which by coincidence is precisely the time you've been visiting the library,' Miss Preece said now, smiling back at her companion and thinking how the child had improved in that time. It was not just her looks, though she was taking a good deal more care of her appearance, but her self-confidence had improved by leaps and bounds. Now, she did not sidle in hoping to escape notice, but came into the library as of right and treated the books with the loving respect which Miss Preece demanded, though she had never actually put her feelings into words. 'Well, you've worked very hard on your holiday task so I suppose I mustn't grudge you your voyage on the good ship *Water Sprite*.' The librarian laughed rather self-consciously. 'I shall miss our chats; in fact I shall miss you.'

'Will you really? Miss me, I mean,' Hetty said, sounding doubtful. 'I shall miss you and the wonderful books very much, but I do so love being aboard the *Water Sprite*. I don't know if you can understand how free I feel when I'm on the canal. Of course I have to work; I open and close the locks, lead Guinness – he's the horse – along the towpaths and to and from the stables, get Gran's messages when we tie up near a village . . . but it's very different from the sort of life I live during term time.'

'But you're fond of your aunt and cousins, I know,'

Miss Preece said. Having discovered that they lived not far from each other, they had formed the habit of walking home together after the library closed and Hetty had talked freely of her life in her uncle's house.

'Oh yes, Aunt Phoebe is very good to me and the boys aren't so bad. Uncle Alf is always fair, but he doesn't really understand girls. He thinks we all like housework, cooking and knitting.' She giggled. 'He actually thinks reading is a waste of time; can you believe it?'

Miss Preece laughed with her, then picked up the exercise book which contained Hetty's holiday task. She had chosen to write about the life of an Eskimo family and had done it so well that Miss Preece had felt the biting cold in her own fingertips. She thought the child had a gift and was tempted to say so, but then decided she would have to see more of Hetty's work before she tried to judge her ability. She knew there were scholarships to be won for bright children – she had won such a scholarship herself – but there would be time enough to talk of such things when Hetty was older.

'I'm going to take the library membership form along with me, just in case Grandpa knows someone who could sign,' Hetty said, picking up the exercise book and rising to her feet. Miss Preece was conscious of a sudden sinking of the heart. If Hetty did discover someone who could sign the form, she would become an ordinary borrower, would come into the library merely to exchange one set of books for another, and Miss Preece suddenly realised that she would not like that at all. She would miss the companionable walks from the library to their homes, but even more she would miss the time the two of them spent amongst the stacks, searching out at first volumes which would help with Hetty's holiday task, and then other books; tales which Miss Preece had enjoyed as a young girl and now thought would give Hetty the same pleasure that she herself had derived from them. Of course, Hetty had not been able to take the books home with her, but she had settled herself in a quiet corner of the Reading Room, devouring the volumes the librarian had recommended.

Later, they had discussed the plots, and how the author had tackled difficult situations, and Miss Preece had realised that she was once more seeing things as a child does, and marvelled at Hetty's ability to transport not only herself but others to the very heart of the stories she was reading.

Now, however, Hetty cleared her throat and the librarian realised that she had not been attending to whatever it was her companion had said. 'I'm sorry, my mind was wandering,' she said apologetically. 'I was about to ask you what you thought of *Kim*, but then I remembered that you hadn't started it yet. I wish I could let you borrow it for your voyage, but I'm afraid that isn't possible. And anyway, perhaps *Captains Courageous* would have been a more appropriate choice. It's about a voyage, though in Kipling's case it was a sea voyage.' She broke off as another thought struck her. 'Hetty, are you in a hurry to get home this evening? Only I have a rather nice set of

Dickens at home, and I'd be pleased to let you borrow one or two of the volumes. I think you'd like *David Copperfield*, and I'm sure you'd enjoy *A Christmas Carol*. If you'll walk home with me I'll run up to my room and bring the books down for you. I know you'll take great care of them,' she finished.

She expected Hetty to jump at the chance and for a moment saw the child's face brighten, but then Hetty drooped, slowly shaking her head. 'I'd love to borrow 'em, and it's really kind of you to offer, but I'd not have a moment's peace,' she said regretfully. 'Oh, Miss Preece, all that water! I sleep in the *Water Beetle* – that's the butty boat . . . oh, the barge the *Sprite* tows behind it – and when the weather turns nasty the rain comes in no matter how we try to prevent it.'

'Well, I won't try to persuade you, because my set of Dickens is calf-bound and very precious to me,' the librarian said. 'But didn't you say your grandfather had a few books aboard?' She smiled encouragingly at her companion. 'It won't hurt you to try your hand at adult literature for a change.'

Hetty agreed that this was so and presently, six o'clock having struck, the librarian locked the double doors and began her nightly round of the premises, making sure, as she told Hetty, that all was shipshape and Bristol fashion before leaving the building. Hetty, however, intended to call on her friend Lucy, so she and the librarian went their separate ways quite soon after leaving St Domingo Road. Miss Preece continued towards Everton Terrace, hoping that her mother

would be in a good humour, for despite her firm intention not to be bullied old Mrs Preece continued to
grumble and complain, though never as frequently as
she had done before her daughter's rebellion.

Chapter Four

Hetty woke. The room was full of grey light and all at once the recollection that today she was to go aboard the *Water Sprite* came flooding into her mind. That was why she had woken early and why she had felt the first stirrings of excitement!

Very cautiously, she sat up and twitched the curtain back, and was unable to prevent a tiny moan from escaping her lips. Outside, the rain poured down from a grey sky as if it intended to start a new flood, and if there was one thing Hetty hated it was trying to get herself and her belongings down to the wharf and aboard the barge in a heavy rainstorm. As she had told Miss Preece, the cabin of the butty boat was not weatherproof, and though she knew precisely where the leaks were situated, and always placed a bowl or basin strategically, there was little she could do to dry off her light summer coat and shoes, which would get soaked as she made her way towards the wharf. Once aboard she could don the spare set of sturdy oilskins but until then she had no choice but to brave the weather.

The window was steaming up, too, which meant that it must be cold outside, but fortunately Hetty remembered that it was very early. The *Water Sprite* would be taking on cargo at the wharf, probably until noon, and it might easily stop raining well before then.

Satisfied on that score, she snuggled down; no point in meeting trouble halfway. If she could just go to sleep again, she might easily awake to sunshine and blue sky. She heaved the blankets over her shoulders and burrowed into her pillow. She *would* sleep, she would, she would! She closed her eyes and began to think about the month that awaited her. Behind her closed lids she saw Guinness's broad back, the long tow rope and the little cabin with the stove glowing and her grandmother chopping vegetables and throwing them into the big black stew pot. She saw her grandfather at the tiller, heard the water slapping gently against the barge . . . and slept.

She awoke for the second time when the alarm sounded. Hetty's bed was directly under the window; she raised her head and peered through the misted windowpane and saw that it was still pelting down. Oh, and it's perishin' August, she thought. It's not fair. She swung her legs out of bed, reminding herself that she had a lot to do today.

Rather to Hetty's surprise, when she left Salisbury Street she was accompanied not only by her two cousins but by Gareth from next door. Reaching the barge, she leaned over and banged on the cabin doors, then ran along to the butty boat. It was already laden with what she took to be either wool or cotton, and as she jumped aboard the craft she saw her grandfather, who had been fastening the canvas cover, straighten up, a hand to the small of his back.

'I'm here, Gramps!' Hetty called joyfully. She jumped into the well and opened the door to the small cabin, slinging her bulging haversack on to the small bed. The rain had ceased only half an hour earlier but she saw, with pleasure, that there were no utensils on the floor and realised that the leaks must have been mended.

Returning to the well she remarked on this fact to her grandfather, reaching over to give him an exuberant hug which he returned, laughing as he kissed her cheek. 'That's right; we thought as the old *Sprite* was in dry dock, so to speak, we might as well get the leaks in the butty boat mended at the same time. But haven't you noticed what we've been and gone and done to the old gal? I knew your cousins were unlikely to spot the change, but I'm surprised at you, young woman.' He climbed laboriously out on to the quayside, then shook hands with Tom and Bill, obviously thinking them too old for grandfatherly kisses. 'Pity it's been raining, because the cabin's a bit small to hold a crowd,' the old man said genially. 'But I dare say we can all get in if we squeeze up a bit, only we won't do that until your gran's got the grub on the table. I know she's prepared a Lancashire hotpot, with a heap of spuds, so I reckon you'll none of you say no to a helping.'

Gareth began to say rather awkwardly that he wouldn't dream of eating their food . . . he hadn't been asking for an invitation but had merely accompanied his friends, but before he had finished the sentence the cabin door shot open and Gran stood there, grinning at them and waving a wooden ladle. She was a small, bird-like woman with curly grey hair and a face tanned and seamed by constant exposure to the weather. Hetty jumped down into the *Sprite* and gave her a loving hug. 'You would feed the five thousand, given a chance, Gran,' she said. 'Oh, Gran, I love your Lancashire hotpot but I'm quite willing to share my helping with Gareth, horrible though he is to me, because he's come all the way from Salisbury Street to have a word with Gramps about getting work on the canal and I thought . . .' She looked around her, suddenly struck by something. 'Where's Guinness? I know you stable him while you're loading, but it looks as though you're ready for the off . . .'

'Aha, she's spotted what's different,' her grandfather said. 'We decided it was time we modernised the old barge, so we've had an engine installed and we've got the loan of a young lad who knows about engines to help out until your gran and myself grow accustomed.'

Hetty's mouth dropped open. 'Gramps, how could you?' she said in a shocked voice. 'You've always said engines were filthy modern inventions which you didn't want any part of, and Guinness is the best horse on the whole of the Leeds and Liverpool, you know he is.'

'True; as soon as folk on the canal knew we had taken to motor power they came calling, hoping we meant to sell the old feller,' her grandfather told her. 'I refused all offers, of course, but I agreed to lend him to a young couple who had just inherited their grandfather's barge.

Whenever we see the *Winchester Wanderer* we keep our eyes open for Guinness, and I promise you he's in grand shape.'

'Oh, then that's all right,' Hetty said, though she still felt a trifle uneasy. 'Do I know the people who've got him, Gramps?'

'No, because until they inherited the *Wanderer* they worked the Grand Union,' her grandfather explained. 'But we're bound to meet them some time over the next few weeks ... now stop chattering and get everyone into the cabin, so we can get outside of that hotpot your gran's been preparing all morning.'

Hetty obediently herded the assembled company into the tiny cabin, helped her grandmother to dish up and then joined her grandfather, who had taken his plate out on to the stern. He greeted her with his usual cheerful smile as she sat down beside him and began to attack her own food. 'Good girl,' he said approvingly. 'Anyone would have thought you'd spent your entire life on the old *Sprite*, instead of having to live mostly ashore for the past ... let me see, let me see ... how many years is it?'

'Too many,' Hetty said a trifle gloomily, for her grandfather's news had shaken her more than she wanted to admit. 'Gramps, who is this feller – the one who's coming along to show you about engines? And where will he sleep? Only there's not room for another person in my butty cabin, even if the other person was a girl, and was willing to share. I've – I've always hoped that when I was old enough to be truly useful I'd live with you and Gran again, aboard

65

the *Sprite*, but if you've already engaged another worker . . .'

'So you shall; live with us I mean, if you really want to,' Gramps said heartily. 'But I've always rather hoped, you being so clever, that you'd have a proper career ashore. Your mam meant to become a librarian, you know, but it wasn't to be.' He sighed, then brightened. 'But it's too early to worry about such things; you're only twelve, after all. Plenty of time to decide on your future.'

'I used to think I'd like to teach, but I've changed my mind. I want to be a librarian, just like my mam; only of course I want to live on the canal as well,' Hetty admitted. 'Oh well, as you say, I am only twelve. But if this boy is going to become a member of the *Sprite*'s crew there won't be a place for me, even at holiday times.'

'Don't you worry about young Harry. Naturally, he'll sleep in the butty boat when you aren't around, but for the next four weeks he'll have a bit of a tent on the bank whilst you're with us,' Gramps said at once. 'He's the eldest son of a barge master . . . remember Mr Collins, the Number One aboard the *Swift*? They've a grosh of kids – four sons as I recall – so when Mr Collins heard I was looking for someone to give me a hand wi' my new engine, just for a few weeks, until I've got the hang of it, he was all too keen to lend me Harry, in return for the lad's keep.'

'I remember Mr Collins,' Hetty said slowly, after a pause for thought. 'But I don't recall Harry. However, if you and Gran think he's all right . . .'

Her grandfather assured her that she would soon get to know and like Harry, as he and his wife did, but secretly Hetty was not so sure. She remembered Mr Collins, a big, blustering man, and she remembered his dirty, ill-clad sons and his rough, sharp-tongued wife. But she had not met any of the Collinses for years and very much hoped that they were now as pleasant and suitable as her grandparents seemed to think.

Her grandfather looked all around him, then dropped his voice. 'To tell you the truth, Hetty, I felt really sorry for the lad. He's the eldest and his parents have always handed out more kicks than kisses. So when I put the word about that I was looking for someone who knew about engines and the lad came to call on me, I didn't have the heart to turn him down.'

'I see,' Hetty said slowly. 'That explains a lot, Gramps, because I do remember the Collins family, and to tell the truth I thought they were a rough lot. But if you're happy with this Harry . . .'

Her grandfather finished off the food on his plate and stood up. 'Remember, the lad's only been with us for a few days,' he said. 'He joined us in the boat-yard and came with us down to the wharf. You would have met him already except that I've sent him off with some money to buy himself a tent, and one of those sleeping bag affairs. I don't imagine he'll come aboard while your cousins are here, but he'll join us as soon as they leave.' He looked consideringly at his granddaughter. 'Think of him as a rough diamond who needs the dirt cleaning off,' he advised her. 'If I can see that there's a decent young feller under the muck, then surely you, being nearer him in age, will do the same.'

Hetty tried not to look doubtful. 'I'll do my best, Gramps,' she said humbly. 'I'll try and forget he's a Collins, for a start. How old is he, by the way?'

Gramps shrugged. 'I didn't ask, but I imagine he's fifteen or sixteen; a good bit older than you, but you've got to bear in mind that he's had almost no schooling, the Collins setting no store by what they call book learning.'

Hetty, finishing off her own hotpot, stood up as well and handed her empty plate to Gramps. 'You're trying to tell me he can't read or write, aren't you?' she said bluntly. 'Lots of the kids on the canal can't do that. But I wouldn't know one end of an engine from the other, so me and Harry are quits. And now let's get our share of Gran's apple pie before those gannets in the cabin eat the lot.'

Hetty was in the butty boat getting ready to set sail, having seen her cousins off, when someone landed with a thump on the decking. She poked her head out and saw a tall, skinny boy with tow-coloured hair checking the tarpaulin which was stretched across the cargo. Hetty cleared her throat and the boy turned round and stared, then turned back and continued with his work.

Hetty waited for him to acknowledge her presence and, when he did not, said rather stiffly: 'Hello! You must be Harry Collins. I'm ...'

'You're Hetty Gilbert; your gran told me you was

comin' aboard,' the boy said. He gave a malicious grin. 'No doubt you'll gerrin the way an' hold us back, same as any other child would.'

'Don't be silly,' Hetty said sharply. 'I've been around barges and canals all my life.'

'Oh yeah?' the boy said rudely. 'And what d'you know about engines?' He sniggered and lowered his voice. 'About as much as the old feller does, I reckon.'

Hetty's eyes opened wide; he was clearly referring to her grandfather, who had taken him on when many another would have refused to have any member of the Collins family aboard their boat. She was about to remind him of this fact when she saw her grandfather coming along the quayside and immediately the boy's whole attitude underwent a lightning change. His face, which had been set in a scowl, brightened into a cheerful smile and he called out: 'Is we ready to go, Mr Hesketh, sir? I bought a tent, like you telled me, and the other stuff. I've stowed it in the kennel bein' as there's no tackle for the horse now, nor oats an' that.'

Hetty sighed to herself. The kennel, though goodness knows why it was called that, was where barge masters always kept any tackle or food connected with the horse, and this sad reminder that Guinness was no longer a part of the team was still too new and painful for her to accept. However, she was glad that Harry had put his gear there, rather than in her cabin on the butty boat.

'Good lad,' Gramps called back. 'We'd best get started if we're to make the most of the light. I want to get well clear of the city before we tie up.' He saw Hetty at her cabin door and beckoned. 'Come and watch Harry start the engine; you'll be amazed at how much faster the old *Sprite* goes once we get moving,' he said.

Hetty clambered obediently out on to the decking, jumped ashore and made her way to the hatch which now housed the engine. She squatted beside her grandfather and watched as Harry came importantly over and began to reach in amongst the mass of metal, talking of flywheels, acceleration cables and governor rods in the manner of one who knew exactly what he was doing. Hetty, who had imagined that one simply turned a switch, revised her opinion. Harry might be a hateful, rude and ungrateful boy, but it seemed that he was necessary, for a while at least, to the crew of the *Water Sprite*.

She squatted back on her heels and saw the two men – if you could call Harry a man, she thought crossly – grin at each other as the engine suddenly burst into life, chug-chugging in the way she had heard other barges do. 'There you are!' Harry shouted above the noise. 'I'll keep an eye on things for a bit whilst you steer, Mr Hesketh, sir. We'll be well clear of Liverpool, Wigan and built-up areas before Mrs Hesketh has boiled the kettle for a nice cuppa to go wi' our supper.' He smacked his lips and turned to give Hetty a friendly smile. 'Your gran makes the best meals I've ever tasted in me whole life,' he said ingratiatingly. 'I's goin' to ask her to give me cookin' lessons so I can stop me mam ruinin' good food when I has to go back to the *Swift*.'

Seeing this as a first overture of friendship, Hetty did her best to forget what had gone before and returned his friendly smile. 'Whilst she's about it, she could give me cooking lessons as well,' she admitted. 'Anyway, you might tell me a bit about engines, Harry. You never know, I might be able to help when you've gone back to the *Swift* and Gramps is trying to cope without you.'

Her grandfather laughed. 'It's a lot more complicated than ever I thought,' he admitted. 'This isn't a new engine, you know, Hetty my love, but an old one which has been reconditioned. I had imagined that I'd be working it after a few days, but now I'm not so sure. With Harry here to tell us what to do, I reckon we can manage on the straights, but when it comes to the big multiple locks – the Bingley Five Rise for instance – I could be in real trouble without him.'

Hetty began to protest that her grandparents had always managed before, and would doubtless do so again, but her grandfather shook his head. 'The engine will save us a great deal of work, but even so, your gran and myself are beginning to get to the age when the hard physical labour of a barge master is too much for us. I think we'll probably need help for several months, and not just weeks; what do you say, Harry?'

'Oh, you'll learn to manage the engine soon enough, when she's runnin' smooth as silk on the cut,' the boy said, 'but there's all sorts of trouble which can crop up – fouling of the propeller, water gettin' in where it shouldn't, just when you're negotiatin' the locks. Yes,

I reckon you're right; I'm happy to say that you'll need my help for a couple of months at least; mebbe three.' He grinned widely, showing a set of shockingly discoloured teeth. Hetty longed to advise him that toothbrushes and paste were not instruments of torture, but should be used daily; however, she said nothing. 'An' I can't say I'm sorry at the thought of enjoying Mrs Hesketh's cookin' for a while longer.'

Hetty cleared her throat. 'Will you teach me about engines, Harry?' she asked. 'I'd like to learn, honest to God I would.'

Harry turned so that his back was to her grandfather, and pulled a truly horrible face at Hetty, sticking his tongue out as far as it would go and pushing his nose up so that it resembled a pig's snout. But his voice, when he spoke, was calm and friendly. 'Of course I'll tell as much as I can, but you don't want to get your hands all mucky with oil. We'll keep the speed down for a bit, so if you fancy a stroll along the towpath, go ahead. If we wanna speed up we'll give you a shout and you can come back aboard.'

'No, I don't think I will, not whilst we're going through towns and that,' Hetty said, deciding to ignore Harry's childish face-pulling. 'I'll walk when we reach the proper countryside; the Pennines are lovely and I know several of the farmers and their wives, so if Gran wants messages I can do that for her. But for now I'll go and help her get supper ready.'

At first, Hetty did make some attempt to understand the engine, which seemed to her a far more capricious beast than any horse, but as the days passed and they pressed further into the hills she began to take an interest in the countryside once more. She saw water voles swimming from bank to bank, kingfishers and dippers darting along and of course the odd rabbit, but she soon realised with some dismay that the silent progress of the *Water Sprite* had vanished with the introduction of the engine. Now the creatures of the canal could hear them coming a mile off, and could keep out of their way if they felt so inclined.

It was wonderful being with her grandparents again, but she soon realised that Harry considered her a threat to his position on the *Water Sprite* and did everything in his power to make her presence seem more of a burden than a pleasure. But he was clever, being careful to sound friendly and helpful when Gramps and Gran were nearby, and saving his spiteful remarks, and the occasional shove, for when he and Hetty were alone.

Poor Hetty, who had longed to return to the canal so much, found herself looking back almost wistfully on the happy times she had spent in the Everton library. Even her home life in Salisbury Street wore a rosy glow when compared with her first few days with Harry aboard the barge. Twice she had nearly ended up in the canal when he had found her sitting on the cabin roof, reading a newspaper, and though she realised that he had only meant to scare her, she did not relish plunging into the water, for she could not swim and did not fancy being dragged out by Harry, to the accompaniment of jeers and spiteful remarks.

To make matters worse, the weather was bad for

the first four days of her longed-for holiday, with the rain falling almost continuously. She was glad that the butty boat cabin roof no longer leaked, but longed for the rain to clear completely, and for a sight of the sun and blue skies, which in her memory had always accompanied her trips on the canal.

However, she told herself grimly that she must simply ignore Harry as much as possible, and had actually begun to do this when something happened to change Harry's attitude to her and hers to him. It was a day when the weather had dawned bright and sunny, and the countryside wore that special look which follows rain, as if every twig, every blade of grass, had been polished in honour of the sunshine. Hetty had got up early to make the most of the good weather, and the four crew members ate a good break-fast. Then Gran suggested that if Hetty was in the mood for a walk, she could visit a farm inland from the canal, where she might purchase a can of milk and some eggs. 'We'll tie up in half an hour, so's you can catch up,' Gran said. Because the barge had been undergoing work ashore, Gran had passed on her three hens and also all her plants to a friend, who was looking after them until they might be returned to the *Sprite*.

Hetty agreed eagerly to go to the farm, and was only slightly surprised when Harry said he would accompany her. 'It'll give you a chance to see how you gerralong wi'out me, Mr Hesketh, sir,' he said. 'And last time I went into the hills around here I saw summat what puzzled me. Young Hetty's allus tellin' me that

74

she knows as much or more than I do meself about the countryside around the cut, so mebbe she can explain, like.'

Hetty, looking out at the towpath and at the canal bank, wondered for a moment just what Harry had in store for her, and then met his eyes and decided that, for once, he was being completely genuine. He was smiling and nodding, his expression very different from that which he usually wore when he looked at her. And this might be the first true overture of friendship he had shown her, so she smiled back at him and nodded an agreement. 'All right, I'll come with you,' she said cheerfully. 'It's so good to see the sun again after four whole days of nothing but clouds and rain that I just can't resist.' She turned to her grandmother. 'But are you sure, Gran? That you and Gramps don't need either of us for a couple of hours? Only suppose something goes wrong with the engine, and Harry isn't to hand?'

'That's the very reason you ought both to go off,' her grandfather called from his position in the stern. 'The water's fairly clear after all the rain so I'm hoping the weed trap is empty and will stay that way, and once I've got her in gear – which I'll do before you young 'uns go off – your gran and myself should manage just fine. But if we don't, you'll come and find us and tell us what we've done wrong, I've no doubt,' he finished, addressing Harry, though he smiled at both his crew.

So presently, Harry and Hetty, one carrying a bucket for the milk and the other a basket for some eggs, set off into the bright morning. Hetty half expected Harry's attitude towards her to become gruff and unpleasant as soon as they were out of hearing of the canal, but this was not so. It seemed that, for once, her companion had something on his mind other than how to irritate her. He told her that the farm they were about to visit had the usual number of half-wild cats, one of which had given birth, about six weeks ago, to a litter of kittens. 'There's two ginger 'uns and two pure white,' he said enthusiastically. 'Me mam and dad would never give house room to any sort o' livestock unless it laid eggs or you could eat it, but I thought mebbe your gran might tek on a kitten; or a pup, even. The old feller's gorra bitch what were due to whelp a month back; they're border collies, rare fine little beasts . . . it 'ud be company for the Heskeths when youse an' meself ain't aboard,' he added almost apologetically.

'Oh, I've always wanted a puppy – or a kitten, come to that,' Hetty admitted. 'But Gramps always said it wasn't fair to have either cooped up on the barge. I wonder whether Aunt Phoebe would let me keep one, though. Other folk on Salisbury Street have dogs or cats, so I don't see why we shouldn't.' She looked curiously at Harry. 'What about your mam and dad? Have they ever kept a dog or a cat on board the *Swift*?'

Harry laughed rather bitterly. 'They wouldn't feed so much as a perishin' mouse, lerralone a kitten,' he told her. 'They'd say it were one more mouth to feed, an' likely drown it when no one were lookin'.'

'Well, we'll ask Gran when we get back to the canal, but I shouldn't think they'd consider it,' Hetty told him. 'And now where's this whatever it was you saw and couldn't make out?'

'Oh, dammit, we was so busy chatterin' that I clean forgot,' Harry said, scowling around him. 'Never mind, I'll show you on our way back to the barge. And now we'd better gerra move on, or we'll not catch 'em up.'

Accordingly, they hurried, and reached the farm in good time. Harry asked if they might look at the kittens, and received permission to visit the big barn, but was told that the pups, all six of them, had only been born a couple of days before. 'T'old bitch won't let you near 'em, being strangers, like,' the farmer's wife told them. 'Next time you're this way, though, she won't be so nervy; then you can have a peek. But you'll find kittens in stables, only take the milk an' eggs afore you go to there, 'cos I were on me way to the dairy when you knocked and I don't want to be having to wait around for you to come back.'

'Right, missus,' Harry said cheerfully, pouring the proffered jug of milk into his bucket and helping the farmer's wife to load Hetty's basket with a dozen big brown eggs. 'The stable's this way, queen.'

Hetty was about to inform him frostily that she knew the way to the stables just as well as he did when she remembered that such a remark would only set his back up, and said nothing. After all, if she wanted her holiday to be a pleasant one, she must not antagonise Harry. Instead, she followed him meekly across the yard and presently was enraptured by the kittens, agreeing with her companion that they must be the prettiest little cats they had ever seen and wishing that they could persuade either Hetty's grandparents, or her uncle and aunt, to adopt one of the delightful little creatures.

After admiring the kittens rather wistfully, the two set off once again in the direction of the canal. Hetty suggested that since the *Sprite* would have got a fair way along the cut by now they might be well advised to go back to the towpath by a different and quicker route, which would bring them out nearer the next lock, but Harry shook his head. 'I want you to see this thing, wharrever it is,' he reminded her. 'It won't take above five minutes. Still, we'd best gerra move on.'

Accordingly, they retraced their steps and presently came to a meadow they had crossed earlier, in which a number of cattle grazed. It was a pleasant place, with several large trees, and it was towards these that Harry headed. He stopped under a mighty oak which spread its branches across a good area of pasture, and stood down his bucket with a sigh of relief, for it was heavy. Hetty followed suit, then looked enquiringly at her companion. He did not speak, but gestured to the tree. Hetty peered up into the branches, but it was heavily foliaged and she could see nothing unusual through the mass of leaves. 'Well?' she said rather impatiently. 'I can't see a thing, unless you count leaves, that is, and acorns of course, only they're not ripe yet.'

Harry peered up into the branches as well, then picked up a fallen stick and used it to part the leaves directly over his head. 'See that thing? It's a bit like a pear, only sort of knobbly, and the wrong colour,' he said, handing Hetty the stick as he spoke. 'You reckon you know more about the country than I do; well, if you know what that is, you're right, because I looked and looked at it last time I came this way, and couldn't make head nor tail of the bleedin' thing.'

Hetty stared up at the strange object. She hated to admit her ignorance, but the fact was she had never seen anything like it before and had no idea what it might be. She tried to give the object a poke with the stick, but missed it by several inches, so next time she tried she moved directly underneath it and gave it a good whack. It rocked on its branch but did not fall, and she was beginning to turn away, suggesting that Harry, being a good deal taller than she, might have better luck in knocking it off its perch, when two things occurred to her simultaneously. She saw that Harry was no longer at her side, but was legging it to the gate leading on to the lane as fast as he could go; and from the object above her head, a most peculiar noise was issuing forth. An angry noise.

In seconds, Hetty realised what it was and realised, too, that Harry must have known that the thing dangling from the branch was a wasps' nest. Poor Hetty dropped her stick, ducked her head into the shelter of her arms, and began to stumble after Harry, but it was too late to escape. Wasps were buzzing round her head, inflicting painful stings on cheeks, brow and nose, and even as she cast discretion to the winds and began to run full pelt, she realised there was one on her scalp and grabbed it out with her fingers, feeling it sting the ball of her thumb.

As she neared the gate into the lane she could hear,

even above the angry buzzing, Harry's cackles of laughter, and she hoped devoutly that the wasps would attack him as soon as she got within range, for despite her tear-filled eyes she could see him rolling around and clutching his stomach, helpless with mirth.

Scrambling over the wooden gate back into the lane, she threw herself at Harry, kicking, biting and punching, becoming even more furious when it seemed as though the wasps did not intend to venture further. Harry tried to fend her off, but he was laughing too much, and when at last he succeeded she saw that he had the grace to look a little ashamed. 'Honest to God, queen, I never thought you'd whack it like that,' he said almost apologetically. 'I thought you'd know it were a wasps' nest. I mean, you're always talkin' about how well you know the canal and the countryside, so I thought you must ha' come across a wasps' nest before.' He wiped his streaming eyes on the sleeve of his ragged jacket. 'So now you know what happens to know-alls what really don't know all,' he concluded, still holding her away from him in a vice-like grip, so that not even her wildest kicks came anywhere near him.

Hetty took a deep, calming breath; her face was on fire and dreadfully painful, and she had a horrid feeling that there might still be the odd wasp either in her hair or amongst her clothing, but she did not intend to say anything about such fears to Harry. Instead, she spoke with an artificial calmness that would never have fooled anyone who knew her well. 'That was a mean trick, Harry, especially when you consider you're three years older than me at least, and always carrying on about how you know everything there is to know about life on the cut. What do you think my gran will say – and Gramps for that matter – when they see my face?' Harry began to look a little uncomfortable, and something else occurred to Hetty. 'And you'd best go and fetch the bucket of milk and the basket of eggs, because if you think I'm going back in that field again you've got another think coming.' She looked over to where the wasps were still buzzing angrily around the oak tree, and gave a gasp. 'Oh, dear – I don't know which one of us did it, although I think it must have been you when you were in such a perishin' hurry to abandon me to the wasps, but someone's kicked over the milk. Still, we've got to take the bucket back, and the eggs of course, so off you go. I wonder what magic trick you've got up your sleeve to stop the wasps attacking you? And of course I wonder how you'll explain away the empty bucket, to say nothing of my stings.'

Hetty was delighted to see that Harry's smirk had turned to dismay; clearly he had not expected his spiteful trick to turn sour on him. In fact, knowing that he would have to cross the pasture once more for the empty bucket and the basket of eggs, she felt almost sorry for him. She waited for him to try to taunt her into braving the wasps once more, and had an indignant refusal on the tip of her tongue, but suddenly he gave her a rueful grin and, leaning over, picked a wasp out of her hair and trod on it. 'All right, all right. I know it were a mean trick, but, as you say, you're a whole lot younger'n me and it annoys me sometimes when you can do things I can't. So I'll fetch the basket and the bucket, and likely I'll end up wi' a mush as red an' swollen as yours.'

'Good! Serve you right,' Hetty said roundly. 'Go on then, and don't think I'll pretend I kicked the milk over, because I'm pretty sure it was you.'

Harry did not deign to reply but climbed up over the gate and set off towards the big oak. Hetty could not help giggling as she saw him tiptoeing across the short, cropped grass. Not even his stealthy progress saved him from the wrath of the wasps, though she saw when he returned to her side that he had only got three stings compared to her own dozen or so.

'I've got the bucket and the eggs,' he said rather breathlessly, climbing over the gate and collapsing at her side. 'I wish ... but it ain't no use a-wishin'. I should have knowed you'd get the better o' me.'

'Ha ha ha,' Hetty said sarcastically. 'I just hope your perishin' face hurts even more than mine does. Only of course it can't, because you've only got a few stings and I've got hundreds.'

'Aye, you're right there,' Harry agreed. One of the wasps had stung his eyelid and now he slanted a look at Hetty, the swollen lid making him look slyer than ever, she thought. 'What'll we say about the milk to your gran, though? I know I've gorra tell about the wasps' nest, but I dunno what to do about the milk. It ain't as if I can offer to let your gran take the milk money out o' me wages, because I don't get none.'

They began to walk along the lane together, heading

for the cut. 'You could tell Gran you'd go without two meals and use the money she saves for more milk,' Hetty suggested cruelly, for she knew how fond Harry was of his food. But when she saw his face fall, she relented and broke into speech once more. 'Oh, it's all right, Harry. When we tell her it was an accident, she'll understand. She was going to make an egg custard – it's one of my favourite things – but now she'll probably make an omelette instead; you can do that without milk.'

'Oh, good,' Harry said gloomily. 'But when she hears about the wasps' nest and sees your face, if she don't turn me off the barge an' tell me to go back to the *Swift*, then she'll likely crucify me, mebbe put the word around that no one else should employ me, norreven if I teaches 'em all I know about engines.'

Hetty looked at him thoughtfully, then looked ahead to where they could already see the water of the cut gleaming through the trees. 'I've had an idea, Harry,' she said, speaking stiffly through her painful and swollen lips. 'If you'll agree to it, I swear I'll not say a word about you egging me on to wallop the wasps' nest. I'll say it fell down while we were looking at it and when we ran away one of us – we don't know which – knocked over the bucket and lost the milk.'

Harry looked at her with deep suspicion. 'If I'll agree to what?' he demanded. 'What's this bright idea of yours? If it's something horrible . . .'

'It isn't; it's not horrible, I mean,' Hetty said quickly. 'Look, I know you can't read or write, and why should you, because I bet your mam and dad never worked

83

out their route on the canal so you could go to school when you moored near a village. I was one of the lucky ones, though. Gramps taught me to read and write before I even started school. If you'll agree to it, I'd like to teach you to read, honest to God I would, and once you're reading, writing is dead easy. Well? Will you give it a go? Or would you rather I told Gramps and Gran that it's your fault my face looks like a pumpkin and we've got no milk?'

Hetty had realised, quite soon after joining the *Sprite*, that Harry was bitterly envious of her ability to read and write, but knew that he would be reluctant to allow someone three years younger than himself – and a girl at that – to teach him anything. On the other hand, when they were sitting in the cabin in the evenings, Gramps and she would take it in turns to read bits out of the newspaper aloud, and Hetty had not been able to help noticing how avidly Harry listened and appeared to enjoy knowing such snippets of information on local affairs as she and her grandfather culled from old copies of the *Echo* or the *Yorkshire Post*.

Now, she looked hopefully at Harry as they reached the towpath. 'Well?' she said rather impatiently when he did not immediately answer. 'I'm warning you, Harry, if you won't agree I'm going to tell Gran and Gramps just what you did, so you can choose: you can either learn to read and write, or take the consequences of getting me in such a pickle, 'cos I shan't be much good to anyone for days and days, with my face all swolled up like a balloon.'

She half expected to Harry to argue and was

pleasantly surprised when he gave her a lopsided grin and nodded his head vigorously. 'I'll do me best to learn,' he said gruffly. 'Tell you what, I'll teach you a bit about the engine an' all – it's a National and not such a bad old thing – provided you don't try an' take my job away.' He spat on his hand, then held it out. 'Shall we shake on it?'

They shook as they reached the towpath and began to hurry along it in the wake of the *Sprite*. 'It's a pity about the milk,' Hetty panted as her companion broke into a run. 'But it can't be helped and I'm sure Gran will forgive us when she sees our wasp stings.'

Hetty was right; Gran fussed round them with blue-bag and a soothing remedy and scarcely bothered about the lost milk. 'Your poor little face, Hetty my love,' she cooed, placing cold compresses on her grand-daughter's burning cheeks and brow. 'Why, Harry, you must have run like the wind to avoid the sort of stings young Hetty has suffered.'

'I did,' Harry admitted. 'And I'm real sorry about the milk, Miz Hesketh, but we was eager to gerrout o' the way o' the wasps, and me legs is longer than young Hetty's here.'

Gran agreed with this, and if Hetty occasionally saw her giving Harry a rather quizzical glance she said nothing and seemed to heartily approve when Hetty explained that she and Harry meant to take a look at the newspapers when they had a spare moment. Hetty had harboured secret doubts that Harry would find reading easy, but she was wrong. He was a good deal brighter than he appeared and was soon picking out words, then sentences, then whole paragraphs, and when they reached Leeds Gramps went ashore and came back with a number of books which he had got from the tuppenny box in St Ann Street, thinking they might prove of interest both to his engineer, as he persisted in calling Harry, and to his granddaughter.

After this, Hetty began to enjoy her time on the *Water Sprite*, now that she and Harry were no longer at loggerheads. She knew that they were not pals, exactly, still regarding each other too warily for that, but there were times when Harry was explaining something about the engine, or they were exploring the countryside together, when they got on pretty well. She knew Harry was jealous of the warm relationship between her and her grandparents, but understood that the contrast between the Heskeths' affection for her and the Collinses' for Harry must be painful to the boy. However, despite such feelings, he taught her as much as he could about the engine and she did her best to absorb the information, while always quick to assure Harry that she did not mean to do him out of a job by using her new knowledge except in an emergency.

The reading was a different matter, for once Harry was reasonably proficient he scarcely needed her help at all, save when he came across long words whose meanings he did not understand. Quite often, Hetty did not understand them either and was glad to borrow the Heskeths' dictionary, so they both became more knowledgeable as a result.

Despite Harry's having been on the Leeds and

Liverpool canal for most of his life, he had little knowledge of the countryside beyond the towpath itself and
some of the fields nearest at hand. Though he and his
brothers had searched the hedgerows for nuts, berries,
wild plums and crab apples, had dug up root vegetables and no doubt robbed waterside orchards and
hen roosts, they had not gone further inland in their
search for food. Hetty, who had always been given
much more freedom than the Collinses had allowed
their sons, was happy to show Harry where the fattest
blackberries could be found when autumn came, as
well as the best nuts, and where they might find hens'
nests deep in the hedgerows and help themselves to
the odd egg or two.

She was, in fact, delighted to take up her old life
where it had left off, and though she missed Guinness
it was nice not to have to watch Gramps legging his
way under low bridges or long tunnels whilst she or
Gran untacked the horse, gathered in the towrope
and tacked him up again when the *Water Sprite* had
emerged. Once, she had dreamed wistfully of the time
when she would be grown up and could lie flat on
her back on the roof of the *Sprite*, put her legs in the
air and "walk" the barge along under the narrow
bridges as Gramps did, but now she realised that such
a task would probably be beyond her strength. Harry
with his long, strong legs might have managed it, but
she was pretty sure it would have proved too much
for her. She knew also that it had been getting too
much for Gramps, for though he never complained she
had seen how tired he had been as he scrambled upright

when they emerged from beneath the bridges, and how worried Gran had looked when they approached another.

With the engine, however, legging through the tunnels was now a thing of the past. And it was the engine which had enabled them to reach Leeds in record time and would mean that she could spend her whole month on the canal, for in previous summers she had sometimes had to leave the *Water Sprite* and catch a train back to Liverpool in order not to miss the start of the autumn term.

That had occasionally happened even when she was on the canal for the whole of the summer holidays, since when they were carrying a mixed cargo and stopping off at every village with supplies for local shops and inhabitants, their journey had taken considerably longer. Once, Guinness had cast a shoe, and when they reached the nearest blacksmith it had been discovered that the horse had developed a foot abscess, which had needed treatment and rest. On another occasion, Gran had been injured when a gale had sprung up and slammed the cabin door on her hand; they had had to turn the *Sprite* round and go back to the infirmary in Leeds, where the wound had needed cleaning and stitching. But now it was amazing how much less time the journey took, with the engine put-putting away and even able to continue to do so after dark, if the Number One so wished.

It was three weeks before Hetty's face was more or less back to normal, which coincided with their return to Liverpool once more, and the end of her holiday. The time had flown and she had felt the usual little ache of disappointment at the thought of school and life ashore. But now, she reminded herself, there was the Everton library and her friend Miss Preece, so though she would miss the *Water Sprite* and Gramps and Gran, she did have something nice to return to. When they reached the wharf, they would unload the cargo they had carried from Leeds – it was cotton – and take aboard their new cargo of sugar. Hetty had a strong suspicion that as soon as they were ashore Gran would give her a note and send her hurrying off to Salisbury Street to let Aunt Phoebe know that they had arrived. Loading and unloading both the *Water Sprite* and her butty boat always took time; there were papers to be filled in, people to see and of course money to change hands. Whilst all this was taking place, Gran would be making a delicious meal in the *Sprite*'s little cabin and Hetty knew that the letter she would be carrying would also include an invitation to Aunt Phoebe, Uncle Alf and the boys to come down to the wharf and have supper with the Heskeths.

Since it was a weekday, Uncle Alf would certainly be working, though he might get home in time to join them later in the evening. Aunt Phoebe would be working as well, of course, but Hetty knew that she would cast aside her ironing in good time to join her parents and niece on board the *Water Sprite*. Like Hetty's mother, Aunt Phoebe had been brought up on the canal and thoroughly enjoyed visiting the barge when she was in Liverpool.

Hetty's thoughts were interrupted by her grand-father's voice addressing her. 'Hetty, my love, get ready to moor up as soon as we near the wharf. You go to the bows and my engineer here will see to the stern.' Gramps grinned cheerfully at his youthful crew. 'Harry, you'll know best when to cut the engine so we don't ram the boat in front, because there's bound to be a queue waiting to unload. I dare say you'll want to visit your mam and dad if they're moored up ahead of us. Want to go along and take a look?'

Hetty saw Harry pull a face and guessed that he had no desire to find his parents, but as soon as the boat was moored he jumped on to the towpath and walked slowly off towards the wharf. Hetty was about to follow him, since she was curious to see what sort of greeting he would receive from his family, when Gran called her. 'Hetty love, I've a letter here for your Aunt Phoebe. We'll be here a while – you know what it's like when we're changing cargo – so I'd be much obliged if you'd take this note along to Salisbury Street right away.' Her grandmother nipped nimbly off the boat and thrust the letter into her granddaughter's hand, along with a number of pennies and ha'pennies. She beamed at Hetty. 'You know what's in the letter because it's the same as always. I've made a rabbit stew, something you don't get often when you live in Salisbury Street, and I'm asking the family to come down to the old *Water Sprite* and share it. Your aunt and uncle are both rare fond of rabbit stew, and there's Bakewell tart for afters.'

'And the pennies? What's the pennies for?' Hetty

asked, though she knew perfectly well, for this had also become a ritual when she was leaving the *Water Sprite*.

Gran chuckled and dug Hetty in the ribs. 'As if you didn't know! It's to buy some sweeties for your cousins. It's a good job Bill and Tom aren't really interested in the canal, otherwise we'd have to take them to Leeds and back instead of you,' she added teasingly. 'Now off with you, girl, and don't linger, because the stew will be cooked to a turn in an hour. Since it's a fine bright evening, we shan't all have to cram into the cabin, but can eat our food sitting on the decking.'

'I'll hurry,' Hetty promised. 'I know Bill and Tom are more interested in cars and buses than in barges, but they enjoy visiting the *Sprite*.'

Gran smiled and nodded. 'Oh aye, mebbe you're right, but there's plenty of time for that. Now off with you, and don't go handin' over the sweets the minute you see your cousins, else they won't have no room in their stomachs for my rabbit stew.'

Hetty hurried off and was soon entering the familiar kitchen, which was redolent with the smell of freshly ironed linen for, as she had guessed, her aunt was working. As soon as Hetty appeared, however, Aunt Phoebe stood her irons carefully down on the hearth, gave her niece a hug, and took the folded note. 'Make a pot of tea, chuck, and gimme a cup,' she said, unfolding the pages. 'I'm that thirsty wi' ironing all them tablecloths on such a hot day I could drink the Mersey dry.'

'Where's the boys? Gran's asking you all to the *Water Sprite* for supper,' Hetty said, pouring boiling water on to a spoonful of tea leaves in the pot. 'I know you'll come, particularly on such a lovely evening, but I wasn't sure whether Uncle Alf would be able to make it.'

'Oh aye, he'll come along as soon as he can; I'll leave him and the boys a note propped up agin the clock, so they'll be bound to see it,' Aunt Phoebe said gaily. 'Oh, I do love me mam's cooking! Wharris it this time? Something good, I'll be bound.'

'I shan't tell you, then it'll be a surprise,' Hetty teased. She waited for her aunt to finish reading the letter, and then asked, 'Did Gran tell you I'd been attacked by wasps? I guess my face is still a bit swollen, though it's nowhere near as sore as it was at first.'

Her aunt nodded, and sipped her tea. 'Oh aye, she told me. Said she reckoned there'd been some skul-duggery from that young feller what's givin' them a hand wi' the new engine, 'cos she said he weren't stung above three or four times, whereas you could scarce put a pin between your bites.'

Hetty laughed ruefully, running her fingers across her roughened cheeks. 'They weren't bites, Auntie, they were stings. It's gnats or mosquitoes that bite, because they're after your blood. But wasps sting just out of nastiness.'

Her aunt gave a disbelieving snort. 'Just out of nastiness indeed! It says in this here letter as you was interferin' wi' a wasps' nest, so what you got you axed for, young woman.'

Hetty was forced to laugh, though she did so reluctantly. 'I couldn't tell Gran or Gramps, because it would have been tale-clatting, but I don't mind telling you, Aunt Phoebe,' she said. 'Harry – that's the name of Gramps's helper – took me across a meadow and showed me this thing hanging in the branches of an oak. He said he didn't know what it was, but I reckon he did because when I poked it with a stick he ran off like lightning, back to the lane, which was when the perishin' wasps came swarmin' round my ears, so you see it was really not my fault.'

Aunt Phoebe finished her cup of tea, then scrawled a note for her husband and sons and propped it against the clock. She stuffed her mother's letter into the sideboard drawer and reached her light coat down from its hook on the back of the door. The two of them checked that the fire was dying down, then let themselves out through the front door, locked it and pushed the key on its string through the letterbox before hurrying down the path. 'How d'you like the *Sprite*'s new engine?' Aunt Phoebe said as they walked along the pavement. 'I dare say you missed poor old Guinness, but that's progress for you. Your grandpa may be an old man, but he believes in keeping up to date so far as his barge is concerned. And how did you get on with young whatsisname, when you were aboard the *Sprite*, I mean? Harry, didn't you say?'

'Oh, Harry and I got on all right; he's not as bad as I thought he was at first,' Hetty said. 'But you'll see him for yourself quite soon now.'

But Hetty was mistaken. When Aunt Phoebe and

Hetty reached the wharf, Gran came ashore to greet them, her expression troubled. Hetty glanced around her. 'Where's Harry?' she asked. 'I want to introduce him . . .'

'He's gone,' Gran said bluntly. 'And don't ask me where, because I don't know.'

Chapter Five

Standing on the wharf, staring at her grandmother, Hetty could scarcely believe her ears. Harry had *gone*? Whatever could Gran mean? So far as Hetty could remember Harry had been intending to stay with them until her grandfather was thoroughly at ease with the engine, and though the older man had certainly learned a lot she was pretty sure that when Harry had left the *Water Sprite* to go in search of his parents there had been no intention, on either side, of his remaining with the Collinses and simply abandoning the Heskeths.

So Hetty repeated: 'Gone, Gran? What do you mean? You aren't trying to say he's gone for good? The last time I spoke to him he was keen to stay as long as possible, even talked about Gramps giving him a proper job as a paid crew member when he had proved his usefulness. Besides, it's only a few hours since he walked up the wharf and I went off to Salisbury Street. Look, I'm sure he's probably only yarning with his brothers, or his parents even. He's probably forgotten the time – you know what he's like – and will be back here well before you sail.'

Gran shook her head dolefully. 'No, chuck, you're wrong there. You'd best read this – a little lad gave it to me not an hour ago.'

Hetty took the dirty little scrap of paper her grand-mother held out. She read it, then whistled softly beneath her breath and, seeing Aunt Phoebe's puzzled look, read it aloud. '"I've gorra berth aboard a ship. They's payin me. You'll do awright. Sorry. Harry."'

After a moment's silence, Aunt Phoebe spoke. 'He's gone all right,' she said indignantly. 'Well, the evil-minded, two-faced little tyke! Oh, Mam, wharrever will you and Pa do? There's no way the two of you can manage the *Sprite*, the butty boat and the new engine; you'll have to get some help. Wharrabout young Hetty here?' She turned to her niece. 'How much did you manage to learn about the engine? D'you reckon you could run it with your grandpa?'

'I could try ...' Hetty was beginning when Gran shook her head reprovingly.

'You will not do any such thing,' she said firmly. 'Gramps and I have moved heaven and earth to make sure you get a good education, and we don't mean to let you waste it, just because one foolish young lad thinks he'd be better off earning money instead of just getting his keep for a few weeks. I don't understand it, because Harry knew right well that we meant to employ him as a third crew member just as soon as we could afford to do so. But there you are, there's no point in crying over spilt milk. Harry has gone and we've got to replace him. Furthermore, we'll want a feller who can help with the heavy work, as well as take over the engine if something goes wrong.'

'There's plenty of strong-looking fellers what have been helpin' with the loadin' and unloadin' still hangin' around the wharf,' Aunt Phoebe pointed out eagerly. 'Any one of them would jump at the chance of a job aboard. What pay would you be offerin', Ma?'

Hetty felt horribly embarrassed, because she knew very well that the sum her grandparents paid Aunt Phoebe for her own keep was a generous one and meant that the Heskeths could not afford a man's wages. She was not even sure they could run to the sort of money a boy would earn.

Gran, however, tightened her lips, glanced around, and was beginning to answer when Gramps emerged from the cabin and jumped up on to the wharf, giving his daughter a reproachful look as he did so. 'Employ one o' them lazy layabouts?' he asked scornfully. 'Why, they're only hangin' round here because no one with any sense would give 'em a permanent job. Besides, a grown man might try to take over as Number One, and that I would not countenance.' He looked at Aunt Phoebe. 'Now if you know of a likely lad, around fifteen or sixteen . . .'

Aunt Phoebe sighed. 'It's no good suggestin' Bill or Tom, though they're the right age; Bill's gorra job wi' his da' in Cammell Laird's an' he's earnin' good money, and there's a factory makin' parts for aeroplanes out at Speke what's took Tom on as an apprentice for the next five years. It suits him better than working in the green-grocer's on Scotland Road, that's for sure.' She put a hand on her father's arm. 'Look, Pa, we're doin' all right for the old readies now both boys are workin', so don't you go sendin' me any more money for the gal here, 'cos we can manage just fine wi'out it.'

Gramps snorted and began to reply, but Hetty cut across him. 'Hang on a minute; what about Gareth, Aunt Phoebe?' she said urgently. 'I know he and meself didn't gerron, but we're both more sensible now. He's a bit older'n Bill and he's real interested in engines, always has been. But I suppose you're going to tell me he's got a job now, same as Bill and Tom.'

Aunt Phoebe, however, shook her head. 'No, he's been right unlucky – now his dad's not working regularly there's no one to put in a word for him, if you understand me. I'll warrant he'd jump at the chance of some practical experience in a real job, and one on the canal at that. At least there's no harm in askin'. I'll nip round there . . .'

'No you won't,' Hetty interrupted. 'I'll go. You help Gran to get the grub ready, and by the time the boys and Uncle Alf arrive I'll be back with Gareth's answer.'

She did not wait for her aunt's agreement but set out at once, and presently she was knocking at the Evanses' house. Mrs Evans came to the door and smiled a welcome when she saw who her visitor was. 'Hello, ducks. Did you have a nice holiday with your gran and grandpa?' she asked cheerfully.

'Yes thanks, Mrs Evans. I always enjoy myself aboard the *Sprite*,' Hetty said politely.

'That's nice,' Mrs Evans said. 'But if you're after our Gareth, he's gone up to the technical institute on Stanley Road to sign up for an engineering course which is due to start in a couple of weeks. He probably won't be home for another twenty minutes or so, but you're very welcome to wait in me kitchen. You can have a cup of tea and watch me makin' an apple pie, if you've the time to spare.'

'No thanks, I won't come in if you don't mind,' Hetty said. 'I'll walk to meet him, then we can talk as we come back.'

'Right you are; I dare say Gareth will be glad of your company,' Mrs Evans said. 'And you can have that cup of tea when the pair of you get back here. In fact you can have one o' me shortbreads, 'cos they'll be out of the oven by then.'

Hetty thanked her and set off, and ten minutes later saw Gareth's red head as he came loping along the pavement towards her. He spotted her when she waved and waved back, then skidded to a halt beside her and ruffled her hair. 'How you doing, queen?' he said. 'Did you know your perishin' cousins are both in work? I wanted to apply for an apprenticeship, same as Tom did, but they wouldn't consider me until I were sixteen, which ain't for a couple of months. So I'm going to fill in time doin' an engineerin' course at the tech. I'd rather get practical experience, but with a hundred fellers chasin' every job, you've got to know someone before they'll even interview you.'

'I don't know about that,' Hetty said, momentarily diverted from her real purpose. 'I s'pose Uncle Alf put in a word for Bill, but we don't know anyone out at Speke, so far as I'm aware.'

Gareth snorted. 'Perhaps you'd forgotten that Tom's bezzie is Ivan Franklin, an' Ivan's pa is in the offices out there,' he said derisively. 'I'm tellin' you, Hetty, these days it's who you know, not what you know.

Mind you, it might have been different if I were older, but I don't reckon anyone'd give me a job without I knew someone already workin' there. But where's you goin', young Hetty? You're a fair way from the canal, but I suppose you've left the *Sprite* and are back in Salisbury Street. Are you doin' messages for your aunt? But you've got no bag . . .'

'No, I'm not doing messages; I came to meet you,' Hetty interrupted. She fell into step beside Gareth, walking back the way she had come and looking up into his face as they went. 'Gareth, d'you remember sayin' you'd like to work on a canal barge? Well, there's been a bit of an emergency . . .'

She was still watching Gareth's face as she spoke, and now she saw his eyes light up and his mouth curve into a smile. 'Tom told me they'd taken a feller on to help with the engine – you don't mean to say he weren't no use?' he said incredulously. 'But I thought he were well experienced, knew all about engines . . .'

It was Hetty's turn to snort. 'So he did; know all about engines I mean,' she said bitterly. 'I can't say I liked him much at the beginning, but we were getting on all right by the time we were on our way back. Then we moored up and he went off without a word. Next thing we knew, a little kid handed Gramps a scrappy note. It was from Harry and just said that he'd been offered a berth on one of the ships in the docks, and he's took it.'

Gareth's eyes rounded and he whistled beneath his breath. 'Without giving your grandpa no warnin'?' he said incredulously. 'That were a rotten thing to do.'

'Yes, it was,' Hetty agreed fervently. 'Of course Gramps has learned a lot more about the engine than he knew before he met Harry, but the truth is, Gareth, that my grandparents are getting on a bit, and what with the butty boat and the new engine, they've got their work cut out to manage, even when things are going right. If things go wrong – well, I dare not think what they'd do. If I could go back with them I reckon they'd be OK, but of course they won't hear of me missing school. So Gramps asked Aunt Phoebe if she knew of anyone who might be willing to take a berth aboard the *Sprite* and I thought of you at once. Only I didn't know you'd signed up for the tech.'

'I told you before I'd be happy to join the *Water Sprite* just for me keep, until I'd learned enough to be useful,' Gareth said excitedly. 'I wouldn't want a wage; the tech won't pay me to attend classes anyway, so I wouldn't be losin' anything. And my mam wouldn't have to feed me, so that 'ud be a savin' for them 'cos as you know I loves me grub.' They had been walking along the pavement quite briskly, but now Gareth broke into a trot. 'I'll have a pal of mine deliver a note to the Institute, explaining about the job; if I get it, that is. Only we'd best go down to the wharf right away, or they might offer it to someone else.'

Hetty, panting along beside him, thought this unlikely but refrained from saying so, and they continued to hurry towards the *Water Sprite*.

When they had eaten the rabbit stew and polished off Gran's famous Bakewell tart, and the visitors had left,

Gramps despatched Gareth to fetch any belongings which he might need on the journey to and from Leeds and Hetty began the part of the proceedings she disliked most: she started to empty her cabin on the butty boat.

It always surprised her how many strange things she had managed to acquire during her time aboard, and today was no exception. Birds' eggs, carefully blown and meticulously cleaned, a couple of pots of blackberry jam which she and Gran had made, a wonderfully brilliant kingfisher's feather and others from jays, pigeons and magpies were just the start of her careful hoarding. There was a corn dolly, given her by a farmer's wife for helping with their harvest, flowers which she had dried and pressed, and a great many other things. Once, her aunt had suggested she should either leave such mementos behind or throw them away, but although Hetty had only been ten at the time she had had more sense than to agree to this. Everything she brought back with her from the *Sprite* carried a memory with it, and all through the winter and the following spring she gloated over her birds' eggs, dried flowers and other treasures, valuing them for the memories they brought with them as much as the objects themselves.

By the time Gareth had explained to his mother about his new job and filled a haversack and a large canvas bag with his belongings, the butty boat cabin was cleared and ready for his occupancy. He had taken the Heskeths' advice and brought old clothes and warm ones, for though the weather was pleasant now it would not remain so during the months ahead. They docked in Liverpool every few weeks, but quite often the turnaround might take place when the Evanses were working or shopping; at any rate, when they were not at No. 9 Salisbury Street, so it behoved Gareth to pack with care all those things which he was sure he would need.

Hetty was amused, and rather touched, to see that he was taking his engineering manuals along with him, though she doubted whether the information they contained would refer to the engines which powered the canal boats. However, she realised that Gareth was ambitious, so studying the manuals would help him when he came to apply for other and more prestigious jobs.

When Hetty had finished clearing her belongings from the cabin, it occurred to her to wonder whether Harry had really left on the spur of the moment, or whether he had planned his flight. If he had done so, the kennel would be empty, but when she opened it up she found that Harry had not lied. There was the sleeping bag which Gramps had paid for, and the oilskins which were an old set of her grandfather's. In addition, there were two skimpy, much patched jerseys, a pair of dirty, well-worn canvas trousers and some enormous wellington boots, which Hetty remembered he had slopped around in when she had first joined them.

Hetty gazed into the kennel, gnawing an uncertain lip. She supposed that the only things Harry had actually owned were the two ancient jumpers and the canvas trousers; should she stand them on the wharf so that if he returned he would not be able to accuse them of stealing his property? Undecided, she tugged out the sleeping bag and her heart gave a little hop. Harry had always pretended to be so grown up, so superior and knowing, but there, at the back of the kennel, was a collection of objects very similar to those she had just taken from the butty cabin. Birds' feathers, some pretty stones, three freshwater oyster shells and a paper bag with several humbugs in it. Poor Harry! He had been trying to cram his childhood into the few weeks of freedom he had enjoyed both on and off the *Water Sprite*. He had pretended to laugh at her when she had shown him how what looked like a magpie's plain black feather turned a brilliant fluorescent green when the sun caught it. He had denied any interest in her pressed flowers, or her corn dolly, but all the time he had been collecting, just as she had.

Gramps came out of the cabin and Hetty called him. He came over, his brows rising. 'What's the matter, my dear? Want another bag to put your stuff in? You always carry away with you more than you bring, and Gran's bottled some wild plums for you to take back to your aunt, so leave room for them.'

'Right you are, Gramps,' Hetty said. 'But what am I to do with Harry's things?' She flourished the clothing, but left Harry's collection tactfully hidden away behind the oilskins. 'They aren't much, but they are his, and I wouldn't like him to think we'd took 'em. Shall I stand them on the wharf?'

'No indeed; they wouldn't be there by morning and

we'd never know who had pinched 'em. It isn't as though we're moored up in open country, or even beside one of the villages.' He patted his granddaughter's cheek. 'I can see from your expression that you can't believe anyone would want such badly worn garments, but there's kids – and men for that matter – haunting the docks who'll steal anything not nailed down.'

'Well, I can't imagine anyone wanting Harry's old jerseys and kecks,' Hetty objected. 'It's not as if the weather's turning cold . . .'

'It may not be cold yet, but folk who don't have much have to think ahead,' her grandfather assured her. 'Believe me, when the really cold weather starts, there's kids who'll be glad to go to bed clad in every stitch they possess – every stitch they can nick for that matter. So just you shove all that stuff back into the kennel. If Harry doesn't want them, we'll turn them out on the wharf next time we moor at the 'Pool.'

'Right. You know best, Gramps,' Hetty said, throwing the clothing back into the kennel. Then she returned to the butty boat where Gareth was stowing away his gear, still lit up with excitement. He turned and grinned at her. 'Thanks ever so much for thinking of me, Hetty,' he said happily. 'I've took a look at the engine and with your grandpa's help I'll be workin' it meself in a couple of days. The firm who sold it to Mr Hesketh gave him a manual, so I've told him when we moor up for the night, I'll start studying it. I already know most of the technical terms, so I reckon by the time we reach Leeds I'll know near on as much as that feller Harry did.'

'Well of course Harry couldn't . . .' Hetty began, then stopped herself. She had been about to say that Harry had been unable to read until fairly recently, and then he had never so much as opened the engine manual, saying dismissively that he did not need to do so. Hetty had guessed that he realised technical terms would be beyond his capabilities, so had not pressed him. Truth to tell, she had tried to read the manual herself, but had understood only one word in ten and had given it up as a bad job.

Now Gareth raised his eyebrows. 'Harry couldn't what?' he asked. 'Don't say he lost the manual?'

'No, no, nothing of that sort,' Hetty said hurriedly; she was not good at thinking on her feet, so to speak. 'What I meant to say was, he didn't have any patience with what he called book learning, so he didn't even bother to glance at the manual. And I have to admit he didn't seem to need it. He knew all the names of the bits and pieces under the engine cover, and which did what. To tell the truth, he was a frightful know-all. Gramps was very patient with him, but it couldn't have been easy taking orders from someone young enough to be your grandson when you've spent your life on the canals and know just about everything there is to know. Yet Gramps never got impatient, not even when Harry tried to tell him something he knew well. If it had been me, I'd have reminded him he was only on board to help with the engine, but Gramps just smiled and carried on with whatever he was doing.'

Gareth chuckled. 'Well, he won't have to put up with me knowing too much; it's likelier that I'll know too little,' he observed. 'I say, I love my little cabin; I can't wait to climb into my bunk when we're moored up tonight. I bet you'll miss it horribly, won't you?'

Hetty was about to reply truthfully that she would indeed when she realised that she was not nearly as unhappy at leaving the canal as she had been on previous occasions. Of course she was looking forward to seeing Lucy, and exchanging stories of their holiday adventures, but she was also looking forward to seeing Miss Preece and the Everton library. Before, the only books Hetty had been able to lose herself in were school texts, but now Miss Preece had made it plain that she could have the run of the library and read anything she chose, so long as she did so in the Reading Room. It was a shame, of course, that she could not take the books home, but she had speedily realised that this was not totally to be regretted. Had she taken the books into her aunt's sometimes chaotic house, all sorts of dreadful things might have happened: tea could be spilt over a volume, a spark from an unguarded fire might burn a hole in a precious cover, a flying foot might land on a page when a book fell to the floor, wrenching it from its place.

Besides, at home she had her chores to perform and her messages to run, whereas as soon as she entered the library a hush descended. She would greet Miss Preece politely, smile or exchange a quiet word with her assistant, select the book she wanted and make her way to the Reading Room, where she was already well known to the habitués. Then she would open her book and immediately enter a different world. She would follow the characters through whichever Wonderland the author had chosen to depict, entranced and enchanted, yet conscious that she was learning with every page she turned.

From time to time, people she did not know would come into the Reading Room. Sometimes it would be just one visit, at other times a man or woman would come on an almost daily basis for a week or even a fortnight, but the people Hetty thought of as regulars quickly became known and recognised by her. In winter, Miss Preece had told Hetty that some of the old men, and one or two of the old women, came in to keep warm, for the old-fashioned and rather noisy radiators kept the enormous room so hot that Hetty always shed her coat before entering. Others came to follow serial stories in the periodicals, or to settle down comfortably for a good read of past copies of the *Echo*.

Now, Hetty's thoughts of her beloved library were interrupted. 'Hetty Gilbert! I axed you if you were sorry to be leavin' the old *Water Sprite*.' It was Gareth's voice, sounding somewhat ill-used. 'I know it ain't the same now, because your grandpa has told me that in the old days your main job was lookin' after that there horse, but even so . . .'

'Sorry, Gareth, sorry; I'm afraid I was dreaming,' Hetty said apologetically. 'Of course I'll miss the barge, but as you say, it's old Guinness I miss the most. And to tell the truth, I'm looking forward to going home so that I can visit the library, because I've missed books while I was on the canal.'

Gareth stared at her as though he suspected that she had gone raving mad. 'Books?' he said incredulously. 'You've missed *books*? But books is school, you little eejit. No one in their right minds even thinks about books in the school holidays!'

Hetty opened her mouth to try to explain that the books she missed were not like the ones they read in school, but more like magic doorways through which one could enter a strange and mysterious land. There, one could have adventures which few could even imagine, for they were outside the experience of any but the author. Hetty began to speak, then stopped. It was useless; Gareth would simply never understand. However, he was still looking at her enquiringly, so Hetty dredged up a reply of sorts. 'Yes, I'll miss the *Water Sprite* and her crew like anything, but I shall keep telling myself that in less than a year I'll be back aboard,' she said briskly. 'As for the engine, I don't think I'll ever really understand it, and I don't think Gramps does either. But now I'd best let you start loading the cargo and get back home, or else Aunt Phoebe will think I've run away to sea like horrible Harry!'

Miss Preece was in the library, sitting at her desk with a tottering pile of books on her right and a much smaller pile of request slips on her left. The books on her right were all on special order and had been sent through from the central library from what they called 'the stack', which was where they kept books for which there was no room on the shelves. Both

Mr Gower and Miss Preece were proud of the fact that they were, in the main, able to supply all the books their borrowers ordered either from their own shelves or from the stack, even though it meant a lot of administrative work. Borrowers had to sign for rare books from the stack, but the librarians thought this a good thing since if the books were not returned within the stated period, they were easily traceable.

So Miss Preece was working away happily, glancing at the pile of books as it shrank, when Mr Gower came up to the desk. 'I see you're busy, Miss Preece, but I've just made a pot of tea,' he said. 'Would you like to share it with me?'

Startled, Miss Preece looked at the books still waiting to be married up with the request slips. She was about to point out that she still had a good deal of work to do before she could take her lunch break, but then changed her mind. She frequently made tea and took a cup up to Mr Gower, but this was the first time he had ever suggested doing the same in reverse. It would seem rude indeed to turn his offer down.

Accordingly, she gave him a quick little smile and stood up. 'Thank you, Mr Gower, I have to admit I'd really love a cup of tea,' she said. 'I know it's a quiet morning, but can Miss Ryder cope if we're both in the office together?'

Miss Ryder was a trainee librarian who was spending time at the local libraries. She was a small, bespectacled girl, very serious and anxious to please, and both Mr Gower and Miss Preece found her a great help.

Now, Mr Gower gave Miss Preece a small, wintry smile and led the way into the office. Miss Preece glanced at the counter and saw the trainee standing by it, looking hopefully out through the glass doors at the sunny street; the girl had admitted she loved date-stamping the books, discussing the volumes the readers had selected and replacing the ones that had been returned. The sort of sunny day they were enjoying now would mean few people either bringing books back or borrowing new ones; Miss Ryder would probably have a pretty boring time, in fact.

They reached the office and Mr Gower held open the door for her, indicating the tray standing on the desk. 'You'd better pour, Miss Preece,' he said, seating himself in the visitor's chair. He cleared his throat, took the cup she handed him, then stood it down on the desk. 'I've often meant to ask you where you go when you have lunch. I frequent Miss Eliza's Dining Rooms on Heyworth Street.' He looked fixedly into his cup of tea as though it were a crystal ball and he could read the future in its murky brown depths. 'I've often thought it would be pleasant if we could take our lunch hour together.' He paused as though expecting Miss Preece to reply, but she said nothing, too surprised and embarrassed to speak. Mr Gower shot a quick glance at her beneath lowered lids. 'Of course, when I go to Miss Eliza's, I take a book, but I would much prefer to have a companion, and I expect you feel the same.'

Miss Preece would have liked to be honest and admit that sharing a meal with Mr Gower was the last thing she wanted. The two had a fairly amicable working relationship, but Miss Preece thought crossly that she would die of embarrassment if she had to spend one of her precious lunch hours seated opposite Mr Gower at one of the small tables in the nearby Dining Rooms. However, it would never do to say so. Instead, she made a sort of muttering murmur which she hoped he would accept as a reply, and picking up her cup took a large mouthful of tea, only discovering that it was far too hot when it was too late. She could not quite prevent herself from spluttering, so produced a hanky from her sleeve and manufactured a sneeze, then had to mop her streaming eyes whilst staring resentfully at her colleague.

'Miss Preece? Are you all right? I'm afraid I didn't put any sugar in your tea – I wasn't sure if you took it or not – so perhaps it was that which disagreed with you. I'm so sorry; I didn't mean . . . I was just trying . . .'

Miss Preece began to assure Mr Gower that she was quite all right and then, despite her resolve, began to giggle. 'I'm sorry, Mr Gower, but the tea was dreadfully hot and burned my mouth,' she explained, doing her best to banish her mirth. 'Like yourself, I occasionally have a meal at Miss Eliza's, but I'm well used to eating alone, so I can't say it worries me.' She hesitated, then took the plunge. 'But what made you mention eating out, Mr Gower? Come to that, why have you made a pot of tea? You usually leave that to me, or to Miss Ryder, if you and I are both busy.'

Mr Gower looked hunted and his rather long,

serious face took on a pinkish hue. 'I wouldn't have said anything, except that I've noticed, these past few days, that you seemed . . . oh, I don't know . . . easier, not so formal. And I thought . . . I hoped . . .'

'Well, I'm very sorry if I've given you a false impression,' Miss Preece said firmly. She had decided that, since she had no desire whatsoever to be on lunching out terms with him, she should make it clear. 'But I'd better tell you straight out that I'm really quite content with my own company. I don't mean to be rude,' she added hastily, 'but I was a solitary child and I'm afraid I'm a solitary adult, too.'

She had kept her eyes fixed on Mr Gower as she spoke and was pretty sure that the look which crossed his face when she finished speaking was one of relief. She realised that the incident must have been even more embarrassing for him than it had been for her, and because of this she leaned forward across the desk and spoke urgently. 'I've just thought, Mr Gower, that there is a reason why I might have seemed less formal in the last couple of days. Do you remember the young girl who used to come to the library at least once most days? She couldn't find a responsible person to sign her library membership form, so of course she couldn't borrow books, but she was really keen on reading and I soon realised that given the opportunity she would soak up knowledge like a little sponge. I dare say you remember that I gave her permission to use the Reading Room, bringing her schoolbooks. She used the information she culled here to write her holiday task, and made an excellent job of it. When that was finished, she began to read what I would call children's classics. If you remember, and I'm sure you will, you said you thought it was all right for her to do that.'

She paused, looking interrogatively at her companion, and Mr Gower nodded. 'Yes, I remember,' he said. 'She was a scruffy little kid when she started visiting the library, but she had cleaned herself up and looked quite respectable by the time she'd been working here for a couple of weeks. Only after a bit she disappeared, and you went back to being – well, not so interested in our borrowers. You changed, but now you've changed back! What happened?'

'Oh, she went to her grandparents for a month,' Miss Preece said at once. 'I was surprised how much I missed her. We'd got into the habit of walking a part of the way home together and discussing whichever book she was reading. Then sometimes she would tell me about her family. Her grandparents work the canal, taking goods from Liverpool to Leeds and vice versa, and they take the girl – she's called Hetty Gilbert, by the way – with them for a month each summer.' She looked across the desk at Mr Gower and knew that her eyes were sparkling with excitement and her lips curling into a smile. 'School starts again in three days, so Hetty will be back in Liverpool any time now. And I've no doubt she'll be slipping through the library doors just as soon as she's able.'

Mr Gower gave Miss Preece a broad and friendly smile; it was as though Hetty's story had banished his embarrassment and allowed him to show a perfectly natural interest in the child's doings. 'And because you know she'll soon be back, you've become as you were before she left,' he said triumphantly. 'You must introduce me to Miss Hetty when she comes in again. If you're busy, send her up to the reference library; there's a great deal to interest an intelligent child up there, and it might do me good to try to find books which she would enjoy.' He gave a creaky chuckle, which sounded as though it were not often used. 'Most of my readers are students or professors, who already know a good deal about the subject they are studying. It'll be a change to have a fresh young mind, eager to learn.'

When she returned to the main library, Miss Preece realised that she would never regard Mr Gower in quite the same light again. She had thought of him as dry and desiccated, believing his only interest to be in his work amongst the books in the reference library. She had never questioned where he went in his lunch hour, nor who made his sandwiches when he ate his lunch at the library. She had imagined him to be dull, authoritarian and indifferent to those beneath him, but now she realised that like herself he was shy, almost diffident, and with the thought came another, even more surprising. Mr Gower, she told herself, had hidden depths. In future, she must realise one should never take anyone at face value. Immediately, she remembered Hetty, and began to look forward to hearing the story of her voyage on the refurbished *Water Sprite*.

* * *

School started the next day, and as soon as it was over Hetty rushed home to collect any messages her aunt might have for her, intending to visit the library just as soon as she possibly could. But when she entered the kitchen she realised that something had changed, though she could not for the life of her have said what it was. She looked across at her aunt, her brows rising. 'What's happened? The kitchen looks . . . well, different.'

Her aunt pulled a rueful face. 'You've gorrit in one, chuck,' she said grimly. 'We wouldn't say nothing in front of your gran and grandpa, but we've had a bit of a shock.'

Hetty began to speak, but her aunt cut across her. 'Paper tablecloths!' she said grimly. 'Paper napkins an' all, only they calls 'em serviettes. Next thing we know, it'll be paper tea towels.'

Hetty grasped the point at once. At this time of day the kitchen should have been piled with clean and well-starched table linen. Now it was empty and the fire beside which Aunt Phoebe usually heated her irons no longer blazed. 'Oh, Aunt Phoebe, I'm so sorry! How many of your cafés and restaurants don't need you any more?'

'The two biggest,' Aunt Phoebe said gloomily. 'And mark my words, others will follow suit soon enough, 'cos it's a big saving. We're going to have to pull in our horns, Hetty, so it's blind scouse tonight. And of course we have to pay out for Tom's apprenticeship . . . still, I dare say we'll manage.'

'So you don't want any messages this evening?'

Hetty asked hopefully, throwing her school bag down on the stone-tiled floor. 'If you're sure I'll just nip up to the library . . .'

Aunt Phoebe said rather listlessly that she had done her own messages earlier in the day and Hetty slid out of the doorway before her aunt could change her mind. She and Lucy had spent their dinner hour telling each other all their news, but now Hetty guessed that Miss Preece also would be agog to hear of the happenings on the *Water Sprite*.

As she entered the library, she saw that there was quite a queue of people returning their books and getting out new ones. Miss Preece was date-stamping the books going out and exchanging occasional murmured remarks with her readers, but when she saw Hetty a big smile crossed her face.

Old Mrs Rennet, who collected books for practically everyone in her street, was handing in a tottering pile of new borrowings for stamping, but she turned to see whom Miss Preece was greeting with such pleasure and cackled as her eyes met Hetty's. She turned to address Miss Preece. 'I see your little friend is back again; she's been gone a fair while this time.' She turned back to Hetty. 'An' I know where you've been. When I were a young girl, your gran was one of me bezzies. We'd go off to magic lantern shows, museums, theatres . . . oh, all sorts together. I were that cut up when she took to goin' about wi' a boy from the canal, 'cos I thought I'd never see her again. But I were wrong; for many a long year she'd come visitin' me for a crack whenever the barge was down at the docks. So I reckon you've been on the canal with Jim and Dulcie. Am I right?'

Hetty beamed back at the old lady, nodding vigorously. 'That's it, Mrs Rennet. But things have changed on the canal. Gramps had an engine put in recently so I'm not as useful as I was when they were horse-drawn. Still, I suppose in a way it gives me more freedom . . .'

Miss Preece finished stamping the last of Mrs Rennet's books and began to pack them into the old lady's large canvas bag. Then she turned to Hetty. 'You'll find the book you were reading when you were last here in the top drawer of my desk,' she said in a low voice. 'If you need anything else, wait until I'm free and I'll see to it.'

'Thanks Miss Preece,' Hetty murmured. She could see by the length of the queue that she would have plenty of time to read her book before the library closed.

After about half an hour, Miss Preece came into the Reading Room and beckoned to Hetty. 'Put the kettle on the gas ring and make Mr Gower and myself a cup of tea, there's a good girl,' she whispered. 'My assistant is off today and I'm sure Mr Gower must be longing for a cup, as I am. Make yourself one as well, of course,' she added. Hetty placed her book down on the table and went into the little office, feeling a surge of pride as she lit the gas under the kettle, first checking that it was full of water. It was nice to be trusted, to feel a part of the library, almost a member of staff, and presently she carried a cup of tea to Miss Preece, though she waited to deliver it until the older woman had finished for the time being with her queue of borrowers. Then she carried the second cup up the stairs, going cautiously so as not to slop tea into the saucer. She had remembered that Miss Preece did not take sugar, but that Mr Gower, who had a sweet tooth, liked two lumps in his tea. If it had been morning they would each have had two ginger nuts with their drink, but she had seen by the clock in the office that the library would be closing in rather less than half an hour and knew that Miss Preece and Mr Gower would then be going home to their teas and so would not want biscuits.

'Good afternoon, Mr Gower,' she said demurely as she arrived in front of the librarian's desk, placing his cup down upon it as she spoke. 'Miss Preece asked me to bring your tea up; she's still quite busy.'

Mr Gower picked up the cup, took a sip and gave Hetty a wintry smile. 'Thank you,' he said, and Hetty was agreeably surprised since quite often in the past he had merely grunted when she had performed some small service. 'Did you have a nice holiday?'

More and more surprising. Was it possible that he had missed her? But it did not do to take such things for granted. 'Yes thank you, Mr Gower, I had a lovely time,' she said politely. She needed to keep on the right side of him, since she guessed that, had he wished to do so, he could have forbidden her library sessions.

However, when it was time to close and he came downstairs, he seemed happy enough to see her replacing books on the shelves and generally helping Miss Preece, and presently the three of them left the building, Mr Gower locking up. On the pavement, he fell into step with Miss Preece and for one awful moment Hetty thought that he might be going to accompany them on their walk home. She did not dislike Mr Gower, but she thought him dull company and was longing for the moment when she and Miss Preece might be able to catch up on each other's news without the presence of a third party to inhibit them.

However, he only walked a few yards with them before bidding them a polite good evening and crossing the road, heading in the opposite direction from that which Hetty and Miss Preece would take. Hetty was unable to suppress a sigh of relief, which made her companion look sideways at her with a little smile hovering. 'Don't you like my revered colleague?' she asked teasingly. 'He isn't as grim as I once thought him, though no one could accuse him of being exciting company, exactly.'

'I don't think he likes me much,' Hetty said cautiously. 'Though he thanked me for his cup of tea, and asked if I'd enjoyed my holiday. He's never been that friendly before.'

Miss Preece laughed. 'He is really terribly awkward, for all he's extremely intelligent. Why, when you think we've worked together for almost eight years, and I still know practically nothing about his home or his background, you can see how very shy he is.'

'I don't suppose he knows much about you, either . . .' Hetty was beginning when Miss Preece stopped abruptly, a hand flying to her mouth.

'Did we lock the little side door?' she said, turning

round too quickly for a tall man approaching them at a smart pace along the pavement.

Hetty gave a warning shriek, but it was too late. Miss Preece cannoned into the man and crashed to the ground, scattering her possessions across the paving stones and giving a moan of pain as she did so.

Chapter Six

The man who had collided with her only just managed to save himself from falling across her. Hetty dropped to her knees. 'Oh, Miss Preece, are you all right? You went down with such a crash ... I thought ...' She glared up at the tall man and then began to try to lift the librarian to her feet, addressing the stranger as she did so. 'It was your fault, dashing along the pavement at such a speed. Are you blind? You went straight into her; the least you can do now is help me to get her up!'

She managed to get her friend into a sitting position, but before she could do anything more the man bent down and addressed Miss Preece in a far from friendly tone. 'For God's sake stand up, and stop sitting on the pavement like a street urchin! You're an intelligent woman and know very well you went down nice and easy. Come along now, get up. I'll give you a hand but I don't intend to carry you because you aren't injured, just shaken up, and I'm already late for my appointment.'

Miss Preece glared up at him and Hetty saw that her cheeks were flushed with annoyance and her eyes very bright with it. When she addressed the tall man, it was in an icy tone. 'My young friend is right; if you were in such a hurry to get to your appointment you should have been all the more careful to avoid other people. As for helping me up, you needn't bother. I can manage perfectly well by myself.'

'Then why don't you?' the man said rudely. 'Instead of still sitting there, looking quite ridiculous I might add, and dirtying the skirts of that rather smart coat.'

Hetty was so cross that she would have liked to slap him. She knew very well that Miss Preece would have a struggle to get up because of her club foot, which was wedged underneath her. If the stranger had been gracious, had apologised and tried to help her to her feet, Miss Preece could have got up easily enough, but as it was her pride, Hetty realised, would not allow her to admit that she needed help.

She was about to ask the man to go away when, with an impatient sigh, he reached down, put his hands beneath Miss Preece's armpits, and jerked her to her feet. Hetty grabbed Miss Preece's stick, which she'd been sitting on, and quickly put an arm round her friend's waist as she began to sway. Miss Preece started to speak, but then the man seemed to see the stick for the first time. 'I'm sorry, I didn't realise you were a cripple,' he said, and even to Hetty's ear he sounded more critical than ashamed. 'I still think you brought it on yourself, though, suddenly stopping the way you did, but I suppose I'd better accompany you home.'

This remark seemed to add steel to Miss Preece's backbone. She straightened into ramrod stiffness and glared at the stranger with even more hostility than he had shown to her. 'Thank you, but I am *not* a cripple.

I merely use the stick when I'm overtired,' she said. 'As for accompanying us, you will do no such thing. Good evening!'

The man started to expostulate, then turned away impatiently, saying over his shoulder: 'All right, be independent, because that just goes to show that you aren't hurt at all.' He turned back towards them; he was not wearing a hat, but he raised a hand to his brow in mock salute. 'I'd best leave you, madam, before your glare turns me into a pillar of salt.'

Hetty saw that her friend was fighting an urge to smile and presently she was able to do so, for the stranger had disappeared. However, when they began to walk, Hetty realised that Miss Preece had been too sanguine; she took one tottering step forward and gave an involuntary groan. 'I – I think I've twisted my knee,' she said breathlessly. 'Has that horrible man gone? Are you sure? I'd sooner die than accept assistance from such an uncouth and unpleasant person. But I'm afraid, Hetty my dear, that I shall have to prevail upon you to come at least as far as my front gate. If I have my stick and your shoulder to lean on, I think we'll manage, so if you wouldn't mind . . .'

'Of course I wouldn't mind,' Hetty said at once, and as the two of them began their slow progress along the pavement she began to smile. 'I wonder how he guessed you were an intelligent woman? No disrespect, Miss Preece, but sitting on the pavement, with your coat all dusty . . .'

Miss Preece giggled; there was no other way to

describe the sound which bubbled from her lips and it was the first time Hetty had heard her giggle, or known that she could. 'I can't imagine,' she said. 'One thing's for sure, though: if we ever meet again I'll know him right away, won't you?'

Hetty thought of the man who had knocked Miss Preece down. He was tall and broad-shouldered, with close-cropped, curly dark hair grey-streaked at the temples, black eyes and olive skin. He had thick, black brows which met across the bridge of a Roman nose that had been broken at some stage, and his mouth and chin both proclaimed determination, even arrogance. He wasn't at all good-looking – he was downright ugly in fact – but Miss Preece was right: once seen, never forgotten, Hetty thought.

She began to say so, but soon all her energy had to be concentrated on helping Miss Preece stumble along the pavement in the direction of her home. It took time, but at last they reached Everton Terrace. Hetty swung open the front gate and would have turned away, but her companion clutched her arm and Hetty saw that the bright colour engendered by the stranger's rudeness had quite faded from her face, leaving her pale as milk. 'Don't go, dear,' she said breathlessly. 'I'll never get up the steps, let alone unlock the door and reach the nearest chair, without your help. Oh, poor Hetty! It was just my wicked pride which stopped me from letting that – that barbarian bring me home. And now it is you who are suffering.'

Hetty laughed, but shook her head. 'Sit on the steps while you find the key in your handbag,' she instructed.

'Then I'll let you in and help you along to your kitchen. I expect you'll want to go to the kitchen?'

'Yes please,' Miss Preece said faintly, producing her front door key from the depths of her handbag. 'My mother always waits for me there.'

'Right,' Hetty said briskly, taking the key, inserting it in the lock and pushing the front door open. She had only once heard Miss Preece mention a mother, and had not realised that they lived together.

Miss Preece had managed to get to her feet as the front door opened and Hetty helped her to mount the steps. They entered the hall together, Hetty assisting the older woman out of her coat and shedding her own jacket at Miss Preece's command. As soon as the front door closed, however, a querulous voice could be heard. 'Agatha? Aggie, is that you? Why are you so late? If you ever had a thought for anyone but yourself, you would know how worried I become when you're late. Do you know what time it is? I haven't even made myself a cup of tea, since I was expecting you every minute . . .'

The voice stopped abruptly as Hetty helped Miss Preece into the kitchen and sat her down on an upright kitchen chair before turning to look at the other occupant of the room. Hetty had formed no mental picture of the old woman, but now she saw that Mrs Preece was tiny, scarcely taller than she was herself. She had snowy white hair which she wore in a big soft bun on the nape of her neck, a softly wrinkled face, all pink and white, and snapping black eyes which were now flickering from her daughter to Hetty. 'What's all this?'

the old lady said aggressively. She shot a repellent glance at her daughter. 'Since when have you invited scruffy street urchins into my house? And what, pray, is the matter with you? I've not had my tea . . .'

Hetty was so indignant that she began to explain that Miss Preece had had an accident, but the librarian hushed her. 'Mother gets irritable when she's worried; don't let it upset you, my dear,' she whispered. 'If you'll just put the kettle on and make us all a drink, then I'll calm Mother down. Don't say anything about my fall' – she smiled rather wanly – 'or I'll never hear the last of it.'

Hetty said she understood and went across to the cooker, lighting the gas beneath the kettle and giving Mrs Preece a curious glance as she passed her chair. She was wearing her school dress and thought she looked rather neat, so the old woman's description of her as a scruffy street urchin had hurt, but then she thought of the way Mrs Preece had spoken to her daughter and decided that she would concentrate on making the tea and escaping as soon as possible.

'The tea caddy is on the mantelpiece and the milk is on the cold slab,' Miss Preece said, as the kettle came to the boil. 'Can you manage, Hetty? Only I have a horrid feeling that if I stand up I might easily simply fall down again.'

'Of course I can manage,' Hetty said cheerfully. 'Only where is the cold slab?'

'It's in the pantry,' Miss Preece said, pointing to a door to the left of the kitchen window. 'And on the shelf above it you'll find a biscuit tin with a picture of King George and Queen Mary on the lid. Put a selection on a plate and we'll all have a couple with our tea.'

Hetty did as she was asked, pouring the milk straight from the bottle into the three pretty cups that she had taken from the dresser. Then she replaced the milk bottle on the marble slab, ignoring Mrs Preece's remark that in this household one poured milk into a jug before bringing it out of the pantry.

Miss Preece, however, after several sips of tea, addressed her mother in a firmer voice than she had used since entering the house. 'What rubbish, Mother,' she said briskly. 'And it isn't even true, you know. It would only make for more washing up, and since such domestic tasks fall to my lot rather than yours, I wouldn't dream of filling a milk jug just in order to wash it up later.' She turned to Hetty. 'What do you think of our house? I was born here, so I'm used to it, but I dare say you'd like to look round presently. I'm proud of our garden as well.'

Hetty began to say that she would like this very much but was interrupted by Mrs Preece, who had drunk her tea thirstily, crunched down several biscuits, and now dabbed at her chin with a pretty lace handkerchief which she produced from the sleeve of her purple wool dress. 'Are you going to start our evening meal, Agatha?' she asked aggressively. 'You've not invited this – this child to share it with us, I trust? Mrs Simpson made shepherd's pie with the cold mutton left over from the joint, but she didn't cook it; it's in the oven, awaiting your return.' She chumbled her jaw impatiently. 'And you've still not explained why you were so late, nor who this young person may be,' she added, and Hetty realised that the aggression had gone from the old woman's tone, to be replaced by bewilderment.

Miss Preece must have realised it too for she smiled at her mother, and when she replied it was in a softened tone. 'I'm so sorry, Mother. How very rude you must think me. But the truth is, I slipped coming out of the library and twisted my knee. This young lady is Hetty Gilbert; she spends a good deal of time in the library, helping the staff when we are busy and reading or doing her homework there because the library is quiet. Today, she and I left the library together, and when I fell Hetty was on hand to give what help she could. In fact, without her I can't imagine how I would have got home.'

Mrs Preece sniffed, but gave Hetty a small and rather grudging nod. 'I see. I suppose my daughter feels no need to tell you that I'm Mrs Preece and that this is my house,' she snapped. 'However, we have now been introduced, which is something, I suppose.'

Miss Preece heaved a sigh. 'You're not very generous, are you, Mother? We shall be very much in Hetty's debt if she'll be good enough to light the oven so that our supper can start to cook. And knowing Mrs Simpson there will be plenty for three, particularly since my fall has quite taken away my appetite.'

Hetty was on her way across to the oven, but at these words she turned quickly towards her friend. 'It's all right, honestly, Miss Preece. My aunt will have a meal on the table by now, so I shan't have to share your shepherd's pie,' she said. 'Do you have a taper which I can use to reach the gas at the back of the oven? Only I don't fancy trying to light it with an ordinary match.'

Miss Preece began to reply, but then to Hetty's astonishment the old woman got creakily to her feet, stumped slowly across the kitchen and snatched the box of matches from her hand. She twisted the gas tap impatiently, lit the match, and tossed it into the oven. There was a mild explosion and a squeak from Miss Preece before the old woman shut the oven door firmly and returned to her chair, though not before Hetty had seen that the shepherd's pie was both large and luscious and could have fed three people easily.

'That was rather dangerous, Mother,' Miss Preece said reprovingly. She turned to Hetty. 'Thank you very much for all your help, and I do hope your aunt won't be worried when you're not in at your usual time. Are you sure she'll have kept a meal for you? Well, in that case, perhaps you'd better take your jacket and hurry home. Do tell your aunt . . .'

'Not so fast, Agatha,' the old woman cut in peremptorily. 'How do you think you're going to get up the stairs to your bed? *I* don't intend to risk my health trying to push a great girl like you up that steep flight.'

Hetty turned and addressed the old woman directly for the first time. 'Don't you have neighbours you can call on?' she asked bluntly. 'What about this Mrs Simpson, the one who made the shepherd's pie? Surely she'd give Miss Preece a hand if she were asked. And to be honest,

I think a nurse, or even a doctor, ought to take a look at Miss Preece's knee. Probably all it needs is strapping up, but I can't do that and neither can you.'

The old lady sniffed once more. 'You may be right,' she said grudgingly. 'But who do you think is going to fetch Mrs Simpson? *I* certainly cannot do so, and I don't suppose Agatha – Miss Preece, I mean – will put herself out in the matter.'

'Put herself out?' Hetty cried, her voice vibrating with indignation. 'What a nasty old woman you are! If she can't climb the stairs to her bedroom, how do you expect her to get to a neighbour?' She pointed an accusing finger. 'You managed to walk when you wanted your supper cooked; what's to stop you fetching Mrs Simpson? Or telephoning from the box at the end of the road for a doctor or a nurse?'

Mrs Preece was so astonished that her mouth simply dropped open, though no words came out. But Miss Preece began to try to get out of her chair, saying as she did so that she could probably crawl up the stairs and that her knee, though painful, would be better in a trice.

This, however, was more than Hetty could stand. 'I'll go for Mrs Simpson if you'll tell me where she lives,' she said. 'And then I'll go home.' She turned to glare at old Mrs Preece. 'But I shall come back tomorrow, early, to get Miss Preece tea and toast and see if she's fit to go into work. If she is, I'll fetch a taxi, because I don't think that she should try to walk until her knee is better. And I dare say Mrs Simpson will give an eye to you.

To Hetty's surprise and relief, Mrs Preece gave a short bark of laughter. 'You've got spunk, I'll give you that; a deal more than my daughter has,' she said. 'If you'll share our supper and then help us up to our rooms, I dare say we'll manage without calling on Mrs Simpson. I won't fetch her round now because she's paid to come in at ten o'clock each weekday morning to help me dress and get me downstairs; I don't want her thinking she's indispensable.'

'Right. But I'll just nip out and get one of the local street urchins to take a note to my aunt, explaining that I'll be late home and won't want feeding,' Hetty said, very tongue in cheek. She saw Miss Preece smile guiltily, and grinned back. The old harridan shouldn't have things all her own way, she decided. 'Oh, and incidentally, Mrs Preece, your daughter has plenty of spunk, she's just too kind and polite to use it against you!'

After that, surprisingly Hetty thought, things went pretty smoothly. She poured the Preeces another cup of tea, handed round the biscuits again, scribbled a few words on a half-sheet of paper, accepted Miss Preece's offer of a sixpence to pay the deliverer of this missive, and left the two women sipping their tea, the tin of biscuits between them, whilst she found a young lad in Abbey Street who was willing to take her note to Aunt Phoebe. Then she returned to the house, checked that the shepherd's pie was beginning to brown nicely and laid the table for three, chatting inconsequentially of her holiday on the canal as she did so. She half expected old Mrs Preece to cut her chatter short, but to her pleasure both women listened eagerly.

'And what about the engine?' Miss Preece asked as the three of them settled themselves at the kitchen table. 'Can your grandfather work it alone now, or does he still need young whatsisname – Harry, didn't you say?'

'No, he does still need help, but Harry's left and Gareth Evans has taken his place,' Hetty said. 'And I'm afraid Gramps and I are in the same boat . . .'

Miss Preece laughed. 'So you are. In the same boat, I mean,' she said gaily and Hetty saw old Mrs Preece shoot her daughter an astonished look. What a shame it was, Hetty thought, that a mother and daughter should not be able to appreciate each other's good points, let alone share a joke, though she realised that the fault lay in the older woman rather than in her friend.

Miss Preece smiled at Hetty. 'I'm sorry, I interrupted; you were about to tell us how you and your grandfather view the new engine,' she said. 'Fire ahead. I find the whole business fascinating.'

Thus encouraged, Hetty took a mouthful of shepherd's pie and thought hard. 'I think Gramps and I – and Gran of course – really do appreciate that the engine has made our lives easier,' she said at last. 'But we miss Guinness – he was our horse – and despite not being a living thing the engine seems to need an awful lot of attention. It's water cooled, whatever that may mean, and has to be cleaned and oiled at regular intervals. Harry truly understood it, but Gareth does know quite a lot about engines too and I think he and Gramps together will be able to cope.'

'And is Gareth happy to remain on the *Water Sprite*?' Miss Preece asked curiously. 'If he's keen on engines, which he obviously is, I should have thought he'd want wider experience than he could get aboard the barge.'

'You're right, of course,' Hetty said. 'But jobs are hard to find, Miss Preece, and Gramps is going to pay Gareth a proper wage, though not a very large one. But between ourselves, I wouldn't be surprised if Gramps isn't looking to retire some time in the next two or three years. If he does that, and sells the barge, then Gareth may have no choice but to move on.'

'I don't see why your grandfather can't insist that whoever buys the barge should employ the lad,' Mrs Preece said suddenly and Hetty was amused to realise that the old lady had cleared her plate whilst she and Miss Preece had scarcely disposed of half their own portions. 'Isn't that the sort of thing he's likelier to do?'

Hetty considered this, then nodded slowly. 'You're right, of course; I'm sure Gramps would try to keep Gareth in work. Normally, however, the barge would go to a son or grandson, maybe even to a nephew, but neither Bill nor Tom has the slightest interest in working the canal. If a relative took it on, it would be on the understanding that he paid the rent of the house into which Gramps and Gran would move, but that doesn't apply to a stranger, of course.'

Miss Preece leaned forward. 'But suppose Gareth

took over the *Water Sprite*? If your grandfather trusted him, he could pay for the barge by instalments, which is just another way of saying he would pay the rent,' she suggested.

Hetty shrugged. 'It's an idea,' she acknowledged. 'But anyway, that's all for the future. I don't know why I mentioned it at all, because Gramps never actually said he was going to retire. It was just a feeling I had that things were going to change.'

Miss Preece finished her meal and stood up, though shakily, and limped across to the stove. 'Never meet troubles halfway,' she said briskly. 'That's our motto, isn't it, Mother? And now I'll put the kettle on and we'll have another cup of tea to give Hetty strength to help us up to our rooms!'

She was smiling as she spoke, and to her relief Hetty saw that the old lady was actually smiling as well. So perhaps she really is fond of her daughter but doesn't like showing it, she thought hopefully, getting up and beginning to clear the table. 'I'll just wash up the crocks and put them away and then I'll give you both a hand up the stairs.'

As she made her way home that night, Hetty reflected that it had certainly been an interesting day. She had learned more about Miss Preece than she had ever expected to know, and of course she had met the dragon, though in fact old Mrs Preece was not as fierce as she tried to make out. Hetty had helped her up the stairs at nine o'clock, her usual bedtime, for the old woman was not only light but also a good deal more agile than she cared to admit. She occupied a large and luxuriously appointed bedroom overlooking Everton Terrace, and though she had not let Hetty help her to undress, she would not be left whilst she changed into her night things, but had sat Hetty on a comfortable chair in the bay window, bid her severely to keep her eyes on the passing scene and not to look round until ordered to do so, and then kept up a constant stream of chat whilst she shed her purple wool dress and various undergarments and donned a long-sleeved, high-necked winceyette nightdress.

'Now you may help me into bed and drape a shawl round my shoulders,' she had said. 'Well, well, you're not a bad child after all. In fact you may come and call upon me whenever you're in the neighbourhood and we'll share a cup of tea and some biscuits.'

'That would be very nice, but when I'm in this area I'm usually heading for the library,' Hetty had pointed out. 'But of course I only go to the library when I know your daughter is there, so at weekends I'd be happy to pop in. If you were needing someone to do your messages, then I'd be glad to help out.'

She got up from her seat to help the old lady into bed and to drape her shawl round her thin old shoulders, and had been about to head for the door when old Mrs Preece grabbed her arm. 'Not so fast, young lady! Pass me my hairbrush and the ebony mirror lying on the dressing table. Ever since I was a little girl I've brushed my hair a hundred times before putting it into its bedtime plait, and I certainly don't mean to give up my beauty treatment just because my daughter was clumsy enough to slip on the steps. Do you see that little blue glass dish by the mirror? Pass it to me and I'll put my hairpins in it.' She glanced up at Hetty, an almost puckish smile curving her lips. 'Sit yourself down, my girl; this won't take above ten minutes and I'm sure you can spare an old lady that much of your time. I take it you're not in a hurry to get off?'

Hetty snorted but sat down again. 'A fat lot you'd care if I was desperate to get back to my aunt,' she declared roundly. 'Is there anything else your majesty would like before I go to help your daughter?'

The old lady cackled. She had already unpinned her bun and brushed her hair so vigorously that it had formed an aureole around her head. 'My daughter always brings me a cup of hot milk and a piece of short-bread when she comes up to bed herself, so you might as well do the same,' she said. 'Ninety-seven, ninety-eight, ninety-nine, one hundred.' She brandished the hairbrush. 'Put it back on the dressing table, there's a good girl, and don't forget my shortbread when you bring me the hot milk.'

'I won't forget,' Hetty promised. Then she left the room at speed, for she had a sneaking suspicion that the old lady liked company, particularly the sort of company to whom she could give orders, and she did not intend to abandon her friend.

Downstairs, she and the librarian had exchanged speaking looks. 'I'm sorry,' Miss Preece said apologetically, 'but my mother sees so few people, apart from myself and Mrs Simpson. And though you might not think it, she's taken to you. I'd not be surprised if she asked you to call again.'

'She's already asked me,' Hetty admitted. 'She's not as nasty as she pretends, is she, Miss Preece? Oh, and I'm to make her a glass of hot milk and take it with me when I help you up to bed . . . with a piece of short-bread. She's got a good appetite, hasn't she?'

Miss Preece laughed. 'Excellent,' she admitted. 'She's small and skinny, but I used to tell her she packed away enough food at mealtimes to make a navvy envious.'

'I bet she didn't like that,' Hetty said, fetching the milk saucepan from the rack on the wall and carrying it through to the pantry. She realised she felt quite a member of the family and smiled to herself. Old Mrs Preece little knew how she and her daughter had already enriched Hetty's life; what a lot she would have to tell Gran and Gramps the next time the *Water Sprite* moored up in Liverpool!

When she emerged from the pantry, Hetty had suddenly remembered her aunt's bad news regarding the paper tablecloths. The smile must have faded from her face, for Miss Preece said anxiously: 'What's the matter, my dear? I'm sure the milk must still be fresh; it was only delivered yesterday.'

'The milk's fine,' Hetty said, pouring some into the saucepan and setting it on the stove. 'Only I've just remembered . . .'

At the end of her recital, she looked hopefully at Miss Preece. 'Will all the other cafés follow suit, do you suppose?'

Miss Preece thought for a moment, then shook her head. 'No, I'm sure they won't; most of them will see it for the false economy it is, because paperware will be thrown away, not reused,' she said. 'But it doesn't really matter, because from what you've told me your aunt is a resourceful woman. She'll find other work, perhaps more congenial work too, and will soon wonder why she had ever needed to take in such quantities of laundry.'

Hetty thought Miss Preece was probably right, and her anxiety had disappeared like frost in June by the time she reached Salisbury Street. She pushed open the kitchen door to find her aunt sitting at the table eating a large slice of fruit cake, with one hand resting possessively on an enamel mug of strong tea. 'I've gorra job, chuck,' Aunt Phoebe said as soon as her niece entered the room. 'I'm to be an assistant baker at Rudham's on Heyworth Street. Me chief job will be cake decoration, a thing I've always loved doin', and the money's pretty good. Oh, I'm that pleased!'

Hetty darted across the room and gave her aunt a hug. 'Miss Preece said it would be all right,' she said exultantly. 'Did you get my note?'

'I did,' her aunt said, lumbering to her feet and fetching another mug from the dresser. She poured tea into it, added a generous spoonful of condensed milk and pushed it towards her niece. 'The lad delivered it just as I arrived home after me interview. I were that pleased with meself that I give him sixpence for his trouble.' She chuckled. 'I gather this Miss Preece of yours had a fall; all right now, is she?'

'I think she can manage now,' Hetty said cautiously. 'I didn't know until this evening, but Miss Preece lives with her mother, so if there's need no doubt old Mrs Preece will alert a neighbour. But oh, Auntie, they've got a beautiful house on Everton Terrace, with a proper garden and everything; I wish you could see it! They've got a grand big kitchen, a walk-in pantry and at least two other rooms downstairs, though I didn't go into either of them.'

'My word, you're going up in the world,' Aunt Phoebe said. 'And I gather from your note that they fed you?'

'Yes, I shared their supper, which was shepherd's pie; it was delicious,' Hetty said. 'Then I washed up the crocks for them and put everything away because Miss Preece was still too stiff to do much for herself. And then I helped them up the stairs to their bedrooms, the old lady first, and Miss Preece next . . .'

'A bedroom each!' Aunt Phoebe exclaimed. 'But couldn't her mam give her a hand? I know you're strong as an ox, queen, from helping on board the *Water Sprite*, but you won't come to your full strength for a few years yet.'

'I don't think the old lady is nearly as strong as I am,' Hetty said. 'And she really is old, Aunt Phoebe, much older than Gran, I should think. But anyway, as I was saying, I helped them both up the flight and then I came home. I say, Auntie, you should see their bedrooms! The old lady's room is as big as our kitchen and parlour put together, and there's proper carpet on the floor, ever so rich and soft. Miss Preece's room isn't quite so large, but she has rugs scattered over polished boards instead of carpet, which I thought looked even nicer. And I should think there are at least two other bedrooms, though of course I didn't get to see them.'

Aunt Phoebe whistled softly. 'It just goes to show that one half never knows how the other half lives. Carpet in a bedroom. Fancy that!' she said, rather enviously. She grinned at her niece. 'But don't you go gettin' ideas above your station.'

Hetty smiled, then sighed. 'I shan't,' she promised. 'But oh, Aunt Phoebe, wouldn't it be nice to have a house like that!'

Chapter Seven

August 1937

Miss Preece was working in her tiny vegetable patch at the back of the house. She had always enjoyed gardening, was good at it, and now she was digging up the tangle of pea haulms and adding them to the compost heap, so that they might rot down and be dug into the soil when winter came.

When the patch of soil which had contained the peas showed only rich black earth, Miss Preece limped over to the long row of runner beans and examined both the flaunting scarlet flowers and the tiny fuzzy beanlets which would, she judged, be ready for picking in another couple of weeks. She had pulled a handful of radishes and was about to cut a lettuce, since they were having steak pie and salad for their supper, when the back door shot open and her mother's head appeared round it. Miss Preece could see the older woman beckoning but was reluctant to leave the garden, so she merely raised her voice to a shout. 'I shan't be a minute, Mother. I just want to gather some tomatoes . . .'

Her mother's voice, sharpened by excitement, cut across her words. 'Do hurry up, Agatha! The girl will be here in ten or fifteen minutes and we should have supper on the table by the time she arrives. The pie's in the oven, but I can't wash the lettuce or prepare the radishes and tomatoes until you bring them in.'

Agatha Preece smiled to herself, reflecting that since Hetty had entered their lives her mother had become a changed person. And probably I've changed quite a lot, too, she thought, raising her voice to assure her mother that she would be indoors, complete with salad stuff, in less than five minutes. She began to select the ripest tomatoes, then went back to the house. When she entered the kitchen, she saw that her mother had spread the table with their very best linen cloth. It had been embroidered many years previously by her great-grandmother with a riot of sweet peas, roses and sprays of lavender. Usually, this precious lace-trimmed posses-sion was only produced on Christmas Day, and Miss Preece, who had opened her mouth to comment on its presence, saw the warning glint in her mother's dark eyes and merely said approvingly: 'How festive the table looks, Mother! I expect Hetty will enjoy the extra space of our kitchen after being cramped up in the *Water Sprite* for three whole weeks.' She smiled at her mother. 'Mind you, that little cabin is the cosiest and best-planned place you could possibly imagine. Well, you saw for yourself how neat and homely the whole barge is.'

Old Mrs Preece sniffed, but could not quite hide the little smile which tugged at the corners of her mouth. As her daughter well knew, the old lady had been thrilled to receive the Heskeths' invitation and had thoroughly enjoyed her visit when they had gone down to the wharf to see Hetty off.

Miss Preece had enjoyed her own first visit to the barge several weeks previously, even more than she had expected. She had taken a box of cream cakes, guessing that such things would be regarded as desirable but unnecessary luxuries by an elderly couple with little cash to spare, and had been delighted with the wonderful neatness and use of space on board the *Water Sprite*. In fact, she admired everything, and when she mentioned that her mother would be as intrigued and delighted with the canal barge as she was herself the invitation to 'bring the old lady along the next time we're moored up here' was quickly extended and as quickly accepted.

'Agatha Preece, will you stop dreaming! I've asked you twice if that's the last of the lettuces and you took as much notice of me as though I were the wind.'

'Sorry, Mother. No, it's not the last of the lettuces. Would you like me to pull another? Only I thought, with the pie and the new potatoes . . .'

Her mother was at the sink, swishing the leaves about in a bowl of water, and after having thought for a moment she shook her head. 'I only asked in case we needed more, but I'm sure this will be quite sufficient,' she said.

Miss Preece saw that her mother was pink-cheeked and smiling, and thought again how strange it was that the girl once described by her mother as a 'scruffy street urchin' should have made such a difference to the lives of two supposedly sensible middle-class women.

144

Hetty had begun by simply turning up every now and then to make old Mrs Preece a cup of tea and ask if she could do any messages. But after a few weeks she had actually suggested that the old lady might accompany her on her short shopping expeditions. Agatha, who had said the same thing herself many times, was astonished, but pleased, when her mother had agreed with seeming reluctance to the scheme. She had warned Hetty that the older woman might change her mind after the shortest of walks, but Hetty said that if that happened she would either demand help from a passer-by or simply hail a taxi cab and bundle Mrs Preece into it.

'But she's very independent, isn't she, Miss Preece?' she had said with a twinkle. 'I don't imagine she'll want to admit defeat so easily.'

Miss Preece wasn't so sure, but in the event, Hetty was seen to be right. When she came knocking at the front door the old lady donned her coat and hat, picked up the ebony stick which she used out of doors, and set off with her young friend. She soon proved to be as keen to argue over prices as Hetty herself, and a good deal better than Miss Preece, who usually paid whatever sum was asked.

There had been other changes too; having had a taste of freedom on her shopping expeditions with Hetty, it seemed that Mrs Preece had decided she might venture as far as the nearest tea room when the weather was fine. She usually arranged to meet an old crony there, and the two elderly ladies would select a window table from which they could watch the passing scene.

They would order a pot of tea for two and either fancy cakes or scones, and would spend a pleasant hour gossiping or simply discussing the news of the day.

At first, Miss Preece was not told of these expeditions, learning of them through chance remarks let drop in the library, but after a while Mrs Preece started mentioning her outings, her tone half defiant and half triumphant. Her daughter congratulated her on her improved health, and old Mrs Preece actually admitted that she felt all the better for her little outings.

And her mother was not the only one to benefit from this unusual friendship, for Miss Preece congratulated herself that it was partly due to her help and influence that Hetty was now at the High School and studying for her School Certificate. Miss Preece had discovered, through the good offices of Hetty's teacher, that there were scholarships available for bright girls, and knowing of Hetty's ambition to become a librarian one day she had talked to her young friend, suggesting that she herself should coach Hetty for the scholarship examination. Hetty, having no desire to work in a factory or a shop and a very urgent desire to better herself, had agreed enthusiastically to the scheme. So she began to go to the library as soon as she left school during term time and spent most of the day there during the holidays, except for the three weeks each year that she spent with the Heskeths on board the *Water Sprite*.

At first, Miss Preece had almost resented Hetty's three-week absences in August, but soon realised that the girl – for she was a child no longer – actually benefited from a complete break. She had headed the list of scholarship winners and was usually amongst the top three or four in her class, and, as Mrs Preece reminded her daughter, 'all work and no play makes Jack a dull boy'.

Now, Miss Preece crossed to the oven and checked that their supper was perfectly cooked before turning off the gas and sliding the pie on to a pretty china plate. Hetty's made a difference to me, too, she thought, placing the pie in the centre of the table. Why, if it hadn't been for her chattering away and telling me the plot of the film at the picture house, I might never have discovered that Mr Gower enjoyed the cinema as much as I do myself; the reference librarian had paused to listen to Hetty's enthusiastic description of the film she had just seen and the day following had suggested that Miss Preece accompany him to a showing of *The Scarlet Pimpernel* that very evening.

Miss Preece had stared, feeling her face gradually growing hot with embarrassment. Mr Gower sometimes chatted to her, but he had never extended an invitation before, and clearly felt as uncomfortable as she did herself. She realised that it was up to her to be gracious, to put him at his ease. She had begun to say that it was most kind, but he had interrupted.

'I wouldn't have asked, only it stars Leslie Howard and Merle Oberon,' Mr Gower had mumbled. 'I heard you telling to the youngster how much you admired Mr Howard's acting . . . and I do so hate going to the cinema alone,' he had finished.

And all of a sudden, Miss Preece realised that she,

too, would like to go to the cinema with a friend, to share a small box of chocolates perhaps, and afterwards to discuss the film, for going alone made one feel friendless and awkward. So she had thanked Mr Gower for his offer and agreed with his suggestion that they should go straight to the Electric Palace on Heyworth Street after work the next day. 'Mrs Simpson, our neighbour, always prepares our evening meal and I'll get Hetty to pop round to keep my mother company,' she had told her colleague, giving him her friendliest smile. 'It will be a real treat; thank you very much, Mr Gower.'

Looking back, she remembered that their first trip to the cinema had been a little awkward, but others had followed and soon she and Mr Gower had become far more at ease with one another. She had always insisted on paying her share – going Dutch, they called it – and thought that Mr Gower had enjoyed these occasions as much as she had, though he never actually said so.

It was strange, however, that they had never become really friendly; Miss Preece supposed that it was because they were so different. In fact, she thought now that apart from their liking for the cinema, they had absolutely nothing in common. She loved visiting parks, going into the country of having a day by the sea, but most of all she loved to read because for her it was an escape, her limp and club foot no longer seeming important. But she knew that fiction, her first love, was regarded by Mr Gower as a frivolity. It was a shame, but Miss Preece knew she could never confide in him about her secret ambition, which was one day to write a novel herself. When she got into bed at night, her mind presented her with plots, scenarios and characters, and tucked away at the very back of her wardrobe was a collection of exercise books in which she wrote down the thrilling adventures which obsessed her at any particular moment. She had never told anyone, not even Hetty, about those exercise books and had no intention that they should ever be seen by eyes other than her own, but it would have been nice to speak of her ambition to an intelligent man.

Publishing her scribbles, of course, she thought was quite impossible. Despite her job, she was sure that writers had to have special training or knowledge which she did not possess. No, the stories in the exercise books were simply her escape route from the dullness of her everyday life, and only as such did she value them. But she would have enjoyed discussing her favourite authors with Mr Gower whilst they drank their tea and ate their biscuits.

However, when Hetty returned . . . Miss Preece smiled to herself. Then they could discuss books till the cows came home!

Hetty came up from the wharf, went straight to her aunt's house to drop off her belongings, and then headed for Everton Terrace. She always had a heap of stories and experiences to tell the Preeces when she returned from her lovely three-week holiday on the canal, but on this occasion they would be rather different. For a start, she had arrived at the *Sprite* to find that Gareth

Evans had accepted an apprenticeship with an engineering firm, and in his place her grandparents had
taken on a young lad, not yet thirteen, called Benny,
who knew a little about engines. He was willing,
anxious to please, and always the first ashore when
they reached a lock, tugging his windlass out of his
belt and beginning to wind the paddles open as soon
as her grandfather put out the fenders and began to
pole the barge into position.

His knowledge of engines, however, was not sufficient to allow him to do all that was necessary, so Hetty
had found herself spending far more time in the engine
room than she had anticipated. The great flywheel took
the combined strength of herself and Benny to get it
moving, which left her grandfather in charge of the
starting handle and the compression lever. It was hard
work getting the flywheel into action, but when the
engine began to cough and thud she knew they were
well on the way to starting.

However, when her grandfather had emerged from
the engine room she had not been able to help noticing
how very white and tired he looked, so it was no surprise,
when they moored up one evening and he had sent
Benny to the village for supplies, when he had turned
to her and given her an affectionate hug. 'You're a grand
girl, Hetty Gilbert, and I know you'll understand that
what I'm going to tell you is as sad for me and your
gran as it will be for you. I've arranged for a pal who's
been down on his luck to take over the *Sprite* and the
Beetle before winter comes. Your gran and myself will
move into old Uncle Matthew's place, because he's

happy to let us live with him rent free until Luke can afford to pay me a hire fee. I'm pretty sure you've realised that we're getting too old for this game. In the past it's been my job to keep the boats moving when we're moored and the canal ices up, else the ice would crack 'em like walnuts, but young Benny doesn't have the strength, and I need my sleep; old folk do.' He had grinned at her, then reached over and rumpled her hair. 'I know you love the *Sprite* and the *Beetle*, but I dare say, what with your studies and so on, you wouldn't have had many more holidays aboard. And Luke's a grand chap. He's in his forties and strong as an ox, so he's happy to keep young Benny on too. He used to work for the Company, but the barge was old, so they withdrew it from service and of course Luke lost his job and his home.'

'Poor chap,' Hetty had murmured. 'Do I know him, Gramps?'

'Bound to,' her grandfather had said after some thought. 'He's got twin sons, they're around twelve, and two small girls; I'd say eight and ten. His wife's Bessie; a big, yellow-headed woman, always smiling, only this latest bit of bad luck has wiped the smile off her face.' Her grandfather had grinned at Hetty. 'It broke out again when she heard our offer.'

'Is he a very tall chap with blond hair?' Hetty had asked.

'Yes, that's Luke; I thought you'd know him.'

'And what exactly did you offer? If you don't mind telling me, that is,' Hetty had added hastily. 'I don't mean to be nosy, Gramps, but I can't help wondering.'

'I said that if they could cope with the pair over the winter then we'd settle a definite sum and they could take over the barge and the butty for good,' Gramps said. He had looked wistful. 'If I'd had a son of my own . . . if Bill or Tom had been interested in taking over . . . but I'm telling you, queen, Luke's the next best thing.'

'Good. So long as you won't be struggling to manage,' Hetty said. 'And I'll be able to visit you often, because Uncle Matthew lives in Burscough, doesn't he?'

'That's right,' Gramps said. He looked relieved. 'I've been dreading telling you, Hetty my love. But you've taken it well . . . I knew you would. And now you must make the most of the next couple of weeks, because I'm afraid this will be your last holiday aboard the dear old *Sprite*.'

Now, wending her way through the busy streets, Hetty thought that she had never worked as hard as she had on this last trip; but she also realised that she had learned a lot. If she ever had to help aboard a barge, she would be almost as well qualified as her grandparents. Not that she meant to undertake such work; she was going to be a librarian!

'Agatha! What a dream you are, girl. I've just told you that I've spent most of the day whilst you were in the garden finishing off the trifle. Hetty loves trifle. Shall I put it on the table, or leave it where it is?'

'Oh, leave it where it is by all means,' Miss Preece said, hiding a smile. She had seen the trifle earlier in the day and knew that her mother had put hot custard on to the set jelly so that now it would have to be poured into the dishes. But Hetty was a tactful creature and Miss Preece knew she would eat – or rather drink – her share of the treat without once mentioning its liquid state.

'What are you smirking for?' old Mrs Preece said sharply now. 'I put it in the fridge after I'd added the custard; it should have set by this time.'

Miss Preece was about to say that the trifle would round off the meal nicely when there was a tap on the back door. She hurried across to open it and there was Hetty, tanned, bright-eyed and smiling. The two greeted one another, then Hetty came right into the kitchen and, whilst Agatha took the pie from the oven, went over to Mrs Preece and gave her a kiss on the cheek. She didn't kiss me, Miss Preece thought rather ruefully, but then I'm not a sweet, white-haired old lady who needs to know she's loved, or if not actually loved, at least well liked. At that moment, however, Hetty, having exclaimed that the pie looked absolutely delicious, took Miss Preece's hand and gave it a squeeze and all the librarian's envious thoughts disappeared. She and Hetty were good friends and trusted one another; who could ask for more?

'Sit down, Hetty, my dear,' old Mrs Preece commanded as soon as their greetings were over. 'I expect you've a great deal of news to tell us. How are your good grandparents?'

'They're quite well, thank you, Mrs Preece,' Hetty said politely. 'But as I'd been expecting, things on the

Water Sprite have changed since last year. I'll tell you all about it just as soon as we've eaten that pie, because I know it's rude to speak with a full mouth.'

At last Hetty finished her meal and heaved a satisfied sigh. 'That was delicious. Thank you very much,' she said. She looked from Miss Preece's face to that of the older woman and began her story. 'As I must have told you several times, my grandparents have been thinking of retiring for some time . . .'

'Well, I'm very sorry for your grandparents, of course, but I think they're doing the right thing,' Mrs Preece said as Hetty finished her story. 'But I suppose you'll miss your voyages?'

'Yes, I shall, but as Gramps pointed out, once I'm in college – if I get there, that is – I'll have to work so that I can earn money to buy books and so on, and that would have put an end to my trips on the canal anyway.'

'True; even I had to do that whilst I was at college,' Miss Preece remembered. 'I was fortunate, though; I got a job helping to catalogue a new library section. And of course there was my legacy . . .'

Hetty pricked up her ears, but Mrs Preece cleared her throat loudly and began to talk of what she had been doing during her young friend's absence, and the subject of Miss Preece's legacy was allowed to drop.

It was not, in fact, until the two of them set off for a walk in the cool of the evening that the subject of the legacy was raised once more. 'You must have wondered why my mother changed the subject when I mentioned my legacy,' Miss Preece said. 'I've never mentioned it before, but the house was left to me, not to my mother, by my great-aunt Agatha. She had married a rich businessman who owned several properties in the better parts of the city; our house was one of them. Great-aunt Agatha was not able to have children, but when I was born she said that if I were named for her, then she would leave me some of her property. By then she was a widow, you understand, and known to be what they called in those days "a warm woman". She died when I was ten and left me the house on Everton Terrace, where we now live, and a sum of money sufficient to see me through my schooling and through the university of my choice, and to keep us very comfortably now.'

'Golly,' Hetty said, awestruck. 'But why doesn't your mother like you to mention it?'

Miss Preece chuckled. 'For one thing, she's a little resentful that I own the house she lives in, which is understandable. And for another, and this is even more understandable, she does not want our neighbours thinking we are any different from themselves, and I do agree with her that this would be a mistake. Only Mrs Simpson comes and goes freely in our house, and she is a good woman and very grateful for the money we pay her, so she says nothing, even if she's guessed that we have a private income. But neither she nor our neighbours know that we are property owners, and even if Mrs Simpson has guessed, she knows better than to spread such news abroad.'

Hetty nodded. 'Yes, of course she would say nothing. She often speaks of her invalid husband and though she says his pension is adequate, it's the money she earns from looking after your mother which allows her to command what she calls "the little luxuries of life". And I know you're very good to her; she told me it was you who bought Mr Simpson's wheelchair . . .'

'Oh, never mind that; Mrs Simpson is very good to us,' the librarian interrupted hurriedly. 'And now I have a favour to ask of you, Hetty dear. It seems rather hard when you're only just back and no doubt longing to get on with your studies, and I wouldn't ask if it weren't important . . .'

'Oh, Miss Preece, you know very well I'll be happy to help in any way I can,' Hetty cut in at once. 'Only tell me what the problem is.'

'It's not exactly a problem . . . the truth is, I've been invited to attend the opening of a new exhibition hall at the museum. They've managed to get the loan of some very rare and valuable manuscripts from the British Library, so as you can imagine I'm very keen to accept the invitation.'

'Yes. It's an honour to be invited, I'm sure,' Hetty said, and was rewarded by her friend's delighted smile.

'Well, it is really. I worked there when I was at university and in fact my special subject was old, hand-decorated manuscripts. So you see . . .'

'But what's it got to do with me?' Hetty asked, genuinely bewildered. 'I know nothing of such things; I don't believe I've ever so much as set eyes on an – an illuminated manuscript. Isn't that what they call them?'

'That's right. And of course I realise that you probably have no particular interest in such things – and it's by invitation only, anyway. They're serving a buffet luncheon, and in the afternoon a panel of experts will answer questions put by the audience. After that, they will be serving tea and biscuits, so it will be an all day affair. But the opening is next Saturday . . .'

'So?' asked Hetty, still more bewildered. She could not imagine why such an event should concern herself. However, it would be impolite to say so. 'How can I help?' She was suddenly struck by inspiration. 'If you want me to come over and get Mrs Preece her lunch, spend some time with her . . .'

Miss Preece smiled. 'Well, it's a little more than that, Hetty. Once a year my mother goes by coach to a seaside resort on the North Wales coast. She meets an old friend who lives there and they compete in a whist drive – as partners, you understand. It's one of the highlights of Mother's year; a last fling before winter sets in and she might find herself confined to the house for days or weeks on end. So I'm sure you understand it is rather important to her.'

'I see,' Hetty said slowly, still not seeing at all. 'But if you're out all day and she is too, what is the problem?'

'Well, in previous years I've always accompanied her, sat next to her on the coach and so on. Oh, I won't pretend I spend the whole day with her, because I'd be bored to tears and besides, my mother wouldn't like it. No, I spend the day pleasantly enough, joining them for luncheon and high tea, and accompanying Mother

157

on the journey home. On this occasion the difficulty would arise when the coach returns to the Pier Head, because we never know at what hour it will decant its passengers . . .'

'Oh, I *see*,' Hetty said, enlightened at last. 'Then if I go with your mother, and come back with her too, I'll be on the spot and able to see her safely home. It's a fair walk, but there are always taxi cabs waiting for passengers at the Pier Head . . .'

'That's it,' Miss Preece said, sounding relieved. 'Dear Hetty, if you truly wouldn't mind going, I should be so grateful. I have already paid for my ticket, which I shall give you. It's divided into four sections, one for the journey there, one for the journey back, one for your luncheon and one for high tea.' Miss Preece produced a stout-looking piece of pink card from her pocket, perforated into four sections, and handed it to Hetty. 'I shall give you some spending money . . . no, no, don't object, you will be doing me a great favour . . . and tomorrow you and Mother can discuss the details. Did I mention that you'll be going to Llandudno? Have you been there before? It's my favourite of all the seaside resorts.'

Hetty, admitting that she had never visited Llandudno, in fact had never even been to New Brighton, felt excitement bubbling up within her. She asked, rather shyly, whether Mrs Preece had been consulted and was delighted when the librarian assured her that all was arranged, save for her own agreement. Hetty hugged herself. She was going to the real seaside! 'Oh, Miss Preece, I can hardly wait for

Saturday,' she breathed as they turned back towards Everton Terrace.

Hetty had set her alarm clock – a present from her uncle and aunt for passing the scholarship examination – for an early hour, but was already awake when its little bell began to tinkle. She lay for a moment, staring at its small face and wondering why it had gone off an hour before its usual time. She glanced at the window, saw the sky beginning to flush with sunrise and all of a sudden remembered. Saturday had come at last! She was going to Llandudno with old Mrs Preece. They would travel in a large cream-coloured coach, have their lunch in a posh restaurant and generally enjoy a wonderful day out. Miss Preece had impressed upon her that she must be sure to visit the Great Orme, riding to its summit in one of the specially constructed trams that catered for visitors. The librarian had said that the view from the top was incredible, especially if one ascended at sunset.

Then there was the pier, which she believed to be one of the longest on the North Wales coast, and the lovely shops, and the beach . . .

Hetty jumped out of bed, hurled her nightdress on to the floor, splashed water into the basin, and began to wash. This was going to be a day she would never forget, and she and Aunt Phoebe had planned together so that Hetty would be as smartly turned out as anyone else on the coach. Aunt Phoebe had bought her – from Paddy's market, naturally – a primrose-coloured linen dress, very much in the modern mode, with a straight skirt ending in a frill of tiny pleats, short sleeves and a sweetheart neckline. It had seemed to Hetty that it had cost a great deal of money, but she and her aunt had shared the price and thought it worth every penny.

Now, she dressed carefully, brushed her hair till it shone and descended the stairs at a gallop. In the kitchen Aunt Phoebe and Uncle Alf looked up and smiled as she hurried into the room. Aunt Phoebe immediately began to dish up porridge whilst Uncle Alf poured her a mug of tea and nodded approvingly as he pushed it towards her. 'You look grand, queen, pretty as a picture,' he said. 'My, that's a rare smart get-up. That old woman should be proud to have such a friend.'

Hetty, gobbling porridge, grinned at her uncle. She knew that Mrs Preece would be in her best, knew also from what Miss Preece had told her that the majority of the folk on the coach would be elderly and would pay little attention to a fifteen-year-old girl who was not even a whist player. Still, it was nice to be admired, particularly as Uncle Alf seldom noticed such mundane things as his niece's appearance. 'Thanks, Uncle Alf, but I shan't be the only one in my best,' Hetty said, finishing her breakfast and jumping to her feet. 'Thanks, Aunt Phoebe, that was delicious. I reckon I'll be late home so don't wait up for me; just leave the key in its usual place.'

She snatched her jacket from its peg and was soon hurrying along, heading for the Pier Head, since Miss Preece was ordering a taxi which would take her and her mother to the coach stop. Indeed, when Hetty arrived, the first thing she saw was Miss Preece helping her mother into a large, cream-coloured coach. The librarian turned and smiled as Hetty joined her. Thinking she must be late, she began to apologise, but Miss Preece laughed and shook her head. 'Mother likes to be one of the first aboard so she can choose her seat,' she explained. 'Unless you particularly want to sit with her, you can choose your place too, but if I were you I should join the other young people right at the back of the coach. Tell Mother where you're sitting and help her down when you reach Llandudno. You'll find her whist partner will be waiting and the two of them will go off together, happy as sandboys.'

This proved to be absolutely true. When she got on the coach, Mrs Preece greeted her warmly enough, but said she had arranged to sit with another whist player for the journey to Llandudno. 'It's not as though there's no one your age aboard, because several young people have already taken over the back seat,' she said. Her eyes scanned Hetty from head to feet, then she smiled. 'My dear girl, I've never seen you look so smart! You do us credit, indeed you do. Now off with you; go and make friends with folk your own age.'

Hetty was only too glad to obey, for she already knew at least one of the back seat passengers, a girl called Julia, who was in the class above hers at school. There were a couple of lads who looked to be around fifteen or sixteen, and another girl, probably a little older. Hetty walked down the aisle towards them a trifle shyly, but Julia looked up and beamed. 'Hello, Hetty! What a bit of luck you being on our coach,' she said happily. 'We were wondering if we could get someone we knew to take the last place on the rear seat. I say, I do like your dress!'

Hetty smiled. Julia was a small, plump girl with dark feathery curls, and she was clad today in blue gingham to match her eyes. Hetty took the vacant seat offered and sat down beside the other girl. 'You look very nice too,' she said generously. 'Wasn't it a piece of luck you having a spare place on the rear seat, though? I'm accompanying the old lady sitting right at the front of the coach, but all I have to do is make sure she gets to the whist drive, then the day's my own.' She looked shyly at the other girl. 'Do you have plans? I s'pose I couldn't go round with you, could I?'

'Course you could,' Julia said at once. 'Llandudno's a lovely place, but not a great deal of fun on your own, I shouldn't think. We aren't giving an eye to anyone, but there were half a dozen empty places on the chara-bancs so we nagged our mothers to buy us tickets, and here we are.'

She delved in her pocket and produced a pink ticket, similar to the one which nestled in Hetty's jacket. 'You know Amanda, I suppose? She's in the year above me and a prefect . . . Amanda, this is Hetty, who's also at our school.'

Amanda grinned. 'Hello, Hetty. The feller sitting next to me is Billy Williams and the chap on the end is my brother Jack.'

Hetty smiled at the boys and they began discussing what they should do when they reached Llandudno, soon drawing Hetty into the conversation, even though she had never visited the town before. They agreed emphatically that they must visit the Great Orme and also the pier, and Hetty scarcely noticed when the coach jerked into motion, so busily engaged was she in enjoying the company of her new friends.

She particularly liked Amanda's brother, Jack, and was glad when he suggested that the two of them might spend some time on the beach. 'We're a bit big for donkey rides,' he told her, grinning. 'But I reckon we're neither of us too old for a paddle. Then we might build a sandcastle, or go along the beach a bit further, where it's all rocks and pebbles, and see what we can find. Ever seen a starfish? Or a sea anemone? I once found a sea urchin,' he chuckled reminiscently, 'it were the thrill of me life, I'm telling you. Going to come with me? Or do you want to go round the smart shops? Julia and Amanda think they're young ladies and too old for the beach, but you look like a girl with a bit more sense.'

So when the journey was over the five of them already knew just where they should head. 'Only first I have to take Mrs Preece to the hall where the competition is to take place,' Hetty confessed. 'So perhaps I'd better arrange to meet you somewhere in say half an hour's time.'

But this was not necessary, since, as Miss Preece had foretold, her mother's whist partner was waiting for her at the stop and pounced as soon as Hetty helped the old lady to alight.

'We may not see you at lunchtime,' Mrs Preece told Hetty briskly. 'But we'll meet up again for high tea, which is taken at six o'clock on the dot, so if you want your share be sure to arrive promptly.'

Miss Milner was a good deal younger than her partner, a brisk, grey-haired woman in her early fifties, Hetty guessed, with a wide, humorous mouth and shrewd, pale blue eyes. She gave Mrs Preece a kiss, telling Hetty that they had been whist partners now for eight years, shook Hetty herself heartily by the hand and then disappeared in the direction of a large hall into which a number of elderly ladies and gentlemen were disappearing, though there were younger folk also heading in that direction.

'The prizes are real good,' Hetty heard one of the younger women remark. 'Last year I paid for a week's holiday in the town wit' me winnings.'

As soon as the little group of friends set off, Hetty turned to Julia. 'I assumed that we'd go to the hall where the competition is being held for our lunch,' she said, rather puzzled. 'I know we go there for high tea, because old Mrs Preece told me so . . .'

'Yes, because by six o'clock, when high tea is served, the competition is over,' Julia explained. 'But if you look closely at the portion of your ticket which entitles you to lunch . . . well, look at yours and tell me what you see.'

Hetty complied and saw that the words *The Seagull*, *The Wintergardens* and *The Frolicks* were printed across the bottom of the section which applied to lunch. She turned puzzled eyes on her new friend. 'What does it *mean*?' she asked plaintively. 'I don't understand.'

Julia chuckled. 'And you one of the clever scholarship girls,' she remarked. 'They're restaurants, silly, and the token allows you one main course, one pudding and one cup of tea at any of them. I don't think we'll go to the Frolicks because all the little old ladies from the town go there, and we won't go to the Wintergardens on Gloddaeth Street, because that's where the whist drive is being held. But the Seagull serves the best fish and chips in Llandudno, as well as the biggest puddings. It's a good walk, but well worth it.' She glanced at her small watch. 'Want to take look at the shops as we go? Only we might as well get lunch out of the way. Then we can split up and do whatever we want until we head for the tram and the Great Orme.'

As Julia had said, the meal at the Seagull was very good indeed, and afterwards Jack and Hetty set off for the beach, so full of food that Hetty doubted if they would be able to reach the sea, let alone paddle in it. The tide was out, but somehow her energy – and Jack's – came back as, shoes and socks in hand, they padded across the firm wet sand to the rocks where they found tiny crabs, flat fish no bigger than a penny, sea anemones which clutched your finger if you held it near enough to their waving tentacles, and many beautiful sea shells, which Hetty collected eagerly, pushing them into the pocket of her linen jacket.

They met the others on the pier as agreed and discussed at great length whether they should go up the Orme before or after high tea, finally deciding to hurry straight to the Wintergardens and enquire of the coach drivers what time the vehicles left for the return journey. 'If it's fairly soon after tea is finished, then we'll have a straight choice between filling our stomachs with grub or rejoicing in the beauties of the sunset,' Billy said. 'I know which I'd rather do, but then I always was a great one for me food.'

The others all laughed at him, particularly a tall, handsome boy, Hetty thought probably seventeen or eighteen, who appeared to have joined the others whilst they were exploring the shops. Amanda, looking rather self-conscious, introduced him as 'my boyfriend, Cyril', and it appeared that he had borrowed his father's car and intended to take Amanda home at the end of the day. 'So you'll have more room on the back seat if you want to cuddle and canoodle,' Amanda said, and was set upon by Jack and Julia, who thought the suggestion quite revolting.

At the Wintergardens they were told that there should be plenty of time after tea to go up the Great Orme before the coaches left, so they made their way first to the large conference hall where the whist drive was being held, and their high tea would be served. As soon as she saw Hetty, Mrs Preece, pink with excitement, displayed her winnings: a large box of chocolates, a beautiful little oil painting in a gilded frame and a pound note in a tiny velvet purse. Naturally enough, Miss Milner had shared in her partner's success and both ladies were delighted with their day out.

When high tea was finished, Hetty and her new friends caught the tram and spent longer than they perhaps should have done on top of the Orme. As Miss Preece had said, the views were spectacular, and Hetty felt tears come to her eyes as she gazed out across the ridged sand below to where the tide was slowly creeping back, and beyond the sands to the mountains, dark blue against the brilliance of the sky.

Presently, they went to the small café on the summit, where Cyril bought them all ice creams and then hustled them aboard the tram, saying that if they wanted to catch the coach they should really get a move on. Hetty thought he was joking, having no idea of the time since she did not own a wristwatch, but when they got to the coach park outside the great bulk of the Wintergardens she was dismayed to find that some of the coaches had already left. She grabbed Julia's arm. 'Don't worry about saving me a place; I've simply got to find Mrs Preece and make sure she's all right,' she gabbled. 'Goodness, how the coaches are filling up! But I don't mind where I sit so long as I can keep an eye on old Mrs Preece.'

'Okay, we won't save a place for you then,' Julia said. 'I say, Hetty, you'd better move quickly else you'll be on a coach with all the old biddies who can't hurry even if they want to.'

'I'll do my best,' Hetty said, and ran towards the Wintergardens. Inside, it took her a few minutes to ascertain that neither Miss Milner nor Mrs Preece were amongst those still strolling around and gossiping, and by the time she got back to the coach park only two vehicles remained. Hastily, she ran alongside the one about to depart and saw Mrs Preece sitting in her favourite front seat. The old lady beckoned and Hetty banged on the side of vehicle, for the door was shut, but to her dismay the driver either did not hear, or chose to ignore her.

Heaving a frustrated sigh, Hetty ran to the following coach, which was drawing up before pulling off the park on to the main road, and the driver obligingly opened his door just long enough for her to tumble aboard. She glanced towards the back seat, but it was fully occupied with young people she did not know, so she handed her pink ticket to the driver, who tucked it into his pocket. Then she took the only remaining seat and plumped herself down, addressing the elderly lady who occupied the window seat.

'Excuse me; I came on a coach to accompany an elderly lady to the whist drive, but she's on the coach in front of this one. I couldn't get aboard, the driver wouldn't wait . . . but can you tell me if all the coaches will reach the Pier Head at about the same time? Only I promised I would look after her, see her back to her own home.'

The woman seated beside her was red-faced and hugely fat and took up at least three-quarters of the seat, but she was clearly well disposed towards her young companion, smiling and patting her hand. 'Don't worry, cariad. These coaches is like beads on a necklace, they follows one another that quick,' she said, in the loud voice of one who was somewhat hard of hearing. 'You'll be wi' your pal in no time.'

A little reassured, Hetty told herself that all would be well. It was a wretched nuisance that she had missed the coach upon which Mrs Preece was travelling, but no doubt Mrs Preece would wait for her at the Pier

Head. She settled back in her seat, and began to think what a lot she would have to tell Miss Preece – and Aunt Phoebe – when she reached Liverpool once more. It was warm in the coach, and presently Hetty's head began to nod. She told herself sternly that she should not fall asleep, that she must remain alert so that she might explain to Mrs Preece how she had managed to temporarily lose touch with her.

Next to her, the fat woman began a conversation with the woman on the seat in front, but since she spoke in Welsh Hetty let the words flow over her and soon, despite her resolve, slept. The coach rumbled on, the women chattered and laughed, the driver threw in an occasional remark and Hetty, in her sleep, told herself that as soon as they reached the Pier Head she would dash from her present coach to the one which contained Mrs Preece.

When at last the vehicle stopped, Hetty awoke. The coach was rapidly emptying and the fat woman was struggling to her feet so Hetty followed suit and hurried along the aisle and down the steps, looking blearily about, then frowning in puzzlement. Where were the familiar jostling crowds, the taxi cab rank, the tall buildings? There were no street lamps, though light gleamed from a number of windows, and trees crowded close to the road . . . and all around her people were hurrying away, calling out in a foreign language . . . Welsh, of course.

Oh my God, Hetty thought, horrified. I've got off the coach too soon; this must be simply a drop-off stop. I'd best get back aboard . . .

Too late; the coach was already rumbling off, the people dispersing. Desperately, Hetty grabbed the arm of the nearest woman. 'Please, where is this?' she asked. 'It's not Liverpool, that's for sure.'

The woman chuckled. 'No, not much like Liverpool this,' she remarked. 'You'll be looking for Mrs Llewellyn's place I dare say; I heard her tellin' someone on the coach she'd got her nieces from Liverpool staying for a few days.' She detached Hetty's hand from her arm and pointed down the road. 'See the house with the red curtains? That's the place you'll be wanting.' And with that, she hurried off.

Hetty went to follow her, then realised that the woman had disappeared into one of the nearby cottages. She ran towards the roadway, looking rather wildly for someone – anyone – who might help her, but the village street was deserted. Hetty had never felt so alone in her whole life. She had no idea where she was, save that this was a long way from Liverpool. She knew it was late at night; was it too late to approach one of the cottages and explain her predicament? Above her she could see through the branches with their burden of turning leaves that the sky was clear and that myriad stars twinkled in the darkness. The moon, a delicate crescent, floated on high, seeming to taunt her, for surely it was the same moon which shone down on Liverpool. Oh, if only she had not allowed herself to fall asleep! If only she had remembered that this was not just a pleasure trip, that she had promised Miss Preece, who had been so good to her, that she would take care of her mother, see her to her very door when they reached the city once more.

Hetty groped her way to a low stone wall, sank down upon it and burst into tears.

Chapter Eight

She was still sobbing helplessly when a voice spoke, giving her such a fright that she uttered a small shriek. The voice was not one she had heard on the coach, and to her relief it spoke in English. 'What's the matter, lass?' he asked, for though Hetty could not see his face through the darkness under the trees, she could tell that the speaker was a man; a young one, she thought.

She peered up at her questioner. She could see very little save that he was tall and seemed to have upon his head a strange contraption, which she thought for one startled moment to be a pair of enormous spectacles, for though the frail crescent moon was casting its beams on the scene, the silvery light was interspersed by deep shadows from the leafy branches. However, she was in no position to refuse help from whatever quarter. She scrubbed desperately at her eyes and spoke with all the calm she could muster. 'I'm sorry I shrieked, but you startled me. The fact is, I must have got off the coach too soon because I'm heading for Liverpool and wherever this is, it's certainly not the Pier Head! Oh, if only I could have got the driver's attention! But he didn't realise I was trying to get back on board.'

The man shook his head. 'No, lass, you've got

hold of the wrong end of the stick, so you have. The coach you've just climbed down from isn't going to Liverpool, it's going back to Llandudno. I'd arranged to meet it and take a young lady, who should have been aboard, to her home in the next valley. But when I asked one of the passengers what had happened to Cerys, she told me the girl had changed her mind and not gone on the trip after all.' He chuckled suddenly. 'So we're both here under what you might call false pretences.'

Hetty heaved a deep, tremulous sigh. 'What'll I do?' she asked. She could feel another sob rising in her throat and tried to conquer it. 'It's not just for myself that I'm worried. I only came on the trip to look after my friend's mother, who is a very old lady. We got separated when the coach she was on left without me. I got on the next one to leave, thinking it was also bound for Liverpool, and didn't discover it wasn't until – well, until just now. Oh, whatever am I to do? I dare say it's too far for me to walk?'

The young man chuckled again. 'I doubt you'd make it by breakfast time if you had to walk,' he said.

'Is there a taxi?' Hetty asked eagerly. 'I haven't any money, but my friend would pay when we reached her home. If the taxi driver could take me to the Pier Head, then we could pick up Mrs Preece and no one need know that I've let them down.'

'There's no taxi,' the stranger said promptly, 'but just for tonight I'm St George, ready to slay any number of dragons to rescue a fair maiden. Would you care to mount my fiery steed, Miss Liverpool? I reckon I can get you to the Pier Head before the coach has even begun to disgorge its passengers.'

'Could you . . . would you . . . ?' Hetty breathed. 'Do you have a car, then? I did look up and down the street but I couldn't see a car anywhere.'

The man grinned; she could see the flash of his teeth, white against his dark face. 'No, not a car.' He moved forward into a shaft of moonlight, so that she could see him more clearly. 'Guess again, cariad.'

Hetty stared and saw he was actually wearing a helmet, and what she had taken to be spectacles were . . . goggles! 'You've got a motorcycle,' she said triumphantly. 'Oh, mister, would you really take me all the way back to Liverpool? I'd pay for your petrol if you'd come with me to my friend's house.'

The young man shook his helmeted head at her and then held out a large, leather-gauntleted hand and took hers. 'St George wouldn't dream of taking money to slay such a tiny dragon,' he said reprovingly. 'But I may ask for payment in kind, however. And now we'd best be on our way if you want to reach the Pier Head before the coaches arrive there.'

Hetty had no idea what he meant by payment in kind but followed as he led her to where his motor-cycle was propped against a wall. He lifted her on to the pillion and then settled himself in the saddle, instructing her to put both arms round his waist and hold on tight, but promising that he would keep his speed down since she had never ridden pillion before. He revved the engine and shouted over his shoulder that she was to give him a pinch if she wanted him to stop. Then he turned on his headlight and the machine nosed out on to the village street and they were off.

It was a magical ride. The road dipped and swayed through the mountains for a short way and then purred along the wider main roads, and all the time the silver moonlight shone down on them and the perfumes of the night teased Hetty's nostrils. Conversation was impossible, for though he had promised to keep his speed down, as soon as he realised that his passenger was enjoying the ride he speeded up, and it did not seem a very long time before he shouted over his shoulder that the lights ahead were the lights of Liverpool.

And then they were in the tunnel and roaring out into the city streets which Hetty knew so well. True to his promise, they arrived at the Pier Head just as the coaches began to arrive. The young man got off his bike, kicked the stand and lifted Hetty down, and whilst he held her in his arms, smiling mockingly down at her, he suddenly bent his head and kissed her lightly on the forehead.

Hetty gasped and thought for one awful moment that her legs were going to refuse to bear her weight, but she managed to stand unaided, and thanked him from the heart for his kindness. 'And if giving me a kiss was what you meant by payment in kind, you're welcome,' she said frankly. 'If you'll wait a moment, I'll fetch Mrs Preece and put her into a taxi, then you can come back with us to Everton Terrace and at least let me pay for your petrol and make you a hot drink before you ride back to Wales. I can't accept such kindness from a stranger, honest to God I can't.'

But the young man was shaking his head and grinning again as he climbed aboard his motorbike. 'You've not recognised me, have you, chuck?' he said softly. 'Ah well, it's always the same. Tell your grandpa I were asking for him . . .'

Hetty darted forward, a hand out to grab his arm and a question on her lips; who could he possibly be? Someone who knew Gramps, obviously . . . but who? She opened her mouth to ask him, but he was away, with a mocking wave, leaving her staring after him.

The coach carrying Mrs Preece arrived a bare two minutes after Hetty herself, so she had to put her rescuer out of her mind and concentrate on looking after Mrs Preece. The old lady was tired and consequently crotchety, wanting to blame someone for the late arrival of the charabanc on which she had journeyed. She complained that the big bag she carried was too heavy for her old arthritic arms, but when Hetty settled her into a taxi and reminded her that the weight was due to the number of prizes she had collected, the old lady gave a grudging smile and presently, discussing her various hands of whist and the tricks she had taken, she began to smile and look forward to her arrival home where, Hetty guessed, she would boast of her prowess and expect her daughter to appreciate the excellence of her play.

'I dare say the girl enjoyed her day away as much as I did mine,' she confided as the taxi rumbled through the lamplit streets. 'Agatha doesn't complain, I'll give her that, but a whole day without me tagging along will have given her as much pleasure as my day in Llandudno has given me.'

'I'm sure you're right,' Hetty said. 'And thanks to you, Mrs Preece, I had a wonderful day as well. We went up to the top of the Orme and watched the sunset. We walked the full length of the pier and played the machines, and we had really good meals as well. I don't think I've ever enjoyed a day more and though the opening of a new section of the museum would bore you and me to tears, I'm sure Miss Preece will have loved every moment.'

Miss Preece's day began as soon as she had waved her mother and Hetty off in their coach. It looked as though it would be a lovely day, and though Miss Preece knew that she herself would be within indoors it was nice to know that her mother and Hetty were unlikely to find themselves battling high winds or rain. Not that bad weather would bother her mother much, Agatha reminded herself with an inward chuckle, remembering one occasion when it had rained cats and dogs and she herself had spent the entire day sheltering beneath a huge umbrella, feet and fingers like ice. Her mother, however, had entered the Wintergardens before the rain had started and had left it, burdened with prizes, after the rain had ceased. She had raised her eyebrows at her daughter's sodden shoes and damp coat and told her quite briskly that 'A girl of your age ought to have sufficient sense to stay under cover, even if it meant spending the afternoon at the cinema; there's the Odeon or the Palladium, both handy for the Wintergardens.' She had smiled suddenly, impishly. 'Or you could have come into the hall and watched us playing whist,' she had ended.

That had been two or three years ago, however, and since then they had been lucky with the weather. But today, Miss Preece reminded herself as she hurried back to Everton Terrace, today is a day for me and I intend to make the most of it.

Back at the house, she dressed with extra care. She had known that to be invited to the opening was quite an honour when Mr Gower had expressed both surprise and a degree of envy. 'I don't see why you've been singled out,' he had said, somewhat peevishly, when she had shown him her invitation. 'But I suppose it's because you specialised in illuminated manuscripts at university. Someone told me that you not only repaired manuscripts which were as much as four hundred years old, but you copied with great accuracy some which were too fragile to be shown to the public.' He had given her his thin, wintry smile. 'You must tell me all about the exhibition on Monday morning, before the library gets busy.'

'I don't suppose there will be much to tell,' Miss Preece had murmured. 'And anyway, the British Museum is lending the exhibits for a whole month, so you will be able to see them for yourself.'

'I should prefer to do so in the company of an expert,' Mr Gower had said archly, causing Miss Preece to go red as a beetroot. She had mumbled that no doubt each exhibit would have its own history printed in the catalogue and had hurried away, embarrassed not only by her blushes, but by Mr Gower's reproachful look.

When she had first realised that Mr Gower would not be attending the event, however, she had feared she would be lonely, for though she had questioned other members of the library service, it appeared that none of them had received an invitation. She had relied upon Mr Gower's companionship, but as the days passed she came to realise that the event would be far more of a treat without his constricting presence.

So now, in her own bedroom, she selected her very best suit. She had bought it for a friend's wedding, many years ago, and had only worn it a couple of times, but it still fitted her. It was royal blue wool, with a pert little matching hat, black high-heeled court shoes and long gloves. Looking at herself in the mirror, she thought she looked just right and not as though bound for a wedding. She had worn her hair in a neat bun for years now, but decided to be truly daring and do it today in a French pleat, since this would comple-ment the little blue hat.

Presently, hair smoothed down, hat perched on top, she looked at herself again. I still look like a librarian, she thought sadly, then laughed at herself. What a fool she was being! Why should she not look like a librarian, when she was one, and usually proud of it? But she was so pale . . .

Five minutes later she was in her mother's room, guiltily pulling open the dressing table drawer in which Mrs Preece kept her small store of face powder, lip rouge, and various other aids to beauty. Miss Preece, who had never used such things, plonked herself down on her mother's small stool and, after much thought, selected a dark rose-coloured lipstick. She applied it lightly, then scowled at her reflection and applied more. That was better! She tried some rouge on her cheeks, then scrubbed it off. She had never considered her ivory pallor attractive, but now she realised that for some mysterious reason her black hair made rouged cheeks look . . . oh, artificial, overdone, like a Dutch doll she had once owned. One last glance in the mirror told her that she had done her best and must leave it now, though she had plenty of time before she was due to arrive at the museum.

She had eaten breakfast with her mother and now decided that if she remained in the house she would simply grow more and more nervous, turning what should be a pleasurable experience into an ordeal. It was such a lovely day that she would not need her coat, so she set off into the sunshine, telling herself briskly that once she reached the museum she would be sure to find colleagues she knew. Just as she arrived on Shaw Street, a tram drew up beside her and a glance at its destination board showed her that it was bound for Islington, which would take her at least halfway to where she wanted to go. Climbing carefully aboard, she paid her fare, settled herself in a seat and checked her wristwatch. She was going to be early, but what did that matter? She seldom had the opportunity to window-shop at the big stores in the centre of the city; she would enjoy doing so now.

She left the tram and made for the nearest store,

and was peering at a display of summer dresses when she happened to glance sideways and saw a remarkably pretty girl, also examining the wares for sale. The girl was very much a modern miss, and Agatha was interested to see how her jet-black hair had been cut and fashioned to draw attention to the beautiful shape of her head. Almost unconsciously Miss Preece's hand went to her own French pleat. My hair has been ignored for most of my life, she told herself, and before she knew quite what she was doing she had turned round, walked briskly to a hairdressing salon she had noticed earlier and entered its portals.

Half an hour later she emerged, wondering at her own courage; or had it been that of the hairdresser? He had brushed out her long rain-straight locks, tutted at something he called 'split ends' and asked her what style she had in mind. When Miss Preece had shrugged helplessly, muttering that she had come in on impulse, simply wanting a change, he had patted her shoulder, run his fingers through her hair a couple of times, then seized his scissors and started to cut.

The scrunching of the blades, only just below her ear, had frightened Miss Preece so much that she had closed her eyes and kept them closed until the hair-dresser invited her to examine her reflection. Then she had been astonished to see in his mirror a pale-skinned young woman whose short, sleek hair fell in two shining wings on either side of her face and who seemed at first to bear no resemblance to Miss Agatha Preece, librarian of this parish.

The hairdresser had eyed her reflection with satisfaction and begun to brush stray hairs off the shoulders of the cape in which he had enveloped her, saying as he did so: 'It's not a style which would suit everyone, but for you I think it is perfect; you like it?' He had smiled at her through the mirror and had seemed content when Miss Preece could only nod and return his smile, bereft for the moment of speech.

So now, emerging on to the pavement and turning her steps towards William Brown Street, Miss Preece quite literally felt like a different person. A far more sophisticated, self-confident person, who would hold her own in the select company she was about to join. Nevertheless, it would be idle to pretend that she was not both relieved and delighted when, upon showing her invitation and entering the foyer of the museum, she saw coming towards her Susannah Trimble, with whom she had been at university.

They greeted each other with enthusiasm, Miss Preece suspecting that Susannah felt as friendless as she herself did. Then they exchanged news of what they had been doing in the years that had elapsed since their last meeting. Susannah worked at the British Museum and was accompanying the exhibition of illuminated manuscripts from London, first to Liverpool and then to various other venues across the country. She was a tall, earnest young woman with light brown eyes behind thick spectacles, and a great deal of wiry and undisciplined pale brown hair.

After their initial greetings, she looked Miss Preece up and down and, speaking with more than a trace of envy, said: 'I say, Aggie, aren't you smart! I love that suit – wish I had one like it – and I nearly didn't recognise you with your hair cut in that smart style.'

'It's the suit I wore when Mary got married,' Miss Preece explained. 'You must remember Mary Cartwright; she was the only one of us to get a poor degree, but since she caught herself a husband within three months of leaving university, I don't believe she was particularly bothered. As for my hair, it's as new to me as it is to you, since I only had it cut half an hour ago, but I'm glad you like it. And now tell me about this professor who is going to give the talk on illuminated manuscripts; do you work for him?'

'Well, I work in his department, but only for one of his junior staff; the prof is a very important person,' Susannah said. 'Well, he's giving the main lecture, which should tell you something.' She giggled. 'Come to think of it, I was wondering why you were here, but of course I've just remembered that you specialised in illuminated manuscripts when we were both in college. In fact, when I went to the interview for my present job, I half expected to see you amongst the applicants.' She gave Miss Preece a wide, ingenuous smile. 'I was jolly glad you weren't there,' she added honestly. 'If you had been, I'd have known I wouldn't have had a hope of getting the job, and I do love it. Why didn't you apply, Aggie?'

'Oh, my mother would never have consented to move to London,' Miss Preece said at once. 'She's spent all her life in Liverpool and would simply say she was too old to live amongst strangers. And anyway, I enjoy being a librarian, though I'm sure it isn't as exciting as your work. Now tell me about this professor. I expect he's quite old?'

Susannah laughed. 'No, he's quite young, or young for a professor at any rate,' she said. 'He's not yet forty, and very highly regarded by . . .'

But Miss Preece was no longer attending. She was staring across the crowded foyer at the man who had just entered; tall, with crisply curling dark hair touched with grey at the temples, and a harsh but unmistakable face. Even as she gasped and clutched Susannah's arm, the other woman turned to follow the direction of her gaze.

'That's him, that's Professor Galera. But you recognised him, didn't you, so you obviously know him . . .'

'No, I wouldn't say I knew him, exactly,' Miss Preece said, trying to shrink behind the other woman. Of all the rotten luck! Professor Galera was the man who had knocked her down as she had left the library some three years before. For a moment she was panic-stricken, fearing that he would approach her, demand what right she had to be attending this function, perhaps even turn her out. Then common sense reasserted itself; he could not possibly remember her after so long. If she kept her walking stick out of sight and tried to reduce her limp, he would simply pass her by, and anyway she was not the only woman in Liverpool with a limp. She had only remembered him because he was so striking, with his high-bridged nose, dark complexion and aggressively jutting chin. She turned to Susannah. 'I – I think he's probably come

184

into the library at some time, and that's why he seemed familiar at first glance.'

Susannah pulled a doubtful face. 'It's possible, only I believe this is his first visit to Liverpool. He has a brother who's said to be very like him; he was in Liverpool for a short time a couple of years ago, but apparently he went to Spain to join the International Brigade when the Civil War started, and he's there still. The professor is talking of going to Spain as well, but perhaps it will come to nothing. It's really only a rumour at present.'

'Oh, I see,' Miss Preece said. So the professor could not possibly be the man who had knocked her down in the street; it must have been his brother. But Susannah was looking at her curiously, so she hastily broke into speech once more. 'Galera's a Spanish name, isn't it? I suppose that's why he's rather dark-skinned.'

Susannah raised her thick straight eyebrows. 'Yes, you could describe his colouring as Mediterranean . . . his father came from Spain originally.' She lowered her voice to a confidential murmur. 'All the women who work at the museum would give their eye teeth for a smile from him. Don't you think he's most awfully attractive?'

Miss Preece was about to say unequivocally that far from finding him attractive she considered him plain as a pikestaff – in fact she thought him down-right ugly – when the big double doors at the end of the wide hall were thrown open and a tall, thin man in a black suit, wearing a monocle on the end of a gold chain, clapped his hands for attention and announced that he would be obliged if everyone would form a queue and begin to make their way into the lecture hall.

Susannah had linked arms with Miss Preece, and now she bent her head to whisper, 'The man with the monocle is the fellow who organised this whole affair, and has done it pretty well, according to my boss. But we must stick together, Aggie; what a bit of luck my spotting you as you entered the foyer! I'll introduce you to my colleagues when the lecture's over. You'll like them; they're a friendly bunch.'

As Miss Preece emerged from the museum that evening, flushed with pleasure and looking forward to telling Hetty and her mother what a wonderful day she had had, she felt a hand on her arm and swung round to find the professor himself smiling down at her.

Returning the smile, she found herself wondering how she could ever have mistaken him for the bad-tempered, impatient man who had knocked her down. To be sure there were superficial likenesses; both men had curly, dark hair, greying at the temples, and were above average height, but when the professor smiled his dark eyes gleamed with humour, and his voice when he spoke was pleasant. She could not remember her attacker, as she now thought of him, smiling at all, but if he had done so she knew it would have been mockingly. However, looking up into the dark face above her own, she raised her eyebrows. 'Yes, Professor? I do hope you aren't going to scold me for asking so many questions!'

He laughed, and Miss Preece's heart did a double

somersault. Why on earth had she ever thought him ugly? Certainly, he was not handsome, but he had a craggy attraction which she had dismissed, denied, because he had reminded her of that other. But he was laughing still, shaking his head. 'My dear madam, I blessed your courage, because there's nothing more embarrassing for a speaker than asking for questions and hearing only a deathly silence. What is more, your questions were searching and intelligent; helpful, in fact. So I wanted to express my gratitude before you left.'

Miss Preece smiled but shook her head. 'It's kind of you to say so, but if I'd not spoken up, someone else would have done. The man in the velvet smoking jacket, for instance . . .'

'Ah yes, what we might call an enthusiastic amateur. But your interest is of a more practical nature.' He hesitated, looking up and down the road. 'Is someone meeting you? Might I walk you home, as we used to say when we were young?'

Miss Preece felt the hot colour invade her cheeks, and was about to invent a reason to refuse this perfectly acceptable suggestion when the professor said hastily: 'If I were not leaving the city tomorrow I would ask you to join me for a meal so that we might discuss my work and your own in more comfortable surroundings. But I'm engaged with friends tonight and then giving lectures at Durham University, York and Edinburgh before going, as I intend, to Spain, so . . . may I walk you home, Miss Preece?'

'Of course,' Miss Preece said at once, telling herself

that to refuse would be both rude and churlish. 'But you're surely not going to embroil yourself in that dreadful war! It would be extremely dangerous.'

'You are very right, and I agree that to go to Spain as things are at present must seem strange,' he said. 'But I have a younger brother – twelve months younger than myself, in fact – of whom I am very fond. He joined the International Brigade at the start of the Civil War, but for the past three months I've heard nothing from him. As you must realise, Spain is in a terrible state, but there's a little village in the Pyrenees where the peasants have never faltered in their support for the Republicans. If I can make my way there, I might get news of Michael. But I mustn't bore you with my troubles.'

'I'm not bored,' Miss Preece assured him. 'War is always terrible and civil war, they say, is the worst. You must be dreadfully worried about your brother – someone told me he is very like you. You both obviously knew the country very well before the conflict started; but I've never been out of England and have always been intrigued by Spain. My grandfather was a Spaniard, you see, which accounts for my interest. If it wouldn't upset you, can you tell me a little about the country and its people?'

Apparently nothing loth, the professor began to tell her of the Spain he had once known. He spoke of vineyards laden with purple grapes, of citrus groves flaunting their golden globes in the hot sunshine, and of the poverty-ridden peasants, labouring ceaselessly in those same vineyards and citrus groves. But despite what seemed like idyllic conditions, the landowners had refused to pay their workers a living wage and in desperation the peasants had risen up, starting the bloody conflict which became the Civil War.

'How dreadful,' Miss Preece breathed, stopping outside her house. 'Of course I knew there had been injustice . . . but, Professor, you will be in great danger if you go to Spain now.'

The professor nodded. 'I shall behave with extreme caution, I assure you,' he said calmly. 'I know the country well, and have many friends there . . . but I see we've arrived at your home.' He held out a hand. 'Goodbye, Miss Preece. I hope we may meet again, and continue our talk when I return from Spain.'

Miss Preece took his hand and was about to thank him for his company when something occurred to her. Normally, she would not dream of asking anyone she did not know well into the house, because usually her mother would be present, gimlet-eyed and inquisitive. But this was the one day of the year when she could invite anyone she knew with impunity. Old Mrs Preece was in Llandudno, playing whist, the house was always neat and tidy, she had baked scones the day before and knew there was fresh milk in the pantry and a slab of butter beneath the wire cover on the slate shelf. But what would her mother say if she discovered that her daughter had invited a strange man to share a cup of tea and a chat?

The professor was turning away. It was not as though he were a young man, or a handsome one, Miss Preece reminded herself; he was not old enough to be her father, but he was probably ten years her senior, and anyway, why should she worry? Her mother need never know that she had entertained such an eminent person in their home; my home, Miss Preece reminded herself emphatically, as she put a detaining hand on the professor's arm, hurrying into speech. 'Professor Galera, I wonder if you would like to continue our discussion over a cup of tea? It just so happens . . .'

Chapter Nine

When Hetty and old Mrs Preece arrived at the house on Everton Terrace and let themselves in, there was no sign of Miss Preece. But she must have heard the front door opening, or possibly their voices, though they had done their best to speak quietly, for whilst Hetty was filling the kettle at the sink and old Mrs Preece fetched milk and sugar for a cup of tea they heard footsteps descending the stair.

The kitchen door opened and Hetty swung round, ready to say she was sorry for their late return, and relieved that thanks to her mysterious helper she had no need to apologise for missing the coach. She was beginning to say she hoped they had not woken her friend when she stopped short, blinking with surprise. 'Oh, Miss Preece, I hardly recognised you, with that marvellous hair-do,' she gasped. 'It's incredible how – how different you look. But you never said you were thinking of having it cut; I'm sure you never breathed a word.'

Miss Preece's hand went up to her hair as though she was as surprised as Hetty to find it cut short. But she only said: 'I'm glad you like it, my dear. After your coach left, I found myself at a loose end. I can't think, now, why I went into the hairdressing salon, but as soon as he saw me the hairdresser took it for granted that I was a . . . well, a customer, I suppose you could say. He asked me how I wanted my hair cut; I just stared . . . then I said I'd leave it to him, and this is the result.'

Hetty opened her mouth to tell Miss Preece again how the new style suited her, but was forestalled by the old lady. 'Ridiculous! Trying to pass yourself off as a flapper, and you in your thirties,' she said peevishly. 'No one would take you for a respectable business-woman, which is what you are when all's said and done.'

Hetty saw a pink flush creep up the librarian's neck and invade her face, and felt really angry with old Mrs Preece. How could she say such a cruel thing? And it wasn't even true; Miss Preece might be – was – a re-spectable businesswoman, but that did not mean she had to be dowdy. Fortunately, however, Hetty realised in time that it was late, that Mrs Preece was tired, and had probably been startled at the change the new hair-style had wrought. So she swallowed the blistering words of reproof which were on the tip of her tongue, and merely shook her head chidingly at the old lady. 'Are you trying to say that your daughter's new hair-style doesn't suit her?' she asked gently. 'Because if so, your spectacles need changing! Why, she looks really pretty, as well as years younger.'

Mrs Preece sniffed, but had the grace to look a little ashamed. 'I was taken aback,' she muttered. 'Old folk don't like change, even when it's for the better.'

'Then you do admit it's for the better?' Hetty said,

lighting the gas under the kettle and going over to the pantry to fetch the biscuits, for she knew Mrs Preece would not dream of drinking a cup of tea unaccompanied by her favourite ginger nuts.

When she returned, mother and daughter were seated at the kitchen table, both smiling now as Mrs Preece began to range her prizes along its surface. The older woman looked up and jerked her chin at her daughter. 'Yes, I dare say it is better; she won't have to spend so long brushing it out and coiling it up,' she said. 'It's got a grand shine to it as well; I like that. When I was young, Mr Preece used to say that my hair shone like polished jet.'

'You must have been very alike,' Hetty observed, helping herself to a couple of ginger biscuits and slipping them into her pocket. 'But having seen you safe home, Mrs Preece, I'd best be getting back to Aunt Phoebe.' She turned to the librarian. 'Did you have a good day? I had a wonderful time; I'll tell you all about it when we next meet, but I really must be going now. I didn't realise I should be this late back. Of course I told Aunt Phoebe not to wait up, only knowing her I expect she'll do so anyway.'

'I had a fantastic time,' Miss Preece said eagerly. 'We'll exchange experiences when you come to the library on Monday. But I don't mean to let you walk through the dark streets alone. I'll just see my mother into bed and then I shall treat you to a taxi ride.'

'You won't find a taxi on Everton Terrace at this time of night,' Hetty said. She looked at the kitchen clock and saw, to her surprise, that it was only a quarter past ten. 'Why don't you walk down to the main road with me if you're truly worried that someone might hit me over the head and carry me off to a ship bound for the Far East and the white slave trade.' She grinned at her friend. 'Come to that, if you do come with me, we might both get hit over the head and carried off to the Far East.'

Miss Preece joined in her laughter. 'I'll borrow Mother's spectacles and the old cloche hat she wears when it's raining,' she said gaily. 'Oh, Hetty Gilbert, you do me a power of good!'

Hetty was beginning to reply that it worked both ways, that Miss Preece did her a power of good as well, when the old lady spoke up. 'In my opinion, Hetty's changed our lives,' she said, sounding as surprised as she must have felt. 'A few years ago you would never have joked and laughed the way you do now, Agatha, my dear.' She turned to Hetty. 'I'm tired, but I've had a lovely day thanks to you.' She rose creakingly to her feet. 'And now you sit down, drink your tea and eat a few biscuits whilst Agatha here helps me out of my dress and corset.'

Miss Preece smiled at Hetty. 'Can you wait?' she asked. 'I really won't be more than five minutes.'

Hetty assured her that she would wait and Miss Preece was as good as her word, so it was less than ten minutes later that the two of them left the house and set off down the road in the direction of Salisbury Street. They emerged on to Netherfield Road and, without consultation, slowed their steps and glanced at one another. 'You first,' Hetty said encouragingly.

'My day was longer than I anticipated, so it will take longer to tell. And something happened which . . . but I won't jump the gun. Go on, Miss Preece; how was your day? Pretty good, I imagine.'

Miss Preece took a deep breath. 'I'll tell it like a story, from the very beginning, and I know you'll be interested because I met someone we know, or rather someone I thought we knew, only I was wrong.'

She told the story well and clearly and when she spoke of Professor Galera's brother, who was so like him, and said that she thought he was the man who had collided with her outside the library, Hetty whistled softly beneath her breath. When she admitted to inviting the professor into her home, Hetty clapped a hand over her mouth to muffle a laugh. 'You *were* daring,' she said admiringly. 'Is that why you used make-up? Your colouring is so dramatic that you scarcely need it, but I thought I could see traces of rouge on your lips.'

Miss Preece's hands flew to her cheeks. 'No, of course it wasn't,' she said. 'I did put on a very little lipstick before I left the house after breakfast, though, thinking it would give me courage to face the day ahead. I suppose that was why I had my hair cut as well, and it certainly worked. I've always been shy, reluctant to stand out in any company, but today I didn't hesitate to ask questions and join in discussions. By the time the professor had to leave – he had a dinner engagement with colleagues at the Adelphi – I felt I'd known him for years.'

'And when are you going to see him again?' Hetty

asked innocently, and smiled as the colour flooded her friend's face once more. 'Oh, go on, Miss Preece, don't expect me to believe that he singled you out and accompanied you home just because you know a lot about illuminated manuscripts. He liked you, and wanted to get to know you better. It's as plain as the nose on your face – or rather on his face, from what I remember.'

'Hetty Gilbert, you are awful,' Miss Preece said, but she was laughing. 'I'm sure his interest in me was purely as someone with similar interests to his own. Anyway, since he's off to Spain in less than a week, he could scarcely try to make an arrangement to meet.' She looked quickly at Hetty, then down at her feet, one so normal and the other in its hefty, built-up boot. 'Though to tell you the truth, he did tell me he would write, possibly from Spain, but certainly when he reached England once more.'

Hetty gave a little crow of triumph. 'I knew it, I knew it! It's about time you realised that you're very attractive, Miss Preece. Why, with your hair cut in that new style, and . . .'

'And that reminds me, Hetty,' Miss Preece cut in, her colour heightening once again. 'Isn't it about time you dropped "Miss Preece" and started calling me Agatha? I know you're a good deal younger than me, but we've known each other for a couple of years now, and I think of you as my friend.'

'It's awfully nice of you to suggest it, but when you're helping me with my schoolwork you're a sort of teacher, and when I'm working in the library, you're my boss,' Hetty said rather shyly. If she had to own

196

the truth, she would have to admit she was embarrassed by the mere suggestion that she might use Miss Preece's first name. However, it would never do to say so. 'If we could get round that . . .'

'We can, of course,' Miss Preece said briskly. 'I'll be Agatha when we're alone and Miss Preece when others are present. Would that suit you?'

'Yes, that would be ideal,' Hetty said gratefully. 'And now, Miss Pr— I mean Agatha, I'll tell you what happened to me, which was as strange, in its way, as what happened to you. And I don't mean it was strange that the professor took to you, but that it seems quite likely we met his brother years ago, when you and he were heading in the same direction but still managed to collide with one another.'

'I did not collide with him; he collided with me,' Miss Preece said with dignity. 'I disliked him from the first moment I set eyes on him, which is odd when you consider how very charming I found his brother. I know Susannah – and the professor himself – said how very alike they are, but I assure you, Hetty, that the likeness can only be superficial. The professor has a gentle expression, full of humour and interest in those around him. His wretched brother was clearly only interested in himself. I doubt whether I registered with him; probably he'd not recognise me if we met tomorrow, face to face. But I'm sorry, I interrupted; you were about to tell me . . .'

The story of Hetty's day in Llandudno was soon told, but the mistake over the coach, her subsequent despair and her rescue by the 'motorbike man' had

Miss Preece assuring her that beside Hetty's, her own adventure paled into insignificance.

'Surely you have some idea who your rescuer was?' she asked, after Hetty had described her wild, moonlit ride. 'You seemed to think it was someone who knew you well. Tell me again who it might have been.'

'I've thought and thought, but the only conclusion I've reached is that it could have been almost anyone who worked the Leeds and Liverpool Canal,' Hetty said. 'If I'm going to start with my first possible guess, it would have to be Jez, who was my best friend from the time I was about four until his father and mother took over a narrow boat on the Grand Union Canal. He used to help Gramps with Guinness, our horse; we became really good pals, but we've not met for years. He's at least two years older than me, which would make him about the right age for the man on the motorbike.'

'Jez,' Miss Preece said thoughtfully, clearly committing the name to memory. 'That's an odd sort of name, isn't it? I don't believe I've ever heard it before.'

Hetty laughed. 'It's short for Jeremy,' she explained. 'Canal folk are like Liverpudlians; they shorten or nickname everyone.'

'I should know; at school they called me Aggie, which I hated,' Miss Preece – Agatha, Hetty reminded herself – said ruefully. 'And I've heard some older customers refer to the library as the Evvie . . . Next name please!'

'Gareth Evans,' Hetty said. 'You know, Miss . . . Agatha, I mean. He lived next door to Aunt Phoebe,

and was apprenticed at some sort of motor factory . . .
I think they made cars, or aeroplanes, or something.
But his family moved away a couple of years ago,
when his dad finally got a job outside the city. So as
far as I can remember, Gareth must have gone when
his parents did.'

'Did he go to Wales?' Agatha asked. 'Not that there
are a lot of jobs for motor mechanics in little Welsh
villages.'

'Don't know,' Hetty admitted. 'The point is that I've
not seen Gareth for ages, so it could have been him.
And I suppose it could have been horrible Harry, the
fellow who walked out on Gramps, do you remember
me telling you? Only why should any one of them not
tell me his name? It seems . . . oh, peculiar, to say the
least.'

'It does,' Agatha agreed, as they turned into
Salisbury Street. 'But you'll find out in due course,
I imagine. Next time you pay a visit to your grandfather, you could sound him out. He might know
something – whether any of the three lads you've
mentioned owns a motorbike or lives in a small Welsh
village, for instance.'

Hetty was much struck by the good sense of this
idea. Presently they reached her aunt's house and bade
one another good night. 'I feel bad about letting you
walk back home alone,' Hetty said anxiously, with one
hand on the front door knob. 'Are you sure you'll be
all right? I know it's only a short walk, but . . .'

'I'll be fine. See you on Monday,' Miss Preece said.
'Goodnight, Hetty, and good luck with your hunt for

your St George and his mettlesome steed.' She looked a little self-conscious. 'And not a word to anyone, particularly my mother, about Max . . . I mean Professor Galera.'

'I won't say a word,' Hetty promised as she opened the front door, which would only be locked, she knew, when Aunt Phoebe was making her way to bed. But as she closed it behind her and walked up the short hall to the kitchen, she was thinking, So his name is Max, is it? And you want me to think he's only interested in your knowledge of illuminated manuscripts! Pull the other one, Miss Agatha Preece!'

As she had expected, she found her aunt sitting up for her, and on impulse she decided to confide in her about the young man on the motorcycle. She told her all about missing the coach, catching the wrong one, and being brought home on the back of a motorbike by someone who had not wanted to give her his name. She tried to make it sound jokey, but could not have succeeded very well since her aunt frowned thoughtfully, looking hard at Hetty as she did so.

'Don't worry, love,' she said at last. 'It *is* an odd thing, but I reckon the feller just didn't want to be thanked. Some folk is like that. And you think he knew you? Well, the only feller I can think of is young Gareth what lived next door, but then I never really knew your pals on the canal. I reckon you ought to pop round to Burscough tomorrer, see whether your gran or grandpa can shed light. Go straight after church on a Sunday and you'll always find them home, and old Matthew, too.'

'Thanks, Auntie, I'll do that,' Hetty said gratefully. 'I suppose it isn't important, but I'd like to know just who the chap was. And now I'm for bed, because I'm worn out.'

She expected to fall asleep the moment her head touched the pillow, but perhaps because she had twice retold the story of her exciting ride home on the unknown's motorbike or perhaps simply because she was so tired, sleep eluded her. She tossed and turned whilst her mind went over and over her wonderful day, and then she started thinking of all the boys, now young men, whom she had known whilst a part of the crew of the *Water Sprite*, and wondering which of them, if any, had been kind enough to bring her back to Liverpool in time to accompany Mrs Preece to Everton Terrace.

When she heard the church clock strike midnight she got out of bed and thought about going downstairs and making herself a hot drink, but decided against it on the grounds that she would undoubtedly wake her aunt and uncle. Instead, she went to the window and pulled back the curtains, then opened the pane fully and looked out at the sleeping street below. Nothing stirred, not a cat, not a scuffer walking his beat, not a late reveller reeling home after a lock-in at the local pub. Sighing, Hetty climbed back into bed, then threw the covers off; she was too hot, that was the trouble. If she lay with just the sheet over her . . .

In seconds, she was asleep. And dreaming. She was walking through a beautiful wood, only when she looked more closely at the trees which surrounded her they were not trees at all, but young men, all of whom were wearing full motorcycling gear complete with helmet and goggles. It was night, but instead of being a delicate crescent this moon was full, making the silver light stronger and the shadows deeper, blacker. A little frightened, she kept to the path which wound its way between the trees and the thick undergrowth, but she soon realised that the young men who stood talking and laughing amongst themselves were not interested in her, though they glanced at her as she passed them by. She knew, suddenly, that one of these men was important to her, and that the reason she was here was to discover which of them it was. She went up to the nearest young man, and as she stretched out her hand to touch him he grinned at her and for an instant she saw his face, lean, tanned, a lock of dark hair hanging across his forehead. But it was not the face she sought and rather regretfully, for he was a pleasant-looking fellow, she shook her head and moved on to the next, the next, the next.

She found him. She put her arms round his neck, trusting as a child with a well-loved adult, and looking up into the face above her own said simply: 'So it *was* you, after all! Oh, why didn't I recognise you, when I do believe I've loved you all my life long!'

He said something; she thought it was, 'Wake up, silly!' and suddenly she was awake and in her own bed, with Aunt Phoebe shaking her shoulder and saying laughingly: 'What a dream you was havin', queen! But if you're goin' to visit Burscough today you'd best gerra move on or you won't have time for no breakfast, and there's a bowl o' porridge wi' your name on it coolin' on the kitchen table.'

Hetty shook her head violently and sat up, feeling extremely foolish. 'What did I say, Auntie?' she enquired apprehensively. 'I was dreaming about my trip to the seaside . . .'

'You didn't say nothin', or not that I could make out,' Aunt Phoebe said, going over to the washstand and pouring water into the round blue basin. 'Come along, show a perishin' leg!'

Hetty slipped obediently out of bed and stripped off her nightdress as her aunt left the room, shutting the door firmly behind her. Splashing cold water into her face, she tried to remember the dream, and presently some of it came back to her, but not all. She could not remember so much as one feature of the young man who had held her in his arms and smiled down into her eyes with such teasing affection. She could not remember whether she had spoken to him or he to her. And by the time she was descending the stairs and beginning to look forward to her porridge and toast, the dream had disappeared like snow in spring, and all she could think of was her visit to her grandparents and her hope that they might be able to throw some light on her mysterious motorcyclist.

After she had eaten her breakfast, Hetty accompanied her aunt and uncle to church, then checked the times of the buses out to Burscough. She had only visited her grandparents twice since they had moved in with Uncle Matthew, because the journey was quite expensive and the times not always convenient. But today she was visiting with a purpose and hopped aboard the half past eleven bus, knowing that her grandmother would insist that she share their dinner, and knowing also that there would be plenty of food for an unexpected guest since Gran always over-catered.

When she arrived at Burscough she could not resist walking down to the towpath and glancing first to her left and then to her right, hoping to see a barge managed by people she knew, but despite the fact that it was a fine and sunny day the water was empty save for a flotilla of ducks and a solitary barge – engine driven – chugging away from her, already almost out of her sight. Sighing, Hetty turned towards Uncle Matthew's neat little slate-roofed red-brick house. If she had been able to warn the occupants of her arrival she would have gone round the back, but since she was not expected she went to the front door, plied the brass knocker vigorously, opened the door and stepped inside just as her grandfather emerged from the kitchen, releasing a wonderful smell of roast beef, roast potatoes and Yorkshire pudding, which made Hetty's nostrils twitch even as she ran towards her grand-father's welcoming arms.

'Hetty, my love, it's as good as a tonic to see your smiling face,' her grandfather said, hugging her warmly. 'You're just in time for dinner; Gran must have guessed you were coming because she's roasted parsnips along with the potatoes, and we all know they're your favourites.' He gave her a kiss, then turned his head to shout over his shoulder: 'Dulcie, my dear, it's our Hetty. Get out another plate and a set of eating irons! Well, well, well. When I woke this morning and saw the sunshine, I nearly accepted old Joshua's suggestion that I should go for a ride – just as far as the next bridge, you know – in his barge. He's had a new engine installed, the very latest thing, but something must have told me not to take him up on his invitation today, and wouldn't I have kicked myself if I'd gone with Josh and missed seeing my favourite granddaughter!'

Hetty laughed, kissed his cheek, and ran over to where her grandmother was just dishing up. 'Dear Gran, it's too bad of me to arrive at dinnertime, but I knew you'd probably cooked enough food for an army and wouldn't grudge me a bite.' She kissed her grandmother's rosy, wrinkled cheek, then went over to Uncle Matthew, already seated, his empty plate before him, and gave him a hug. 'Sorry, Uncle Matt; this is your house I'm invading, but I hope you don't mind!'

'Course I don't, since your gran is the best cook in the world, and would feed half the neighbourhood given a chance,' Uncle Matthew said. 'Nice to see you, queen. Sit yourself down and prepare for a treat, 'cos there's a treacle puddin' for afters – and if roasted parsnips is your favourite, then treacle puddin' is mine.'

At her grandmother's request, Hetty helped her to dish up, ladling potatoes, cabbage and carrots on to each plate, whilst her grandfather carved the joint of beef and Gran produced from the oven a square tin, bubbling with Yorkshire pudding, and cut the contents into four large pieces. Hetty smiled to herself as a large pot of home-made horseradish sauce and another of rich beef gravy were handed round the table. Aunt Phoebe did her best, but no one could cook a roast like Gran. When everyone was served, Uncle Matthew bent his head and said grace and Hetty loaded her fork and began to eat.

Presently, she thought it only fair to say that she had come to visit them since she had a problem she hoped they might help her to solve, but as she knew he would, her grandfather shook a reproving head at her and put a finger to his lips. 'You know our rules, young Hetty. Casual conversation of an easy nature is allowed at the dinner table, but anything which needs consideration waits till we've done the washing up.'

Hetty laughed. 'I thought that was just aboard the *Water Sprite*,' she protested. 'But it's fair enough, Gramps; I'd much rather have your full attention, so I'll abide by the rules. I say, Gran, when we've had our dinner, can I have some stale bread to feed the ducks? There were a whole lot of them on the canal as I passed.'

Her grandmother agreed that there were always a few crusts left for the ducks, and then conversation lapsed as the family polished off their main course and started on the treacle pudding, helping themselves from a large jug of custard.

'I'll wash up!' Hetty said eagerly, collecting crockery and cutlery and carrying the heavy kettle across to the sink, but her grandmother shook her head and handed her a string bag full of stale bread.

'No you don't, queen, you go and feed the ducks. Your Uncle Matthew, your grandfather and myself have got washing up down to a fine art. We take it in turns to wash the crocks and pots, dry them and put them away. Today, I shall wash, Uncle Matthew will dry and Gramps will put away. Then I shall make a nice pot of tea and we'll discuss your problem whilst we drink it. Off with you now.'

Hetty took the bag of scraps and was soon casting a positive feast before the ducks and wondering whether her grandparents would be able to help in the identification of her mysterious rescuer. Returning to the kitchen, she found the tea poured and everyone seated round the table, eyeing her with considerable curiosity. 'Sit down and tell us your problem, and we'll see if we can help,' Gramps said encouragingly. 'Only I just hope it isn't a mathematical one, or anything to do with history, because neither your Gran nor myself were any good at schoolwork.'

Hetty laughed. 'As if I'd bring you that sort of problem when I'm having special coaching lessons from Miss Preece at the library,' she said. 'No, this is something quite different . . .'

Hetty explained, giving as many details as she could about her rescuer; he was tall, broad-shouldered and, so far as she could judge, quite slim, though it was difficult to tell, clad as he was in leathers. Her grandparents wanted to know if he spoke with a Liverpool or a Welsh accent. Hetty frowned thoughtfully, for it was a question that had puzzled her every time she thought about it. 'Well, at one point he called me "cariad", at another "chuck", and he also referred to me when he first spoke as "lass". The Welsh say "cariad" – I think it means "my dear" – Liverpudlians say "chuck" and Lancastrians call one "lass". So that isn't much help.'

Her grandfather nodded wisely. 'He really didn't want you to recognise him, did he?' he asked. 'A lot of Scousers speak with a trace of a Welsh accent, or even a Lancastrian one, but in view of the fact that he wouldn't tell you his name I think he misled you purposely by using forms of address common to Wales, Liverpool and Lancashire.'

'Yes, I think you're right,' Hetty said, after some thought. 'But wait until I tell you his parting shot! It's that which makes me wonder if you can guess who he was.'

However, when she came to the last part of her story, where the young man had said, 'Tell your grandpa I were asking for him . . .' she could tell at once by the expression on her listeners' faces that they were no wiser than she.

'Could it have been Jez?' Gramps suggested. 'We've not set eyes on him for years, so I suppose he might well ask after us. But then so would Gareth – and he's Welsh, and wanted to get work in Wales if he possibly could after his parents moved away from Liverpool. Or there was Jimmy . . . or Frank; you were pally with them at one time. Goodness, Hetty, it could be almost anyone!'

'I s'pose it wasn't Harry? The fellow who walked

out on us without giving us so much as a hint that he meant to leave?' Gran put in rather timidly. 'Honest to God, queen, with so little to go on, I wouldn't like to hazard a guess. But does it really matter? If he didn't want you to know who he was, I imagine he had a good reason. Didn't you say he had come to the village to take a girl called Cerys back to the next valley? If Cerys is his girlfriend, then he might not want her to know that he had given you a lift all the way back to Liverpool. Some girls can get really jealous over the tiniest thing.'

'Or he might be married,' Uncle Matthew chimed in. He was a small, gnome-like man, totally bald but with bushy side-whiskers, a moustache and a small pointed beard. Because of his many years on the canal he was brown and wrinkled as a walnut, and now he grinned at his great-niece, looking as mischievous as the gnome he resembled. 'If he's wed to some pretty young Welsh lass, I'd say your gran's guess is right and he wouldn't want you putting it abroad that he'd brought you all the way back to Liverpool and not accepted a penny piece, in case it got back to his lady wife.' He chuckled wheezily. 'There's the answer to your puzzle . . . and if he truly recognised you, why did he call you Miss Liverpool and not Miss Gilbert? And most gals of your age have grandparents; I tek it he didn't say "Gramps" did he?'

'No, of course he wouldn't, because Gramps isn't *his* grandfather,' Hetty said, giggling. 'But I suppose you're right; if the chap didn't want to be recognised then trying to find out begins to seem like – oh, I don't know, like prying.' She turned to her grandparents, both of whom, to her secret amusement, were nodding and smiling and looking just like Tweedledum and Tweedledee from *Alice's Adventures in Wonderland*. 'You agree with Uncle Matthew, I can tell.'

'That's right, sweetheart,' Gramps said at once. 'You don't want to get obsessed with finding out something that isn't in the least important. Otherwise, when next year comes and you're taking your school certificate, you'll find yourself studying the faces of your fellow students instead of answering the questions.'

Hetty giggled again, but Gran trotted round the table and gave her shoulder a comforting squeeze. 'If you're meant to find out who rescued you, then find out you will, in the fullness of time,' she said. 'It's a bit like that old adage, though – a watched pot never boils. Just you put the whole episode out of your mind and the solution will come of its own accord. You see if I'm not right.'

Hetty agreed to do this, and was glad she had decided not to mention that the young man had kissed her just before they parted. She had told no one this, not even Agatha Preece, and since she had now decided to put the whole matter out of her mind she was glad of the omission. Her rescuer's kiss had been, she knew, a teasing kiss, not a proper one at all, a kiss meant to make her even more curious as to his identity. Well, Mr Mystery, you've fallen down on that one, she told him inside her head. Because I dare say you just guessed that most girls have grandparents, and drew a bow at a venture, as they say. So I won't think about it any more, I won't, I won't!

Determinedly, she began to ask Gran how she liked living in a proper house instead of a barge, and presently Gramps took her outside to see his vegetable patch and to pick a bag full of apples from the trees at the end of the garden. 'They're Bramleys, cookers, which means that Phoebe can make a nice apple pie with 'em,' he instructed his granddaughter. He led her to another tree and stretched up to gather some of the rosy, sweet-smelling fruit. 'And these are Coxes, which you can eat just as they are.'

'Thanks, Gramps. I'll have a Cox or two on the bus going home,' Hetty said, tucking a couple into her pocket. 'Isn't it good that you and Gran are so happy, living with Uncle Matthew? And he's happy too; I've never seen him look so healthy and cheerful.'

'Aye, we do well enough, the three of us,' her grandfather said. 'And don't forget the advice of three old 'uns, my dear. Stop thinking about that young fellow with the motorbike and, as your gran says, you'll find out who he is, and why he acted so mysteriously. And when you're ready to go and catch your bus just say the word and we'll walk you down to the stop. We like to take some exercise each day; does us all good. I've talked about getting us a dog, but nothing's come of it so far. Maybe in the spring . . .'

Hetty and Gramps strolled on, chatting comfortably, but when they returned to the kitchen Hetty gave a squawk of dismay. 'Look at the time, Gramps,' she said, pointing to the clock on the mantel. 'If I'm to catch the next bus . . .'

'What's the hurry, queen?' Uncle Matthew asked. 'You've not visited us for an age, and Dulcie's made a lovely salad and a pile of cheese butties, to say nothin' of a fruit cake what 'ud do for a perishin' weddin'. There's another bus in a couple of hours.'

'Oh, but I really shouldn't eat all your lovely food, and I've not brought so much as a sugar lump . . .' Hetty began, but was firmly told not to be so foolish.

'We miss you even more than we miss the *Sprite* and the *Beetle*,' Gran said rather plaintively. 'Next summer, you can come and stay with us, can't she, Jim? Of course, we don't have a barge any longer, but we've a nice little row boat; we could take a picnic out into the real countryside . . . you'd enjoy that, Hetty love.'

Hetty agreed that she would and it was tentatively arranged that she should spend at least a few days at Burscough when next summer arrived.

'Unless there's a war by then,' Gramps said, but Hetty did not think he was serious. Why should there be a war? True, there were terrible things happening on the continent according to the newspapers, and Miss Preece – I mean Agatha, Hetty reminded herself – had talked about a war in Spain, but that was a long way away and besides, Hetty had not been attending very closely.

So she promised gaily to come to Burscough the following year for a holiday and hopped aboard the later bus when it stopped to pick her up, waved vigorously to her relatives and sank into a seat, reminding herself that she had vowed to stop wondering about the motorcyclist.

But dreams, of course, were a different matter; no one could control their dreams.

Chapter Ten

If old Mrs Preece noticed how eagerly her daughter awaited the arrival of the post each morning after her trip to Llandudno, she made no comment, and Agatha was grateful, for it was not until halfway through November that the first letter arrived from Spain. Not that it was the first letter, for the professor – or Max, as he had signed himself – had clearly written several times before, since he referred to previous correspondence. But in a country torn by civil war, Agatha supposed it was scarcely surprising that a great many letters never reached their destination. And at least this one had done so, when she had almost given up hope.

It came through the letterbox accompanied by an electricity bill and a couple of circulars, and Agatha thrust it into her pocket and went into the kitchen with a thumping heart. He was alive! She had told herself over and over that he must be safe because he had no part in that bitter conflict, but everyone knew that innocent civilians were constantly being killed; how could she be sure that he was not one of them?

She entered the kitchen and put the electricity bill and the circulars down on the table. Mrs Preece, sprinkling brown sugar on her porridge, reached for the envelope containing the electricity bill, slit it open and pushed it across to her daughter. 'They're very quick off the mark; the man only read the meter last week,' she said. 'You'd better check it, though I've never known them make a mistake. Shall I pour you a second cup of tea? We're earlier than usual, so if you want to help me dress, you could pop round to Mrs Simpson and tell her she won't be needed until lunchtime. That will save us a few pennies.'

Agatha could have screamed. Not only did she know how much their neighbour relied on the money they paid her, she was also aware that if she hurried, she might arrive at the library before it opened, which would give her time to read her letter in comparative privacy. If she stayed to help her mother dress, however, it would probably be lunchtime before she could so much as glance at her correspondence.

But her mother was looking at her, clearly expecting her to agree to cancel Mrs Simpson, and this Agatha was determined not to do. Instead she said reprovingly: 'How can you be so mean, Mother! You can't expect Mrs Simpson to always be available if you cancel her on a whim, and anyway, I like to get in to work before the public begin arriving. Besides, you're always telling me that Mrs Simpson has got helping you dress down to a fine art. Last Sunday, you said it took me twice as long as it takes her to get you into your Sunday-go-to-meeting outfit.'

Mrs Preece sighed but capitulated, so her daughter was able to arrive at work and take her place behind her small desk a good ten minutes before the library would be open to the public. She was disappointed to find that the envelope only contained one small sheet of stained writing paper, but even so, she eagerly prepared to peruse the lines written in the professor's neat hand. There was no address either on the page or the envelope, so she would not be able to reply, but she supposed that it might be dangerous for him to receive a letter from England. She spread out the closely written sheet and began to read.

Dear Miss Preece,

As I told you in my previous letters, I had had no luck in tracing Michael and was beginning to think the worst, so I'm doubly glad to be able to pass on my good news. As soon as the weather began to improve I set off for the village I mentioned when we met – no names no pack-drill is important here, since I imagine that letters to other countries might be opened and read – and at last got news of Michael. He was wounded some time last year but not badly enough to be repatriated, and is now fighting fit again. So wherever I've gone I've put the word about that I'm in Spain and eager to meet up with him; indeed I hope to do so in the not too distant future.

Things here are very bad; everything is scarce. The air raids are terrifying. The aircraft fly in at dusk and wreak enormous damage on Spanish cities, which seems madness since at this rate there will be little left for whichever side wins. Not that there is any doubt, as I expect you realise; the Nationalists have everything on their side.

*I understand that only about one in ten letters
addressed to England arrives at its destination, so God
alone knows whether you will receive this, but I'll write
constantly, hoping at least some of my missives get
through.*

*I think of you often and long for our next meeting
more than you would believe,*

Sincerely,

Max Galera

Agatha read the letter through three times, trying
to pick up information between the lines. She could
not now remember the name of the little village in the
Pyrenees which he had mentioned when they had last
met, but it did not matter. What mattered was that he
was alive, or at least had been when he had written
the letter. He had not put an address on it for obvious
reasons – she supposed that he was constantly moving,
never in one place for long – but now she saw that it
was dated, for there were figures in a tiny cramped
hand at the foot of the page, not at the top as one
would expect, and she realised, with some dismay, that
the letter had been written at the end of July, more
than three months ago.

Because of her intense interest in what was
happening to the professor, she had begun to read
everything she could lay her hands on about Spain
and, consequently, understood his reference to the
weather, for in common with most English people she
had always assumed Spain to be a country of perpetual
sunshine; how else could they grow crops such as

oranges, lemons and grapes? Now, however, she knew better. Madrileños, as the citizens of Madrid were known, had a saying regarding their weather: 'Our city has nine months of hell and three months of winter,' they told anyone who was interested, and the rich who owned the great houses and ran the city were careful to leave it as soon as the weather grew extreme.

I wonder if he's in Madrid now, Agatha thought, folding the letter and popping it into her handbag. No, I'm sure he can't be because we're into November and he says as soon as the weather grew clement he began his search for Michael all over again. And though he hasn't actually found him, he's had news that Michael's alive and well. Oh, how I wish I could help him in some way! He says everything is scarce, which must mean food, clothing, and perhaps even ammunition. If only there was an address to which I could send a parcel; as it is, all I can do is pray for his safety, and that of his brother too, of course. But perhaps now one letter's got through, others will follow. If only there was something I could do to help!

It was a sunny Saturday at the end of July, nearly nine months after Agatha Preece had received the first of the professor's letters, when Hetty bounced into the library, feeling like a prisoner loosed from her chains. She had taken her last examination for the School Certificate in June, term had now finished and it seemed as though the whole summer stretched ahead of her, full of exciting and enjoyable things.

She was leaving this very day to honour her promise

to her grandparents and Uncle Matthew and spend a couple of weeks in the little house in Burscough, though she would not be with them for the entire fortnight. Gramps had already contacted an old friend of Hetty's, Sally Brimelow, who had also left the canal in order to live with relatives so that she might complete her education. When she had heard that Hetty would be staying with her grandparents and would be hoping for a few days aboard a barge, she had begged that Hetty might join the *Maid Marian* so that they could spend time together. Mr and Mrs Brimelow had now retired, leaving the *Maid Marian* to their sons, Nathaniel and Benjamin, so Hetty would be joining a young crew and, as Sally said, because Hetty was experienced it would make things easier for the boys, as well as more fun for Sally herself. She was to travel with the *Maid Marian* for a couple of days, able to give a hand through the multitude of locks around Wigan and return to Burscough by rail.

Also, she and Miss Preece meant to have what the older woman called 'a little jolly' of their own during the month of August. Agatha said it would be to celebrate Hetty's obtaining her School Certificate, but Hetty told herself that if she failed it would be a consolation prize. Agatha had arranged for her mother's friend, Miss Milner, to stay at the house in Everton Terrace for a couple of days to keep her mother company, whilst she and Hetty went down to Llandudno. Agatha had booked them into a bed and breakfast house on North Parade and Hetty, who had never had a proper holiday, was looking forward to it with much excitement.

Her stay in Burscough, however, was to come first and now she had arrived to say her farewells, both to Miss Preece and to her assistant, for though Hetty helped out unofficially the powers that be had decided that the Everton library was too busy for Miss Preece to manage alone and had appointed Miss Maria Thorpe as assistant librarian.

Slipping behind the counter, Hetty began to collect the returned books, saying quietly as she passed Miss Preece: 'Don't look so worried! I expect you saw the newspapers before you arrived at the library, but it may not be as bad as it sounds, and anyway, your professor might be miles away.'

Agatha smiled with difficulty. 'I've been telling myself just that all morning,' she said quietly. 'But if it's true that the Nationalists have managed to split the Republican territory in two . . . well, things were bad enough before, but now, from what the reporters are saying, it's just a matter of time before the Republicans are crushed and have to surrender. And incidentally, how many times have I told you that he's not *my* professor?'

'About a hundred,' Hetty said. 'And don't forget, your . . . I mean *the* professor isn't involved with either side . . .'

'Of course he is,' Miss Preece snapped. 'How can it be otherwise when his brother is a captain in the Republican army?' She sighed, stamped the books before her and pushed them across to her customer, then turned to smile at Hetty. 'Oh, I'm sorry, my dear; I've no right to take my worries out on you. But I had quite a long letter this morning – I'll let you read it whilst we have our sandwiches – and from what Max says, it's a hopeless cause. Still, once the Republicans have surrendered, at least our men will be coming home.'

'Oh, Agatha, I only came in to say goodbye,' Hetty said, dismayed. 'Have you forgotten? I'm off to Burscough on the eleven o'clock bus so I won't be here for lunch.'

'Oh dear,' Miss Preece said. 'The newspaper reports put it right out of my head. Well, have a lovely time with your grandparents and enjoy your trip on the canal.' She gave Hetty a smile, but it was a poor effort. 'By the time you come home again, the news may be much better. After all, the Republicans still hold Barcelona and Madrid, and Franco has always sworn that he would never let anyone treat Madrid as his allies have treated other Spanish cities.'

Hetty swooped on a pile of returned books, then smiled brightly at her friend. 'Well, aren't I daft; buses go from Liverpool to Burscough more than once a day! I'll catch one this afternoon; it's not as though I gave my grandparents my time of arrival, so that means I'll be here to read your . . . *the* professor's letter over lunch. Only I'll have to nip out now and buy myself some sandwiches . . .'

'You will do nothing of the sort,' Miss Preece said firmly and Hetty was relieved to see a little colour return to her friend's cheeks. 'I shall treat the pair of us to lunch at the Priory Tearooms and I won't take no for an answer.'

Hetty laughed. 'You won't have to; I'm always hungry and the food at the Priory is delicious,' she said. 'And now I'd better return these books to their correct places on the shelves since someone is bound to want to take them out if I don't. Do you know, I'm really going to miss the library whilst I'm with my grandparents.'

'You're an official borrower now, don't forget,' Miss Preece said, date-stamping busily. 'You can take two books provided you don't go dropping them into the canal, or feeding them to the ducks.'

'I know; but two books will only last me a couple of days and I'm away for longer than that,' Hetty pointed out. 'Oh, I do hope the news from Spain will be better by the time I get back.'

Over a delicious lunch, Hetty read Max Galera's latest letter and realised at once why Miss Preece was so worried. In his previous letters, the professor had written cautiously, seemingly reluctant to give much detail in case they might fall into the wrong hands, but now it seemed caution had been thrown to the winds.

He had begun the letter by saying that in future he would give a truthful account of what was happening, for he, and others fighting for the Republicans, were beginning to suspect that the outside world knew nothing of the terrible events taking place in Spain. The remark 'I, and others fighting for the Republicans,' proved pretty conclusively that the professor was by no means simply an observer, but was taking an active part in the war. After that, he went on to describe the bombings carried out by German aircraft and the horrendous killings of innocent civilians in a way which he had never done before. His penultimate paragraph said that he was sending the letter back to England with a trusted friend who would make sure that the letter reached Agatha safely.

Hetty noticed that her friend had folded the very end of the letter so that it was hidden, and did not attempt to read any further, merely handing the sheets back to the librarian. 'No wonder you looked so pale and ill when I came in this morning,' she said quietly. 'Oh, Agatha, I'm so sorry to be going off on a pleasure trip when you are in such distress. But it's not as though I could do anything to help . . .'

'There's not much I can do to help either,' Agatha said ruefully, tucking the letter back into her handbag. 'I wish to God I could write back to him and tell him that there are honest reporters who have returned to England with stories of Franco's wickedness and treachery, but I can't even do that. All I can do now is pray that Mr Galera – both the Galeras, I mean – will come home safely when it's all over.' She beckoned to the waitress for her bill, slipped a threepenny piece under her empty plate and went over to the cash desk.

When they parted outside the library, Agatha told Hetty to enjoy her holiday and begged her to write often. 'It would cheer me up immensely to receive news of your doings, because I don't mind admitting that the professor's letter has cast me into gloom,' she said frankly. 'I've decided to write a covering note and then send a copy of the letter to the *Echo*, hoping that they will publish it on their letters page. The more people who know about what's going on in Spain the better, and it's the only way I can think of to help.'

Despite sharing Miss Preece's feelings of gloom after she had read the letter, Hetty had managed to dismiss it from her mind by the time she stepped down from the bus in Burscough and found her grandfather waiting for her. He beamed and gave her a big hug, then insisted on carrying her small suitcase, though she refused to let him take the rucksack which contained her sleeping bag and pillow.

'Looking forward to your canal trip?' he said jovially as they strode along the pavement. 'Sally popped in to arrange things and says they'll pick you up at the end of the week, which gives you some time with us before you go off. Is that all right?'

'Oh, Gramps, you are good,' Hetty said gratefully, as her grandfather outlined the arrangements he had agreed with Sally. 'This is going to be a wonderful holiday, honest to God it is.'

'We thought you'd be pleased,' her grandfather said as he pushed open the back door and ushered Hetty into the kitchen. He shut the door and turned to his wife, who was stirring something over the stove. 'Here's our guest, arrived just in time for a helping of rabbit stew and some of Matthew's home-grown potatoes. We've discussed the tentative arrangements I made with young Sally and it seems Hetty is in agreement with our plans.'

Gran turned from the stove as Hetty rushed across

the room, seized her in a warm embrace and gave her a smacking kiss on the cheek, which Gran pretended to wipe off whilst beaming quite as broadly as her husband had done. 'Go on, you foolish creature, you nearly made me drop my spoon,' she said. 'And don't forget that it was me who met Sally and mentioned that you were coming to stay, which of course made her suggest that you might join them on their barge.'

'Thank you, Gran; you're a wonderful woman,' Hetty said, laughing as her grandfather pulled a rueful face, telling his wife that she was a show-off. 'I've brought my sleeping bag and pillow, but shouldn't I take some food aboard? I don't want to be a charge on Sally's brothers. I've been saving up . . .'

'So have we,' her grandfather cut in. 'You'll be coming back by rail so we shall give you your ticket money, and your grandmother has been baking for what seems like weeks, only whenever I try to have a taste she says: "Hands off; that's for my girl's canal trip!"'

Hetty joined in the laughter which followed and was about to protest again that she should make a contribution when the door opened and Uncle Matthew came in, bearing a large cabbage and a bunch of carrots. He waved the vegetables at Hetty, then came over and gave her a kiss. 'I've been and gone and got meself an allotment,' he said proudly. 'I growed these veggies meself. I would have give 'em to you to tek aboard the *Maid*, only if I did you'd have to run alongside, because your gran's already prepared enough food to feed the crew for a month. Now sit yourself down, queen, and tell us all the news from the big city.'

By the time Hetty went to bed that night she had told her grandparents and Uncle Matthew all that had happened since her last visit, and had learned all their news in exchange. One particular item had been very welcome: Luke Daley, who had taken on the *Sprite* and the *Beetle*, was doing very well and now paid the Heskeths a weekly rent. Gramps assured Hetty that they had not expected the money to be paid over so quickly and added that he and Gran were downright rich compared with many other retired boaters.

This eased Hetty's mind considerably, since she knew that Gramps still paid Aunt Phoebe for taking care of her and had worried that the old people might be going short, but this was clearly not the case. And as soon as I'm earning I'll make it up to them, Hetty told herself, snuggling into her pillow. Of course, since I mean to go to university I shan't be able to have a full-time job for years, but friends have said that most students take jobs in the long vac, so I'll give all the money I earn to Aunt Phoebe and Uncle Alf, and Gran and Gramps.

When, later in the week, Sally beat a brief tattoo on the back door and then popped her head into the kitchen, Hetty, packed and ready, was waiting for her. She rushed towards the other girl, gave a hug and pointed to the table, which was covered with boxes and bags of food. 'Can you get your brothers to come up and give us a hand?' she said breathlessly, struggling into her rucksack and trying to pick up one of the biggest boxes. 'If you and I try to carry it all, we won't have the strength left to climb aboard the barge, let alone do anything useful.'

Sally laughed even as Grandpa demanded: 'What's wrong with me, young woman? I could carry this little lot with one hand tied behind me . . .'

'Yes, of course you could, but I forbid you to try,' Hetty said, putting the box she had begun to lift back on to the table as Sally said that she'd fetch the boys, and disappeared once more. Hetty, who had never known the boys well, greeted them politely when they appeared, and thanked them for agreeing to take on a passenger.

Nathaniel, the eldest, grinned at her but shook his head. 'You ain't a passenger, young Hetty, you're what I might call the cabin girl,' he said breezily. 'And that means you get to do all the dirty work.' He eyed the groaning kitchen table and whistled beneath his breath. 'On second thoughts, seeing as how your gran seems to be provisioning the barge for the next six months, maybe you *are* a passenger!'

He laughed, and Hetty laughed with him. She thought the two boys were very alike, though neither resembled Sally in the slightest, for her friend was blonde, fair-skinned and blue-eyed, whilst both young men were dark. 'Don't forget I'm no stranger to the work of the *Sprite*,' she told him. 'I mean to be useful, honest to God I do.'

Presently, fully laden, having thanked the Heskeths profusely for their generous contribution, Nathaniel – only he had told Hetty to call him Nat – gave the order to cast off, whilst his brother started the engine and Sally took the tiller. As she felt the steady thrum of the engine, Hetty felt excitement begin to course through her. They were off! It was a brilliant sunny day, with only the gentlest of breezes stirring the leaves on the trees, and she was in good company, for both young men seemed pleased to have her aboard and Sally admitted she was downright delighted. 'My brothers are grand fellers but it'll be good to have another girl,' she assured Hetty. 'When we moor up of an evening, we play cards or read or do jigsaws, but sometimes the boys go off to the pub with the other fellers and leave me behind. Most of the boat women are middle-aged with families, and all they want to talk about is cooking or kids. It'll be a real treat to have someone me own age who'll discuss the things which interest me.'

'Hasn't it been lovely?' Sally said four days later, as she and Hetty watched the boys tying up alongside the wharf. 'Not one drop of rain has fallen since you joined the *Maid Marian*. We got through the locks much faster than usual, which gave us time to explore the villages and do a bit of shopping ... oh, how I shall miss you, Hetty.'

'I'll miss you as well,' Hetty admitted. 'What are you going to do now you've left school, though? We won't lose touch again, will we?'

'No, we won't,' Sally assured her. 'I'm going to try to get a job in a factory. The pay's pretty good, they say, which would be helpful because now that Mam and Dad have retired, money's a bit tight. The alternative is becoming the third member of the crew on the *Maid*. If I do manage to get work away from the canal, my brothers will have to find a lad looking for a berth, because the barge and the butty really need a crew of three or four. Still, the chances are that all such a lad would want is the experience and his keep, and a bit of pocket money.'

'It would be better for you, because boatmen never pay their children a proper wage,' Hetty agreed. 'In a way, I'd like to join you and get a decent job, but it wouldn't be fair. Gran and Gramps have scrimped and saved so that I can go to college and become a librarian, and I don't mean to disappoint them.'

Sally sighed, then picked up her friend's rucksack and helped her to struggle into it, before both girls jumped down on to dry land. The boys joined them, and Hetty thanked them sincerely for her lovely holiday. 'I wish you could have come all the way with us,' Ben said gruffly. 'Still, we'll be passing through Burscough on our way back to the Liverpool docks; mebbe we'll stop off so we can tell you how the rest of the voyage has gone.'

Hetty opened her mouth to reply but was forestalled by Nat. 'Don't be so stupid, Ben; by the time we get back to Burscough, Hetty will have returned to her aunt's house, and that's nowhere near the canal.' He turned to Hetty. 'Will you be back in school by then? If not, why don't you come down to the wharf? We'll be there mebbe a day or two because we're unloading cotton goods and taking on a mixed cargo, which always takes longer to stow aboard.' He struck an attitude. 'Hetty Gilbert, I hereby invite you to eat your dinner with us Brimelows aboard the *Maid*, when we next reach Liverpool.'

Ben snorted. 'He'll want you to cook his perishin' dinner an' all,' he warned her. 'Now *my* invitation comes wi' a box of chocs an' a posy of flowers.' He copied his brother's exaggerated bow. 'If you do come down to the docks, pretty lady, I invite you to accompany me to the cinema of your choice. How about that, eh?' he said, speaking in an exaggeratedly posh accent.

Hetty laughed. 'Thank you both kindly, but I'm afraid that I shall be far too busy studying for my next lot of exams to accept any invitations, once I'm home.' She turned to Sally. 'Don't forget you promised to come and visit next time you're in Liverpool.'

'I won't forget, only you don't seem to spend an awful lot of time in Salisbury Street,' Sally observed. 'From what you've told me, when you aren't in school, you're at the Everton library! So I can only visit after closing time, which I suppose is around six in the evening, is it? Still, I'll do my best to come then. In fact the boys might accompany me, then we could all hear each other's news.'

Hetty agreed to this, for to refuse after the hospitality the Brimelows had shown her would have been downright insulting. Then she picked up her case, and she and Sally turned to head for the station. Hetty had only gone a couple of steps, however, when her suitcase was taken out of her hand. 'I'll come to the station with you,' Nat said. 'And I'll wait with you until your train arrives. Sal and Ben can give an eye to the *Maid*.'

Hetty had little choice but to relinquish her hold on the suitcase, but when Ben joined them and began to try to relieve her of the rucksack, and Nat immediately stood her suitcase down and began to tug at the straps around her shoulders as well, Hetty told them sharply to leave off. 'I feel like a flaming bone between two dogs,' she said, only half laughing. 'Sally's going to walk me to the station, though there'll be no need for her to wait, so you boys had better get back to the barge before some young thief realises she's unmanned and climbs aboard to see what he can steal.'

'Ben can go,' and 'Nat can go,' the two young men chorused. Sally started to giggle, but Hetty, far from giggling, had to bite her tongue on a number of sharp retorts. However, when Sally picked up the suitcase and Hetty readjusted the rucksack, both young men took the hint and rather sulkily said that they had best return to the barge.

Hetty and Sally continued on their way, and when she was sure that they were well out of earshot Hetty turned apologetically to her friend. 'I hope you don't think I was being awfully rude, Sally, but I'm not looking for a boyfriend; I'm far too busy with my schoolwork and working in the library on a Saturday. If you could just tell your brothers that I like them both very much, but only as friends . . .' Her voice trailed away and she looked anxiously at Sally, fearing to see disapproval written on the other girl's face, but instead saw only a mixture of sympathy and curiosity.

'Oh, Hetty, I do understand, and I'm most dreadfully sorry that they've made things difficult for you,' Sally said remorsefully. 'But you know most girls chase after Nat and Ben and would give their eye teeth for a smile, let alone an invitation to the flicks! They're both good-looking, wouldn't you say? And fun to be with, which may be even more important than looks. I don't believe either of them has ever had an invitation refused, so I suppose that's why they behaved rather badly. Do you like one of them more than the other? If so, I think perhaps you should accept one and turn the other down. Only a couple of times on board the *Maid* they very nearly came to blows, and that's never happened before . . .'

'Oh, Sally, it must have done,' Hetty said. 'Brothers, even when they're the best of friends, always disagree and fight from time to time. I know Tom and Bill did. If Nat and Ben don't they must both be saints, and I'm jolly sure that neither of them is any such thing.'

Sally laughed. 'Of course they fought when they were young,' she agreed. 'As you say, all brothers do. But since they've grown up, and especially since they've taken over the *Maid*, they haven't even had a cross word. They were always good pals and agreed without any fuss that though Nat is the official Number One – he's twenty-two and Ben's not yet twenty – they would share the command of the barge. Nat is Number One from Liverpool to Leeds and makes all the decisions, whilst Ben is Number One from Leeds to Liverpool. It's worked really well and I'd hate to see it go wrong just because they both think they're in love with the same girl.'

The two had been walking briskly along the road that led to the station, but at her friend's words Hetty stopped dead in her tracks. 'In *love*?' she squeaked. 'Did you say "in love", Sally Brimelow? Good Lord! I know I knew them vaguely from being on the canal with my grandparents, but I never *really* knew them until four days ago. No one falls in love in four days; that's being quite ridiculous.' Even as she said the words, however, a picture flashed into her mind. A dark face above her own, the moon shining silver between black-branched trees, and a voice saying softly: *For tonight I'm St George, ready to slay any number of dragons to rescue a fair maiden.*

Sally's eyes widened. 'You've remembered someone who fell in love all in a moment,' she said triumphantly. 'You know it happens, you must do. Why, I could see it in your face. Who was it, eh? Not yourself!'

Hetty's mind shot back to Miss Preece and the professor. It was not cheating to dismiss her own recollection of that weird, moonlit experience, because no one could call that falling in love, she told herself; it was not even infatuation. If she had fallen in love with anything, it was the moonlight, the thrilling pillion ride and the speed of their going. She could scarcely claim to be in love with someone whose face she had never seen and whose voice she had not recognised. But Miss Preece now ... 'You're right; I *do* know someone who fell in love at first sight,' she said. 'I've told you about my friend Agatha, the librarian at

Everton library; well, I believe she fell in love with a professor from London who gave a lecture at the Liverpool Museum when his department loaned them an exhibition of illuminated manuscripts.'

Sally gave a crow of amusement. 'That isn't falling in love, that really *is* infatuation,' she said. 'Besides, I don't believe professors do anything so – so low as falling in love. I suppose they must get married or there wouldn't be any little professors, but I'm sure they go about it in quite a different way from ordinary people.'

By this time they had reached the station and Hetty had bought her ticket and been told that the train would arrive in less than ten minutes. Sally sank on to a bench, putting down the suitcase with a sigh of relief, but Hetty, though she sat down too, felt quite cross with her friend. 'I never said the professor fell in love, though I think he probably did,' she said. 'I said it was Miss Preece. Did I tell you that the professor has gone off to Spain? He's joined the International Brigade and he writes to Miss Preece whenever he can, though she doesn't receive half the letters he sends. But anyway, this whole discussion started because you said your brothers thought they were in love with me, and I'm sure you're wrong. At least, I hope so, because though they're very nice and I like them both, as I said before, I don't want a boyfriend.'

Sally was beginning to reply when her voice was drowned by the clatter and shriek of an approaching train, and Hetty was glad to get to her feet, give her friend a kiss and shout her thanks again as she climbed aboard. It was such a short journey to Burscough that there was little point in removing her rucksack, so she perched on the edge of her seat and thought back over the last four days.

Sally had been right about the weather, which had been brilliant, and she thought she had been as useful as it was possible to be in such a short time. She had also met old friends, exchanged news and been warmly greeted by villagers who remembered her from past trips with her grandparents. But the truth was that the increasing warmth shown towards her by both Brimelow boys had made her life rather difficult and she realised now that she was glad to get away. Much though she had enjoyed most of her little holiday, it had made her see that she would never willingly return to work on the canal. It was a hard and narrow life compared with the one she had in mind, which was to go to college, graduate and become a librarian.

She did not, however, intend to let the awkwardness she now felt because of the boys' behaviour affect her friendship with Sally. The other girl now lived with her parents in Seaforth, a good tram ride from Salisbury Street, but they could always arrange to meet up somewhere in the city centre; it did not much matter, so long as they did not again lose touch. For, ever since she won the scholarship to the high school, Hetty had been aware that she had no best friend in a similar situation to her own. She had joined the school at the age of thirteen, when most of her fellow pupils had already formed the strong friendships which would continue throughout their time at school. Thanks to the companionship of Miss Preece, she had not realised how she missed having someone of her own age to go about with, but now she was determined to keep her friendship with Sally alive, regardless of the awkwardness caused by the Brimelow boys' mistaken belief that they had fallen in love with her.

And then there was her own recollection of that extraordinary ending to her day trip to Llandudno. She had been true to her vow to put the whole thing out of her mind, had honestly done her best to do so, but she had been unable to prevent the dreams. At least once every month or so, the dream would return. Once again, she would climb off the coach and watch it roar into the distance, then look round, only to find herself alone. As she had done in reality, she would panic, begin to cry, and then find herself addressed: *What's the matter, lass?*

Sometimes the dream was caused by something which had happened to her in the real world; a moonlit walk, a windy night, even a film at the picture house. At other times the dream would bear little resemblance to the event itself. There would be fiery dragons, green, gold or glinting silver, which shot flame from their gaping mouths, threatening her, setting fire to trees and undergrowth; but before she could become seriously worried she would hear again that amused and mocking voice: *For tonight I'm St George, ready to slay any number of dragons to rescue a fair maiden. Would you care to mount my fiery steed, Miss Liverpool?*

Only in this dream it was never a motorbike but a

great white charger, and she always woke before she could obey his command to mount.

The train drawing to a halt at Burscough Junction brought Hetty's mind abruptly back to the present. She picked up her suitcase and jumped down on to the platform. She had not expected to be met since she had been unable to even guess at her time of arrival, but as she began to walk along the lane which led to Uncle Matthew's house she saw Gran's small dumpy form ahead of her, and hurried to catch her up. Gran was burdened with two large shopping baskets and Hetty was just wondering why her grandfather had not accompanied his wife when there was a shout from behind her.

'Dulcie, my girl, just you put those baskets down. I stopped to have a word with Freddie Mimms – he was coming out of the post office – and off you charged. And don't tell me those baskets aren't heavy, because . . .' He broke off, having drawn level with his granddaughter, and grinned at her. 'Well, well, well, if it isn't our little Hetty! Now here's a dilemma: do I take that suitcase or relieve your gran of those baskets? If only I had two pairs of hands . . .'

Gran turned to wait for them and Hetty, giving her a kiss, pointed out that she was perfectly capable of carrying her own suitcase. 'But I do think Gran might let you take at least one of her baskets,' she observed, and presently the three of them set off once more, Gramps striding along with the heavier basket in his right hand, whilst he and Gran shared the weight of the other one between them.

When they entered the kitchen, Uncle Matthew, who was sitting at the table peeling potatoes, insisted that the three of them should sit down whilst he made a pot of tea. 'And Hetty can tell us all about her canal trip,' he said, smiling at her. Hetty sighed with pleasure as she slipped the rucksack off her shoulders. She had had a lovely time with Sally, but it was good to be back.

Chapter Eleven

It was a hot day towards the end of August and Hetty was alight with excitement, for she had just gone to the high school where the results of the recent examinations were being displayed on a large board in the main hall. She had approached the board with some trepidation, screwing up her courage to face the fact that she might have failed. But in the event, she did not even have to read the result for herself, since as soon as she appeared one of her classmates called out to her. 'Haven't you done well, Hetty Gilbert! You've passed with distinction! In fact we've all done pretty well. Three distinctions, two credits and seven passes; not bad, eh?'

Hetty agreed that it was not bad at all, then walked up to the board and read the delightful result for herself. Yes, it was true. Pamela hadn't been teasing, so now she was all set to try for her Higher. Other girls were hanging around chatting, but Hetty knew that she must tell her family before she did anything else, though Miss Preece would be anxiously awaiting the result. After all, it had been she who had not only encouraged Hetty but coached her in maths and science, both subjects not at all dear to Hetty's heart. However, Hetty knew her duty and turned her footsteps towards Heyworth Street.

Uncle Alf would be at Laird's on the other side of the Mersey, so he would have to wait until he returned that evening to hear the good news. Aunt Phoebe, however, was still at Rudham's, where she was highly regarded, and Hetty knew that when she entered the shop and asked for her aunt she would be taken at once to the small office whilst the rest of the staff would cluster in the doorway, as eager as Aunt Phoebe to know her results.

Because of the heat, Hetty decided to catch a tram and was soon entering Rudham's, asking if she might speak to her aunt. The middle-aged woman behind the counter beamed at her. 'Course you can, chuck; you know where the office is. Tek a seat in there while I get your aunt from the kitchen. And I don't have to ask you how you gorron 'cos I see'd you hoppin' off the tram with a grin like the Cheshire cat fair splittin' your face. But don't you tell me nothin', 'cos it's only right your auntie should be the first to hear the news. After all, she's been as good as a mother to you.'

'Thanks, Mrs Huxtable,' Hetty said, ducking under the counter flap and heading for the office. She had barely entered the small room when her aunt joined her there, dusting the flour off her hands.

'Go on, tell me the worst,' she said, trying to sound worried but failing dismally. 'I guess you scraped through; you certainly deserved to do so, the way you've worked these past few months.'

'I didn't scrape through,' Hetty said, chuckling to see her aunt's face fall and then brighten as she added:

'I passed with distinction. Oh, Aunt Phoebe, the relief!'

'Hetty Gilbert, you wicked girl, letting me think even for one moment that you'd failed,' her aunt said, flinging both arms round her niece and leaving large white fingermarks on Hetty's threadbare school blazer. 'Now look what you've made me do! Oh Lor', I'm that excited I forgot I'd been making puff pastry.' She turned to Mrs Huxtable, who was hovering in the doorway. 'Did you hear that, Mrs H? Passed with distinction! That means she'll go into the sixth form and start studying for her Higher.' She hugged her niece again. 'Gran and Gramps will be so proud; they'll say you're as clever as your mam was. She'd have been proud an' all; she'd have said you was a chip off the old block. And now you'd best telephone the post office in Burscough, because Gran and Gramps will be pacin' up and down the pavement waitin' for your call.'

Hetty said she would go to the nearest box at once, and presently set off along Heyworth Street with a large box of cream fancies beneath one arm, a present from Mr Rudham. He had come into the shop just as she was about to leave, and upon hearing her news had insisted on giving her the cakes.

Hetty rang the number of the telephone box outside the Burscough post office and the receiver was snatched up so quickly that she guessed Aunt Phoebe had been right; Gramps had been hovering, possibly for hours. She told him the news, received his excited congratulations, and then set off for Everton library where Agatha Preece refused to be surprised by the result, though she could not hide her pleasure. 'You deserve your success,' she told Hetty. 'No one could have worked harder than you've done, my dear. Unless you have another appointment, I'll treat you to lunch at the Priory to celebrate.'

'That would be lovely,' Hetty said gratefully. 'Have a cake! I'm taking the rest back to Salisbury Street, but I can spare you and Maria, and Mr Gower of course, one to eat with your elevenses. I shall be off to Burscough on the first bus tomorrow, to celebrate with Gran and Gramps, but I'll take them chocolates, I think.' She laughed. 'I must be the only pupil in the whole of Liverpool who is looking forward to the end of the summer holidays and the start of the new term!'

April 1939

Max Galera looked down at his brother's sleeping face and decided not to wake him yet. After all, what was there to wake up for? The Republicans had clung desperately on to Madrid, their last stronghold. They had continued to fight through the worst winter anyone could remember, with constant blizzards, deep snow on the plateau and, very soon, almost no food. Despite Franco's promises, the Luftwaffe had attacked the city relentlessly, night after night, until there was nothing left worth bombing. And now that winter was beginning to withdraw its cruel claws and the wind was growing softer as spring crept in, the Republicans had surrendered and the Nationalist troops had begun to pour into Spain's capital city.

What will happen to us, the members of the International Brigade? Max asked himself. Britain and France had recognised the Franco regime in February, and international recognition had followed. Now, Max guessed, Franco would show no mercy to those who had fought him to the bitter end, so it behoved him to get himself and his brother out of this damned, doomed city. Already the red and yellow Nationalist flags flew everywhere, and citizens who wanted to preserve their lives were hastily scrabbling round for any red and yellow material which could become a makeshift flag, for whatever their true allegiance now was no time to display it.

The brothers had found shelter of a sort in the cellar of a bombed house. At first they had shared it with others, but now that the war was over the Madrileños must have decided that to be caught anywhere near members of the International Brigade would be asking for trouble, so the brothers had the cellar to themselves. But it would not be safe for long; sighing, Max reached out and shook his brother's shoulder, watching as the younger man's eyes opened. At first his gaze was bleary with sleep, then it sharpened into recollection of their plight.

He sat up, staring at Max. 'What'll we do?' he said huskily. 'I'm damned if I'm going to stumble up to the nearest Nationalist soldier and try to surrender. They'll shoot first and ask questions afterwards.'

He yawned cavernously. 'Ah, God, I could eat a horse!'

'You probably have . . . eaten horse, I mean,' Max said drily. 'Certainly they say folk have been eating rats, and it's a while since I saw a cat or a dog on the streets. But food isn't important . . .'

'It is to me,' Michael muttered. 'It's bloody important. I'm telling you, Max, everyone has to eat to survive, and survival is very much on my mind right now.'

Max grinned. 'I agree, and in order to survive, we've got to get out of this city pretty damn quick. It's a good thing our uniforms have become little more than rags. No one looking at you would suspect for one moment that you were an officer in the International Brigade. And since we both speak fairly good colloquial Spanish, my plan is this. We make our way through Spain to the Pyrenees, cross the mountains and reach France. From there it should be relatively easy to contact the British authorities, who will surely help us on our way to a Channel port. What do you think? Have you a better idea?'

Michael shook his head. 'I think you're right, and it's our only chance of avoiding arrest by the Nationalists,' he said resignedly. 'But to an extent, I think we shall have to play it by ear, take chances when they're offered. Agreed?'

His brother nodded and rose to his feet. 'Agreed,' he said. 'And now we'd best get started.'

* * *

'It's mid-June and the Republican army surrendered in April, so surely the Galeras ought to be back by now,' Agatha Preece said, clearly speaking with all the casualness she could muster. 'Some of the International Brigade are back already, so I've heard. If only communications weren't so poor!'

It was a bright Sunday afternoon and Agatha and Hetty had come up to Prince's Park to feed the ducks and stroll amongst the well-tended flower beds, but it had been obvious to Hetty from the moment they had met that Agatha had only one thing on her mind – Professor Max Galera, and his brother.

Now, Hetty gave what comfort she could. 'It's a big country, Spain, and from what you've told me the Galeras won't be able to hop on a train or even walk openly up to a frontier. Of course it will take time to make their way on foot, but as soon as it's safe to do so I'm sure the professor will write and let you know what's going on.'

'Yes, I'm sure you're right,' Agatha said, her tone clearly doubting the words her lips were speaking. 'But Franco's a monster, Hetty. He's killed his own people by the hundred – the thousand – so why should he hesitate to kill a couple of Englishmen who are alone and penniless in his country?'

'Why should he do something which isn't in his best interests?' Hetty countered. 'From what I've read in the papers, he's got troubles enough at home. And don't forget Hitler. He's still saying that the ally he most wants is Great Britain, so if Franco behaved badly towards Englishmen in Spain Hitler might force him to apologise. Franco wouldn't want to be humiliated like that in front of his followers. I've not read *Mein Kampf*, but a friend of mine told me that Hitler believes the Germans and the English are natural allies, whereas the Spanish are different. We're Aryans, whatever that is, whilst Spaniards are Latins, if I've got it right. And remember, the professor isn't exactly a nobody, is he? If he's captured – which I'm sure he won't be – he'll know how best to contact the British embassy and get himself sent home. Just you relax a bit, Agatha, and one day, hopefully quite soon before you drive us all mad, there'll come a knock on your door and the prof will seize you in his arms and all your troubles will be over.'

Agatha gave a watery laugh. 'You ridiculous child! No one will seize anyone in their arms, particularly not myself,' she said. 'And if there's an embassy in Spain still standing I'll be very surprised. Or did you mean the one in Paris?

'Well, when he gets to any embassy he'll be able to write you a letter,' Hetty said. 'Don't worry so, Agatha! Mr Galera's resourceful and intelligent. He'll get home all right.'

'I just hope he does so before we're all at war,' Agatha said gloomily. 'We can't let Germany continue to invade any country in Europe that swine Hitler fancies. Mark my words, Hetty, it'll be France next, and then what chance will the professor have to get back to England?'

'Oh, don't even think it, Agatha,' Hetty said. 'France isn't a tiny country; they've got an army and a navy, and an air force as well. They aren't going to sit down and let the Huns overrun them. Now for goodness' sake stop raising imaginary worries, when there are real ones in plenty.' She looked around her at the wide stretches of grass and lake, the bright flowers, the people strolling quietly along the paths. If her friend was right, and she feared she was, England was as much at risk as Agatha's professor.

'I'm sorry, I'm afraid I'm poor company this afternoon,' Agatha said stiffly. 'I'll change the subject. I see the tea room is open; shall we treat ourselves to a pot of tea and a scone?'

'Yes, that would be lovely,' Hetty said, but hard though she tried to prise her mind away from the Galeras, it refused to obey her commands. She and Agatha had spent hours with maps and atlases spread out before them, trying to guess where the brothers were. Now, she saw in her imagination great towering mountains, white-topped with unthawed snow, and two tiny figures, clad in rags, plodding ever upwards. Yes, they must be in the Pyrenees by now, she told herself. And once they reach France . . .

Max was the first to see the cave, which was not surprising, because he had once known these mountains well. Others who had crossed the Pyrenees had done so with a guide, but he and Michael had both spent time here before the war had started and remembered the path they had to follow well enough. To be sure, the going had been hard, but at least in these mountainous regions there were no Nationalist strongholds. Max imagined that General Franco had not considered the tiny, poverty-stricken villages to be worth annexing, so though the land was poor and crops consequently sparse, they had been met not with refusals to help, but with offers of such food as the villagers could spare, and with advice on which mountain passes they should take.

Max had wondered why the Luftwaffe had bothered to bomb such a remote area, for he doubted very much that they could have known or cared where their bombs landed here. In one case, bombs had closed a pass that he and Michael had intended to take, but when he questioned one of the peasants the answer was a simple one. 'They jettison any bombs left over rather than risk trying to land with such a dangerous cargo. We asked a Republican pilot whose aeroplane was shot down by the cursed Nationalists. He escaped to France by crossing the mountains, as you are doing yourselves.'

Now, Max regarded the cave thoughtfully. It would give them shelter for the night ahead, but he had hoped to reach the village in the valley where he and Michael had stayed several times when in the area. But it was already dusk and he knew that if they did not take regular periods of rest, the wound in Michael's leg would begin to trouble him. Nevertheless, it must be a shared decision, so he glanced at his brother, his eyebrows rising. 'Well? Press on or rest here?'

Both men carried bedrolls and they still had the remains of the iron rations with which they had been provided by the women's militia just before leaving

Madrid. Max thought the girls heroines, every one, and knew that without the bedrolls which the militia had also provided, together with a small sum of money, it was doubtful if he and Michael would have made it even to the foothills of the Pyrenees. When the girl in charge of the militia had first offered the food and bedding he had tried to refuse, saying that her organisation's need was greater than his and Michael's, but the girl had pointed out that possessing anything connected with the army, now that the Republicans had surrendered, would be dangerous.

'From this moment, we will revert to being simple citizens of Madrid,' she had told him. 'I shall claim to have worked behind the counter in one of the big shops which the Nationalists have destroyed. I shall wave a red and yellow flag and smile at the soldiers, the ones I aimed my rifle at yesterday. Then, when it is safe to do so, I'll go back to my village outside Barcelona, and await my opportunity for revenge. I will work on the land as my family has done for generations, for a pittance which will scarcely feed me, let alone provide clothing. So take the food and the bedrolls, friend, and never forget us, as we shall never forget you of the International Brigade.'

Michael was still gazing dubiously at the cave. He took a few steps towards it and grimaced. Max guessed that his wound had made itself felt, and knew he was right when Michael turned to him. 'I reckon we'd do best to get a night's sleep,' he said. 'After all, when we reach the village we'll be able to relax for a day or two before setting out again. Let's have a look inside first, though, to make sure it's dry and will hold both us and our gear.'

The cave was dry and as comfortable as it was possible for such a place to be. The men settled down in their bedrolls, for despite the fact that summer was well advanced it was cold at this height and would get colder when darkness came. Max surveyed their food and was glad they had charged their water bottles at the last stream they had crossed and did not have to go searching for water. They ate one of the hard ship's biscuits, and dissolved a couple of milk tablets in Michael's water bottle which they shared between them, saving the contents of Max's water bottle for the morning. Very soon Max was relieved to hear his brother's breathing grow even and knew that he slept.

Max, however, could not sleep. His mind raced ahead to the village before them, which both he and Michael had once known so well. It was the nearest thing to civilisation that they would come to whilst still in the mountains, and Max thought wistfully of the little inn with its tiny, cramped bedrooms, and the straw pallets and rough brown blankets that had once seemed so harsh and inadequate, though now he guessed they would feel like the height of luxury after weeks of sleeping on thin bedrolls, laid out on the hard earth.

The village was surrounded by tall trees, so the main room at the inn was always warm and welcoming, with a huge log fire burning on the hearth and very likely a haunch of mutton roasting on a spit above it.

There would be beer – wonderful, cool beer – and a long loaf, baked by the innkeeper's wife and spread thickly with butter provided by the big herd of goats. And there would be good company and much laughter, for the village was far enough from civilisation to have been little affected by the war. Bartering was the easiest way to obtain goods which could not be made or grown in the village. Goat's cheese and butter were exchanged for fruit and vegetables from either France or the Spanish plain, though the villagers had a vineyard, close to a nearby river so that during the months of summer drought the vines could be watered without too much effort. Max and Michael had always stopped at this particular village when, as boys, they had come to the area on climbing trips. Now Max was looking forward not only to the creature comforts the village would provide, but to meeting and greeting old friends, to hearing their stories and relating his own.

We'll set off early in the morning, as soon as we've had a hot drink and the last of the biscuits, he told himself. As they journeyed, they had picked up twigs and pieces of dry wood with which they could make a fire, because Max was a great believer in starting the day with a hot drink. Tomorrow, he planned drowsily, we'll use the last dried milk tablets and the last scrap of cocoa. Such a drink would be a real treat, he thought, just before sleep claimed him.

Next morning they set out as the sun rose, flushing the sky with delicate pink and gold. The cave was high up, and from its eminence they could just see the tips of the trees which grew, they knew, in the valley.

They were both in high good humour, for today would be the beginning of easier times for them both. When they left the village, they would be using a clearly defined path, which led downhill all the way into France. And once they were in France, Max could allow himself to think of the girl Agatha, that strange, Spanish beauty who had turned out to be neither strange nor Spanish, despite her looks. All the time he had been with the International Brigade he had thought of her often, talking to her inside his head, writing letters and keeping a diary to show her when he reached England once more. But once he and Michael had started what he thought of as their retreat, he had done his best to put her out of his mind. He dared not have any sort of distraction; he must be alert, thinking in Spanish as well as speaking it, for the Nationalists were hunting down anyone who might have fought against them. But once we reach France, the first thing I shall do will be to write her a letter, he told himself, as he and Michael began their descent into the valley.

They were walking companionably side by side when Max shot out his hand and grabbed Michael's arm, drawing his brother to a halt. 'Something's wrong,' he murmured. 'Something's missing, though I'm not sure what. And there's an odd smell . . . I think we'd better leave the path and go down through the trees, though I'm damned if I know why I'm so uneasy.'

Michael cocked his head on one side, then spoke

succinctly. 'No dogs,' he whispered. 'Have you ever got this near to a village – any village – without the dogs warning of your approach?'

Max frowned thoughtfully. His brother was right. It was not only the innkeeper who kept dogs to round up his goats. Every peasant with a few acres of land had a dog. He turned to his brother. 'What'll we do?' he murmured. 'Do we go on?'

'We must,' Michael said, equally softly. 'We've got to find out what's happening.'

Slipping quietly through the trees, the two men continued to descend.

An hour later, they stood outside the inn and Max was not ashamed of the tears which ran down his cheeks. The village had been laid waste, the inn burned to the ground, bodies thrown in a heap and inadequately covered with leaf mould. Not a soul remained, not a dog or a hen. And it had happened recently, probably no more than three or four days earlier. Presumably, the Nationalists had come this way in search of anyone who might be fleeing from their regime and had chanced upon the village. Perhaps the dogs had barked a warning and the innkeeper, or one of the peasants, still not having much news of the outside world, had let his allegiance show. It would have been enough to condemn him, but why, in God's name, had they destroyed everything?

As they approached vultures rose, then looked at Michael and Max and settled once more to their disgusting feast. Michael tried to scare the big birds away, but Max stopped him. 'They're nature's way of cleaning up,' he told his brother. 'If we could bury the bodies ourselves I'd help you chase them off, but we've no tools and it would take the pair of us weeks. I know it horrifies you, but we must let ill alone.'

Now, he and Michael climbed down to the vineyard and found it desecrated also, the vines and the tiny grapes uprooted and trampled. They returned to the village, but could not bear to remain within the square, with its stink of death and destruction, so sat down on a great fallen log in the surrounding trees and looked sombrely at each other. 'There's nothing we can do here,' Max said at last.

Michael nodded and got to his feet. 'Right. Then we'd best get on our way,' he said, giving his brother the travesty of a smile. 'We'd rather relied on provisioning ourselves here for the last leg of the journey. Now, all we can do is fill our water bottles and tighten our belts.'

'We ought to have taken some of the grapes, even though they're not ripe,' Max observed. 'But it's not as bad as all that; I've still got a chunk of that cheese which we were given at the last village, and a few biscuits. I always keep something back, just in case, you know.'

'Good old Max, always covering us for any eventuality ...' Michael was beginning, when the sound of someone, or something, approaching them from the direction of the river made both men slip behind the trunk of the nearest tree. 'What the devil ... ? I could have sworn ... oh, Max, look who's here. All right, old chap, we won't hurt you.'

The 'old chap' was a leggy mongrel pup, with fly-away ears and round, terrified eyes. His ribs stuck out, and when he saw the two men he fell on his belly and crawled towards them, but showed no inclination either to bite or flee when Michael dropped to his knees and began to stroke the silky brown fur.

Max laughed and held out his hand, which the pup promptly licked. 'Poor fellow; the one survivor,' he said ruefully. 'He was probably off on an illicit rabbit hunt when the Nationalists came. I said the attack must have happened in the last three or four days, and this chap proves it. He'll hang around for a bit, but then he'll make for the nearest village. He's a bit young to hunt for himself, but he'll soon learn to eat anything: grubs, a squirrel's hoard of nuts, even under-ripe grapes, like the ones down by the river. Peasants don't feed their dogs; the bitch teaches her litter to fend for themselves.' He looked quizzically at his brother. 'Do you want to take him on? We're going to have a job to feed ourselves ...'

'We can't possibly leave him here; it would be worse than killing him outright,' Michael said indignantly. 'He won't be any trouble; as you said, peasants don't feed their dogs, they fend for themselves. And once we reach France ...'

Max laughed and put down a hand to caress the pup's pricked ears. 'I wasn't suggesting for one moment that we should abandon the mutt,' he said mildly. 'Besides, he'll follow us whatever we say.

And now let's get started on the rest of our journey. We'll have to see if we can train Chappie here to hunt for us as well as himself; now that really would be useful!'

When Agatha Preece awoke one bright morning in early August it was already beginning to be hot, which was a nice change, she told herself, for the previous week had been miserable. She got out of bed, washed and dressed, and, as she did every morning, wondered. Where was he now, the professor? Was his brother still with him? She was sure he must have crossed the Pyrenees by this time. Perhaps he was actually in France!

She approached her mother's bedroom, only to find that that lady was already up and presumably downstairs, since the room was empty. Agatha smiled to herself. Most people, as they aged, grew less capable, but her mother was proving the exception. Admittedly she came down to the kitchen wearing a smart navy blue dressing gown over her nightie, and did not usually dress until Mrs Simpson was on hand to help with such garments as corsets and back-fastening dresses, but at one time she would simply have lain in bed until her helper arrived. Now she preferred to get up, help her daughter make the breakfast and discuss the day's doings.

During the holidays, whenever Hetty was able to do so she called at the house on Everton Terrace and, after chatting with Mrs Preece for a while, suggested that she might either do the older woman's messages or accompany her round the shops. Agatha was truly grateful to her young friend, since such little expeditions gave her mother something to think about beside her arthritis and the frightening things that were happening on the continent.

Everyone was expecting war – conscription had started in May – and this had made Mrs Preece remember the war to end all wars, in which her husband had been killed. He had been an officer in one of the Pals' Batallions and, along with many of his friends and relatives from the East Lancashire Regiment, had died on 1 July, 1916, at the battle of the Somme. Agatha had been eleven at the time and could still remember her mother's grief and her brave efforts to hide her sorrow from her only child.

Now however, entering the kitchen, Agatha pushed such thoughts out of her mind. Mrs Preece was at the cooker, just pouring water from the kettle into the big brown teapot. She looked up and smiled as her daughter came into the room. 'Morning, Agatha. It's nice to see the sun for a change. You'll not want porridge on such a sunny day, so I've set out the cornflakes and I'm just starting to make some toast.' She turned to give Agatha a wicked, twinkling look. 'There's a letter from your boyfriend; you'll want to read that before you'll even look at your breakfast, I dare say.'

Agatha jumped. She had never actually admitted that the letters from Spain, which arrived so infrequently, were from a man, let alone someone who was interested in her; why should she? After all, it was possible, despite his affectionate words, that the professor merely wrote to her in order that someone knew what was happening in Spain. She opened her mouth to tell her mother she had got the wrong end of the stick, but the sight of the much-handled envelope, propped up against the marmalade jar, drew her like a magnet. What did it matter if the professor only regarded her as a friend? What mattered was that the letter would prove he was alive.

She reached for the envelope, but her mother was before her, handing her a cup of tea and picking up the envelope. 'Just sit down and have a sip of your tea,' the older woman commanded. 'Then you shall have your letter. And if you wonder how I know that it's a man who's been writing to you, and a man of whom you are already rather fond, then you shouldn't keep his letters in your underwear drawer.'

Agatha, in the very act of opening the envelope, stopped short to stare. 'Mother, how dare you read my letters!' she exclaimed. 'What were you doing, searching through my underwear? Really, I thought better of you.'

Mrs Preece bridled. 'Daughters shouldn't have secrets from their mothers,' she said defensively. 'Anyway, I wasn't searching for anything. I was putting away the clean linen which Mrs Simpson had just ironed when something rustled. Of course I didn't realise it was letters, I thought the lining of the drawer had got caught up in one of your petticoats, so I went to smooth it down, and . . .'

'And took one letter, at least, out of its envelope and no doubt read every word,' Agatha said. She knew she should have been furious, but all such emotions were cast aside in her eagerness to read the missive in her hand. 'Well, if you've read the letters, you must realise that the professor and I are just good friends. And now be quiet and let me read this one in peace.'

Mrs Preece gave a cackle of amusement. 'Just friends indeed!' she said scornfully. 'Oh, they ain't love letters; how could he write love letters when he must have known he could be killed at any moment? But if you read between the lines . . .'

'Shut *up*!' Agatha almost screamed. Her eyes scanned the page swiftly then rose to meet her mother's enquiring gaze. And when she spoke her voice was high, like a child's, and tears ran down her cheeks. 'They're alive!' she said. 'Oh, Mam, they're in France and will be home just as soon as they can get to a Channel port. Oh, thank God, thank God!'

'I guessed as much,' Mrs Preece said placidly; and untruthfully, Agatha thought, but was too happy to say so.

She put the letter down beside her untasted tea and rose to her feet. 'I don't want any breakfast, I'm too happy and excited. If I hurry, I can get to Salisbury Street and tell Hetty the good news before the library's due to open.' She rushed round the table and gave her mother an exuberant hug. 'I forgive you for reading my letters and being such a bossy old woman,' she said. 'Why, I dare say Max and his brother will be back in England next week, or the week after. And he's promised to come up to Liverpool just as soon as he can, so you'll meet him and can judge for yourself what sort of man he is.'

'He's a brave one if he's courting you,' her mother said, but her eyes were twinkling. 'When will you realise, Agatha Jane, that you're really a very pretty woman?'

Her daughter bent over to kiss her cheek and Mrs Preece pushed her away. 'Get on with you!' she said with pretended annoyance. 'And since you're going round to Salisbury Street, you might tell young Hetty I've a fancy to go shopping this morning, if she's free.'

Agatha, taking her light coat off the peg and beginning to put it on, had her fingers on the door handle when a thought occurred to her. 'Mother, I want you to promise me, on your word of honour, that you won't say anything to anyone about Max and Michael coming home, and please don't air your opinion that there's more between Max and myself than friendship. Will you give me your word?'

Mrs Preece chuckled. She held up a finger, licked it and drew it across her throat. 'See this wet, see this dry, cut my throat if I tell a lie,' she said. 'I won't say a word, except to Hetty of course. I take it I may mention the matter to her?'

'Well, I suppose I can't stop you discussing when and how he'll get home, but please don't fill Hetty's head with a lot of nonsense about Max being more than a friend,' Agatha said. She opened the door and slipped into the hall. 'I'll see you this evening, and don't forget your promise.'

Although the letter had come from France, there had been no address to which Agatha could write, since Max told her that they would be on the move once more as soon as his letter was posted. *But once we're in England I'll be in touch again, hopefully in person*, he had written. *We're going straight to London, of course; various people want to interview us. Spain's attitude to Germany looks like being pretty important if war does come, and I'd say there's not much doubt of it. We'll both volunteer as soon as we may . . . but that's for the future. Take care of yourself, and we'll be meeting very soon.*

On 25 August, another letter arrived. Agatha read it over her breakfast, then turned a tragic face to her mother. 'You'll never guess what he's done,' she said bitterly. 'He's volunteered to join the Royal Air Force, and they've accepted him. Apparently he's had a pilot's licence for several years. But despite his experience he's had to go for basic training and won't get any leave for a number of weeks. Oh, and I've so looked · forward to seeing him again!'

'Never mind, my dear,' Mrs Preece said, with a rare show of affection. 'At least he's volunteered for the air force and not the army; all that mud and those terrible trenches . . .'

Despite her unhappiness, Agatha gave a rather watery laugh. 'That was the Great War, Mother. I think this one will be very different. Oh, I forgot to say that Michael's volunteered for the air force as well, and he was accepted too. I thought the professor would be too old, but I'm clearly wrong. Come to that, I never asked him his age, and he never volunteered the information, why should he?' She sighed deeply. 'Well, it's no use fretting; what's done is done. I must just look forward to his first leave.'

Hetty was sitting on the bench outside the Burscough house, with Aunt Phoebe on one side and Uncle Alf on the other. Gran was in the kitchen with Uncle Matthew, making everybody a cup of tea, and Gramps was just emerging through the back door with a plate of buttered scones.

Inside the kitchen, the wireless was playing softly, for today was 3 September 1939, and at a quarter past eleven, Mr Chamberlain was going to make an announcement.

Gramps was holding out his plate of scones and beginning to ask who would like one when Gran hushed him and turned up the wireless set. 'Someone's just said that Mr Chamberlain is about to make his announcement to the nation,' she said, coming into the garden behind her husband. She set the wireless down on the doorstep and sank into a deckchair. 'Now listen, because this is going to be important.'

Hetty obeyed, though she felt dismay and even fear when she heard what Mr Chamberlain had to say. His deep, sad voice spoke of Herr Hitler's invasion of

Poland and Britain's demand that he withdraw from that country. However, he went on: '. . . no such undertaking has been received and consequently this country is at war with Germany.'

Chapter Twelve

For a moment, there was complete silence, each one wrapped in his or her own thoughts, for Gran had switched the set off as soon as the announcement was finished.

Now, Aunt Phoebe leaned across Hetty and took her husband's hand, and Hetty saw the affection between them as an almost physical thing. She remembered that Bill and Tom were both in the forces, Bill in the Navy and Tom in the RAF, and that at this moment both her aunt and her uncle would have no thought to spare for anyone but their boys.

And I suppose it's the end of my studying for the Higher School Certificate, Hetty told herself. I'll have to do war work; make aeroplanes or parachutes, or guns, and I can't say I'm sorry because from what Professor Max says in his letters to Agatha Germany is ready and eager for war, and we are neither. If only people had listened to the Republican army and the men of the International Brigade, to say nothing of that politician – what's his name? Oh yes, Winston Churchill. Surely somebody in authority, as well as Mr Churchill, must have guessed when Hitler began annexing Austria and Czechoslovakia that he wouldn't stop there. Gramps said we were ill prepared in 1914;

it seems to me that we never learn and that we're ill prepared all over again. So the least I can do is to help the war effort in any way I can.

She looked across to where her grandmother sat in the deckchair; Gramps was standing beside her, his hand on her shoulder, and once again Hetty saw that in this moment of crisis their love was strengthening them, giving them purpose.

Around them the garden glowed. The bed of brilliant dahlias buzzed with bees, and butterflies fluttered from full-blown rose to bud, whilst above her head the trees still flaunted the dark green leaves of summer. Above them again, puffs of white cloud drifted across the brilliant blue of the sky. Only yards away, the canal lapped lazily against the bank as a rowboat drifted past.

Five minutes ago we were at peace, and now we're at war, Hetty told herself. But the flowers go on growing, the bees still visit the flowers and the fish still dart to and fro in the canal. Yet the war will change all our lives: complicate some, simplify others. Oh, dear God, I wonder how long it will be before it won't just be puffs of cloud up in that beautiful blue sky, but Hitler's Luftwaffe?

She glanced round at her family and felt a rush of love; they were taking it well, assimilating the facts without fuss. Even as she watched, Gramps gave his wife's shoulder a hard squeeze and then bent over her, offering the plate of scones. 'Come along, Dulcie; take a scone while young Hetty here nips into the kitchen and helps Matthew pour us all a nice cup of tea. No sense in half starving ourselves and letting good food go to waste.' He grimaced. 'I dare say we'll be glad of a scone or two once this war gets going!'

It was a chilly December day; the view from the Preeces' kitchen window was blanketed by fog and Agatha, sipping a cup of tea whilst her mother made toast, thought that she had seldom felt more miserable. She had been so thrilled when the professor had arrived back in England, but that had been weeks and weeks ago, and she had still not seen him. Now that he had a permanent address – well, perhaps permanent was not the right word, but at least an address to which she could write – they had exchanged letters pretty frequently, but it seemed a meeting was not yet possible. He was working intensively, for besides his air force training he was being cross-questioned frequently over what had been happening in Spain, and although his most recent letters had hinted that he hoped to get leave quite soon now, he had not mentioned a date. Agatha had reminded him that the library was on the telephone, and he had rung her twice, but on both occasions their conversation had been stilted, since presumably he was as aware as she that others were listening.

'Agatha Preece, I've asked you twice if you'd like another piece of toast, and all you've done is stare out of the window as though you could see through the fog!' Her mother's voice was sharp with annoyance. 'Do pay attention, girl!'

Agatha was beginning to apologise, to say that she

would like another piece of toast very much, when she heard the post come through the letterbox. She would have jumped to her feet and hurried to fetch it, but before she could do so her mother put a restraining hand on her shoulder and slapped a slice of toast on to her plate. 'For goodness' sake, girl, eat your breakfast; I'll fetch the post, unless you want to be late for work that is.'

Agatha sighed but began to butter the toast, knowing that Mrs Preece would bring the letters back to her more quickly than she could do herself. Mrs Preece re-entered the kitchen and put a letter down in front of her daughter. 'Needless to say, it's from your friend; though what sort of a friend he is when he's been in England for two months and still not visited you, I can't say,' she said, and Agatha heard the trace of bitterness in her mother's voice with understanding. She had never had a close friend whom her mother did not know, so it was natural enough that Mrs Preece should resent this unknown man who seemed to have considerable influence over her daughter. She thought of explaining again that Max could not just go wherever he liked now that he was in the air force, but took a bite of toast instead. Perhaps he really is just a friend, she told herself rather sadly; I'm beginning to believe that now he's back in England he may wish he'd never promised to write to me from Spain. However, she reached for the letter and opened it, scanned the single page briefly, then laid it down and turned to her mother, her hands flying to her hot cheeks. 'He's coming up to Liverpool on a flying visit, a few days before

Christmas,' she said, unable to keep the excitement out of her voice. 'He'll be on his way to Durham, where his father lives now he's retired. Apparently he and his brother will both have leave then, and they'll have a family Christmas. His mother died years ago and his father remarried, but I've told you that, I'm sure.'

Mrs Preece sniffed. 'You've told me remarkably little,' she said stiffly. 'Do the sons not get on with their stepmother?'

Agatha shrugged. 'I don't know, he's never said. But he does say he has something important to tell me; I wonder what on earth it can be?'

'Oh, it'll be something to do with the war,' Mrs Preece said dismissively. 'Nothing happens these days which isn't connected with the war. He'll probably suggest that you should join up, do your bit for your country, as they say.'

Agatha felt the hot blood rush to her cheeks once more. How could her mother be so cruel? She knew very well that none of the services would accept a woman with a club foot. She opened her mouth to say so, but before she could speak Mrs Preece got up from her seat and came round the table to put an arm round her daughter's shoulders. 'Oh, Agatha, I'm so sorry! That was a horrible thing to say, and of course I know very well that you wouldn't dream of joining up and leaving me to take care of myself. Please say you forgive me.'

Agatha was touched. Her mother seldom apologised for the unthinking words she uttered when in a temper. She got carefully to her feet and smiled. 'Of course I forgive you. I expect you're longing to meet Mr Galera, and to tell you the truth I am as well, since I can scarcely remember what he looks like,' she lied. 'And now I really must get a move on, because although Mr Gower will open the lending library for me, and remain downstairs until I arrive, it always puts him in a bad temper. He doesn't really like people, you know, which is why he's the reference librarian, I suppose.' She laughed. 'Up in the gallery, he doesn't have to mix with the hoi polloi, as Maria and myself do.'

'And Hetty,' Mrs Preece reminded her daughter, as Agatha finished her toast and began to put on her thick winter coat. 'She's not moved out to Burscough yet, has she? Only I know there was talk of her doing so when her aunt and uncle rented the house in Birkenhead so that they would be nearer the shipyard. I shall miss Hetty terribly, particularly if she moves away from the city.'

Agatha paused, a hand on the doorknob. 'I think she'll probably get war work in Birkenhead and continue to live with her aunt and uncle, which will mean she only has to hop on the ferry to be back in Liverpool,' she said comfortingly. 'After all, if Laird's need workers so badly that they're prepared to take on her aunt, then I should think they'd jump at the chance of employing Hetty.'

'But you said her aunt was doing some sort of cleaning job,' Mrs Preece pointed out. 'Hetty's clever; she could be a bookkeeper or – or a typist, I'm sure.'

'That's right; and working in the shipyard would

certainly count as helping the war effort,' Agatha said. 'She's coming to the library later today, though, so no doubt she'll be able to tell me what she's decided. She talked to someone at school about getting factory work, but they told her that if she does that she won't be accepted in any of the services when she's old enough to join up ... look, Mother, I must fly or I really will be late for work, but I'll ask Hetty to come back here with me for supper, and then we'll both hear what she's decided to do.'

'And you can share *your* news,' Mrs Preece said complacently. 'Tell her that your boyfriend's written to say he's coming to see you at last.'

Agatha cast up her eyes and pulled down the corners of her mouth. 'Very amusing,' she said sarcastically. 'See you later, Mother!'

Hetty got off the bus at the stop nearest Uncle Matthew's house and heaved her shopping basket and the large sack she carried from one hand to the other. It was a cold day and the fog had not lifted but her coat, though by no means new, was warm and she stood her burdens down for a moment to turn up its big fur collar. It had been a smart coat once, navy blue and tight-fitting, but because of the blackout Hetty, who was not good with her needle, had laboriously stitched a length of white tape round the waist and diagonally across the back and front, so that she could be seen at night.

She reached the cottage but did not attempt to go round the back since she had not told the old people that she meant to visit them, and always felt it was a bit of an intrusion for someone not expected to walk straight into someone else's home. Instead, she headed for the front door, rapped smartly upon it and entered the small hallway. She made for the kitchen, calling out as she did so: 'It's only me, Hetty. Are you in, Gran and Gramps?' As she spoke the last few words, she pushed open the door to find her grandmother and Uncle Matthew sitting on either side of the table, methodically slicing runner beans. They smiled a welcome and Gran got up and went to fill the kettle at the sink, whilst Uncle Matthew helped Hetty out of her coat and told her that she had arrived just in time to share their elevenses.

'How lovely; but where's Gramps?' Hetty said eagerly. 'Oh, gingerbread; my favourite.' She beamed at her relatives and emptied her shopping bag out on to the table, though she did not attempt to lift the sack which she had stood down as soon as she entered the room. 'I was passing the greengrocers on Heyworth Street and Mr Gaulton called out to me to pop in for a moment. He wanted to know if I could do with some cooking apples which were past their best, and a big bag of shallots, if I knew someone who didn't mind crying for a week.'

'Thanks very much, Hetty my love,' Gran said eagerly, beginning to gather up the big green apples. She patted the sack of shallots lovingly. 'I don't mind shedding a few tears if it means getting jars and jars of onions pickled. But I wonder why the greengrocer couldn't sell 'em?'

'Apparently folk are holding back from buying vegetables or fruit which needs bottling or pickling, because it's quite hard work and takes time,' Hetty said. 'I knew Aunt Phoebe wouldn't thank me for giving her extra work even if it did mean lots of pickled shallots and bottled apples, because moving house is far harder than I dreamed it would be. First, we went over to Birkenhead and scrubbed the new house from attic to cellar . . .'

'Was it very bad, queen?' her grandmother asked sympathetically. 'I remember when Gramps and I were first married and took on a little house in Bootle, it was downright filthy; I wouldn't like to say the number of bars of soap we used, nor how many scrub brushes we wore down to the wood before we could move in.'

'Well, it's done now,' Hetty said. 'The actual move took place yesterday, and of course as soon as the house in Salisbury Street was empty we had to scrub every floor and clean down everything there, and when I said that the new people would do it, Aunt Phoebe primmed up her mouth and said she wouldn't have folk thinking her a slut . . . but where *is* Gramps?'

Uncle Matthew was replying that her grandfather had taken some scones to an elderly neighbour when the back door opened and he surged into the room, talking as he came. 'Dulcie, Matt, we've got a guest to share our elevenses, so put out an extra cup . . .' He stopped short, staring at Hetty. 'Well I'm blessed! Here's young Sally Brimelow wanting to get in touch with you, Hetty my love, because she doesn't have your Birkenhead address, and here you are, large as life and twice as lovely!' He turned back to Sally. 'Take that coat off, my dear, or you won't feel the benefit when you go out again.'

Hetty smiled at her friend. 'Hi, Sal. It's lovely to see you. I was going to write out our new address and pop it through your mam's letterbox on my way back from Burscough.' She took another cup from the dresser, and poured milk and tea into it. Sally, having shed her coat and hung it on the hook by the door, accepted the cup, sat down and took a piece of the gingerbread Hetty was offering.

'Scrumptious,' she said happily, through a full mouth. 'Hetty, I've gorra proposition to put to you. But first of all I'd better explain what's happened to the *Maid Marian*. You know Mam and Dad retired when the boys took over? Well, when Nat and Ben joined up, Mam, Dad, Uncle Bert and my cousin, Sammy agreed to return to the canal and the *Maid*, because barges will be an important part of the war effort, taking stuff from the docks to the mills and vice versa.'

'Hang on a minute,' Uncle Matthew said. 'As I recall, Bert's son must be around eighteen, ain't that so? So surely he'll be called up? Conscription came in months ago.'

'Sammy's eighteen awright, and a big strong lad, but a trifle simple; tuppence short of a shillin', in fact,' Sally said bluntly. 'That's why they don't want him in the forces. But on a barge, with his parents who understand him and will take the greatest care of him, Sammy'll be

273

invaluable. Provided you explain carefully just what you want him to do, he's as useful as any other feller.'

'I understand,' Hetty said quickly. 'But what's all this got to do with me, Sal? Or with you, for that matter, since with Sammy to do the heavy work a fifth member of crew would be unnecessary, I'd have thought.'

'True. But, Hetty, I went to the Company to ask if they had any berths for someone experienced in working on a canal barge and the man who interviewed me asked what I knew about narrow boats. Naturally I said that I imagined they were very similar to the larger boats – the barges – which are used on the Leeds and Liverpool canal, and he said very probably I was right and would I consider a berth aboard one of them. Apparently with all the young men going off to the armed forces there is a dreadful shortage of canal people who know what they're doing, particularly on the Grand Union and Oxford canals. He said that if I could find another young woman who had had boat experience, and one other girl who was eager to learn, then he would be willing for the three of us to take over a boat on the Grand Union, plying between the London docks and Birmingham or the mill towns. He said we'd be issued with special ration books so we wouldn't have to register with a particular shop, and he'd talk to the authorities about us getting extra rations anyway, because some of the work – don't we know it – is very hard and needs a fair amount of strength.

'And oh, Hetty, I thought of you at once! You've

274

always loved the canal, and I dare say the Grand Union isn't that different from the Leeds and Liverpool, and I've already got a girl who's keen and has helped out with a boat now and then. Her name's Alice, and if you're agreeable, then I'm to arrange for the three of us to be interviewed by the man at the Inland Waterways HQ who is responsible for getting the crews together. We'll have a practical test aboard, just to make sure that you and I can manage the change from a barge to a narrow boat, and then he'll decide which of the pair of us is sufficiently experienced to act as Number One, though I mean to suggest that you and I take it in turns, as my brothers did. That's if you're interested, of course.'

She reached across the table and grabbed Hetty's hand, her blue eyes fairly blazing with excitement. 'It's a great opportunity, honest to God it is! If we go into a factory, or join one of the women's services, then we'll spend the war being told what to do – jumping when someone else says jump – but aboard the canal we'll be our own boss, and we'll be helping the war effort far more . . . oh, more *personally* than if we were stuck in an office or peeling spuds in a cook-house, like my cousin Cynthia.'

Hetty looked at her relatives, trying to subdue the smile which threatened to break out and give her feelings away. To be in charge of a boat, to help the war effort by using the only expertise she possessed! It was what most girls would give their eye teeth for . . . but she would hear what Gramps and Gran thought before making up her mind. She looked interrogatively at the three elderly people seated round the big kitchen table. 'Well? What do you think? There's been no mention of pay, but I'm sure the authorities wouldn't expect us to do important work for nothing. Gran? As the only lady present – apart from me and Sally – you go first.'

'Well, if I were you I'd take it on,' Gran said. 'I just wish you'd be plying on the good old Leeds and Liverpool, but in time of war one goes where one is most needed. Yes, I'd sign on as boat crew if I were you, love.'

'Gramps?' Hetty said, her smile breaking out, despite her resolve. 'What do you say?' She shot a glance at Sally, who was raking a hand through her wheat-gold curls, anxiously watching Gramps's thoughtful face.

'Same as your gran,' Gramps said promptly. 'Like her, I wish it were the Leeds and Liverpool, because we'd get to see you more often, but beggars can't be choosers. Doubtless you'll get leave, though how they'll arrange it I wouldn't like to guess. When we were on the canal, even a day's holiday had to be planned weeks in advance . . . but you go ahead and take the practical test, which you'll sail through with flying colours. That's my advice, and I guess Matt here will say the same.'

Uncle Matthew nodded his agreement, his rosy little goblin face creasing into a broad smile. 'I just wish I'd had a chance to work the canals durin' the last little lot,' he admitted. 'But I were sent to France wi' the East Lancs regiment, so I were lucky to come out of it wi' a whole skin. You tell 'em yes, queen, and I reckon you'll not regret it.'

Hetty promptly shot across the kitchen and hugged her friend exuberantly, then stood back and let out her breath in a long sigh of relief. 'Phew! I'm so glad we're all agreed, because the minute you mentioned it, Sal, I knew I'd be happier on the canal than I could ever be in a factory or one of the armed forces. I wonder what the big differences will be between a barge and a narrow boat? Apart from the measurements, I mean.'

'Well, we'll soon find out,' Sally said. She took the cup of tea Gran was holding out and sipped it gratefully. 'Marvellous, just what I wanted! Thanks, Mrs Hesketh. And now Hetty and meself had best make tracks to the nearest phone box because we need to get in touch with Alice before we can arrange the interview. I wonder how soon it'll be before we're in our new home – and have our orders, of course. Honest, Hetty, I can't perishin' well wait!'

Because of the arrangements the two girls had to make, it was well past her usual time when Hetty arrived at the library. In fact Miss Preece, Miss Thorpe and Mr Gower were leaving the building as Hetty came hurrying up St Domingo Road.

'Just where have you been, young lady?' Miss Preece asked with mock annoyance as Hetty joined them. 'I'm used to my little helper arriving in time to put books away and check the files . . . and today we've had rather a lot of distractions, haven't we, Miss Thorpe?'

Maria Thorpe nodded shyly. She was a meek, mouse-like little person in her mid-twenties with shiny light brown hair that was always escaping from the bun at the nape of her neck, and pale, short-sighted blue eyes. Now, she smiled shyly at Hetty. 'I've volunteered for the WAAF, Miss Gilbert, and today I had a letter saying I'd been accepted,' she said. 'I'm to await another letter telling me where to go and when, but I asked the lady in the recruiting office and she said she thought I'd be gone soon after Christmas. So of course I had to tell Miss Preece, though I don't think they'll be able to get anyone in my place.'

'And I was relying on you, Hetty,' Miss Preece said. 'Oh, goodnight, Mr Gower; see you in the morning.'

Mr Gower gave the three women his usual thin smile and crossed the road, and as soon as he was out of hearing Hetty told the two librarians her own news. 'We're to report to the Inland Waterways office the day after tomorrow,' she said. 'Sally's done all the arranging; I've met this Alice Smith – she's nice, just as Sally said – so now we've got to get through the interview and the practical test, and then I suppose we'll move into whichever barge – boat, I mean – they've decided to let us take over. I'm thrilled, and so are the other two!' Hetty looked hard at Miss Preece. 'You look very flushed.' She gave her friend a wicked grin. 'Anything exciting in the post this morning?'

Miss Preece gave a non-committal answer, changing the subject quickly to what she meant to do if the library authority really could not find her an assist-ant. Turning to Miss Thorpe, she said: 'But Mr Gower and myself managed before you joined us, so I dare say we can manage again. Of course it will be hard on a Saturday, though we may be able to get another schoolgirl in on a temporary basis.' She turned her dark eyes enquiringly on Hetty. 'Or will you have weekends off? If so, you could nip up from the docks and give us a hand.'

Hetty shook her head. 'Not possible; the boat to which we shall be assigned will be plying on the Grand Union canal, a long way away from here. It would have been lovely if it had been on the Leeds and Liverpool, but there was no question of that.'

'But of course you'll get leave, what my mother says they used to call furlough in the last war,' Miss Thorpe said. 'You aren't allowed even an hour off – according to my cousin – when you first join up, but that's the Royal Air Force; it may be different for the canals.'

Hetty sighed. 'This war is all wait and see,' she said resignedly. She looked up at Miss Preece. 'I'm hoping you're going to invite me for supper. Aunt Phoebe was going to buy fish and chips, as it's her first day in the new house, and I told her not to get me any because I've no idea what time the ferries leave and if there's one thing I really hate, it's fish and chips which have gone cold and are put in the oven to warm up.'

'Of course you're invited to supper,' Agatha Preece said at once. 'I can just imagine what my mother would say if I didn't ask you to share our meal. She'll be desperate to hear all about the canal boat, too.'

They reached the corner where their way parted from Miss Thorpe's, and as soon as the assistant librarian had left them Hetty turned impulsively to her companion. 'Go on, Agatha, tell me what's happened,' she urged.

'I'm sure you've had a letter and I just hope it was good news.'

'It is,' Miss Preece said, and Hetty saw a smile begin. 'Max is coming up to Liverpool on Wednesday the twentieth. He's going to meet me from work and suggests that he should take Mother and myself out for a meal so he can get to know her. But he'll be in Liverpool all day Thursday – he's booked in at the Adelphi – and suggests that I take that day off so that we can spend it together. I'm really excited, Hetty, because although I know very well he's just a friend . . .'

Hetty gave a crow of amusement. 'Just a friend indeed! Why are you so shy of admitting that he's something more? It's been clear as daylight to everyone but yourself that he likes you very much and wants to get to know you better. Is he coming here with his brother? Do you remember when he collided with you and was so . . . oh, so snooty.'

Agatha Preece sniffed. 'I know nothing about his brother, nor do I want to,' she said loftily. 'And as for Max being interested in me – as a woman, I mean – time alone will tell.'

Agatha awoke on 20 December as her alarm tinkled its morning message. For a moment she wondered why she felt so excited, then remembered. The professor was going to meet her from work and come back to Everton Terrace with her. She would introduce him to her mother, they would share a cup of tea and a chat, and then Max would take them back to the

Adelphi, where they would have a meal. When Mrs Preece was young she had often been taken to the Adelphi, but Agatha had never entered its imposing portals and told herself that she was looking forward to that experience almost as much as to seeing Max again after so long.

It was not true, of course. In fact her main feeling was a worry that after so long he might not recognise her. She guessed that it was why he had chosen to meet her from work. It would have been awkward if he had suggested coming straight to the house on Everton Terrace, because she knew her mother too well to expect that Mrs Preece would let them meet alone at the front door, even for five minutes. As soon as the doorbell sounded she would be toddling up the hall, elbow to elbow with her daughter, determined to see this man with whom Agatha had been exchanging letters, some of which Mrs Preece had read. After discovering that her mother knew where she had hidden her correspondence, Agatha had taken the letters to work and prised up a floorboard in the ladies' lavatory, secure in the knowledge that only herself, Maria and Hetty ever entered, since it was not available to the general public. Then she had placed the letters in a manila envelope, written her own name in large, clear capitals across it, and replaced the board.

Now, Agatha got out of bed, smiling at the mental picture she had just conjured up of herself and her mother trundling as fast as they could towards the front door, like a couple of racehorses stretching their necks as the winning post came in sight. But in fact, she was rather dreading the meeting between Mrs Preece and the professor. Limping heavily along the landing to the bathroom, she just hoped that her mother would be on her best behaviour and would remember that the professor was her host. She went over to the gas geyser which hung above the bath, picked up the box of matches from the windowsill, struck one and turned on the gas. She hated this part of the proceedings, because if the gas blew the match out before being ignited, the whole business had to be gone through again, and the smell of gas frightened her. In the summer Agatha washed in cold water, but at this time of year she usually lit the geyser and had a shivery, strip-down wash, and since she could see through the window that the frost on the trees was undiminished, she knew that it was even colder outside than in.

The gas geyser, however, behaved beautifully for once and was now hissing away merrily. Agatha considered a bath, then decided against it. No need to give her mother ammunition; it would be just like her to greet Max by saying gaily: 'Aha, you're the young man who is so important to my daughter that she takes a bath first thing in the morning and uses all the hot water, so that her poor old mother has to boil a kettle for her own ablutions.'

The fact that this would be untrue would be immaterial to her mother, but best to play safe and act as she always did. Accordingly, Agatha had a strip-down wash, then hastily donned her underwear and dressing gown and returned to her room, for the bathroom was icy. She had already selected a white blouse and dark blue skirt and jacket and now she put them on, brushed her hair and picked up her handbag, then went downstairs. She had secretly hoped to reach the kitchen in time to make her breakfast – porridge this morning, as well as toast and coffee – before her mother put in an appearance, but old Mrs Preece must have heard her daughter lighting the geyser for no sooner had Agatha put oats, water and a couple of splashes of milk into the saucepan than the kitchen door creaked open and Mrs Preece hobbled across the room and picked up the loaf.

'Morning, Agatha. I'll start the toast,' she said briskly. 'I guessed you'd get up earlier than usual today, seeing as how your young man will be arriving in the city this evening.' She looked her daughter up and down with a gimlet eye. 'You look very smart, dear. I've always liked you in dark blue.'

'Morning, Mother,' Agatha said, hoping her disappointment did not show; it would have been so nice to read last night's *Echo* and eat her breakfast in peace, but clearly this was not to be. 'I believe, however, that the professor is already in Liverpool, having caught the milk train at some ungodly hour this morning. Didn't I tell you?'

She knew she had not done so and acknowledged, though only to herself, that she had kept Max's arrival quiet because she did not want her mother doing anything embarrassing, such as ringing the Adelphi and demanding to speak to Professor Galera. When she had voiced this fear to Hetty, however, her young friend had shaken her head, putting such thoughts to flight. 'Your mother is a holy terror, but I don't believe she'd ever do anything to hurt you,' Hetty had said. 'She might think it amusing to embarrass you, but she'd never go behind your back, let alone speak on the telephone to a man she's never met. Why, she's downright scared of the thing, which is why she held out when you wanted to have one installed.'

At the time Agatha had acknowledged the truth of Hetty's remark, and now, stirring porridge, she thought remorsefully that it had been too bad of her even to let such a thought cross her mind. But Mrs Preece did not seem to have taken offence because she had not been told the time of Max's arrival, and was whipping two slices of toast out from under the grill and reaching for the loaf to cut two more slices of bread.

'Ah, then if he's here already you think he might surprise you and arrive at the library earlier than planned,' Mrs Preece said shrewdly. 'Well, what does it matter, when all's said and done?' And then, to Agatha's surprise and pleasure, she added: 'I'm proud of you, my dear. You do me credit. And though I wasn't too sure how I felt about it when you first had your hair cut, I like it now.'

Agatha had arranged with her assistant that she would leave ten minutes before the rest of the staff so that she and Max might meet by themselves. Accordingly, she bade Miss Thorpe goodnight and put on her thick winter coat, but she left her head bare since she was still afraid that the professor might fail to recognise her if she wore her hat. However, it was far too cold to leave off her scarf, so she wrapped it round her neck as she left the library, descended the five steps with a thumping heart and looked anxiously around her.

She had been tempted to abandon her stick, to try to disguise her disability, but had decided that this would be sheer foolishness. Besides, it would be open to misinterpretation; the professor might think she intended to use his arm as a crutch. Indeed, she might be forced to do so, for though it was not a long walk from the library to Everton Terrace, a walk she did every working day, she went at her own pace and the professor, having longer legs, might stride out.

Agatha suddenly remembered that there were three entrances to the library; he might be waiting at any one of them. There were a number of people walking along the pavement, but the only person standing still was a tall man in an RAF officer's greatcoat and cap. Even as her eyes flicked over him, she did a double take and felt her heart quicken, for he was smiling and coming to meet her, a hand held out. Agatha limped towards him, transferring her stick from her right hand to her left, and presently they were shaking hands and she was telling him that for some reason it had not occurred to her that he would be in uniform. 'But of course I recognised you,' she added hastily. 'Apart from the fact that you're very brown, I don't think you've changed at all.'

'Nor have you. You're as . . .' he looked down at her face and seemed to change his mind over what he had been about to say, 'you're as neat and trim as I remember you,' he ended rather feebly. He made

as if to offer her his arm, and when she did not immediately slip her hand into the crook of his elbow added:
'Do you prefer to go by tram to your home, Agatha?
I would hail a taxi, but I haven't seen one with its flag
up since I arrived here twenty minutes or so ago.'

'I always walk to and from work; it's not far, only
about half a mile,' Agatha said, horribly aware that
her voice sounded stilted. 'But if you've been hanging
about in the cold for twenty minutes, perhaps you
would rather catch a tram. I'm stuck in the library all
day so I like to get a bit of exercise and fresh air when
I leave the place.' They were standing on the pavement in front of the library and now she looked seriously up into the dark and craggy face above her own.
'Why didn't you come in? It's warm in there.' She gave
a little chuckle. 'I know it's an old building and the
radiators are old too, but they're pretty efficient. And
there's a reading room equipped with a fair number
of newspapers and magazines. You could have waited
in there.'

The professor shook his head. 'I didn't want to; I
was afraid of missing you. But by all means let us
walk. I could do with some exercise too.'

The two of them set off along the pavement and
presently they reached Everton Terrace and Agatha
slowed. Should she warn him that her mother could
be difficult? But it seemed unfair to old Mrs Preece –
and to the professor – to put him on his guard against
something which might never happen. With her hand
actually on the garden gate, she hesitated, then spoke.
'My mother is what you might call a character,

Professor,' she said timidly. 'When she's nervous, and meeting strangers always makes her nervous, she can become a little brusque. If this happens, I do hope you won't take it amiss.'

The professor laughed. 'I have an extremely crusty old father myself,' he said. 'And why have I suddenly become Professor again after we agreed to address each other by our first names? I'm far more likely to take offence over that than over anything your mother might say to me.'

'Oh, that's all right then,' Agatha said with a gaiety which even to her own ears sounded a little false. 'To tell you the truth, M-Max, it feels a bit cheeky to call you by your first name, but I'll do so in future. After all, you called me Agatha just now.' She opened the gate and led him up the path, unlocked the front door, and ushered her companion inside.

Once indoors she realised, without surprise, that her mother must have been watching for her, since the parlour door shot open and Mrs Preece appeared in her best dark purple dress. Agatha hastily introduced the professor and her mother smiled graciously, then held the parlour door invitingly open. 'Good afternoon, Professor Galera, how nice to meet you at last! Do come through; now you've arrived my maid will bring in the tea.'

Agatha and Max shed their coats and went into the parlour whilst Mrs Preece rapped lightly on the kitchen door. When she returned, her daughter gave her an accusing glare. 'Really, Mother!' she murmured under her breath. 'Whatever made you say such a thing?

As if two women, living alone, would even think of employing a maid. I suppose you bribed some poor girl . . .'

There was a rattling in the doorway and Mrs Simpson wheeled in a tea trolley containing all the equipment needed for tea, including a plate of buttered scones, another of biscuits and a third upon which reposed a large fruit cake. To Agatha's horror, she bobbed a sort of half-curtsey and began to hand round the dainty side plates which Agatha had only ever seen through the glass of the china cabinet, whilst Mrs Preece started to pour three cups of tea. Agatha looked at the professor and saw his lips twitch even as Mrs Simpson began to manoeuvre the trolley across a ruck in the carpet . . . where it lurched, gave a protesting creak as one of its wheels folded inward, and deposited fruit cake, scones and most of the biscuits upon the parlour floor. The teapot slid, heading for a similar fate, but Mrs Preece grabbed it just in time to avert disaster.

'Oh, bugger!' the 'maid' squawked, dropping to her knees and beginning to pile the well-buttered scones back on the plate. She raised a pink and rather sweaty face to Agatha's. 'I told your mam I'd mek a pig's ear of it, but she were that keen to impress your feller . . .'

Agatha blinked at their neighbour's sudden Scouse accent, then picked up the fruit cake and slammed it back on to its plate, and turned to her mother. 'No wonder the wheel gave way,' she said crossly. 'I don't believe this trolley has been used for twenty or thirty years. And now I think you'd better introduce Mrs Simpson to my friend. After all, she *is* our next-door neighbour.'

By this time, the professor also had dropped to his knees to collect the scones, many of which had fallen buttered side down, and Agatha could see that he was doing this in order to hide his amusement. But when Mrs Simpson staggered to her feet and held out a buttery hand he shook it gravely, though a moment later Agatha saw him surreptitiously wiping his palm on the lace tablecloth with which her mother had decorated the top of the trolley. She glanced angrily towards her mother, the words *Pride comes before a fall* hovering on her lips, but Mrs Preece gave her no opportunity to speak.

'Dear, dear, dear, what a dreadful thing to happen,' the old lady said gaily. 'That trolley has been in my family for a hundred years. What a good thing it was that I'd already poured the tea, because if that had landed on the carpet I should have been most distressed.' She took the plate of scones from its place, gave them a penetrating glance and then, with obvious regret, returned the plate to the trolley and smiled sweetly at the professor. 'I dare say you'd not fancy a scone, though they were freshly baked this morning,' she said. 'However, I'm sure my maid . . . my neighbour, I mean, will cut you slice of the fruit cake, if you would prefer it.'

The professor regained his seat and his composure and, though he thanked Mrs Preece, declined the treat. 'I've booked a table at the Adelphi for seven o'clock and your daughter tells me you're on the telephone, so if you don't object I mean to ring for a taxi, for we really should be leaving just as soon as I've finished this delicious cup of tea.'

By now everything had been restored to the trolley, though it still leaned at a precarious angle. Mrs Simpson, with many a mutter of 'I told you so' in Mrs Preece's direction, took one end of it whilst Agatha took the other. 'You'd best carry the teapot, Mother,' Agatha said stiffly. 'It would be too bad if that hit the deck as well.' She was dying to get her mother to herself so that she could tell her what she thought of her behaviour, but by the time the three of them, and the trolley, had reached the kitchen, she realised that this would scarcely get their evening off to a good start, and decided to swallow her spleen, for now, at any rate. Instead, she thanked Mrs Simpson with real sincerity for her help, and began to say how sorry she was for what had happened, but Mrs Simpson waved her apology aside. 'It were a bit of fun, and no harm done,' she said, and giggled. 'That there's a poem, ain't it, Miss Agatha? And your feller took it well, wouldn't you say? I likes his looks; reckon you could do a lot worse.'

'He's not my feller . . .' Agatha started, then gave up. Whatever she said, the professor would be known as 'Miss Preece's feller' whenever his name came up. Better to ignore it for now and tell Mrs Simpson, later, not to listen to her mother's flights of fancy.

As they parked the trolley by the sink, Mrs Preece set down the teapot and hurried back to the parlour.

Agatha turned to Mrs Simpson. 'I'd love to help you to clear up this mess and put everything away, but you heard what the professor said; even if a taxi arrives within five or ten minutes of his telephone call, we shall only just reach the Adelphi by seven o'clock,' she said. 'But if you'd like to leave it – the washing up and clearing away, I mean – then Mother and I will tackle it when we get home.'

'Don't you worry, queen,' Mrs Simpson said comfortably. 'Your mam's already paid me to do an extra two hours, so I still owe you some time. You go off and enjoy yourself . . .'

Agatha cut in hastily before Mrs Simpson could end the sentence with 'with your feller', since she could hear sounds from the hall indicating that the professor was ringing for a taxi. Very soon, warmly clad in coats, hats and scarves, they set off for the Adelphi.

Chapter Thirteen

When Agatha entered Fuller's on Ranelagh Street next day, where she and Max – she must remember to use his first name – were to meet, she was delighted, but not at all surprised, to find him seated at a window table waiting for her. He was the sort of man, she now realised, who would always be early for an appointment rather than late, and since she herself was of the same kidney she thought it augured well for their friendship.

Smiling, she walked slowly over to the little table and took the seat opposite. 'Good morning, Max. I trust you had a good night's sleep. I must tell you that my mother thinks you are a prince amongst professors.' She chuckled. 'You certainly know how to treat crotchety old ladies!'

Max tutted reprovingly, but his eyes twinkled. 'Your mother is not a crotchety old lady, or at least she was not crotchety last evening. In fact she was very good company, although to tell you the truth I could have wished her at Jericho if it had meant more time for you and me to get to know one another.'

Agatha felt her cheeks grow warm, but told herself briskly that he was just being polite. The trouble was she knew so little about young men ... not that the professor was young, exactly. Looking at him attentively across the table now as he ordered two cups of coffee from a hovering waitress, she thought that his time in Spain had aged him.

As the waitress departed to get their order, Max leaned across the table and took her hand. 'It was a trifle awkward last evening, with your mother present, to talk about our plans for today,' he said. 'But first of all I must remind you that I'm on my way to Durham, which is where my father and step-mother now live. Michael is already there and we mean to have a family Christmas together. So, much though I would like to spend more than a couple of days in Liverpool, I'm afraid it isn't possible. You see, I'm on embarkation leave. I expect you know what that means.'

Agatha felt a stab of dismay chill her blood. 'It means they're sending you abroad,' she said in a low voice. 'Oh, Max, I thought that it was the army and Navy who went away from Britain, not the air force. Where will you be going; is it far?'

'I'm not supposed to know where I'm going, but because I'm a flying instructor I suspect it might be either South Africa, Rhodesia or North America.' He gave her a rueful grin. 'First I spend more than a year writing to you, then I see you for a couple of days, and now I'll have to start wielding my pen all over again.'

Agatha gave him a timid smile. 'I like receiving letters, but of course it would be much nicer if we could meet,' she said shyly. 'Now that the first awfulness of

293

knowing we're at war has passed, it's easy to think that life is simply going to go on as usual. But it won't, of course; you know that better than anyone, and I suppose Michael must as well. Is he going abroad too? Are you both on embarkation leave?'

'No, Michael is aircrew, a navigator in a Wellington bomber. He's got four days' leave, which is why he's already in Durham. Because I've got longer, I'm expected to do the round of relatives and old friends, but I snatched a couple of days so that you and I could meet. I wish you could come up to Durham. Is there . . .'

'Coffee for two,' the waitress said, cutting across what Max had been about to say. 'Nothing to eat, sir? We've some fresh baked scones, just out of the oven.'

Max raised his eyebrows at Agatha and smiled as she shook her head. The waitress moved away and Max leaned towards Agatha once more. 'I'll never hear the word "scones" again without thinking of your mother. How beautifully she carried it off! But did she honestly believe that anyone employs servants in this day and age? I thought even the royal family were having staff difficulties.'

Agatha laughed. 'When my mother gets the bit between her teeth, nothing daunts her,' she observed. 'But what were you about to say when the waitress interrupted?'

'I was wondering whether it would be possible for you to get some leave – time off, I mean – so that you might come up to Durham for a few days. I'd like you to meet my father and my stepmother, but most of all

I'd like to introduce you to Michael. He's supposed to be very like me, though personally I can't see it.' He looked hopefully at her. 'But if you could come up to Durham, you could judge for yourself.'

Agatha looked down at her hands. The last thing she wanted to do was to meet Michael, if indeed Max's brother had been the man who had knocked her over, blamed her for the collision and then called her a cripple. But she certainly did not intend to let the professor know about that long-ago incident. After all, Michael must have changed considerably in the five years which had elapsed since then; and anyway, Max's suggestion that she should visit Durham was out of the question.

She began to mumble, then took a deep breath and met Max's eyes squarely. 'It's awfully kind of you to ask me, but I'm afraid it's quite impossible,' she said. 'My assistant librarian has been accepted by the WAAF and might leave me at any time and in any event, I have to give the authority a fair amount of notice even to have a day off.'

'I guessed what your answer would have to be, but I thought it was worth asking,' Max said, giving her a rueful smile. 'It was a bit of a cheek to suggest it, I suppose, but I've met your mother, so why shouldn't you meet my father? However, I accept that it's impossible at present; let us say it's a pleasure deferred, because I'm bound to get back to Britain sometime, and when I do I'll make straight for Liverpool and do my caveman act and carry you off to Durham, even if the library authority refuses to give you leave.'

Agatha laughed; she could not imagine the urbane man seated opposite her dressed in animal skins with a big club over his shoulder, but when she said as much he shook his head at her. 'That just shows you don't know me very well yet,' he said. 'I'm a devil when roused, and any sort of opposition brings out the worst in me.'

He was trying to frown, but his eyes twinkled and Agatha, remembering her collision with his brother, almost said that caveman tactics must run in the family, but bit the words back; she must forget the whole sorry incident. 'Then I won't oppose you, so long as you don't irritate me beyond bearing,' she said laughingly instead. 'And now, what are your plans for today? You said something about shopping for Christmas presents . . .'

'I want you to help me choose something pretty for my stepmama and something warm and useful for my grandmother,' Max said. 'And then we'll have lunch somewhere nice and I thought we might go to the cinema this afternoon, if there's anything showing that you'd like to see. But once I've bought my presents, the day is our own.'

'I'll do my best to help you choose,' Agatha said, but her thoughts, as they left Fuller's and headed for Lewis's, were somewhat chaotic. It had just occurred to her that, according to others, a man did not ask you home to meet his parents unless he was serious. But she must remember that war changed everything, including attitudes. She and Max might never be more than good friends, but even good friends exchange visits from time to time. If he asked her again to go to Durham – if he gave her enough warning, that was – then she really would do her best to go, even if it meant facing the man who had knocked her down and called her a cripple.

Satisfied with her decision, she entered Lewis's with a feeling of pleasant anticipation. Choosing a present for two women she had never met was quite a challenge, but it meant she was at liberty to ask questions about them. After all, colouring, character and likes and dislikes all had to be taken into account when choosing the perfect gift.

She was limping towards the jewellery counter, lured by its sparkling showcases, when Max took her hand and led her in the direction of the lift. 'Grandmother first,' he said. 'I've written down her size in dresses, just in case you see something you think would suit her . . .'

Much later, sitting on a red plush seat in the cinema, watching the main feature draw to a close, Agatha thought over her day. It had been, she decided, the best day of her life so far, for everything had gone beautifully, just as it ought. Even the weather had not let her down, for though it was extremely cold it neither rained nor snowed and the sun shone, pale but persistent, out of a brilliant blue sky.

Presents had been bought – a lilac wool dress for Max's grandmother, a sparkly brooch and necklace for the woman he referred to, rather charmingly Agatha thought, as 'Stepmama', pipe tobacco for his father and some small toys for the children of one of his cousins. These had to be chosen with care, since the children in question lived down south, so their presents would have to be sent by post, but the buying of such things as a cuddly teddy bear and a model railway set allowed Agatha to wander round the toy departments without feeling that everyone was staring at her. Indeed, she hoped that the assistants who served them thought they were buying for children of their own. She noticed that none of them stared at her club foot. Perhaps they never had, but then she had seldom ventured into such departments, having no young relatives for whom to buy gifts.

After making their purchases, they had wandered around the market, enjoying the festive air of Christmas. Agatha had been unable to resist temptation and had bought a few treats for her mother, whilst Max had splashed out on two pounds of walnuts, which he told her his father loved, and two boxes of crystallised fruits for his womenfolk.

They had had lunch at the Adelphi Hotel and Agatha had felt wonderfully sophisticated when the waiter, who had served them the evening before, recognised her and addressed her as 'madam'. After lunch, Max had looked at her shyly, though still with a lurking twinkle. 'Will you think I'm entering my second childhood if I say I'd like to go for a ride on the Overhead Railway?' he had asked. 'A fellow in my carriage on the train coming up from London said it was pretty imposing in peacetime, but even more so now that we're at war. It's the only way a civilian gets to see the docks and the variety of shipping which has come into the port . . . but if you'd be bored . . .'

'I wouldn't; I'd love it,' Agatha had said at once. 'When I was a little girl, my father took me from Dingle to Seaforth and back again, just for the ride. I loved it then, and I shall love it now. I don't suppose you know, not being a local man, but folk call it the Dockers' Umbrella . . .'

Max had laughed. 'I did know; but you can trust a Liverpudlian to find a nickname for just about everything. I wish we had time to visit New Brighton, but there won't be much to see because of the blackout, so I dare say we'll have to make do with a ride on the Dockers' Umbrella.'

Agatha thought that Max's enjoyment had rivalled her own, and hers had been considerably increased by Max's knowledge of the vast variety of shipping in the docks. He had been able to point out corvettes, sloops, merchantmen, destroyers and many others, explaining to Agatha how the fighting ships would accompany convoys of merchantmen as they undertook the perilous crossing of the Atlantic, harassing the wolfpack, as they called the German U-boats, and attacking enemy shipping if it came heading for their convoy.

They had disembarked from the Overhead Railway at Seaforth Sands and walked into the village, where

Max had hailed a taxi, saying that there was little point in taking the Overhead Railway back to the city since they would be unable to see anything because of the blackout. In Liverpool once more, Max had bought the *Echo* and they had consulted the list of films showing at local cinemas. They had made their choice, which was an early performance since Max meant to catch a train to Durham which would leave Lime Street Station just after eight that evening, and they had taken their seats in the darkened cinema side by side, in comfortable companionship.

When Max had taken her hand in order that he might pull her closer, and whispered that he wished the lady in the row in front would take off her hat, she had felt her cheeks grow hot and thought about pulling her hand discreetly away, then decided against it. She had heard girls talking about trips to the cinema when she had been in college, and knew that handholding was the norm. The girls called a trip to the cinema 'four penn'orth of dark', and judging from what some girls said, holding a fellow's hand was almost obligatory if he paid for your ticket. Besides, Agatha realised that the feel of his hand in hers was comforting, and if it was the same for him, why should she deny him such comfort? Very soon he would be far away, in a foreign country, and she had to admit to herself that she would very much rather he remembered holding her hand in the darkened cinema with pleasure than that he should look around him for some more willing cinema-going handholder.

Presently the credits began to roll and the lights went up. Max helped her into her coat, asking her where they should go for a snack since he would not reach Durham until very late that night.

'Honestly, Max, we've been eating all day,' Agatha protested, though only half-heartedly. They had emerged from the warm cinema into a freezing street and the thought of a hot drink was attractive. Furthermore, she was enjoying her very first outing with a man who seemed to relish her company, and did not want it to end. 'Besides, your train leaves in just over an hour, so we can't go far from the station; you'll want to he first on board so you can get a corner seat so you can snooze,' she added.

'Very well. I had intended to take you home, but I'll put you into a taxi, if that's all right, with instructions to the driver to take great care of you,' Max said. 'As you say, we can't go far from the station in search of the aforementioned snack, so we'll go to the buffet; then as soon as my train arrives I'll bag that corner seat you spoke of and get someone to keep an eye on it for me whilst I take you to the taxi rank.' He smiled down at her. 'Agreed?'

Agatha began to protest that she could perfectly well catch a tram – or even walk – but though he grinned at her, he also shook his head. 'None of that independent spirit, young lady,' he said. 'When I say taxi I mean taxi. Remember you've done some shopping yourself and those parcels are quite heavy. Now come along! I know a railway buffet isn't as glamorous as the Adelphi, but right now it fits the bill.'

They found a corner table in the buffet and sat with cups of coffee before them, Agatha at least feeling a little anxious, wondering how they would part. She supposed they would shake hands, promise to write and then go out to the taxi. She had already made up her mind, however, that she would dump her parcels in the cab, ask the driver to keep an eye on them, and rush back to the station. She was suddenly determined that she would wave him off; it was the least she could do in return for such a wonderful day.

At first, conversation was jerky, but then Max began to talk about his fellow officers and Agatha laughed at the exploits he related. She told him that she thought life in the services must be fun and he pulled a wry face, admitting that it was certainly different from anything he had experienced before. However, he could not quite forget Spain and the horrors that he and fellow members of the International Brigade had endured. Agatha, seeing the pain in his eyes, said hastily that the Civil War was best forgotten.

Max seemed about to agree with her, then shook his head. 'No, my dear; forewarned is forearmed. It's foolish of me to deny you knowledge of what happened in Spain and might happen here. I've seen for myself how very ill prepared we are for what is to come. Germany has been ready for war – eager for it – for several years. In his evil, cold-blooded way, Hitler used the Civil War as a sort of practice ground for a larger conflict. I'm proud of the pilots and planes which we do have, but they're a drop in the ocean compared with the Luftwaffe, who will attack with tremendous ferocity. Their bombing is deadly accurate, they seldom miss; it's said that putting a big red cross upon the roofs of hospitals and convalescent homes was madness, because the German pilots use the crosses for target practice and score a bull's-eye every time. I wish I knew some magic formula to keep you and your mother – and everyone I love – safe, but I don't. All I can do is advise you to get into the deepest cellar you can find as soon as the siren sounds, or to a public shelter, of course; I take it they're being built?'

'I believe so,' Agatha said. 'And then there are those Anderson things; we've ordered one as our house hasn't got a cellar, but it's not arrived yet. The government have issued information leaflets saying that if you've not got a cellar, the cupboard under the stairs is almost as good. The library has a large basement area where the staff could go in case of daylight raids, and there's a public shelter being built nearby. So you see we have a choice of bolt-holes.' She smiled at him a little uncertainly. 'Have you any more advice to hand out, Flight Lieutenant?'

Max smiled back. 'Yes, I have. Take a supply of food and a flask of hot tea to whichever bolt-hole is nearest. You'll need to wear your warmest clothing, and I'd advise taking a couple of blankets and pillows with you. I've seen drawings of the proposed public shelters, though I've not visited one yet. They have wooden bunks which are available on a first come first served basis, which is why I said get to some sort of shelter as soon as the warning sounds. And once there, no nipping out to see what's going on until you hear the all clear; a friend of mine in Spain was killed doing just that.'

'I'll do as you say,' Agatha said submissively, but she reflected that she, at any rate, was unlikely to be in a shelter during a raid since she had already volunteered both to fire-watch and to help in any way she could. But it would not do to increase Max's worries by telling him this.

'Oh, God, I wish . . .' Max said fervently. 'But it's no good repining, only it seems all wrong that I'm going off to comparative safety, leaving you – and my family of course – to face up to danger without me. I shall write to you, giving you my new address, as soon as I'm able. Please write back, and often, because every time a letter arrives I shall know you're still safe.'

'I'll write,' Agatha promised. 'And I'll write often, truly I will. But as for leaving us in danger, you must have forgotten that getting to wherever the air force send you will mean crossing large areas of ocean. You told me earlier today how the wolfpack attacks convoys, so you will be even more at risk than we are. And don't pretend that the Luftwaffe wouldn't dream of attacking a British ship, because I'm afraid I wouldn't believe you. So I shall await your first letter just as eagerly as you will await mine.'

Max grinned and opened his mouth to reply just as the rattle and roar of an arriving train made speech impossible for a moment, during which time he got to his feet and pulled Agatha to hers. They headed for the platform, still hand in hand. 'It's my train, I think,' Max shouted above the tremendous din. 'Agatha, I've been meaning to ask you . . .'

A guard, blowing his whistle, came along the platform; doors crashed open and slammed shut and men in uniform poured out, shouting and grinning. Max made for the nearest carriage, hefted his suitcase aboard, then jumped up after it. 'Stay there,' he mouthed. 'Don't move an inch; I'll just put my case on a corner seat, as we said.' Seconds later he was out again, breathing hard. 'Bit of luck; a fellow in the carriage says he'll watch my suitcase for five minutes.'

He grinned at her, a flash of white teeth in his tanned face, for the station was dimly lit, as were the carriages themselves, and caught Agatha's hand. They hurried across the concourse, but as they went under the high arch which led to Lime Street he glanced up and then, to Agatha's complete astonishment, stopped short, pulled her into his arms and, before she knew what was happening, started to kiss her. Agatha melted against him, her lips, at first astonished, beginning to soften beneath his. Then he released her, pointing upwards to the dimly seen arch above their heads. 'Did you see the mistletoe?' he asked, still holding her in his arms. 'You must know that a fellow can kiss a girl – any girl – underneath the mistletoe at Christmas time! Oh, Agatha, my dear, I'm going to miss you! Promise me you'll do as I suggested and take good care of yourself. I hate to leave you when we've barely become acquainted, but I dare not risk seeing my luggage go off to Durham without me.'

Agatha was speechless, her lips still burning from his kiss. Her very first kiss, she realised as they ran, still hand in hand, towards a waiting taxi. Max tugged the door open, gave the driver some coins and pushed Agatha inside. He gave her the briefest of brief waves and disappeared into the station concourse once more. Agatha put her parcels on the seat, then leaned forward and shot back the glass panel which separated the driver from his passengers. 'You will wait for me, won't you?' she said breathlessly, already opening the taxi door. 'There's something I forgot; I won't be a minute, honestly I won't.'

The taxi driver grinned at her, showing a fine display of long, yellow teeth. 'Give 'im a kiss from me, queen,' he shouted. 'I see'd you at it earlier, but I'll wait. He's generous with his dosh, your feller.'

Agatha smiled but vouchsafed no reply, and even as she hurried across the concourse it occurred to her how she had changed after her day with Max. Normally, she would have snubbed the taxi driver, but that was before she had been kissed. Now, as she went towards the train, which was getting up steam, she told herself that it had just been a mistletoe kiss and everyone knows that a mistletoe kiss means nothing. She supposed in a way that it was a thank you for a day they had both enjoyed; she must be careful not to read too much into it.

All around her, she realised, as she crossed to the still stationary train, people were kissing. Men were going away or coming home, women were greeting or bidding farewell. Clearly, Max's kiss had been very much on a par with a handshake; she would put it out of her mind. Yet even as she limped along, searching for his carriage, she could not quite banish the lovely warm glow that his kiss – his closeness – had lit in her breast.

Presently, she spotted Max and rapped on the pane, thinking how unlike her it was to make a spectacle of herself. He turned his head, saw her and got to his feet even as the train began to move. He was mouthing something, she did not know what, but she limped alongside the train, cursing her clubfoot which never allowed her to hurry, always threatening to turn her ankle, if she tried to move too fast, and deposit her on the ground.

He was breathing on the pane, trying to write a message; then he must have realised she was falling behind and for a moment he disappeared, then appeared again, pulling down the sash window of the door and leaning out to wave. She could see he was speaking, but now he was too far away for her to even guess at his words. Nevertheless she remained on the platform, waving and waving until the train was out of sight. Only then did she force herself to leave.

When she reached the arch she looked up, but could see nothing in the dim blue light which was all that was allowed. She wondered for a moment how someone had managed to get a bunch of mistletoe up to such a height, then put it out of her mind, because it was not important. She had had a wonderful, unforgettable day, and though she would still have repudiated even the suggestion that she and Max were more than just friends, she hugged the memory of his kiss, and the warm glow which had followed it, to her breast. She would tell no one, not even dear little Hetty, but she was beginning to believe that perhaps she was not just a plain, foreign-looking cripple, but a woman who could be desirable – perhaps really was desired.

She reached the taxi and was rather touched when the driver hopped out and came round to the rear door, holding it open for her. 'Hop in, princess,' he said grandly, giving her a mock bow so low that his nose nearly touched his knees. He straightened and grinned at her. 'Find the boyfriend?' he enquired genially. 'Bet he were surprised to see you, havin' said his goodbyes earlier.'

Agatha, settling comfortably into her seat, said that her friend had indeed been surprised. 'But this was his embarkation leave so we may not meet for months, possibly years,' she explained. 'I think it's nice to be waved off when you're leaving for foreign parts.'

The driver nodded sagely, selected a gear and stuck his hand out of the window to indicate that he was drawing into the main stream of traffic. Agatha watched the cars and lorries crawling past, their hooded lights making any sort of speed impossible.

She knew Max had paid the taxi driver to take her to Everton Terrace, and now she gathered her parcels together, for the vehicle was nearing her destination. Then she frowned; there was one parcel too many! Hastily, she checked. She had bought crystallised fruits for her mother and Mrs Simpson, as well as a pretty brooch in the form of a tiny bunch of miniature violets for Mrs Preece. Then there was a scarlet woolly hat and scarf for Hetty, and some fruit which she and her mother would eat over the holiday. Heavens, whatever would she do if she had inadvertently picked up one of Max's purchases along with her own? She would have to post it to his Durham address . . . which, she realised with dismay, she did not have! Quickly, she checked the parcels again and picked out the one that she could not identify. It was a smallish, square box, wrapped in brown paper and . . . oh, goodness! Written on it, in Max's clear, decided hand were the words: *Happy Christmas, dear Agatha, and thank you for a wonderful day. Take care of yourself, Max.*

Agatha's hands flew to her hot cheeks. He had bought her a Christmas present and she had not reciprocated . . . oh, God, she should have realised, should have guessed . . . but it was too late for regrets. Unless she could rush up to the shops before the library opened next morning and buy something, despatch it . . .

To where, you fool, Agatha's practical mind asked scornfully. Moments ago, when you thought the parcel might be one that he had inadvertently left behind, you realised you didn't have his Durham address. Oh, what on earth can I do? It was awfully kind of him to buy me a gift, but I wish to God he hadn't!

Chapter Fourteen

Agatha and Hetty met on Christmas Eve to exchange presents, and as soon as they left the library and turned their steps towards Everton Terrace, Agatha poured out the story of the gift which Max had given her and which she had been unable to thank him for, let alone reciprocate. The two friends were walking along Heyworth Street, and doing so with caution for the pavements were frosted. Hetty longed to take Agatha's arm, but knew it would be resented, for her friend was very independent with regard to her mobility.

'That is awkward,' Hetty agreed when she had heard the full story. 'But the professor must realise that you don't know his parents' address and will understand why you can't thank him for his present, let alone buy him something in return. What was it, by the way? The gift, I mean.'

'I shouldn't really have opened it until tomorrow, but I did, of course,' Agatha confessed. She fished in her handbag, which she wore school-satchel fashion across her shoulder, and produced a small box which she handed to Hetty. 'Go on, open it!'

Hetty complied, and gasped. Nestling in tissue paper was the prettiest, daintiest necklace she had ever seen. It was a crystal pendant in the shape of a teardrop hanging from a slender gold chain, and when Hetty looked at her friend she saw tears shining in the older woman's eyes. 'Oh, Agatha, it's beautiful, and it does prove he likes you a lot. You should be really proud; if it were mine, I'd wear it all the time.' Agatha sniffed, pulled out her hanky, and blew her nose. 'But why are you crying, you silly goose?'

'I'm crying because it never occurred to me to buy him so much as a few sweets,' Agatha mumbled. 'Oh, Hetty, I don't even know if he likes chocolates, or needs a warm scarf or gloves! Even if I knew his parents' address, I'd be hard put to it to know what to buy him.'

'You could buy him cufflinks for his shirts, or a cigarette lighter,' Hetty said. 'That's what I bought for my cousins: a cigarette lighter for Tom, because he smokes, and cufflinks for Bill because he doesn't – smoke, I mean. Or you could simply buy him twenty Players, or some pipe tobacco . . .'

'I don't know if he smokes,' Agatha wailed. 'I don't know anything about him. Oh, I feel so mean.'

'Don't be so silly. If he's as nice as you think he is, then he won't expect you to buy him anything, so don't you dare let it spoil your Christmas,' Hetty said as they reached Everton Terrace. 'Hey, I've thought of something! You're on the telephone, aren't you? Ring the operator and ask for his number, and when you get it, ring up, thank him for his present and get his Durham address.'

Agatha thought this a brilliant idea, but it turned out to be a non-starter since Agatha knew neither Max's

father's initials nor his address, and lacking this information the operator refused to give Agatha the number,
even though the name Galera must surely be unusual
in Durham. She had made the phone call as soon as
they entered the house, but by the time they sat down
to the meal Mrs Simpson had prepared for them she
had decided to take Hetty's advice and put the matter
out of her mind. 'He promised to write as soon as he
had his new address,' she said, 'and as soon as he does
so, I shall buy him the very nicest cufflinks available
and send them off, along with a letter of thanks for
my beautiful Christmas necklace.'

When it was time for Hetty to leave, presents were
exchanged and much laughter followed when Hetty
exclaimed with pleasure over her scarlet woolly hat
and scarf, and Agatha did likewise over the identical
set in white which Hetty had bought for her. Then
they had to say goodbye, knowing that this time they
might not meet for many weeks, perhaps even
months. 'But I'll write just as regularly to you, Agatha,
as I will to Gramps and Gran,' Hetty promised. 'I'll
write to Aunt Phoebe as well, of course, but not so
often because I know she hates letter writing and will
only respond to the longest letter with scrappy little
notes.'

Agatha took her coat from the hallstand and strug-
gled into it. 'I'll walk as far as the corner with you,'
she said. 'And you may be sure that I shall look forward
to your letters with real eagerness and will reply at
length, because I know you'll be interested in everything that happens in the library.'

They stepped out into the icy dusk and were at the end of Everton Terrace when, for the first time in her life, Hetty stood on tiptoe and kissed the librarian's cheek. 'Thank you for everything, Agatha,' she said huskily. 'And look out for my letters, because every time we moor up, in London or Birmingham, I'll post one off to you and expect to get one in return. Oh, Agatha, I do hope Sally, Alice and myself will be able to manage the *Shamrock* and the *Clover* when there's no older, more experienced person to advise us.'

Hetty was on the tiller, Alice on the butty boat and Sally dealing with the engine when the blizzard hit them. They had been aboard for two complete trips, fully laden in both directions, and had, Hetty thought, managed very well, despite the deteriorating weather conditions. She had been worried at first that she would not remember the procedure which in days gone by she had been able to follow in her sleep, but this had not proved to be the case. Once they were laden and put-putting in the right direction, even Alice, the only true novice on board, had quickly learned most of the essentials.

Even before the blizzard struck they had begun to lose track of where they were, but now, with dusk about to fall and the wind and snow completely hiding their surroundings, they could easily be in deep trouble. The snow was blowing horizontally in their faces, and even when they switched on the headlight, which was hooded as were road traffic lights, all they could see were whirling flakes. Hetty cast one horrified glance ahead, then raised her voice in a scream. 'I can't see a perishin' thing through the snow, even with the headlight on,' she shrieked. 'Sally, can you hear me? I'm going to steer for the bank, because we'll have to moor up until the storm passes.'

Sally's head popped out of the engine room. 'I heard you. I'll throttle back and give Alice a shout to tell her that we're going to sit out the storm moored up,' she yelled. 'This perishin' storm's no joke, though; it's so dark it could be midnight, but it can't be more than four o'clock, if that.'

Hetty heard the engine noise drop as she steered to where she hoped the bank lay, and to her immense relief she found it, noting that it was a length of towpath, uncluttered by reeds. She steered her craft carefully until the *Shamrock*'s nose bumped the bank, then jumped ashore and tied up whilst Alice did the same for the butty.

By the time they had moored both craft, she and Alice looked like snowmen. Then all three made hastily for the cabin, so that they could discuss what they should do. In the delicious warmth – for they never let the fire in the stove go out – they relaxed for the first time for several hours, rubbing their icy hands and shedding their snow-covered garments as they entered. Quickly, they donned dry jerseys and trousers, then hung their wet things on the rope stretched across the cabin for use when the engine was not running, and looked enquiringly at one another.

They had not intended to moor up for a while, meaning to draw into a particular wharf where a fish and chip van visited on a regular basis. This vehicle kept to a strict timetable and was due this very evening. The three girls had been looking forward to a fish and chip supper, and had done nothing towards preparing a meal. Knowing this, Hetty looked enquiringly at her companions. Since she was acting as Number One for this trip, she felt it incumbent upon her to decide what to do. 'If the weather wasn't so dreadful, I'd vote for going on,' she said. 'But if we can't we can't, and I believe that pressing on when I can scarcely see my hand in front of my face is a recipe for disaster. Colliding with another boat might well be the end not only of the *Shamrock*, but of her crew as well. I know it's disappointing, and if the snow clears and the wind drops then of course we'll press on, but in the meantime we can check over our stores and decide what we'll have to eat. Alice, you're the nearest; what tins have we got?'

Alice got up from the bench on which she had been sitting and lifted the seat to reveal storage space packed with tinned goods. 'There's four tins of soup, two of baked beans and two of spaghetti,' she said. 'They're the ones on top; stuff like tinned peaches and peas and sardines are underneath; I can't see them but I know they're there. So that means either soup or something on toast. We haven't any eggs, and I know we've run out of milk because we were going to buy it at the corner shop when we stopped for fish and chips. We could open a tin of conny-onny for anyone who likes a sweet cup of tea.'

Hetty began to agree that something on toast would fill the chinks, then stopped short and gave a groan. 'We've got no *bread*,' she wailed. 'Don't you remember, Sally? We gave the last couple of slices – they were pretty stale anyway – to those ducks when we were queuing for the lock.' She heaved a sigh. 'Still, we shan't starve, but we mustn't forget to stock up when the storm's over. Only if you ask me, it's set in for the night; how the wind howls!'

Alice shuddered and clutched her dry jersey round her. She was a slender girl with long, shiny hair the colour of polished oak, and a pair of innocent blue eyes. When Hetty had first met her, she had wondered whether the other girl would be able to cope with the physical work of the boat, which demanded a good deal of strength, but Alice, as Sally had remarked, seemed to be made of whipcord and did her share and more of any heavy lifting without waiting to be asked.

Now, Hetty wagged a finger at Alice and intoned, in a hollow voice: *''Twas a dark and stormy night, three men sat round a fire, and one of them said, Antonio, tell us a tale, so Antonio began . . .'*

''Twas a dark and stormy night, three *girls* sat round a fire . . .' Alice and Sally chorused, then broke down in giggles.

'What a night for telling ghost stories this would be,' Hetty remarked, holding out her hands to the stove. 'But I don't think we'd better start frightening ourselves into a fit, because we've got nowhere to run! In fact, I could do with a cup of tea while we vote on what to have for supper. Pull the kettle over the fire, Alice – I filled it up earlier – and . . .' She stopped speaking, for at that moment the girls heard a very loud splash and a shout, and then the boat rocked violently. 'What the devil was that? Not a ghost, I trust!'

All three girls jumped to their feet and Hetty, who was nearest the door, clambered into the well and stared into the teeth of the storm. At first she saw nothing, but then something – or someone – rose out of the water, frightening her so much that she screamed before realising that the dripping figure was a mere man and not some sort of mythological creature come to haunt them.

Hastily she scrambled out on to the bank, closely followed by the other two, and snatched up a boat hook, pushing it in the general direction of the dripping figure. 'Grab hold of that,' she shouted sharply. 'Hold tight and we'll pull you out.' She turned to Sally and Alice. 'Some fool's run straight into the canal,' she told them. 'Ah, he's got the boat hook; give me a hand, girls.' She addressed the dripping, shivering figure, up to his armpits in icy water. 'Don't worry, we'll have you out in two ticks, but for God's sake don't let go of the boat hook!'

The man shouted agreement, his voice scarcely audible above the howling of the storm, and Hetty thanked her stars that the canal was only about five feet deep at this point. Even so, it took the combined efforts of all three girls, and the dripping victim, to get him out of the water, and when at last he stood shivering violently on the bank and was beginning to thank them Hetty cut him short.

'You can tell us how wonderful we are once you're in the cabin,' she told him sharply. 'And you can tell us how you ended up in the canal, as well,' she added as the man tried, rather feebly, to wring the water out of his heavy overcoat.

'Thanks, girls,' he said through chattering teeth. 'God knows what would have happened to me if you'd not been close by. I'm really grateful . . .'

'Don't waste your breath,' Hetty advised. 'C'mon, into the cabin.' She grabbed his hand and towed him to the *Shamrock*, and no more words were exchanged until they were all inside, the man having to bend his head since he was a good six feet tall and narrow boat cabins are low-ceilinged.

Once the doors were shut, Sally whipped one of her blankets from its cupboard and gave it to their visitor. 'Take off your wet things,' she said briskly. 'I dare say you think we ought to go outside whilst you undress, but I'm afraid that's out of the question. Just remove all your upper clothing and then tie the blanket round your waist before you slip off your trousers, and the decencies will be preserved.'

Hetty could not hide a smile and began to help the man out of his heavy coat, for he was fumbling help-lessly at the buttons; it was plain that his fingers were numb with cold. She did not look up into his face, but kept her own gaze lowered until he had stripped to the waist. Then he tucked the blanket round himself, slipped out of his sodden trousers and kicked off his already unlaced boots.

Respectably draped in the blanket, he sat down by the fire and began to rub himself dry with the towel Hetty offered him. 'You must think me the most awful fool even to be out on such a hellish night ...' he began, then stared up at Hetty, his eyes rounding. 'My God, Hetty, is it really you?'

Hetty gasped. Now that she looked closely at the young man, she could only marvel that she had not recognised her childhood enemy at once. 'Gareth!' she exclaimed. 'What on earth are you doing here? The last I heard of you, you were on some sort of an engineering course, then your parents moved away and we didn't hear anything else.' She laughed, and turned to Sally and Alice, who were staring at her open-mouthed. 'Sorry, girls. Have I never mentioned a horrible, red-headed boy who lived next door to us and made my life a misery when I was a little kid?' Gareth made protesting noises, which Hetty ignored. 'Well this is him, Gareth Evans, late of Salisbury Street.' She looked down at the young man, suddenly realising how much he had changed and guessing that she had changed also. 'Gareth, meet my crew; Sally's the blonde and Alice the brunette. And girls, I've just remembered, Gareth used to work for my grandfather aboard the *Water Sprite*, so he knows – or used to know rather – a good deal about canal boats.'

She turned back to Gareth. His water-darkened hair

was beginning to dry to the flaming red she remembered and his face had been wiped clean of mud, and once again she wondered how on earth she had not recognised him straight away. But it had been years since they had last met, and it had not occurred to her that she might meet him here, let alone up to his chest in the canal. She was beginning to ask him just how he had come to plunge into the water when the kettle whistled and Sally leapt to make the tea, whilst Alice produced the tin of biscuits and offered them round.

Hetty waited until everyone was provided with a cup of tea and a couple of ginger nuts, then looked enquiringly at Gareth. 'Well? What were you doing, going for a swim in the canal in the middle of a blizzard? Come on, out with it!'

Gareth laughed and leaned across to where his greatcoat hung, dripping, across the makeshift clothes line. He fumbled in the pocket, then brought out a sheet of paper and held it out to Hetty. 'You won't be able to read this, but I was on my way to the fish and chip van,' he said ruefully. 'The blokes had all given me their orders – they were written on that piece of paper, only the water's washed every word out – and the quickest way from our training camp to the wharf is along the towpath. Having worked on canals myself, I usually enjoy a walk alongside the water and the fellows know it, so even when the snow started they guessed I'd be glad of the opportunity for a change of scene.'

'We were going to have fish and chips tonight,' Sally put in. 'But when the blizzard blew up we were too afraid of an accident if we kept going; a collision is always bad, but in this sort of weather it could be fatal . . .'

'And we really don't know where we are,' Alice said rather plaintively. 'Even when we get nearer to civilisation, where there are landmarks such as warehouses and so on alongside the canal, we won't be able to see them.'

'Yes, but that doesn't explain how you came to fall in,' Hetty said accusingly to their visitor, 'and you a member of the *Water Sprite*'s crew for long enough to be wary of a swim in midwinter. Don't tell me you jumped in on purpose, because I'm afraid I shan't believe you.'

Gareth chuckled and dunked his ginger biscuit into his cup of tea, then bit into it and spoke with his mouth full. 'If you want the plain, unvarnished truth, it was your fault,' he said, grinning round at the three girls. 'I'd crossed several fields and reached the towpath, or rather I thought I had – snow changes everything, doesn't it, and of course I could see very little with it blowing into my face. Usually, I cross on to the towpath by climbing over a stile, but this evening I couldn't see it. The snow was a good way up the hedges and laying fast, so I found a thin bit of hedge and pushed my way through . . .'

'That will please some poor farmer,' Hetty muttered, giving her old enemy an accusing look. Gareth must know as well as she did herself that it was one of the deadly sins of farming to make a hole in a hedge through which stock might escape.

Gareth gave her a shame-faced look. 'Yes, I know what you mean, but I was lost, queen, and beginning to get pretty anxious. I thought I'd reached the towpath – hoped I had, rather – but I couldn't be sure. Then I saw light ahead of me and I just thought I'd found a cottage with its blackout curtains carelessly drawn. I decided I'd best make my way there and ask directions. Then I saw what I thought was a tarmac road and stepped on to it, only to find myself plunging into ice-cold water. I gave a bit of a yell, hoping that someone from the cottage would come to my rescue . . .' he grinned round apologetically at them and drained his mug of tea, 'and the rest you know,' he finished.

'Well, someone did come to your rescue,' Sally said brightly. She took Gareth's empty mug and refilled it from the teapot, then waved a spoon at him. 'Do you want it black, or with conny-onny? Only we're clean out of milk, and bread as well. We meant to buy some when we got the fish and chips, in fact we had quite a little shopping list, but the blizzard put a stop to all that.'

'I'll have it with conny-onny, ta,' Gareth said, grinning broadly. 'Eh, it's good to hear someone talking Scouse for a change. How long did it take you to say shopping, or errands, instead of messages? The first time I said messages, the fellers in my hut thought I were a German spy! Oh, and when I spoke Welsh to a pal who came in for training, I got even more suspicious looks.'

The girls laughed. 'I didn't know you spoke Welsh,'

Hetty said. 'As for Scouse expressions, it's not so bad for us because we're all from Liverpool. But I see from your uniform that you're in the air force, so there'll be men in your camp from all over the country, I suppose. Which branch, or section, or whatever, are you in?'

'I'm a flight mechanic; at the moment I'm working on the kites used for training would-be pilots, which is fairly interesting, but I hope to be posted to an operational station – we call them stations, not camps – once the war hots up a bit and the high-ups get their act together. Things are pretty chaotic at the moment; I expect it's the same with the Inland Waterways Board. Or are they more organised?'

'I don't know,' Hetty said. She turned to her friends. 'What do you think?'

Sally pulled a doubtful face. 'It's difficult to judge, because this is only our third trip, and when things go wrong we blame ourselves.' She grinned at the young man, whose clothing was now steaming gently, and leaned down to turn his coat, since one side was already almost dry. 'Because of the weather we haven't always arrived when expected, which has meant hanging around, waiting for our return load. But you've worked the canals, so you know it isn't . . . it isn't . . .'

Hetty laughed, and helped Sally out. 'Working a canal boat isn't an exact science, as my old physics teacher used to say, and the Inland Waterways people know it and work round it, so to speak. Gramps concentrated on carrying foodstuffs, fleeces, cotton and so on, so the *Sprite* didn't need an enormous clean between loads. But now there's a war on we have to take all sorts, even coal, and as you can imagine cleaning the boat out when she's been carrying coal and is about to be laden with flour or sugar is no sinecure.'

'Gosh, no; how the devil do you do it?' Gareth asked.

Hetty gave him a small and rather grudging smile. Despite the fact that several years had passed, she could not completely forget how the two of them had sparred and argued, and called each other names. And though he was three years the elder, Gareth had some-times used his superior strength to trip her up, or tug a loose strand of her hair, and on one occasion steal her half-eaten apple and crunch the remains of it down, grinning tauntingly as he did so. But he was obviously still interested in life on the canal, though he had been out of it for years. I really must forget the old Gareth and give him a chance to prove he's a different person, she told herself.

'Well, Hetty? How do you manage the clean-up which is necessary between trips?'

Hetty gave herself a shake. 'There's a special wharf with a chute which loads us with loose coal, and one with a scoop crane which removes it at the other end of the trip,' she told him. 'Then we brush and scrub and wash until the boat's impeccable, and go on to another wharf where our return load will be put aboard. We don't do any of the heavy lifting, which is all done by mechanical means. In fact, apart from cleaning down between loads, all we have to do at either end of our voyage is sheeting up . . . and if you remember, that really is a horrible business.'

'I remember,' Gareth said ruefully. 'But do you have the strength to heave the planks which support the canvas sheeting into position? No doubt you fasten the canvases over whatever your load happens to be with no trouble at all, but the planks are damned heavy and difficult to handle because they get slippery, I remember that too.' He looked at Alice, thoughtfully brushing out her long, damp hair, and caught her eye, then raised his brows. 'If you'll forgive me, you don't look strong enough . . .'

All three girls laughed and Sally answered for her friend. 'Hetty and myself thought the same when we first met up, but Alice's fragility is just an illusion. She's as strong as any feller, is our Alice!'

'She needs to be; we all need to be. Just starting the engine, as you'll remember, takes every ounce of one's strength,' Hetty said ruefully. 'But what's worrying me right now is you, Flight Mechanic Evans! What will your pals think when you fail to turn up with their grub? Suppose they send out a search party? I feel we ought to make our way to your camp – sorry, station – just to let them know that you aren't lying in a field somewhere, a frozen corpse, but I don't fancy going out into that blizzard, even armed with a torch.'

'You won't have to; when I saw how bad the weather was, I said I might have to take shelter until it eased. There's a pub quite near where the fish and chip van stops, so they'll think I've gone in there.' He rose to

326

his feet, clutching his blanket, and winced as his head cracked against the cabin roof. 'Ouch! Doesn't it just show how much I've grown since I worked the canals!' He felt his clothes, steaming merrily before the stove, then sat down again. 'They'll be ready to wear in another hour or so.' He grinned engagingly at them. 'I know you've run out of bread and milk, but if I promise faithfully to bring you a supply as soon as the shops open tomorrow morning, can I snitch another biscuit? Honest to God, girls, I'm famished!'

Once Gareth had left them, with promises to walk the towpath next day until he reached the first wharf if necessary, carrying a large canvas bag full of food – they had lent him the canvas bag – the girls settled down for the night, fully expecting to find the weather cleared by the morning.

Hetty was the first to awaken, but though she tried to slip soundlessly from her sleeping bag to take a peep through the little glass panel in the door, the movement woke both Alice and Sally. On this occasion Alice was lying on the floor, whilst the other two girls occupied the narrow wooden bunks, since they took it in turns to use the berths. In summer, one of the girls would occupy the tiny cabin on the butty boat, but in winter they preferred to cram into the main cabin, which was comfortably warmed by the stove.

Sally opened one eye, mumbled something and heaved her sleeping bag up until only the top of her curly head showed. But Alice, whose turn it was to cook, reached for her jersey and pulled it on before scrambling to her feet and lifting the filled kettle on to the top of the stove. 'What's the weather like?' she asked as Hetty rubbed steam from the tiny window. 'The wind's dropped; didn't it howl last night? I thought I'd never be able to sleep, but I dropped off in the end.'

Hetty withdrew from the window, giving a tremendous yawn as she did so. 'I didn't sleep for ages either because I was worrying about Gareth. I kept remembering what I'd said about a frozen corpse and wondering whether we should have let him leave when he did. His greatcoat wasn't too bad, but his trousers and boots were still pretty wet when he left. You're right, the wind has dropped, but it's still snowing. I hope the canal is not frozen – I know it wasn't yesterday or he wouldn't have been able to fall into it, but if there was a hard frost last night I shouldn't think we'll make it to the unloading wharf, and if we miss Gareth he'll have walked all that way for nothing.'

The girls never undressed completely when they went to bed, only shedding jerseys, dungarees and trousers, and since water was at a premium, very little washing was done. Fortunately, a kindly woman at Leighton always offered them the chance of a hot dip, and most of the large towns en route had public baths. The girls took it in turns to leave the boat and make their way to the nearest bathhouse, where, for a small sum, they were able to revel in a tub full of hot water, a bar of soap and a fluffy towel. It was wonderful to get out of garments stiff with oil, dust and quite often, Hetty feared, sweat, which they had worn for at least a week. When the opportunity occurred, the girls washed their filthy clothes and dried them on lines they had erected across the engine room, which was the warmest place when they were under power. Each girl had only one change of clothing because they were so short of space, and though they did what they could they knew they seldom looked their best.

Hetty was just glad that Gareth had been too pre-occupied with his own woes to comment upon the fact that his hostesses had draggly hair, smuts of coal dust on cheek and chin, and hands which were downright filthy. However, if they were stuck here for a bit they could walk into the nearest town and take advantage of the baths, as well as making good all the deficien-cies in their food supply.

'Tea's up!' That was Alice, pouring three mugs. 'I say, Hetty, I think I'll have my hair cut when we reach the city. Washing long hair is a real chore when you have to do it in your bath-time, so to speak. Anyone fancy a tin of baked beans with no accompanying toast? Or we can leave breakfast until we reach civilisation once more and can buy some bread.'

'I'll have mine later,' Hetty said, pulling on her serge trousers and donning her leather boots. She reached for her waterproofs, put them on, opened the double doors and stepped into the well. There was a shriek of protest from Sally as wind and snow blew in and Hetty, giggling, closed the doors all but a crack. She had already taken a hasty look at the water and seen that it was only covered with cat ice, through which the *Shamrock* would make her way with no trouble. She shouted as much to the two girls within the cabin, adding the information that she would be obliged if they'd join her as soon as possible, so that they could get moving. She looked out at the bank, hoping to see footprints that would show her which way Gareth had come and gone, but though the snow was easing off it had been sufficient to cover any tracks made the previous day.

Even as she made her way towards the engine room, however, the flakes ceased to fall altogether. When the other two joined her, she began to give her orders. 'Sally, you push over the compression lever at the count of three; Alice and I will work the starting handle.' She and Alice began to turn the handle and the enormous flywheel, which took up a great deal of space in the cramped surroundings, began to revolve. Hetty and Alice increased the speed until Hetty shouted, 'One, two, three.' Immediately, Sally pushed the lever and the engine burst into life. The other two released the starting handle and they all three scrambled out of the engine room.

Hetty and Sally untied the ropes which attached the *Shamrock* and the *Clover* to the towpath, and very soon they were put-putting up the canal, the boat's progress not in the least impeded by the slight covering of ice. Hetty sighed with relief. Any minute they might come across Gareth, hopefully laden with a large bag of food. Normally, they would have stopped at the first farm they saw, to buy fresh milk and anything else the farm had to offer, but because of her anxiety for Gareth Hetty just wanted to push on, and since she was Number One for this trip it was she who decided how they should proceed.

As they neared the wharf she was relieved to see Gareth's tall, greatcoated figure hurrying towards them, accompanied by another couple, similarly clad. She had seldom thought of Gareth since he had moved away, but now she realised that she liked the new version very much, considerably more than she had liked the old one. Even the memory of his teasing and their constant quarrels seemed to have been softened by time into the sort of treatment brothers and sisters habitually endure. Now that they had met up again, she realised that the old enmity was dead. She and her crew would be travelling up and down the Grand Union Canal for as long as the war lasted, and if Gareth remained at Upper Heyford for the same length of time he would surely want to meet up again to talk of old times and old friends.

Then there were the two fellows with him, even now beginning to grin as they neared the *Shamrock* and her butty. She and Sally often bemoaned the fact that when they tied up near Birmingham they were unable to leave the canal boat unmanned in order to go dancing, see a film or even visit the big shops together. Because it was impossible to render the *Shamrock* and the *Clover* safe from the young thieves who haunted the wharves, they had made it a rule always to have one girl aboard each boat. Hetty knew that none of them had much enjoyed their solitary expeditions, but now that they knew where Gareth was, things might change. The young men even now strolling towards them looked friendly; she would invite them aboard, and if they all got on, perhaps it might be fun for Sally and Alice as well as herself to have a man's company from time to time.

Chapter Fifteen

Gareth had been so late back after his involuntary dip in the canal that the other fellers in his hut had long given him, and their fish and chips, up. Next morning at breakfast they jeered at him for spending the night drinking beer at the local pub, but accepted his far more dramatic explanation. They were intrigued by the fact that his rescuers had been an all female crew of a canal boat, since they had assumed that such craft were manned by large and brawny males.

'Fancy you knowing one of them though, Ginger, you lucky dog!' his friend Phil remarked. 'If I fell in the bloody canal and a woman fished me out, she'd be ninety years old, toothless and the image of Popeye, muscles an' all.' He stared hard at Gareth. 'What were they like, these girls?'

'Young and pretty,' Gareth said promptly. 'Hetty used to be a scrawny kid, more interested in books than blokes, but I wouldn't deny she's changed. All the hard work on the boat has improved her figure . . . she's got a waist and tits and things now, though she's still no beauty. But the other two are little smashers, honest to God they are.'

They were sitting in the cookhouse, leisurely devouring a breakfast of porridge and toast, since they

333

had been stood down due to the heavy snowfall of the night before. Most of the men would go to the NAAFI, write letters, listen to the wireless or possibly play cards, but Gareth meant to keep his promise to shop for the crew of the *Shamrock* and deliver the food to them, even if it meant walking three miles or so to the nearest wharf. He said as much to Phil, who immediately offered to accompany him, as did Eamonn, a large Irishman, another friend who had listened to Gareth's story with considerable amusement.

'I'll be glad of your company, but you needn't think you're going to step in and grab the only girls for miles around,' Gareth said promptly. 'There's a nice little blonde I've earmarked for my own use.'

'She won't have you, feller, once she's set her eyes on me gorgeous body,' Eamonn said in his strong Irish accent. 'All the girls fall flat on their backs when they see my beautiful blue eyes fixed upon 'em. Why should your little blonde be any different? Besides, you said you knew one of the girls already, so she'll be the one for you, Ginger.'

'Hetty's a brunette and I've never gone for brunettes myself.' Gareth said thoughtfully. 'Still, Alice – she's the third member of the crew – is almost a blonde. At any rate, her hair's a lot lighter than Hetty's, so in the unlikely event of Sally actually overlooking my manly charms and going for a bogtrotter instead, I'll have Alice, Eamonn here can have Sally and lucky old Phil can reel in Hetty.'

Phil crunched down his last mouthful of toast, pushed back his chair and stood up. 'If those girls could

334

hear you dividing them up like so many pigs in a sty, you'd neither of you get a look in,' he observed. 'Frankly, I don't care which one I get, so long as she's warm and willing. By the way, before I offer to help you carry all this shopping, how old did you say they were? I don't mean to walk miles just to discover they're three old crones.'

Gareth finished his toast and pushed back his chair, whilst Eamonn hastily gulped the last of his mug of tea. The three of them cleaned their irons and strolled out of the cookhouse.

'Well? How old are they?' Eamonn asked suspiciously as they walked across the frozen parade ground. 'It's all very well to say young and pretty . . .'

'Hetty must be seventeen or eighteen and Alice and Sally look about the same,' Gareth told him. 'Say eighteen at a pinch, but of course the only one whose age I can be sure of is Hetty. As I said, Sally and Alice are very pretty girls, very pretty indeed. And Hetty's brainy, really clever, though I wouldn't call her pretty. She's a bit on the bossy side, sharp-tongued too. But I'm sure you'll like her.'

At this point they reached their hut, pushed open the door and hurried in, though it was very little warmer inside than out. Gareth took his coat down from its peg and jammed his cap down over his springy light red curls, then turned and faced his friends. 'Are you coming or aren't you? It's up to you, but I'm not going to hang around because I may have to walk a good way along the towpath before I find them, and though it's not snowing at the moment there's clouds up there which don't look too clever.'

Neither man answered, but they both began to put on their greatcoats, and presently the three of them set out, heading for the village where, Gareth knew, they would be able to buy bread, milk, and various other commodities. When Gareth had completed his purchases, including a bag of doughnuts as a thank you for his rescuers, they set off across the snowy fields. Gareth warned the others to steer clear of the hedgerows since ditches in deep snow can appear mere indentations, and very soon they reached the snowy stile, climbed over it and were on the towpath. Gareth pointed to the canal. 'I thought that if it was really badly iced up we'd come across the *Shamrock* near here, but it's only what you might call cat ice; they'll have to steer carefully, and put the engine into go slow mode, but they'll reach the wharf ahead of us, though not by more than perhaps half an hour.' He glanced enquiringly at his companions. 'Are you game to go on?'

'Sure and I'm not the feller to be put off by a bit of a walk, now,' Eamonn said at once. He looked up at the sky. 'Though I'd not swear to it that we'll be there before the snow starts again. Do you t'ink they'll invite us in?'

'Bound to, when they see our handsome faces, particularly mine, and all the grub we've bought them,' Phil said. 'Only from what you told us, Ginger, they have to unload this blessed ship or boat or whatever you call it, and I don't fancy being asked to give a hand with great sacks of coal or flour or whatever. The air force is really strict about keeping one's uniform clean and tidy.'

'Didn't I tell you? The loading and unloading is done by huge cranes, so your pretty hands won't get mucky,' Gareth assured them. 'It's not far now to the wharf. Step out, fellers!'

His two companions did as he suggested and began to chat, whilst Gareth grinned to himself. He thought he had done a good job of putting his friends off Hetty and on to Sally and Alice, for he had realised, whilst the girls fussed round him in the *Shamrock*'s cabin, that Hetty grown up was a very different proposition from Hetty the child. Then, he had thought her skinny and plain; now he found himself enchanted by her small, elfin face and pointy chin, by the big eyes, so dark a blue that one had to look twice to make sure they weren't black, and by the shape of her, slender yet strong. Even her hair, which he would once have described, if he had thought about it at all, as lank and mousy, was now thick and glossy and most definitely attractive, the colour of clear honey. Yes, Hetty was a real little smasher, and if anyone ended up asking her out, it must be he.

'Ginger? Is that the *Shamrock* I can see ahead? And the other one . . . can't remember its name . . . yes I can, the *Clover*?' Phil's voice rang out, reverberating across the water, for the figure which had been at the tiller of the foremost boat turned, stared and then waved. 'She's seen us . . . let's run!'

The three young men broke into a gallop, very soon

coming up alongside first the butty boat and then the *Shamrock* itself. 'Ahoy there, *Shamrock*,' Gareth shouted somewhat breathlessly. 'We've got your grub. Can we come aboard?'

Summer came, and the crew of the *Shamrock* rejoiced in the sunshine, the long, light evenings and, it must be confessed, Hetty told herself as she pinned out a line of washing above the cargo of the *Clover*, the company of any number of attractive young men. For her friendship with Gareth meant that he asked her out every time they tied up within two or three miles of Upper Heyford RAF station, and since he and his friends were now joint owners of an ancient car, they could go further afield than had ever been possible on foot.

Today, for instance, she and Gareth had planned to go in the old jalopy into the nearest town to see a flick. Hetty was looking forward to it, though she did feel a trifle apprehensive, because lately Gareth had been, as she put it, 'getting heavy'. This meant that he had not only kissed her rather forcefully when they said good-night, held her hand in the local cinema, and clutched her embarrassingly tightly when they danced together, but referred to her as 'my girl', which was going a lot too fast for Hetty. The mysterious stranger on his powerful motorcycle still intrigued her and made it impossible for her to commit to anyone else, though she admitted to herself that she was growing increasingly fond of Gareth.

Fond, however, was one thing and in love quite

338

another. Last time she and Gareth had gone dancing he had started to tell her that he was in love with her, and it was only by being both quick and tactful that she had managed to avoid a declaration. On this outing she would have to be brave and explain to him that she didn't want to consider herself as anyone's girl, or claim that one man meant more to her than any other. She hated the thought of hurting him, but if their friendship was to continue then it must be just that: a friendship.

Hetty hung the last garment on the makeshift line just as Gareth appeared, a bag in one hand and a broad grin on his freckled face. 'Hi, honey bunch,' he shouted, crossing the towpath and dropping his bag in order to put both arms round her. 'What about a kiss for your feller, eh? There's no one watching, unless you count about thirty cows all peering over that perishin' hedge.'

Hetty pretended to look around her, though with a lurking grin. 'I can't see anyone I'd describe as my feller,' she announced. 'Aha, here comes our audience, so no funny business, LAC Evans!'

Approaching them at a leisurely pace was a horse-drawn narrow boat, and Hetty stopped what she was doing to wave and call out to the elderly woman at the tiller. 'Afternoon, Mrs Buxton,' she said. 'How are you and Mr Buxton? I can see old Rupert is in fine fettle, as usual. We envy you your marvellous horse-power when our engine's playing up.'

The old lady laughed, displaying pink and tooth-less gums. 'We wouldn't see our old feller put out to grass, not for the best bleedin' engine in the world,' she said. 'I dare say you'm faster than us, but not be much, and when it comes to reliability we'd back old Rupe any day. Still, there you are; that's progress I reckons.'

'Are there many horse-drawn narrow boats still plying their trade?' Gareth asked, as the other boat passed them. He jumped aboard the *Clover*, making Hetty squeak a protest as the boat lurched. 'I know about the timber barges because we met one, if you remember, the last time you gave me a ride on your way back to the Smoke, but I didn't think there were many ordinary narrow boats still reliant on a good old nag.'

'There aren't a lot, and they're all manned by experienced boaters,' Hetty chuckled. 'But there are a great many of the big, horse-drawn barges you mentioned which carry timber or steel; loads too long or heavy for an ordinary canal boat. They used to put the fear of God into us when we met one. It just seemed impossible that we could ever get through, because they're all of fourteen feet wide, but the bargees know their business and now we exchange chat as we pass and never hang back or start sweating with fear. But Alice is in the cabin, making a cuppa. Have we got time for one?'

Gareth consulted his watch, then nodded. 'If we're quick,' he said. 'We don't want to walk in halfway through the big feature, though, and the car's parked a couple of fields away so we'll have to get a move on.'

They did so, and arrived at the cinema just as the

queue for the box office was beginning to edge forward. They joined it, and since they both preferred adventure to romance – on the screen, at any rate – they were still discussing the plot of the film they had seen as they made their way back to the car.

'Fish and chips for the whole crew?' Gareth asked as the car nosed its way carefully along the village street. 'The shop's still open and I'm flush at the moment, having not spent my week's pay on make-up or frilly underwear, the way you girls do.'

Hetty giggled. 'I'd like to see you in frilly knickers,' she said. 'As for us spending our money on such things, don't make me laugh! We've forgotten what pretty clothes look like aboard the old *Shamrock*. But we'd appreciate fish and chips if you're sure you can run to it for all of us, and yourself, of course.'

'If I have to starve for the rest of the war I'll buy fish and chips tonight,' Gareth said, bringing the car to a halt outside the small shop. The tantalising smell was the only indication that it was selling fish and chips, for its blackout was rigidly maintained. 'Because, my sweet, adorable Hetty, I've got some news which, no doubt, will dint your hard heart, if not break it. I'm off on a course in a couple of weeks. Me and Robby will soon know all there is to know about Wellingtons – the boots, you know – and when I've taken in all the knowledge available on their engines and passed whatever tests they give us, we'll be posted. Probably to somewhere in Lincolnshire, because that's where most of the heavy bombers fly from.'

Hetty stared at his profile across the darkened car.

She had told Gareth often enough that he was 'just a friend', so why should she feel so dismayed? But she put a hand on his and gave it a little squeeze. 'Well, it was what you wanted,' she said bracingly. 'Fancy the air force teaching you all about footwear! Are they a bit like Spitfires, these Wellingtons? I seem to remember someone saying . . . but no doubt your knowledge of aero-engines will come in useful.'

'Wellingtons, my dear little ignoramus, are not boots, as you know very well, and neither are they fighters; they're bombers, often called Wimpies for some little-known reason, and they're pretty big; very different from the aircraft I've been working on. So I expect not only the sort of goodnight kiss you've always denied me so far, but letters every week and promises of eternal devotion after every phone call. Right?'

'Wrong,' Hetty said promptly, for she had heard the serious note in his voice despite his light-hearted banter. 'I've told you a hundred times . . .'

'We'll have to arrange meetings every few months, or I'll go mad,' Gareth said. He no longer sounded even slightly light-hearted. 'I've told you over and over how I feel about you but we've met so often that I've not pushed it. Now, however, it's time for being a little serious. I suggest that we meet, say in five or six months' time, in some small town or large village halfway between wherever the *Shamrock* happens to be and my Lincolnshire billet. Then I'd like to book into a hotel for a couple of nights as – oh, well, I might as well be shot for a sheep as for a lamb – as Mr and Mrs Evans.' They were still sitting in the car and now he slung an arm round her shoulders, pulling her close. 'Please, Hetty, say you will!'

He accompanied the words with a kiss, his lips so warm and firm on hers that Hetty was tempted to give in, but then she remembered her mysterious motorcyclist and pushed him away. 'I won't!' she said firmly. 'Behave yourself, Gareth! I like you a lot, but – but not in the sort of way you mean. You're great fun, you make me laugh and you've been a good friend, but . . .'

Gareth let go of her and heaved a deep sigh. For a moment he said nothing, then he spoke, his voice very low. 'Does *he* make you laugh?'

For a moment Hetty was bereft of words. Then she said uncertainly: 'What do you mean? Who is *he*? And why should you think I'm – I'm interested in someone else?'

'If you aren't, then that's even more insulting. You should grow up, young Hetty,' Gareth said, and his tone was cold, almost stern. Hetty felt her cheeks flame. Gareth had never been so nasty to her before, and she did not like it.

'I don't know what you mean,' she said, hearing her own voice as cold and annoyed as his and not caring; in fact she hoped that he was upset. He had upset her, hadn't he? 'I never said I liked another fellow.'

'But you do,' Gareth said. 'Come clean; it's better for both of us.'

Hetty took a deep breath. He was right; she knew that in her heart. So, haltingly at first and then more firmly, she told Gareth about the missed coach, the mysterious meeting, and how she had never been able to forget her rescuer.

Gareth listened in silence and then, to her surprise, he turned and gave her a peck on the cheek. 'All right; you aren't in love with a flesh and blood man, but with an idea,' he said at last. 'And since I'm off to Lincolnshire quite soon, we won't try to meet; what's the point? But just for friendship's sake, will you telephone me a couple of times a month? I'll give you the number of my mess as soon as I know it myself. And you'll write?'

Relieved to have got off lightly, Hetty agreed to both ring and write, and then suggested that they might meet, though definitely not as Mr and Mrs Evans, but Gareth shook his head firmly and opened the driver's door of the car. 'Better not,' he said. 'And now let's buy those fish and chips!'

Chapter Sixteen

Agatha was finishing her breakfast after a long night fire-watching when her mother came into the kitchen. 'I've got the post,' the old lady said rather breathlessly. 'I saw the postman coming up the street from my bedroom window, so I hurried down to save you leaving your breakfast and going out to fetch it.' She smiled at her daughter and laid the envelopes in front of her. 'It'll be mostly government leaflets and bills, I expect, but there's one from Hetty. You could read it to me whilst I eat my breakfast; I take it you've left my porridge warming on the back of the stove?'

'Yes, that's right,' Agatha said, getting to her feet. She ladled porridge from the pan into a round blue dish, sprinkled it sparingly with sugar – sugar had been rationed for ages so Agatha usually sweetened her own porridge with golden syrup, but her mother preferred sugar – and set the dish down on the table before the older woman. She picked up Hetty's letter and pushed it into her pocket. 'I haven't got time to read it to you now, Mother,' she said briskly. 'And anyway, I expect there's a good deal of it that wouldn't really interest you. But I'll read it to you tonight, when I get home from work. Do get on with your breakfast; Mrs Simpson was working in the NAAFI last night, so there's only me to help you put on your shoes and stockings.' She stopped speaking to give an enormous yawn, then shook herself. 'Goodness, I'm tired! There were a lot of aircraft about last night but it seems they were on their way somewhere else, thank God, or they were ours, of course. We've not had a really bad raid since Christmas, so we've a lot to be thankful for, especially with the docks so full of shipping.'

Mrs Preece stopped spooning porridge. 'I'm sorry, Agatha, I forgot you were fire-watching last night,' she said remorsefully. 'Why don't you open the library an hour or so later when you're on duty? As for my shoes and stockings, I can manage without both, at a pinch. I can wear my slippers, and Mrs Simpson will pop in around lunchtime to make sure I'm all right. She can help me on with my stockings if I've not managed to get into them myself by then.'

Agatha laughed, stood up and gave her mother's hand a squeeze. 'Oh, Mother, it doesn't take me two minutes to put on your stockings and shoes, and I *like* to do it. As for being tired, that's unavoidable. Mr Gower and I discussed opening the library later but decided it wasn't on; as you know, ever since the war started, our membership has doubled, or even trebled, and a good few of our borrowers are WVS, ARP or fire-watchers, like Mr Gower and myself. They come off duty, get a couple of hours' sleep, and then come out to get their messages and to renew their library books, so we can't let them down by opening late.'

Mrs Preece finished her porridge and took a couple

346

of sips of the tea Agatha had poured out. 'Well, if you're sure you don't mind,' she said, jerking a thumb at the Welsh dresser. 'I left my shoes and stockings down there last night; Mrs Simpson helped me off with them – and my corset – before she went on duty.' She gave her daughter a quick glance from under lowered lids, reminding Agatha of a puppy which has chewed your shoes in the night but doesn't know whether you have yet found the remains. 'Then I can read Hetty's letter when you come home this evening. Eh, how I miss that child!'

Agatha sighed. 'You know very well, Mother, that the letter's addressed to me, but of course I'll be happy to read most of it to you. Only Hetty isn't a child any more, but a young woman, and she may have written things she would rather I kept to myself.'

Mrs Preece pouted. 'I'm a married woman and know about such matters, which is more than you can say of yourself, Agatha Preece,' she muttered. Then, when Agatha did not reply, she gave a little laugh. 'All right, all right, I understand what you're saying. And now let's change the subject. Have you made me a list for shopping? If Mrs Simpson is free this afternoon, she'll come with me.' She looked hopefully at the letter, still sticking out of her daughter's pocket. 'I wonder if Hetty'll manage to get some time off soon. I know you wrote and invited her to use our spare room when she's on leave now that her aunt lives over the water, and it would be a real treat to see that happy little face again.'

'Leave's a bit difficult, because she isn't officially

either fish, fowl or good red herring,' Agatha reminded her mother. 'There are several boats manned by girls who are paid by the government, but they aren't in any of the services. Still, she said in her last letter that she might get away for a week now the weather's so good, so maybe she's writing to tell us when she's coming back.'

Mrs Preece brightened. 'Why don't you just open the letter and see whether she mentions a date?' she suggested. 'It wouldn't take but a minute and it'll save me spending hours wondering how our little Hetty is getting on and whether we'll be seeing her soon.'

Agatha had walked over to the Welsh dresser and fetched her mother's shoes and stockings. Now she knelt down, put on the stockings and her mother's pink garters, buckled the shoes, and got awkwardly to her feet. Then she dug her hand into her pocket, produced the letter, opened it and swiftly scanned the three pages covered in Hetty's round, childish handwriting before meeting her mother's anxious gaze. 'Well, she is getting four or five days off, but I doubt whether we shall see her for more than a couple of hours, if that,' she said regretfully. 'She'll spend a couple of days in Birkenhead with her aunt and uncle and then go on to Burscough to see her grandparents. They are getting on and with leave so difficult, and her time so short, she really should spend most if not all of it with them.'

Mrs Preece sighed. 'I felt sure we'd be seeing her at any moment; it's been months since she was here last,' she said. 'But she's bound to get proper leave soon, I trust.'

Leaving the house, Agatha hurried along Everton Terrace. She was longing to read Hetty's letter and knew that once the library was open to the public she would be too busy to take time out for her personal correspondence. Despite fire-watching, she and Mr Gower always arrived at least fifteen or twenty minutes before the official opening time so that they could prepare for the day ahead, and today, Agatha decided, she would read the letter before she did anything else. She knew the library was tidy, the books in their correct places on the shelves, the stamp already turned to today's date, and the mugs which she and Mr Gower used for their tea washed up and ready. Because of the increase in readers the authority had appointed Mrs Evelyn Hibbert, a widow in her forties, to assist Mr Gower and Miss Preece, and she had settled down and admitted to Agatha that she already loved the job. She lived locally and knew most of the library members, soon grew at ease with Agatha and regarded Mr Gower with deference verging on awe, whilst he treated her with cautious approval. Now it was Mrs Hibbert who made tea or coffee, brushed and dusted, and even stamped the outgoing volumes. She held the fort for Mr Gower when Agatha was rushed off her feet and he came down to help out, and had become a prized member of their little team. Agatha told her mother that she thought Mr Gower had been a little stiff and starchy with Mrs Hibbert at first because she was not, as he pointed out, a trained librarian. However, now that he had grown accustomed to her presence, he was actually beginning to regard their new recruit with approval, which could only be good.

Now, Agatha reached the library and undid the metal gates, climbed the steps, unlocked the glass doors and let herself in. Then she sat down behind the counter, took out her letter and began to read.

Dear Agatha,

Things are hotting up at last! Ever since the BEF were brought back from Dunkirk in June, and the powers that be began to fear an invasion, Gareth has been trying to get a posting to what he calls an operational station and now he thinks he may get his wish. He went on the course to learn about bombers – I told you about it in one of my letters – and passed with flying colours. He came back here for a bit but now his posting has arrived (to RAF Scampton, in Lincolnshire). I shall miss him, but I think it's probably a good thing because as I know I've told you before, he's been getting a lot too serious. Ever since we fished him out of the canal, he's kept track of the Shamrock *and always turned up when we got near Heyford. It's been great fun in some ways to have a fellow to take me dancing, or to the flicks, but it's been getting more and more difficult to keep him at arm's length. Well, not quite that, because we do kiss and have a bit of a cuddle, but that's because I've not wanted to hurt him by telling him to back off. In fact I don't deny I like him a lot, more than any of the other fellows*

I've danced – and flirted! – with, and if it wasn't for someone I met a long time ago, I might fool myself into believing that I love him. But I keep thinking about the man I met on my way home from Llandudno, where your mother had been playing whist. Do you remember my strange encounter? I can't forget that fellow, the one who brought me home, no matter how I try. I know you'll say I can't possibly be in love with someone I only met once and whose name I don't even know and honestly, Agatha, I think that's true. I'm not in love with him, that would be quite absurd, but even writing about him, as I'm doing now, gives me a strange sort of thrill and I'm ashamed to admit that though I enjoy it when Gareth kisses me, I don't get that weird sensation, almost as if the world has stopped turning, which comes whenever I think about my mysterious motorcyclist.

So you see it wouldn't be fair to Gareth to start pretending I'm serious when I know really that I'm not. He's a friend, and a good one, a very special friend, but that's all, so when he goes off to some station miles away it will be a good thing, even though I'll miss him.

Now, to change the subject completely, you asked in your last letter when you might expect to see me. I've got four days' leave coming up but I shall spend it half with Aunt Phoebe and half with Gran and Gramps at Burscough . . .

Agatha skipped the rest of the paragraph, having read it closely earlier in the day, then continued to read.

As you can imagine, approaching London on the canal is pretty scary because the bombing seems fairly continuous when the nights are clear. It's not so bad now, and we've been most awfully lucky since the Luftwaffe could cause absolute mayhem if they chose to target the canals, but they've not done so yet, at any rate, and of course we never tie up for long near the capital – or any big cities, for that matter. And in between towns and cities, the countryside is magical. The corn is being cut and the foxgloves and mead-owsweet send wafts of perfume across to us as we pass, and we've made lots of friends, both amongst the boaters, as the canal folk call themselves, and the farmers and villagers whose homes and businesses we pass on our way. So don't think of us as unfortunate, because we're anything but; neither Sally, Alice or myself would change our lot for that of anyone else at all!

Well, I suppose I'd better sign off and get some work done, but write back as soon as you can. Dear Agatha, I wish I were as fond of Gareth as you are of your Max – don't try to deny it, just be thankful – but it is not to be. Take good care of yourself and as soon as the Inland Waterway people get their act together we have been promised leave and I'll make my way to Everton like a pin to a magnet.

Ever yours,
Hetty

March 1941

'What on earth are you carrying with such care?' Mr Gower asked as Agatha crossed the library floor, heading for the Reading Room. He glanced at his wrist-watch. 'It's not time for elevenses yet, is it? Not that you're likely to take our elevenses into the Reading Room when the front counter is so busy. Why, even the Reference Library has readers, though they're mainly old hands who know what they're doing and don't need a lot of help from me.'

Agatha turned to him, her face lighting up, and Mr Gower thought, not for the first time lately, that Miss Preece was becoming almost pretty, which was strange when you came to think, since she was working harder than she had ever done. The library was busy now from the moment it opened until they closed. Then of course both she and Mr Gower would hurry to their homes, get a meal of sorts, and take up their posts as fire-watchers or, in Miss Preece's case, some-times helping in the mobile canteens which serviced the workers throughout the night.

'Miss Preece? Whatever are you carrying?' Mr Gower repeated, his curiosity thoroughly aroused. 'My next-door neighbour does our shopping and she spotted that Sample's had a good supply of ginger nuts. She knows how fond Mother is of biscuits, so she bought as many as the shop assistant would let her have. I know you like them as well – as indeed do I – so I brought a bag of them to work; they're in the office awaiting your pleasure. Don't say you've bought some as well!'

Miss Preece laughed, then came towards him to show him what she was holding so carefully. 'It's the first sign of spring I always say when the crocuses come out under our apple tree,' she said gaily. 'I put these corms in a pot last autumn and stood the pot in a sheltered corner. I thought it would be nice to put them on the windowsill in the Reading Room; it'll cheer the place up, and since I'm feeling very cheerful, it seemed appropriate.'

Mr Gower looked admiringly at the shallow blue china pot held so carefully between his fellow librarian's hands. The crocuses, purple, gold and white, were indeed a delightful sight, and he was tempted to tell Miss Preece that the flowers were not the only attractive things about to enter the Reading Room; she herself, with her shining bob of black hair, her dark blue eyes and her flushed cheeks, looked to Mr Gower every bit as lovely as the crocuses.

He opened his mouth to say so, but his courage failed him; to be snubbed would ruin the careful, friendly relationship he was building up, so he waited whilst Miss Preece looked around the Reading Room and obviously decided that it was not a suitable place for her beautiful bowl of flowers. She carried them back into the lending library and put them on the extreme end of the counter, whereupon Mr Gower suggested that he might join her, since he was not busy, and could date-stamp the books going out whilst she checked those being returned.

Miss Preece agreed at once, giving him a look so grateful that it encouraged him to ask the question

354

which burned on his lips. 'You're looking very happy, Miss Preece. Has something nice happened?'

He half expected to see her face change into the forbidding mask which had once greeted any attempt of his to ask her a question, but she gave him a flashing smile as they went behind the counter and began to work. 'I've had a cablegram from South Africa, from Professor Galera. He's coming home!'

Mr Gower felt his heart thud into his boots, but when he spoke, his voice emerged calmly. 'Well now, isn't that good news,' he said. 'No doubt we'll be seeing him any day.'

'Well, no, because he could be posted just about anywhere in Great Britain,' Miss Preece said regretfully. 'He'll still be training pilots, I gather, and not flying sorties, which is a relief because that is so horribly dangerous, but training airfields, I gather, are usually in remote areas. Still, I expect he'll come to Liverpool at some stage.'

'Oh, bound to,' Mr Gower said gloomily. 'Bound to come and see you. Well, isn't that nice. No wonder you're excited!'

'Isn't life strange?' Agatha enquired of her mother that evening as the two of them sat in the kitchen, eating the excellent vegetable pie that Mrs Simpson had made them earlier in the day.

Mrs Preece took a mouthful of food and answered thickly. 'What's strange? I say, Agatha, Mrs Simpson is a grand cook. If I didn't know better, I'd think this pie was a pre-war one, stuffed with stewing steak.'

The pie was named after its creator, Lord Woolton, and Mrs Simpson had begged bones from her butcher with which she had made a delicious stock. This she had thickened with Bisto powder and added to the vegetables, making the result a good deal tastier than the original recipe, and much enjoyed both by the Simpsons and the Preeces. 'What's strange is that I've been pouncing on my letters from both Max and Hetty, hoping that one or other of them would be coming home soon,' Agatha said, 'and now Hetty thinks the Inland Waterways Authority are giving her and her crew at least ten days' leave, and Max is being brought back to England so that he can train pilots actually on the spot. Wouldn't you say that that was quite a coincidence?'

Mrs Preece sniffed. 'I don't know about coincidence; Hetty's been promising us that she'll get proper leave for months, but so far all she got last year was four measly days, and she spent them with her grand-parents. I'm not denying that it was her duty to go to the old folk, because they won't be here for ever, any more than I shall, but if I were you, girl, I wouldn't count my chickens.'

'Oh, Mother, Hetty came up to the library when she was free and we had a good old gossip,' Agatha protested. 'And as for the professor, he's bound to get some leave. After all, he's been away for fifteen months, so he must be due for time off. I mean, they get embarkation leave when they're going away, so they should get . . .'

Mrs Preece gave a wheezy chuckle. 'Disembarkation

leave, I suppose you mean,' she said. 'But I'm not interested in Max; it's my little Hetty I want to see again.'

'You will, I'm sure of it,' Agatha said soothingly.
'Just keep watching the post; Hetty's a good girl, she'll
be bound to write when she gets definite dates.' She
glanced at the clock on the mantelpiece. 'I'm helping
out at the NAAFI this evening, but I'll give you a hand
to get into your night things before I leave.'

Mrs Preece scowled at her. 'You'll do no such thing,'
she said crossly. 'It may take me a while, but I can
manage perfectly well, thank you. Mrs Simpson
comes round during the evening so if I need help,
she'll give it.'

Agatha tutted, getting up from the table and
carrying their plates over to the sink. 'Just because
there were no raids in January or February, that
doesn't mean to say there won't be any in March,'
she reminded her mother. 'Not that I think there will
be; why, a couple of days ago there was a flurry of
snow as I came back from fire-watching, the last thing
you'd expect at the beginning of March. And come
to think, unless there's a raid we shut the club at half
past ten, so I'll be back with you by eleven at the
latest. And the raids never start before then, so we'll
have time to get down to the Anderson before
bombing starts.'

'I am *not* going down into that beastly cold shelter,'
Mrs Preece said sharply, her eyes flashing. 'It's cold
and dirty and smelly, and I hate it. If there's a raid –
and I mean if – then you'll find me under the stairs.
I admit that should the house get a direct hit I'll be a

goner, but then I'd be just as dead if a bomb landed smack on the Anderson.'

Agatha sighed but did not argue, since she was well aware of the truth of her mother's remarks. It wasn't so bad in summer, but in winter she thought it quite possible that if they slept in the Anderson shelter they could easily catch their deaths from pneumonia, even if they escaped being blown to bits. So she smiled at Mrs Preece and went over to the stove to fetch the kettle. 'Right you are; I'll join you under the stairs if there's a raid,' she said cheerfully. 'And because you're an obstinate old woman, I'll leave you to wash up our supper things.' She stood the kettle on the draining board, put on her coat and a pink headscarf, and headed for the back door. 'Be good, and I'll see you later.'

Agatha had a good evening at the club, but was not sorry when Mrs Hetherington, chairlady of the local WVS, told her that the clock had struck ten and she might as well go home and get some sleep. 'You're working at the library all day tomorrow and fire-watching at night. There's no sense in staying on here when most of the customers have gone, and we've plenty of helpers to do the cleaning up,' she said. She examined her rota. 'I'll see you again in a week's time. Good night, Miss Preece, and don't forget to put aside a copy of the latest Agatha Christie for me. If I'm too busy to pop in, perhaps you could bring it with you next week.'

Agatha agreed that she would put aside the book

in question – *One, Two, Buckle My Shoe*, an Hercule Poirot mystery – for Mrs Hetherington, and set off for home. It was very cold, with a sharp little wind which caused her to tighten her headscarf and wish devoutly that she had thought to bring the woollen muffler her mother had knitted for her the previous Christmas. Because it was late she thought about catching a tram, but she would need to change, and would still have a good distance to go at the end of her ride, so she decided she might as well walk. Everywhere was in darkness, of course, but she could see enough to make her way through the streets safely and presently passed a house with a beautiful window box crammed with spring flowers, including crocuses of every possible colour. It reminded Agatha of her pretty blue pot with its display and she wondered whether the flowers would still be unfaded when Max came to visit her.

She had brought the crocuses into the library partly to cheer up both borrowers and staff with this first sign of spring, and partly to celebrate Max's return. Apart from that first cablegram announcing that he would soon be coming home she had heard nothing, but this did not worry her; cablegrams would be as strictly treated by the censor as letters, and Max had already told her all that he was allowed to pass on, which was simply that he would soon be back in Britain.

As she walked, she wondered whether she should dig up some more of the bulbs which flourished in her back garden and pot them up to beautify her work place against Max's return. Pheasant eye narcissi were in bud and not only would look lovely but would fill the air of the library with their frail, sweet scent. However, South Africa was famous for its wonderful gardens, so Max was probably accustomed to having blossom all around him and would not be particularly impressed even if she could deck the place with rare orchids. Yet there was something about the homely beauty of the brave little crocuses which pleased her and her readers – Mr Gower, too – so she would leave them on the counter until they withered and were beautiful no longer.

Having made up her mind, Agatha slowed her pace to glance in one or two of the darkened shop windows as she passed. A greengrocer with imagination had got large sheets of blank newsprint from somewhere and drawn pictures of various fruit; next to bananas, oranges and grapes he had carefully written the words *None today*, which made Agatha smile. Tropical fruit had to be brought from abroad, and merchant shipping needed room for far more important cargo.

Despite the lateness of the hour, there were still a good many people about, so when she heard herself hailed she turned her head, guessing that it was a library member wanting company on the walk back to Everton. Glancing over her shoulder but not slackening her pace she saw a tall man dressed in air force uniform, but it was only when he took off his cap and grinned at her, white teeth flashing in his tanned face, that she recognised him. Without giving a thought to her crippled foot, she spun round, crying: 'Max! Oh, is it really you?' and before she could steady herself she was falling, falling, her stick flying in one direction and her bag in another, whilst the pavement seemed to leap up to meet her, cracking her knees and grazing her hands so that even as she laughed with joy she was aware of tattered stockings, bleeding hands and knees, and – for her handbag had flown open – possessions skittering freely across the paving stones.

'Agatha? Oh, my dear, how could I have been such a fool, to startle you so!' He was bending over her, both hands seizing hers in a firm grip, hauling her gently to her feet. 'But when I saw it was really you I just couldn't bear the thought of you disappearing into the throng, so I shouted.' He held her away from him, gazing anxiously into her face. 'Are you much hurt? You went down with such a crack . . . no, no, don't stoop to gather your things; you may leave that safely to me.' He began to pick up her scattered possessions, saying as he did so: 'Do you always throw yourself at the feet of any man who calls your name?'

'Not always, and I'm fine; bloody but unbowed, in fact,' Agatha said gaily. Her heart was hammering out a fast rhythm and though there were tears on her cheeks, for her grazes stung and her joints ached, she thought she had never felt happier. 'But Max, wherever did you spring from? I got your cablegram, but I assumed you'd go to Durham first to see your relatives. I thought you'd not be in Liverpool for several days, perhaps even weeks.'

'Are you sure you aren't hurt?' Max repeated. He had

gathered up all her bits and pieces and bundled them into her handbag, and now he found her stick and her gas mask case and restored them to her. Only then did he anxiously examine her hands, tutting over the blood and the dirt. 'We'll go to the small hotel where I'm booked in for the night; I'm sure someone will clean you up and make us a pot of tea. We can drink whilst we talk – by God, England seems cold after South Africa – and I'll tell you all my news, which is quite a lot. Take my arm, my dearest girl. The hotel is only a few yards further on.'

They reached Maple's Hotel and went inside, where Agatha's hurts were cleaned and bandaged to the accompaniment of much tutting and questioning, and the two of them were settled in the lounge and given a large pot of tea.

So it was over cups of tea that Agatha and Max began to get to know one another all over again after their long months apart. Max insisted that Agatha should start off by telling him all that had happened to her since they had last met, as a good few of their letters would undoubtedly have gone astray. Agatha cast her mind back; how dull her life seemed. In fact the only excitement had been his letters and Hetty's, but it really would not do to say so; instead she told him how she and Mr Gower had shared the task of fire-watching from the turret of Everton library and how she had taken her turn at helping to man the mobile canteens. Max asked her whether the library was still open for borrowers after a night raid had kept the staff from their beds, and was gratifyingly astonished when she assured him that not only did they always open on time, but had grown accustomed to being constantly busy for readers had multiplied, especially during the winter months. 'I think that's about all I've done since I saw you last,' Agatha said apologetically, but Max shook his head and wagged a reproving finger.

'You've sold me short, young lady,' he said accusingly. 'What about the raids at Christmas? One of your letters about that time did get through and it sounded pretty horrendous. Was much damage done?'

Abruptly, Agatha remembered the raids that had taken place in November and December the previous year, which had caused enormous damage and loss of life. For a moment, she relived the terror she had felt then as the bombs whistled down and the flames leapt up, for this had been, so to speak, Liverpool's baptism of fire. Everyone knew that London was bombed every night, that people were living in the Underground, or in public shelters, but this was the first time Liverpool had suffered a sustained attack and even remembering it for Max's benefit brought back the sick horror she had felt on learning of the terrible tragedy which had occurred when the Ernest Brown School in Durning Road had received a direct hit, causing it to collapse inwards into the public shelter beneath. Next day, Agatha had heard that though the rescue services had started work immediately, over a hundred people had died and many more had been seriously injured. Haltingly, she began to tell Max what she had seen and reported from her post every time a new fire started, or a building crashed to earth, but her voice grew shakier with every word.

Max, however, must have realised how recalling such horrors upset her, for he leaned across and stroked her cheek, a gesture so gentle and loving that Agatha felt tears rise in her eyes. 'That's enough, my love; I never meant to make you cry,' Max said. He wiped away her tears with one finger. 'I'm a swine to bring back memories which are best forgotten, especially as I was so far away and so safe.' He looked at her ruefully, raising one dark brow. 'Agatha, my dear, I'm going to tell you something which I should have told you months ago; when we met at the museum opening. I'm afraid it's going to distress you and I know you will be very angry, so would you rather I told you in a less public spot than here?'

Poor Agatha felt her heart descend into her boots. He must be going to tell her that he was happily married, with half a dozen children and a large house somewhere in the north of England. Or perhaps he had married a Spaniard during the Civil War, which would explain why he had been attracted by her black hair and dark eyes.

But he was looking at her quizzically, one eyebrow still raised. Agatha looked round. When they had entered, there had been other people in the lounge. Now it was empty, save for an elderly couple in one corner who could not possibly overhear their conversation. Agatha looked steadily across at him, meeting his gaze squarely. 'Here is fine,' she said quietly. 'Carry on, please.'

Max sighed deeply. 'I've lied to you twice, but I don't mean to do so ever again, and now I'm going to set the record straight,' he said. 'When we met at the museum opening and were introduced, someone had told you that I had a brother very similar to myself. That is true in one way because Michael and I are very alike, though not quite in the way you imagined. Michael takes after our mother; his hair is lighter than mine and his eyes are blue, not brown. He's quite a bit shorter than I am, at least four or five inches, but we are both academically inclined and have similar interests. So do you understand what I'm trying to tell you?'

'Not really,' Agatha admitted. She felt positively light-hearted with relief; he was *not* married! But why should it matter that he had let her believe he and his brother were virtually identical? It wasn't as if ... suddenly, she knew. She could feel a bubble of laughter welling up inside her, knew that her cheeks were pink and her eyes sparkling. 'So it was *you* who knocked me down in the street and were so exceedingly rude,' she said, trying to sound indignant but feeling only relief and amusement mingling. 'But why didn't you tell me, Max? Why not admit it and just say you were sorry? I expect it was just as much my fault as yours, because thinking back I did stop very suddenly, when your brother – I mean you – cannoned into me.'

'It was unforgivable; my only excuse is that I'd arranged to meet Michael at six o'clock and I was already late. It was only afterwards that I began to wonder about you and try to find you again, to explain my rudeness.

But I was only in Liverpool for a couple of days and though I described you to everyone I met, no one could tell me who you were, or where you worked.'

'If you said I had black hair and a club foot, it seems strange that you weren't more successful,' Agatha said somewhat drily, but Max shook his head reprovingly at her.

'I didn't know then about your foot, I only knew you walked with a stick. But anyway, that's beside the point. When we met again, I was so ashamed of my behaviour on the first occasion that I let you believe it was my brother and not I who had knocked you down; you see, I was already attracted to you and was determined to get to know you better, particularly once I'd done some asking around and knew you weren't married or engaged . . .'

Agatha gave a smothered chuckle. 'To tell you the truth, Max, when you said you had something to tell me, I thought you might be going to say you had a wife and a dozen children,' she said. 'So now we know we're both free, white and twenty-one, as the saying goes. But you said you had a couple of lies to confess; what's the second one?'

'I told you in one of my letters that I was nudging forty,' Max said gloomily. 'In fact I'll be forty-three in June this year.'

'I never received a letter telling me your age, but I already knew how old you were from something one of your colleagues at the museum let drop,' Agatha said truthfully. 'And I'm thirty-six, seven years younger than you. But what has age got to do with anything?'

'Oh, dear God, I'm doing it all wrong,' Max said distractedly. 'I meant to tell you that I knew from the first moment we met you were the only girl for me, and . . .'

'Woman, not girl, and – and I felt the same,' Agatha said, feeling the warm blood rush to her cheeks. She was too honest to let Max think his words were not what she had longed to hear; why should she? A woman of thirty-six must acknowledge that her chances of meeting the man of her dreams were few, but to know that Max loved her, as she loved him, was wonderful, and she would be the last person to deny it. She hesitated, then broke into speech once more. 'Ever since you kissed me under the mistletoe on Lime Street station I've . . . I've known you were someone special. Only I didn't know how special, not then.'

Max struck his forehead with one hand and groaned. 'Dear God, Agatha, confessing seems to be the name of the game tonight. There was no mistletoe; I just wanted an excuse to kiss you. Can you ever forgive me?'

Agatha began to giggle, then to laugh out loud. 'Oh, Max, what a pair of fools we are,' she said. 'If we're being really truthful, I'd never been kissed by anyone before, but it was lovely and I really enjoyed it, so you don't have to apologise. You kiss beautifully, but I expect you've had lots of practice, unlike myself.'

'Well, you're going to get a good deal of practice from now on,' Max said with a grin. 'And there's one more thing I need to tell you whilst I'm coming clean, so to speak. Agatha, my dear, I'm not only nearly forty-three;

I'm old-fashioned. I'm being posted to Lossiemouth, in the north-east of Scotland, and if I were ten or fifteen years younger I'd ask you to meet me halfway so that we could book in at some hostelry as man and wife and – and get to know one another. But I can't do that, it's against all my principles; all my upbringing, in fact. So . . . so would you . . . would you marry me? If you say yes I can get hold of a special licence . . .'

'Of course I'll marry you,' Agatha said simply, rising reluctantly to her feet. 'I really must go, Max, or Mother will be half mad with worry, but I've got the day off tomorrow – our new assistant, Mrs Hibbert, will cope – so we can meet then.

The two of them left the hotel, arms round each other's waists, heads very close. Agatha felt happiness flooding through her, its warmth conquering the chill of the March wind. As they walked they discussed their plans for the future and Agatha told her lover that she would have to give notice in good time so that her employers might find a replacement librarian. However, she was sure she would soon find work in Lossiemouth, perhaps even on the RAF station. 'Because now that we're getting married, I shall want to be with you all the time, and there's my mother to consider . . .'

'Your mother must come with us; we couldn't possibly leave her alone in Liverpool whilst the war continues,' Max cut in quickly. 'Lossiemouth isn't large, but I'm sure we'll find lodgings easily enough.' He gave her waist a squeeze. 'Can I come home with you now? I want to tell your mother my marvellous news . . .'

'What news is that?' Agatha asked, then giggled when Max tutted. 'Oh, you mean *our* marvellous news. I'm sure Mother will be pleased once she gets used to the idea, but at first it will be something of a shock . . .'

It was to be a typical wartime wedding, Hetty thought, with Max in his uniform and Agatha in the navy blue coat and skirt which she had worn to attend the museum opening so long ago. She herself was to be Agatha's only attendant, wearing a borrowed dress and court shoes, which were too small and pinched her toes, but none of the shoes and boots she wore aboard the *Shamrock* were in any way suitable. She and Agatha were in the latter's bedroom, putting the finishing touches to their toilet, whilst Mrs Preece, dressed in her best and almost as excited as the bride, pottered about rearranging the little bouquets which Max had had delivered to the house earlier in the day. Hetty's was made up of purple and white violets, whilst Agatha's was lilies of the valley, and Hetty thought she would never again smell their heady perfume without remembering her friend's flushed and happy face and her dark, sparkling eyes.

True to his word, Max had obtained a special licence, which meant that the wedding was being held a mere ten days after the couple had plighted their troth in Maple's Hotel. When Agatha had described the occasion to Hetty she had thought it very unromantic, but when she said as much, Agatha had only smiled and shaken her head. 'When you love someone, and know they love you, everything they do or say is romantic,' she had told her young friend. 'Whenever I look at Max, my stomach turns over.'

'That sounds more like a bilious attack than a sign of affection,' Hetty had said, only half teasingly, but again Agatha had shaken her head.

'No. Love isn't all mistletoe kisses and diamond engagement rings, my dear. When you fall in love, you'll understand.'

Now, Mrs Preece eyed her daughter critically, then smiled and reached up to pat her cheek. 'I dreamed of you having a white wedding, but the war has put a stop to such things,' she said regretfully and then, as Agatha opened her mouth to speak, she placed a finger across her daughter's lips. 'I know what you were going to say, but from the moment I first set eyes on Max I knew you two were made for each other. I suppose I thought he'd wait for peace before popping the question, and I was worried because you were going to be separated so soon after the wedding, but that's because I'm a foolish old woman.' She turned to Hetty. 'They've invited me to go with them to Scotland when the library have found a replacement librarian for Everton. It's very generous of them, and if I can find lodgings I like I may take them up on it. Max says Liverpool is going to be a target for the Huns because it's an important port, and I dare say he's right, whereas Lossiemouth is just a little village on the shores of the Moray Firth. However, a decision of that sort has to be carefully thought out. All my friends are here, and if we leave this house

370

unprotected God knows what we'll find when the war's over.'

'I wish I could offer to rent it from you, but of course it's out of the question,' Hetty said regretfully. 'I shall be back on the canal tomorrow. In fact, Mrs Preece, officially I haven't even left the *Shamrock*. The girls are coping just for three days, so I can attend the wedding.'

Mrs Preece raised her eyebrows. 'Two of them to handle those great long boats? How on earth . . .'

'Sally's boyfriend is on leave from the air force; he's living aboard and doing my job whilst I'm away,' Hetty explained, then glanced at her wristwatch and gave a squeak. 'Goodness, look at the time! We're due at the register office in twenty minutes; the taxi will be here in seconds!'

Agatha picked up her bouquet, gave a last glance at her reflection in the dressing table mirror, and made for the stairs. She had been so busy in the past few days that she had not really had time to be nervous, and now she waited for anxiety to engulf her and was rather surprised when it did not do so. Brides were supposed to be all of a tremble, she reminded herself, but it seemed that she was to be the exception. She felt both calm and happy, and realised that she was looking forward to the small reception which was her mother's wedding present to the happy couple. There would not be many guests: only the Galeras, a cousin of her mother's, Mrs Simpson from next door, and Mr Gower, who was unable to attend the ceremony itself but was coming to the reception.

Agatha helped Hetty to settle old Mrs Preece into the taxi which awaited them at the gate, then slid into the front seat next to the driver. She had met Mr and Mrs Galera the previous evening, when she and her mother had been invited by them to dine at the Adelphi, and had liked them very much, though it had come as a considerable surprise to discover that Max's stepmother was about her own age, a great deal younger than her husband. However, Elinor Galera had very soon put her at her ease, and by the time the evening ended Agatha felt she had found a new friend.

She had felt shy of meeting Michael, who had been told of the deception Max had practised on her at their first meeting, but soon relaxed, finding him very different from her fiancé. Physically, Max was a head taller and a good deal heavier than Michael, and the younger man seemed frivolous compared to his brother at first. He laughed a lot, told jokes, and teased Max, but when she and Elinor went to the ladies' powder room the other woman told her that Michael was quite as serious as Max, but more prone to disguise the fact.

'I know you'll like him very much when you get to know him properly, and that's a good thing, because the brothers are very close,' Elinor said. 'Don't judge Michael on this first meeting, though. He's putting on an act, as I'm told many aircrew do. It's a big responsibility, navigating one of those heavy bombers.'

The screech of brakes as the taxi drew up outside the register office brought Agatha abruptly back to the present. She stepped out of the taxi and suddenly all her unnatural calm deserted her. What on earth was she doing here, she, a confirmed spinster who had never even had a boyfriend, actually considering marriage! Butterflies started to dance a fandango in her stomach and a cold sweat broke out on the back of her neck. She looked round wildly for a way of escape – and saw Max. He was smiling at her, holding out his hand, and she knew all in a moment that he was probably as nervous as she, but hiding it better. She felt a small, tentative smile break out on her face and the butterflies, so active only moments before, calmed down. This was wedding nerves; they would disappear as soon as she was Max's wife – were disappearing already. She handed her small bouquet to Hetty, then helped her mother to alight. 'Is my hat on straight?' she enquired, suddenly anxious. 'Is my nose shiny?'

Mrs Preece patted her arm. 'You look lovely, my dear,' she said huskily. 'In we go. We mustn't keep everyone waiting!'

'Alone at last, Mrs Galera!' Max said, putting an arm around his brand new wife and leading her gently into the bedroom at the Adelphi which they would inhabit for the one and only night of their honeymoon. 'Phew. I never realised before what an ordeal getting married was, but I suppose it's something every bride and groom has to go through. I say, what a dream of a nightdress; where did you get it in these austere times?'

Agatha took the flimsy nightie out of her small case

and turned to look up into Max's dark, intelligent face. 'What a good thing I'm in love with you,' she said, ignoring his question and voicing her own thoughts. 'Otherwise this would be purgatory – being shut up in a bedroom with a man one scarcely knew!'

'Well, yes; but since we *are* in love, we don't need to consider the plight of those less fortunate. Are you tired, sweetheart?'

'Yes,' Agatha admitted. They had smiled and smiled throughout the service in the register office, smiled and smiled at the reception Mrs Preece and Mrs Simpson had arranged, smiled some more as they took up their reservation at the Adelphi. They had come, hand in hand, to their room and had eyed each other speculatively across the width of the delightful double bed. Then they had tidied up, as Max had put it, and gone down to the dining room. The waiter, a spry little man with an avuncular manner, suggested they should have the soup, followed by roast chicken and rounded off with a lemon mousse, and they had agreed, eaten everything eagerly – they had been too nervous to eat at the reception – and then come straight to their room. Now, Agatha reflected that that part had been easy; the difficult part was about to begin. Then she looked at Max's anxious, craggy face and knew, all in a moment, that he was as frightened of doing something wrong as she; possibly more so. 'The nightie?' she said. 'Yes, it's awfully pretty. My gran wore it on her wedding night and she's lent it to me so that I can follow the family tradition. Do you want to get changed into those startling pyjamas in here, or would you rather go down the corridor to the bathroom?'

Max began to speak, then stopped. He crossed the room in a couple of strides, caught hold of Agatha and began to kiss her neck, and then to unbutton her crisp white blouse. When he drew back Agatha smiled up at him and sat down on the bed, the better to roll down and remove her precious silk stockings. 'We've only got this one night, because tomorrow you go off to Scotland and I return to Everton library,' she observed. 'I'd like to be coy and reluctant, but it would be an awful waste of our time together. So let's make the most of it, Max.'

And they did.

Chapter Seventeen

Although Hetty had come back to Liverpool for the wedding, she and Agatha had not had much chance of the sort of heart-to-heart they usually enjoyed, but once she was back on the boat, and Agatha was once more in charge of the lending library, letters began to be exchanged once more. Agatha noted the fact that despite the distance now separating them, for Gareth had been posted to Scampton as he had hoped, Hetty was still in touch with the young man. For all her talk, she was fonder of him than she was prepared to admit, Agatha believed, and was glad. The unknown motorcyclist was just that – unknown – but she, Agatha, had taken to Gareth on sight when he came looking for Hetty all those years ago, and knew that the Heskeths liked him too. However, it was Hetty's business on whom she bestowed her heart; Agatha just hoped that it would not be on someone totally unworthy.

When she picked up her letters one bright April morning and carried them into the kitchen with her, she hoped that the one addressed in Hetty's round, rather childish writing would contain good news. The promised leave had still not materialised, but in her last letter Hetty had mentioned that the girls were expecting a visit from an Inland Waterways official, and were keeping their fingers crossed for a decision. Agatha ripped open the envelope, glanced quickly over the two flimsy pages it contained, then smiled at her mother. 'Wonderful! She's coming back at the end of the month; I'll read it to you when I get back from the library, but isn't that good news? Cheerio, Mother.'

Later, sitting at her desk in the library, she read the letter, smiling to herself.

Dear Agatha,

How strange it still seems to write 'Mrs Galera' on my letters to you, but I'm growing accustomed. In reply to your enquiry we are all well and growing fonder of the dear old Shamrock *with every day that passes. We are an experienced team now (I suppose I should say 'crew') but as we pointed out when the man came visiting from Inland Waterways, just because we are good that shouldn't mean we don't need time off occasionally – proper time off, suffi-cient to get back home to see our people. The man agreed, went away, and the result is that the powers that be have decided the easiest way to give us a decent bit of leave is to lay up the* Shamrock *and the* Clover *for ten days. They'll be in a secure anchorage, in some sort of compound, probably at the London end of our run, so with a bit of luck the three of us will be free at the end of April. They haven't told us yet when or where we are to hand over* Shamrock *and* Clover, *and I haven't looked up the times of trains, but I imagine I should be with*

*you on the 28th or 29th – hope this is all right. I
can't tell you how much I'm looking forward to it.*
   Love,
   Hetty

Agatha pushed the letter into her pocket and stood
up. She would get the kettle going so that Mr Gower,
when he arrived, could have a nice hot cup of tea. Like
herself, he had spent the previous night fire-watching,
and she knew from odd remarks he let drop that his
mother was not only old but also cantankerous. Both
in the previous December and also in March, when
Liverpool had been targeted by the Luftwaffe, old Mrs
Gower had complained of difficulty in sleeping, and,
regardless of the fact that her son had been working
day and night, she had made the raids an excuse for
not rising in time to get him breakfast.

Agatha had telephoned Max the previous evening
and they had talked for fully ten minutes before the
switchboard had informed them sharply that others
were waiting for the line. Now, still feeling a warm
glow, for Max had ended the conversation with the
words 'I love you, sweetheart', she decided that as she
was in early enough she would make tea and toast for
her colleague on the little gas ring in the office. She
knew Mr Gower was going to miss her when she joined
Max in Scotland, so it would be a little attention which
he would appreciate. He had attended the wedding
reception and given her a pretty carriage clock, but he
had not been able to hide his envy of Max.

Feeling self-righteous, Agatha went into the kitchen,

filled the kettle and balanced it on the gas ring, then got half a loaf out of the makeshift breadbin in which they secured their odds and ends of food – the library harboured more than one family of mice – and cut two thick slices. As she lit the gas, however, Mrs Hibbert came in and Agatha, smiling at her, explained that she was making Mr Gower some breakfast, as his mother did not always do so.

Mrs Hibbert tutted. 'I'll do it, so you can get on,' she said, pulling up a chair and stabbing one of the pieces of bread with an ancient toasting fork. There was no butter – butter was rationed, and pretty strictly at that – but margarine would have to do. Soon, the kettle began to whistle and the first round of bread was toasted to a nice brown.

Agatha returned to the counter and began to stack the ordered books into a neat pile, then sniffed; her helper had burned the second piece of toast and was vigorously scraping it. To be sure, Agatha thought, she was tired, but today was going to be a good day. Hetty had written and would be returning to Liverpool in a couple of weeks' time, no doubt full of her adventures on the canal.

Agatha wished she had more exciting news to share with her young friend, but her life seemed to consist of nothing but working in the library all day and then taking part in any war-related work she could do. Now that he was living in Scotland, she and Max had to make do with telephone calls and letters. But even receiving his letters thrilled Agatha, made her feel . . . oh, wanted. So now she sang, and wished that Max were here and not far away. She saw her first borrower approaching, a bag of books in one hand, and scurried back to her place behind the counter. The woman beamed at her.

'Mornin', Miss Preece! I see'd Mr Gower a-comin' up the road; is that burnt toast I smell? Your boss ain't goin' to be too pleased if you've charred his breakfast!'

Cyril Gower blinked with loathing at the sunshine as he got off his tram at the top of Heyworth Street and headed for the library. He felt tired from a night spent fire-watching and stiff from only having had two hours' sleep. He also felt bad-tempered because he had picked up the box of his favourite cereal from the pantry shelf only to find it empty, and when he had decided to make do with coffee and toast, the loaf was stale and the milk in the enamel jug on the slate slab was sour. It was enough, the librarian decided, to put any man into a bad temper; now he would have to do a full day's work on an empty stomach. For a moment he almost wished himself young enough to be conscripted into one of the armed services; he was sure they were provided with breakfast. He imagined a plate piled with bacon, fried bread and delicious, golden-yolked eggs, a pre-war breakfast, but then he thought about marching and drilling, and remembered his flat feet and the miserable little pay packets members of the forces received, and almost decided that being a librarian was preferable.

He was still considering what sort of day lay ahead

of him when the sight of a small boy carrying a model yacht brought to mind the drama of Dunkirk, which had happened in June the previous year, with the rescue of the British Expeditionary Force from the Huns. He remembered the stories in the papers of the men stranded on those long, pale beaches, the little boats, some under sail, going to and fro, back and forth, rescuing those same unfortunates, a modern St Crispin's Day. Mr Gower had almost wished he could have been a part of it, and now he could hear in his mind Shakespeare's stirring words:

> *Then will he strip his sleeve and show his scars,*
> *And say, 'These wounds I had on Crispin's day.'*

But life wasn't like that, not really. For a start, you had to suffer the wounds before you could have the scars, and he didn't imagine that that part of the quotation would be any fun at all.

Sighing, Cyril Gower rubbed his eyes, sore and reddened from staring into the dark sky the previous night for any sign of enemy aircraft, and cursed the sunshine, which had turned the milk sour so that even the consolation of coffee had been denied him. He also cursed his mother, who must have known the cereal box was empty, but who had not bothered to buy more. Then for good measure he cursed the library, the books, and the members, already making their way to St Domingo Road whilst he, damn it, was going to be late.

He had overslept, something that never happened

to him as a rule, not even after a night of fire-watching. He blamed his mother for that too. She should have woken him – she usually did so – but for some reason she too had overslept, and she had not been fire-watching. In fact she had been in bed the previous evening, snoring loudly, before he had even left the house. Making a mental vow to buy a new alarm clock to replace the one his mother had dropped a week earlier, Mr Gower hurried along the road. He knew Miss Preece had been fire-watching as well and wondered if she, too, might be late today. He hoped she would be. If he was actually in the library first, he could demand an explanation for her lateness, tell her fire-watching was no excuse; he himself was extremely tired but had still made it to work on time.

He turned on to St Domingo Road and glanced at the library, seeing at once that the metal gates had been pushed back. However tired she was, Miss Preece must have opened up on time. He climbed the steps and entered the building, feeling a moment of deep disappointment. He had been looking forward to venting his feelings on her by delivering a good telling-off; now it was he who was in the wrong. He could feel an irrational resentment towards his colleague rising within him, and when he smelt burning toast he thought this might well be his opportunity. She had no right to cook herself breakfast when the public were actually choosing books from the shelves. He would tick her off in front of the line of women already waiting to have their books date-stamped; that would teach her! He knew most of the library members assumed he was Miss Preece's boss simply because he was a man, but in fact they were just colleagues; if anything, she was ahead of him in the hierarchy due to the fact that she had a first class honours degree.

Once, he had been sure that Miss Preece admired him, had believed in his heart that if he ever felt inclined to pop the question, she would fall into his hands like a ripe plum. Every woman, he was certain, wanted desperately to be married; why should she be the exception? He had thought, too, that they had a lot in common, both being burdened with old and crotchety mothers, and had imagined that this shared understanding would be a sufficient basis for a long and successful marriage.

Now, however, he went round the counter and tapped Miss Preece sharply on the shoulder. He began to ask her, loudly, how it was that he could smell burnt toast and was astonished when she turned to him with a smile. 'We knew you were fire-watching last night, Mr Gower, and would probably have had little opportunity to get yourself breakfast,' she said. 'So Mrs Hibbert has made you some toast and marg and a mug of coffee; they're in the office, if you'd like to go through.' Mr Gower was so taken aback that he was unable to say a word, but simply stared at her. He felt a great fool when Miss Preece's slim, dark eyebrows shot up. 'What's the matter, Mr Gower? If you're thinking that Mrs Hibbert spoilt your toast, I believe one piece did go up in flames, but that's been thrown away. The two that are left are fine and the coffee will still be nice and hot.'

Mr Gower went over to the library assistant, just about to join Miss Preece at the counter. 'Thank you, Mrs Hibbert; it's very good of you,' he said stiffly. He would have liked to add *but I had my breakfast an hour ago*, but knew this would be ungracious as well as untruthful. Instead he said, addressing Miss Preece: 'I do trust you're not working away there on an empty stomach; I know you were fire-watching last night as well.'

Miss Preece opened her mouth to reply, but jolly Mrs Armitage got in first. 'No, a' course she ain't workin' on an empty stomach, she's workin' on the bleedin' counter,' she said, giving a loud bellow of laughter which set the whole queue off into gales of merriment.

Mr Gower turned away and headed for the office. He told himself it was too early for readers in the Reference Library but the truth was he was famished; his stomach was fairly roaring for food and hot coffee. He sat down on the swivel chair behind the small desk, reached for the mug of coffee and took a cautious sip, and then a couple of big swallows. Then he started on the toast.

It had been kind, he decided, of Mrs Hibbert to make him some breakfast. He had resented her when she had first joined the staff, resented the fact that outside office hours she called Miss Preece Agatha, and the librarian referred to the older woman as Evelyn. Of course, Miss Preece was really Mrs Galera now, but she did not use her married name at work. He thought of Mrs Hibbert's crisply curling grey hair, her neat figure, and her rather sweet smile, and decided that she was a decent little thing. He wanted to tell her to call him Cyril, which would be one in the eye for Miss Preece who had never used his first name, even when invited to do so.

Finishing the toast down to the last crumb and draining the coffee, Mr Gower made up his mind to have rather more courage in future in his dealings with his new colleague. There was a play coming on at the Empire Theatre in two or three weeks' time which he wanted to see. He would invite Mrs Hibbert to an evening performance, then buy her dinner at somewhere really expensive, possibly the Adelphi; he had heard that the food there was still extremely good, despite wartime rationing and shortages. After all, she could only refuse.

Chapter Eighteen

Hetty, Sally and Alice were packing, because the decision to take the *Shamrock* and her butty boat out of commission for ten days meant that all their personal possessions should be either stowed ashore or taken with them when later that day they headed for Liverpool and home. Hetty, cramming her sturdy boating clothes into a large hessian sack which had once held potatoes, thought that much though she loved the *Shamrock* and the *Clover*, she would be downright glad to live ashore for a whole, wonderful ten days.

Not that she would have changed jobs with anyone, for now, with over a year's experience behind them, even the toughest of the locks and the longest of the tunnels held no terrors for them. Despite the fact that the winter just past had been an extremely severe one, the three girls had coped with everything that nature, and the war, had thrown at them. When they were loading and unloading at the Regent's Canal dock, it often seemed to Hetty that it was only by a miracle that the canal had not been breached, but so far, though they had watched the dark aeroplanes roar overhead and the fires leap up, the canal and its craft had been spared.

Because of the severity of the weather that winter, however, raids had almost ceased, though they heard both on the wireless and in letters from family and friends that Liverpool had suffered a bad raid in mid-March. April, however, had been quiet, and since most of their leave would take place in May the girls hoped fervently that the Luftwaffe would not revisit the Liverpool docks.

Now, filling her haversack with things she would want whilst on leave – the hessian sack would be left along with the boats in the secure compound – Hetty voiced what they were all probably feeling. 'I hope to God the bomber's moon stays behind good thick cloud cover in May, the same as it has in April,' she said. 'You won't be in Liverpool long, will you, Alice? Didn't you say your mam and the kids were evacuated to North Wales? Sal and I will be too near the docks for comfort if the Jerries decide to start bombing Liverpool, and from what Gareth tells me, it's on the cards. The 'Pool is the obvious destination for the food and armaments America is supplying, so naturally Jerry will realise it soon enough and attack again. However, let's hope it doesn't happen whilst we're on leave. Everyone ready to go?'

She looked round the cabin, suddenly aware of how much she would miss her companions and their craft. Then the girls stowed their sacks away under one of the side bunks and made for dry land. They would catch a train and be home before nightfall, though Alice would be sleeping with a cousin and would catch the first train next morning, to join her family in Wales.

* * *

Hetty arrived in Lime Street at two o'clock in the afternoon and stood on the platform for a moment, biting her lip. Her grandparents had come out of retirement some months before and were taking a barge up and down the Leeds and Liverpool Canal, carrying anything the government needed moving. 'It's our war work,' Gramps had written proudly. 'We may be old, but we're not useless.'

As for Aunt Phoebe, she was working the afternoon shift today and would not be home until ten o'clock that evening. She had written informing her niece of this, and telling her where the key would be hidden, but Hetty found she had no desire to go through all the rigmarole of crossing the Mersey, only to find herself the solitary occupant of a cold and uninhabited house. Birkenhead had been bombed quite heavily, and though the Luftwaffe were undoubtedly aiming for the docks, the town had taken quite a pasting. Hetty had heard that the great floating crane known as the Mammoth had been sunk, as had two cargo vessels, the *Myrmidon*, which had been carrying government stores, and the *Empire Simba*, with its cargo of steel. Laird's had not been hit, but according to her aunt it would be many months before Birkenhead – the one-eyed city as Liverpudlians rudely referred to it – recovered from the attacks.

So what to do? But already she knew the answer. She would go to the Everton library, dump her haversack in the office and help Agatha if she needed help with her books, or sit in the nice warm Reading Room

388

with several copies of the *Echo* and catch up on local events. And Agatha would tell her how much she missed Max, and how lovely it was being married, for her friend had had a long weekend up in Lossiemouth with her new husband and had told Hetty that it had been a magic time.

Having made up her mind to go to Everton, Hetty set off at once and was lucky enough to catch a tram going in the right direction before she had walked for more than five minutes. Presently, she was running up the steps and opening the library doors whilst taking off her haversack, and beaming as her eyes met Agatha's.

'Hetty!' Agatha said. 'My dear, I'd not expected to see you for another couple of days at least. But how welcome you are! If I give you some money you can trot along to Mr Woolridge's and buy some cakes; doughnuts would be nice, or ice buns. Then you and I – and Mr Gower and Mrs Hibbert, of course – will take a little break because, as I expect you remember, we're on late opening tonight. Mrs Hibbert, I forgot you've not met. This is Hetty Gilbert, whom you've often heard me mention.'

There was no one waiting at the desk, so Hetty went round the counter and held out her hands, palms upwards, towards the librarian, shaking her head as she did so. 'Oh, Agatha, I'd love to help, and buy some cakes, but look at my hands! Crewing a canal boat is dirty work, and though I was lucky enough to have a bath before leaving the compound, I'd not realised that train travel is a pretty smutty business too. I'm sure my hands would do credit to a coal miner, but if I can nip into the Ladies . . .'

Agatha told Hetty to go ahead so Hetty made for the staff lavatery, thinking how nice it was to be welcomed back here as though she truly belonged.

Later, Agatha and Mrs Hibbert ate their doughnuts and drank their tea, taking it in turns to see to the incoming and outgoing borrowers, and Mr Gower, thanking them politely, carried his own share up to the reference section. Whilst they ate, Hetty told her friend a little more about her life aboard the *Shamrock*. 'It's hard work, much harder than you might suppose. But at this time of year the countryside is so beautiful it makes me catch my breath, and in the winter, when we're snug in our cosy cabin with the stove blazing, we feel downright sorry for civilians sleeping in icy bedrooms, with only a couple of thin blankets to pull round themselves.'

Agatha agreed that this sounded pleasant as they washed up their tea things, and then Hetty went off to the Reading Room, where several old men were perusing the newspapers. A couple of women sat on the sturdy wooden chairs against the wall, eagerly reading the periodicals and commenting in low voices on the recipes and knitting patterns which were such an important part of any magazine in wartime. Hetty had brought a book in with her and presently became engrossed, but when Agatha opened the door and announced that the library was about to close she jumped to her feet at once, returned her book to the shelf and smiled at her friend.

'Ready, Hetty?' Agatha asked. 'Won't Mother be delighted when she sees you again after so long! Get your haversack and we'll be off.'

They arrived at Everton Terrace and presently old Mrs Preece was giving Hetty a kiss and urging her to take her things up to the spare room and then come down at once, since she had made a cake that very afternoon and the tea would not take a minute to brew.

'I'm not staying with you tonight, I'm going across the water to my aunt,' Hetty said. 'But I'll be back tomorrow, because Agatha means to get theatre tickets for the new show at the Empire. I wouldn't miss that for the world, because although we're supposed to get a certain amount of time off, we don't linger near big cities. It's too dangerous.'

'The theatre!' Mrs Preece said wistfully. 'Am I to be included in this jaunt?'

'Of course you are, Mother,' Agatha said at once, sounding reproachful. 'As if Hetty and I would dream of leaving you at home! And the weather looks set fair, so we shan't have to bother with umbrellas and wellingtons.'

The three women emerged from the theatre into a calm, moonlit night. The torches which had become an essential accompaniment to any such excursion were not necessary and they made happily for the nearest taxi rank, still talking of the show they had just enjoyed.

'It feels almost like peacetime to go to a theatrical

performance and then go home by cab,' Mrs Preece remarked as they joined the queue. 'Now, young ladies, the theatre was your treat, Agatha, but I mean to pay for the taxi cab to take us home to Everton Terrace.'

'And I'll give the driver a tip,' Hetty said. 'I wish I could make more of a contribution, but us boat women still aren't counted as members of His Majesty's Armed Forces, so though the government pays us we have to provide our own clothing and food out of what is really a very small allowance.'

'I call that scandalous,' Mrs Preece said. Agatha tried to say that they would catch a tram, but since it would have meant a tedious journey with a walk at the end of it she allowed herself to be persuaded, and helped her mother into the taxi when they reached the head of the queue.

'What a lovely night,' Hetty remarked as they climbed out of the cab and waited for Mrs Preece to pay the driver. 'It's a full moon; I do hope it doesn't give the Luftwaffe ideas.'

The words were scarcely out of her mouth before the siren wailed and Agatha hustled them within doors, saying she would go straight up to her room and change since she would be fire-watching until the all clear sounded.

'I'll come with you,' Hetty said quickly. 'I might be able to help . . .'

'You can help most by taking Mother and yourself down to our Anderson shelter, or the public one a bit further along the road,' Agatha said. 'I know it's a bomber's moon, but that doesn't mean the raiders are heading for us.'

Hetty agreed, though reluctantly, and presently they heard the drone of enemy aircraft and she and Mrs Preece hurried to the shelter and began to prepare for the night ahead.

And what a night it had turned out to be, Hetty thought, as she made breakfast and waited for Agatha to return home. The bombs had rained down, the ack-ack batteries had retaliated with all the firepower at their command, and Mrs Preece had insisted that they use the Anderson shelter which had been erected in their back garden rather than going to the public one. There, she had wrapped herself in a couple of blankets and gone off to sleep as confidently as though there were no bombing raid taking place overhead.

Agatha popped in just after the all clear sounded to tell them that she would be home in an hour or so, but was needed to assist in the Smithdown Road area, where a dairy, as well as a number of private houses, had been hit. 'I believe Birkenhead – the town, not the docks – was hit as well; I'll try to find out where the bombs fell as soon as things calm down a bit,' she added, rubbing a hand across her smut-covered forehead. 'But right now there's a good deal of confusion. All I know for certain is that they're bringing a mobile canteen to Sefton Park and need help there, so that's where I'm bound once I've signed off from fire-watching.'

'Then you can have some breakfast and a wash,

I hope,' Mrs Preece said somewhat tartly. She and Hetty had left the shelter as soon as the all clear had sounded, but Mrs Preece, it appeared, had woken feeling hard done by and was not above taking out her ill humour on her daughter. 'I'll put the porridge on; the kettle's already on the boil.'

'Right, Mother, only don't make me any porridge yet, because it will take me a while to find out where I'm most needed, and I must phone Max and let him know we're all right,' Agatha said. She winked at Hetty, who was pouring three mugs of strong tea. 'The library can open late for once. You poor girl, to be home on leave when the Luftwaffe have decided to come back.'

'I'll be happy to help all I can, either by day at the library or by night patrolling the streets,' Hetty said stoutly. 'We've been so lucky on the canal, it's about time I found out what a real war is like.'

She meant every word she said, but later that day she found out what war was like with a vengeance when a far worse blow fell on her, a blow for which, oddly enough, she had been totally unprepared. One of the bombs which had probably been aimed at Laird's or the docks had scored a direct hit on her aunt's little house, and both Aunt Phoebe and Uncle Alf had been killed outright.

'Perhaps it's a good thing that the poor lass has so much to do,' Mrs Preece observed to her daughter as the two of them prepared a rather sketchy supper on the Saturday following the death of Hetty's aunt and uncle. As people had predicted, the heavy raid which had taken place that Thursday was followed by another on the Friday, and since the skies were still clear – and the moon at the full – they feared that they would be blitzed once more during the coming night.

Now, spreading margarine thinly on the slices of bread her mother had cut from the loaf, Agatha agreed, though somewhat doubtfully, that the workload which had fallen on her young friend's shoulders might have its compensations.

Mrs Preece nodded sagely, fetching a jar of home-made strawberry jam from the pantry and placing it in the middle of the kitchen table, next to a pot of Marmite and another of honey. 'There's no doubt being busy is better than being idle at such a time. But it worries me that Hetty hasn't wept; tears help, believe it or not. I remember when your poor father died . . .'

Agatha stopped listening, for she had heard the sad story of her father's death many times. Now, it was Hetty's troubles which filled her mind. The girl had had to get in touch with her cousins, to break the news of their parents' death. Tom had been given compassionate leave and was staying with relatives in Bootle. The other boy, Bill, was at sea somewhere and could not be reached. Then there were funeral arrangements to be made, and before that she had to get in touch with the Inland Waterways Authority to ask them where her grandparents were likely to be found. She knew, of course, that it would be somewhere on the Leeds and Liverpool canal but that meant little; they could be almost anywhere along its considerable length, and when she found them she would have to tell them the dreadful news that their daughter and son-in-law were dead.

Agatha glanced at the clock on the kitchen mantelpiece; it was four o'clock in the afternoon, high time Hetty returned, as she had promised, to the house in Everton Terrace. On the Friday night, she had acted as runner for the fire-watchers in the city centre who were without any form of telephone, and she had intended to do the same tonight, but Agatha had been against it. 'You've got to get some sleep,' she had told her young friend. 'As soon as the siren sounds, you and Mother should go straight to the Anderson shelter. It's not as if you can sleep during the day, because you'll be too busy dealing with your own personal tragedy. Mr Gower and I have requested permission from head office not to open the library on Saturdays for a while, so I shall get some sleep during daylight hours.'

Hetty had said she would see how things turned out, and now the back door opened and the girl herself came into the room. She smiled at the two older women, picked up a slice of bread and margarine, sat down and reached for the jam pot, whilst Mrs Preece poured her a cup of tea. 'The Inland Waterways people have found Gran and Gramps,' she said. 'I spoke to them on the phone, which was better in some ways than having to tell them face to face. They were actually in Leeds and had just loaded up, but someone else will take over the barge whilst they return to Burscough by train. They won't be here until tomorrow, but once they arrive things will be a lot easier. They are devastated, naturally, but Gramps will know far better than I what needs to be done. So if you don't mind, I'll just have something to eat and then go to bed for a few hours. Wake me when Moaning Minnie sounds, if I don't hear it. As for the shelter, I'll see how I feel.'

'All right,' Agatha said reluctantly. 'I suppose if we try to insist that you go to the shelter you'll just meekly agree, and it won't be five minutes before you're reporting to the wardens, or WVS, and offering to help. Well, you know best, dear. And now we'll all eat our tea, such as it is, and prepare for the night ahead.'

Hetty loved staying in Agatha's pretty little spare room, but knew she would find it difficult to sleep. Thoughts of Aunt Phoebe and Uncle Alf, of the way they had accepted her into their family, filled her mind. Easy-going Aunt Phoebe had never made her feel a burden; Uncle Alf had several times introduced her to his friends as 'young Hetty, what's as good as a daughter to Phoebe and me', and the boys had squabbled with her, teased her and protected her when she needed it. Of course she still had Gran and Gramps, but now that they had returned to the Leeds and Liverpool she did not see much of them. Naturally they exchanged letters, but it was not the same. Aunt Phoebe had never been demonstrative, rarely giving either her sons or her niece a kiss or a hug, yet Hetty had known herself loved and felt her loss deeply and painfully.

Climbing into bed, fully dressed apart from trousers, jersey and boots, she plumped up the pillow and lay down, thinking how nice it would be if the moon hid its face behind thick clouds and the Luftwaffe decided to have a night off. Oh, if only they had taken the night off on Thursday; then Aunt Phoebe and Uncle Alf would still be alive.

Hetty had not yet cried for her aunt and uncle; she had been too busy and too shocked, had not perhaps even taken in what had happened and how it would affect her life. But now, suddenly, she felt a sob rise up in her throat and began to weep, and presently she cried herself to sleep.

She woke to the wail of the siren and glanced at her wristwatch. It was half past ten, and as she scrambled into her clothes she saw through the window – for she had rolled up the blackout blinds as soon as she had got into bed – that the darkness of the night was already split by searchlights. As soon as she was dressed she tapped on Mrs Preece's door, which was opened so abruptly that she guessed the older woman had not undressed. Hetty smiled at her. 'I expect Agatha's long gone,' she said. 'But we'd better make sure before I take you down to the shelter.'

'Don't bother; I heard her clattering down the stairs at least half an hour ago, well before the siren started,' Mrs Preece informed her. 'Are you going to stay in the shelter with me? Agatha said you wouldn't . . .'

'I'll get you comfortably settled, then I'll see how

I feel,' Hetty said evasively. 'Agatha showed me where she left blankets and provisions and so on earlier in the evening, and no doubt Mrs Simpson will join you. Come along now.'

Mrs Preece accompanied her down the stairs, and Hetty fetched the large canvas bag containing a flask of tea, jam sandwiches wrapped in greaseproof paper, candles and matches, Mrs Preece's knitting and a couple of books. Then she picked up the two neatly folded blankets and handed them to her companion and they both set off for the Anderson shelter. Agatha had explained to Hetty the evening before that they never left things in the shelter, where they might be stolen, or could get damp and musty, but what she termed 'the emergency bag' was always packed and ready.

Hetty checked that the house was secure, for sadly it was not unknown for thieves to strip a house bare of anything of value whilst its occupants were in the shelter. Then she hustled old Mrs Preece into the Anderson, to find Mrs Simpson already ensconced. They greeted one another, and the two ladies wrapped themselves in the blankets and settled down on the hard wooden benches. Already, they could hear the drone of the heavy bombers and the rattling fire from the ack-ack batteries, but Hetty was amused to see that neither of her companions took the slightest notice. Mrs Preece was pouring tea into enamel mugs and Mrs Simpson was frowning over a knitting pattern. They looked set for the night, and Hetty felt no compunction about leaving them. She bent over and kissed Mrs Preece's soft, wrinkled cheek, then touched her tin hat in mock salute. 'I'm off to give any help I can,' she announced cheerfully. 'I can see you'll be all right for the next few hours, so don't go saving me any grub because if they need me as a runner for the fire-watchers, or to check blackouts are drawn, or to cordon off bombed buildings, they'll give me a cuppa and a wad from one of the mobile canteens. See you soon, my dears!'

Three hours later, Hetty honestly wondered if there would be any Liverpool left by the time the all clear sounded. She had offered her help and had been told to go to a big warehouse near the Bryant and May's match factory, to act as runner should the fire-watchers there spot a conflagration. The bombers dropped incendiaries as well as HE bombs, and Hetty supposed that sometimes, if one acted quickly enough, fires could be extinguished before they did too much damage. Tonight, however, the defendants were overwhelmed. Hetty saw, from her perch on the flat roof of a warehouse near the docks, a barrage balloon in flames being carried towards the shipping by the spiteful wind and heard, only moments later, a deafening explosion, saw flames leap as high as the highest building. All around her there was chaos; she must report to HQ as soon as possible, though there seemed little hope of quenching the conflagration.

Telling the fire-watcher she would be back as soon as she could, she ran down the stairs and dashed to the nearest point to tell of the latest fire, and on the way saw tram lines rearing up like angry snakes, water mains spouting fountains and fractured gas pipes alight, to add to the horrors. Several times she thought of poor Agatha, fire-watching from the topmost turret of the Everton library with its fantastic view of the entire city spread out before her, and wondered how on earth she was getting on. There were so many fires that it would be impossible for the older woman to pinpoint them, but at least she had the telephone downstairs in the library, though she found the spiral staircase difficult, either ascending or descending.

Hetty got back to the building which she had just left to report to HQ and gasped; it must have received a direct hit, for as soon as she got close enough she could see that it was just a shell, its windows gaping whilst flames leapt almost as high as the building itself.

A man in warden's uniform saw her and shouted. 'Don't go near that building, queen! What are you doing out here? Find a shelter, for Gawd's sake; the streets ain't no place for a young girl. I'm goin' to cordon off that building . . .'

'I'm a runner,' Hetty said breathlessly, swinging round to show him the armband she had been given. 'I've just returned from HQ; what happened to the old feller who was fire-watching on the roof of this place?'

The man shrugged helplessly. 'He wouldn't have stood a chance, chuck,' he said gently. 'Now gerroff; I've work to do.' He had a bundle of metal rods under one arm and a coil of rope across his shoulder, and now began to cordon off the building; surely a useless task with so much destruction all around.

Hetty sighed, then decided to make her way back to St Domingo Road. She imagined that the library would be locked, but hoped that the little door at the end, which led up to the turret where her friend was fire-watching, would be open. When someone could be spared, Agatha was given a runner to save her from the horrors of the spiral staircase, and the little door was unlocked then.

As soon as she neared the library, however, Hetty began to feel uneasy. The streets were too quiet, too deserted, and despite the fact that it was May she found that she was shivering, not just with fright but with cold also. And she realised she was lonely, for aboard the *Shamrock*, no matter what might be happening, one was never alone. She hugged her thin coat around her, wishing she had thought to don the duffel she wore aboard the boat in winter, and looked apprehensively up at the sky. It was scattered with stars but the moon had sunk out of sight behind a row of buildings, and, in any case, thick dark clouds were beginning to blot out the stars. Hetty had stopped in order to look about her; now she began to walk again, and even as she did so she heard the drone of an engine. She looked up. Yes, there was an aeroplane, black even against the blackness of the sky, and it was coming towards her, coming fast and low and menacing, seeming to be heading straight for her as though the pilot had her in his sights and meant to shoot her down.

Hetty gave a tiny shriek and began to run, then slowed; which way, which way? She had been heading for the library and now she realised that she was on

St Domingo Road, that the large and imposing building opposite her was the library, though it looked different, somehow sinister, as though it were in league with the pilot of the plane which was swooping lower, lower . . .

Hetty told herself that she should make for the nearby public shelter, but something made her continue to run as fast as she could towards the library. She was outside the main gates now, hesitating, guessing that this entrance would be locked, not knowing which way to turn, sobbing with terror, longing for human companionship, any companionship . . .

Arms closed around her waist, strong arms, and she found herself lifted off her feet. The man carrying her fairly tore round the corner of the library, to the little side door which led directly to the turret. Then he stood her down and rubbed her tear-wet cheek with his own firm, slightly bristly one, continuing to hold her with her back against his chest so that she could not see his face.

'I've got you, cariad; you're safe with me, safe as houses,' he crooned. 'Just relax; the raid's nearly over. Very soon dawn will begin to creep over the rooftops and another day will begin, and when the all clear goes I'll throw you up on my great white charger and carry you off, because today's my day for rescuing fair maidens.'

'Oh, Gareth, how did you find me? I've never been so frightened in the whole of my life,' Hetty gasped. 'And why didn't you tell me it was you who put me on your motorbike and brought me home to Liverpool that night? I feel so ashamed! Fancy thinking that the man who kissed me might be horrible Harry or one of the other blokes from my days on the canal. Oh, darling Gareth, I've been so stupid! But I'm not stupid any longer; I love you, the real you, not the imaginary one.' She twisted in his arms and pulled his head down in order to plant a trembling kiss on his startled mouth. 'Will you ever forgive me?'

'I might,' Gareth said. His voice cracked. 'Oh, Hetty, I've loved you ever since we were kids and I'll love you for the rest of my life! But we'd best get inside because I see a warden coming up the road and he's bound to ask what we're doing here.'

'If we climb the spiral staircase we'll find Agatha at the top,' Hetty said, hanging back as they entered the building. 'You've not met her for years, but she's always approved of you and thought me a fool not to grab you with both hands. But what are you doing here, Gareth? You're supposed to be miles away in RAF Scampton, doing clever things with engines.'

'Your grandfather rang my airfield and told me where you were. He and I have always kept in touch, and I reckon he knew how I felt about you even before I did. At any rate, he rang after your aunt and uncle were killed and told me to ask for compassionate leave, which I got. Naturally I didn't waste a moment but jumped into the old jalopy and came straight to Everton Terrace. The old lady you're staying with with said to try the library, so here I am.' He put his arms round her and squeezed gently. 'Oh, Hetty, Hetty, Hetty! I've been so bloody unhappy, because in a way it was worse

404

that you'd fallen in love with a me who wasn't me . . . am I making sense?'

'No, but I understand what you're saying,' Hetty said dreamily. 'How awful it would have been if I'd not recognised you just now! Worse if I'd gone on looking for someone who didn't exist . . .

They were inside the library now and Gareth was pushing Hetty gently before him up the first half-dozen steps when they heard the *crump* of an exploding bomb and both instinctively ducked, then laughed at their foolishness. Gareth was just saying that he thought the missile had landed at least a mile off when they heard footsteps descending the stairs above them and hastily retreated, for there was no room for two adults to pass on the narrow metal steps.

'It's only us, Agatha,' Hetty called as the footsteps hesitated. 'We met outside the library and Gareth grabbed me and more or less threw me towards the bottom of the turret, but the aeroplane passed over, so that was all right.'

'Oh, Hetty, hasn't it been a dreadful night?' Agatha said, her voice floating down to them as she came lower. 'It looks as though the whole city is ablaze, and all the library windows and the glass doors have gone – blast, though, thank God, and not a bomb or an incendiary. Imagine what would happen to our books and documents if an incendiary smashed through the roof.' She reached the foot of the stair and flickered a small torch briefly into their faces, then politely switched it off, though not before she had smiled broadly at Gareth. 'Hello, young man; it's good to see you. What have you been up to? You both look extremely pleased with yourselves, not to say happy!'

'We are,' Hetty said. 'We're never going to quarrel again and – and one day, we're going to get married!'

ALSO AVAILABLE IN ARROW

A Mother's Hope

Katie Flynn

Along a blacked-out wartime street a girl is scurrying, a basket on one arm. As the sirens begin and the bombs crash down, she is filled with panic and, with a heavy heart, abandons her burden in a sheltered doorway, meaning to return later. Even as she disappears in the resulting chaos, the bundle in the basket begins to wail.

Years later, two young unfortunates meet on a miserable November day. Martin has been desperately trying to hitch a lift along the lonely windswept road and when he sees a weeping girl in front of him, he hurries to catch her up.

Rose and Martin become unlikely companions until they go their separate ways, not expecting to meet again. However, fate decrees otherwise . . .

arrow books

In Time for Christmas

Katie Flynn

Addy and Prue Fairweather live with Nell, their widowed mother, in a flat above her shop on the Scotland Road. The sisters, however, are very different. Addy is dark-haired, plain and always in trouble, whereas Prue is flaxen-haired, blue-eyed and as angelic as her looks imply. To make matters worse, Nell makes no secret of her preference for the younger girl, increasing Addy's jealousy and resentment.

On the other side of the coin, Giles Frobisher and his twin sister, Gillian, live in a crumbling mansion near the sea in Devon. The family have lost most of their money in the Depression, so Giles leaves university and joins the Fleet Air Arm. He meets the Fairweather girls briefly on a visit to Liverpool but they lose touch. When they meet again Addy and Prue are no longer children, and Giles realises he is falling in love . . .

arrow books

ALSO AVAILABLE IN ARROW

Heading Home

Katie Flynn

Claudia Muldoon and her younger sister, Jenny, live with their parents and their gran in her house in Blodwen Street. Both parents have good jobs and the family assume they are settled for life, but then Grandpa Muldoon has a seizure and begs his son to return to Ireland and the family croft.

The Muldoons leave and Gran has to take in lodgers to make ends meet, for the Depression is beginning to bite. In Ireland, however, the Muldoons flourish and the girls love the freedom of their new life, though as they grow up, disadvantages become clear. Claudia has to find work, so both sisters return to Liverpool and to their old pal Danny, who still adores the beautiful Claudia and welcomes them back with delight.

But both girls' lives take an unexpected turn when Danny's friend, the flamboyant and successful Rob Dingle, returns from America . . .

arrow books

To find out more about Katie Flynn why not join the Katie Flynn Readers' Club and receive a twice yearly newsletter.

To join our mailing list to receive the newsletter and other information* write with your name and address to:

Katie Flynn Readers' Club
The Marketing Department
Arrow Books
20 Vauxhall Bridge Road
London
SW1V 2SA

Please state whether or not you would like to receive information about other Arrow saga authors.